BOOKS BY SUZA KATES

The Savannah Coven Series
Whisper of a Witch
Conviction of a Witch
Binding of a Witch
Haunting of a Witch
Possession of a Witch
Deception of a Witch
Suffering of a Witch

The She Series
She Who is Hidden

Single Titles
Hallowed Eve
The Penance Stone

To Madison,
It was great to meet you!

VENGEANCE OF A WITCH
THE SAVANNAH COVEN SERIES

SUZA KATES

Sue Kates

ICASM PRESS

SAVANNAH

Copyright © 2014 by Suza Kates
Cover design © 2014 by ICASM PRESS

All rights reserved. No part of this book may be reproduced in any form or by any electronic or mechanical means including information storage and retrieval systems, except in the case of brief quotations in critical reviews, without permission of the publisher, Icasm Publishing LLC.

This book is a work of fiction. The characters, names, events and places are fictitious and products of the author's imagination or are used fictitiously. Any similarities to actual persons, living or dead, places or events is entirely coincidental.

Published by Icasm Publishing LLC
5710 Ogeechee Rd. Suite 200 #278, Savannah, GA 31405
www.icasmpress.com

Library of Congress Cataloging-in-Publication Data

Kates, Suza
Vengeance of a Witch / Suza Kates
   p. cm.

ISBN-13:978-0-9889809-9-0
ISBN-13:978-0-9912002-0-7 (ebook)
I. Title

Printed and bound in the United States of America

This book is dedicated to the 75th Ranger Regiment with a special thank you to the 1/75 soldiers and support staff. My time with you was a privilege.

ACKNOWLEDGMENTS

For this book I have to thank three very patient and dedicated people, Karen Dale Harris, Sharyn Cerniglia, and my husband David. This book was quite the whirlwind, and all three of you worked around my deadline-induced insanity. Drinks on me in San Antonio!--Suza

THE COVEN

Anna St. Germaine
Hair: Long, straight, sable brown
Eyes: Sapphire blue
Color: Sapphire blue
Cat: "Ivy" gray female with lime green eyes

Anna sees visions of past, present, and future. She is the coven's head witch and is a descendant of the three women who originally banished the demon Bastraal three centuries ago. Her ancestral home is on an island off the coast of Savannah, Georgia and now serves as coven central.

Claudia Grant
Hair: Straight, long, flaming red
Eyes: River green
Color: Coral
Cat: "Rowan Von Ashbi" coloring of an American Wirehair with yellow eyes

Claudia is a history professor who only needs to touch an object to sense its past and previous surroundings.

Hayden Wells
Hair: Brownish red "caramel"
Eyes: Golden brown
Color: Pale pink
Cat: "Daisy" black tortoiseshell with yellow eyes

Hayden is a medium from San Francisco who sees and talks to spirits/ghosts.

Kylie Worthington
Hair: Long, wavy golden-blonde
Eyes: Hazel
Color: Yellow
Cat: Sassafras "Sassy" also a long-haired blonde but with bright yellow eyes

Kylie is a college student who's "on a break" to do her part for the coven and is able to control electricity in any form.

Lucia Ruiz
Hair: Long, wavy deep brown
Eyes: Brown
Color: Red
Cat: "Iris" black Persian with blue eyes

Lucia was born to privileged wealth in Spain and has the ability to find anything that is lost. She is an adventurer, world-traveler, and renowned relic-hunter.

Paige Reilley
Hair: Shoulder-length, white-blonde with ragged bangs
Eyes: Turquoise blue
Color: Turquoise
Cat: Tiger Lily "Tiger" brown and gray with white chest and belly, bright green eyes

Recently discharged from the military, Paige is a soldier in every way with the added abilities of super-strength and speed.

Shauni Miller
Hair: Long, straight, black
Eyes: Emerald green
Color: Green
Cat: "Cuileann" black short-hair with green eyes

Shauni is a nature-loving biologist from Colorado and communicates with animals telepathically.

Viv Sakurai
Hair: Shoulder-length, black, angled bangs
Eyes: Gray
Color: Purple
Cat: Kikoku "Kiko" orange tabby with yellow-green eyes and a grumpy disposition.

Relocated from Chicago, Viv is a physicist searching for an explanation for her own special power of telekinesis.

Willyn Brousseau
Hair: Wavy, shoulder-length, light blonde
Eyes: Pale blue
Color: White/cream
Cat: "Snowball" pure white with golden eyes

Willyn is a nurse, a mother, and a Christian. Raised in Alabama, she uses her healing powers to help those in need. She came to Savannah with an additional package, her young son, Tadd.

THE GUYS

Dr. Michael Black *Whisper of a Witch*

This tall handsome veterinarian fell in love with Shauni in the first book of the series. He has dark blonde hair and gray eyes and is able to read a person's aura. He's a pretty calm guy until someone messes with his witch.

Dare Forster *Conviction of a Witch*

Dark and handsome with deep blue eyes, this male witch came to the coven's island with his own plan. He wanted to partner with one of the women, but he never expected to fall in love. Especially with a gentle, Christian soul like Willyn. Now married, the two have made a family with Willyn's small son, Tadd.

Nick Reagan *Binding of a Witch*

The coven likes to hang out in their favorite pub, and the owner of the bar always liked looking at Viv. His eyes are the color of the whiskey he sells, and his past is one of struggle. One night Nick finally got the nerve to approach the Asian beauty, but he got a lot more than he bargained for. The demon Bastraal had been destroyed once before, and his remains had been buried. Beneath Nick's very own pub.

Trevor Roch *Haunting of a Witch*

One of Savannah's finest, this homicide detective clashes hard with the coven's ghost whisperer, convinced she's a con artist. Hayden has no choice but to work with the annoying man and find a serial killer who's working with the Amara. Staying true to form and following the coven's pattern, the two fall for each other. Against their better judgment.

Ethan Drake *Possession of a Witch*

This demon hunter is well-acquainted with evil and has been chasing his own monster since childhood. When he offers to help the coven with their demon infestation, he has no idea he's about to be taken on the adventure of a lifetime. Lucia Ruiz is hard to resist, and is the one woman who might be able to save him.

Cole Lonergan *Deception of a Witch*

As Trevor's police partner, Cole has been introduced to the coven and all of their secrets. While he admires the women and considers them all good friends, he never expects to feel anything more. But Claudia Grant is a long-legged-wicked-smart witch, and much like his favorite candies, Cole finds himself wanting to take a bite.

Quinn St. Germaine — *Suffering of a Witch*

Quinn is the younger brother of the coven's head witch, Anna. With sable hair and cobalt eyes, he is the masculine and handsome version of the siblings. His knowledge runs to occult history and magickal languages. He assists the coven in all things, and though he has his eye on a particular witch, he does his best to deny it.

1

Paige Reilley lifted her head and sniffed, sure she'd caught a trace of the monster she'd come to kill. When the breeze lifted and curled her way, she took another deep drag of the humid night air, testing for the telltale scent of foul sulfur.

Nothing. No sound or movement, only still as death buildings, trees blanched by moonlight, and the occasional piece of trash rattling across cobblestones. A discarded piece of plastic scraped by her, fleeing the relentless winds.

Paige could relate, for she too was relentless. She now pursued a creature forged in an underworld abyss, one that had come to town tonight for…well, for nothing good. The demon still lurked nearby, she was certain, but whether that knowledge came from her soldier's training or witch's intuition, she couldn't say.

Studying the area, she performed more recon, searching for anything she might have missed on her first couple of passes. By September, the Savannah tourist season was on its last legs, so even the popular City Market was empty at four in the morning. Bars were long closed down, horses and carriages put to bed, and the saccharine scents from the candy store had floated far away.

Scanning the row of buildings on the opposite side, she searched for potential places where an enemy combatant might conceal itself. Buildings of various material and color stood side by side, their rooftops pressed together like a row of uneven teeth.

The storefronts were well maintained despite their age, and Paige admired the proud facades, pretty on the outside, but strong and determined, having prevailed against years of abuse from the elements.

She was well hidden, and no cars would pass her on the tabby walkway, with headlights to reveal her or her prey. The mixture of sand, limestone, and shells dated back to the city's foundation, and though wider than surrounding streets, only pedestrian traffic was allowed on this thoroughfare.

At this hour, though, the boisterous tourists had been replaced by a menacing absence of sound. Only distant traffic contributed a sub-layer to the static silence, as did the gusts ruffling thick, waxy leaves of street-planted magnolias.

Tiny white-bulbed lights hung year-round in the trees but cast little light, leaving Paige to rely on the waxing moon. Even that source of illumination was repeatedly lost to passing clouds, so her instincts, magic, and training would have to do.

But they usually served her best.

A few men were sleeping in the square at the west end. Known locally as "the rail," the park was an accepted gathering spot for the homeless, especially during milder months. The prone bodies, stretched beneath overcoats or blankets, hopefully would remain asleep through her confrontation with the demon.

Other types cruised the park on occasion, engaging in swift narcotics-related transactions. And Paige owed her gratitude to at least one drug dealer who'd been hauled in earlier by a couple of cops on patrol.

They'd noticed the pusher when he'd run screaming into traffic. He'd been more than happy to get off the streets, reportedly babbling to the officers about a "creature" coming at him from the bushes.

The cops had chalked it up to drug-induced hallucinations or mental disease. But Cole, a detective as well as boyfriend to one of Paige's coven, had caught wind of the arrest and, knowing the man was likely telling the stark truth, had notified the witch who happened to be on call.

Paige pressed against the rough brick at her back and counted herself lucky to be that witch. In the gloom of her hiding spot, she smiled, jacking herself up for a fight.

Continuing to scope the shadowed marketplace, she conjured an AC/DC song in her head. *Yeah you…* But she changed the lyrics to fit the situation…*Kill you all—night—long.*

And she smiled.

Over a year ago, she'd come to Savannah only to discover she was fated to defend the city from an ancient evil. It went by the name Bastraal, a powerful demon who'd made his way here centuries before, only to end up banished by the predecessors of Paige's coven.

The same witches who'd banished the demon had also left a prophecy behind. Nine witches. Nine trials. And before they could even make it to Bastraal, an army of enemies to defeat.

The Amara, as they called themselves, deserved to be put down like the monsters they were. And Paige was ready to do more than protect the flanks of her fellow witches. She was eager—excited even—to finally take point.

Just as soon as her time arrived. Her trial. And it had to be coming up any day now.

A subtle scraping sound drifted from her right and abruptly quieted the murderous tune still playing in her head. By her estimation, the noise had originated about two buildings down.

And sure enough, as she homed in on the spot, a tall shape took form. The beast disturbed the shadows with its movement, a bare ripple of darkness that didn't belong. That wasn't natural.

Paige held her breath. *Don't give yourself away. Not yet.*

She could wait as long as it took to make the bastard feel comfortable. Safe and sound. Then when it got careless, she'd make her move.

Patience was not only a virtue in her line of work, but a necessity. It could save lives, namely hers. She might be stronger and faster than the average witch, but these were hellborn creatures she was hunting, a warrior caste of demons summoned by the Amara.

She wondered what the monster's mission was tonight.

Another scuff of beastly flesh over pavement floated to her on the air. The movement came from behind an old wagon on display in the center of the market walk. She picked up on hurried slap-shuffle footsteps, and then, several yards past the antique cart, a murder of crows suddenly burst from a tree to scatter and caw.

The big guy was moving, and was practically leaving a trail of crumbs.

As she tracked the demon's progress, she consciously relaxed the muscles in her back, shoulders, and lean, mean legs. Her arms were slack at her sides, one hand resting loosely below the hilt of the stainless-steel dagger on her hip.

She required no embellishment, fancy design, or shiny jewels for her weapons. All she needed from a blade was a sharp edge and unyielding strength.

She felt the same way about other adornments, specifically jewelry, which only ever seemed to get in her way. But there was one exception, and she wore it now, a silver amulet hanging from her neck. The intricate and sophisticated weave was reminiscent of a Celtic knot.

Eight stones rimmed the outer edge, each of a different color. They represented her sisters, and each one was connected to the heart of the necklace, just as the women were connected to Paige.

The center gemstone was hers, an aquamarine that represented her place in the coven. She valued her place within the circle and respected the color magic had chosen for her.

Plus, she kind of dug the fact it matched her eyes.

A real live female lived inside the warrior's body, though Paige did her best to hide her from the world. The inner girl tended to be too soft, too trusting, and that—as she well knew—could only lead to injury.

The wind shifted then and brought the beast's stench to her directly, reminding her she was on duty. She listened for any noise, any scrape or clatter, that might pinpoint her quarry's location, and then she saw a flash of mottled gray skin as the demon dashed across an intersecting street to the next section of the market walkway. It was putting too much distance between them.

Time to move. Edging along the storefronts, she kept to her own inky shadows, using trees or any other available objects to cloak her position. Her footsteps were imperceptible, and she gave silent thanks that the sheltered moon was now working in her favor.

Dashing across the street, she ducked behind the ivy-covered gazebo that served as an information center. Again she lost sight of the creature. Why was it creeping around, its actions so furtive?

The demons had first carelessly revealed themselves in the city only two weeks ago, during a bachelor party thrown by the men associated with the coven. Unfortunately, the guys' fun had been interrupted, and to hear them tell it, demons had been on every corner, out in the open, and literally running in the streets.

The fear was that Ronja, the dark witch who'd helped the devils cross into this world, had decided to set them loose on Savannah. Secrecy be damned. Thus the coven had assigned mainland shifts, one witch available at all times in case more of the creatures were reported.

But the monster she was tracking now was being far too stealthy to fit that assumption. If the drug dealer's sighting was accurate, this creature could be looking for someone to kidnap. The Amara had done it before, taking victims to use as shells for other types of demons.

The kind that possessed a person and didn't let go.

Shoving the why of the creature's actions down deep for the time being, Paige stilled, allowing every fiber in her body to harden like the tabby pavement beneath her feet. Set solidly into her hidden position, she listened. She prepared.

Suddenly, the wind shifted, rushing from behind to pass over her nape and through her short blonde hair. The breeze would carry her scent past whispering leaves, around the grand old clock atop a black pole, and finally down the corridor created by the two rows of buildings.

It would flow straight to the beast.

She had been paying attention before, but now she was intently focused. Other than the fluttering magnolia leaves, she heard nothing. So she waited. With her breathing controlled and even, she held her relaxed yet ready-to-launch stance.

She was prepped to defend or attack. For her they were one and the same.

Nerve endings along her spine prickled as she sensed the demon's movement. This time, it was headed her way. It had caught her scent and was closing in.

So Paige formulated a new plan, to sit tight and let the fiend track her for a change. Let the freak come willingly to its own demise.

It wasn't long before the demon's rotten-egg rankness struck her full blast, riding on the thick, muggy air. The intensity of the stench indicated the thing had taken her bait. A snuffling noise on the other side of the gazebo confirmed its proximity.

She was waiting…waiting.

Suddenly her head kicked back as a light and airy sensation zipped up her limbs, through her torso, and rushed into what had to be the very center of her brain. Her body felt flooded with effervescence, as if a river of tiny bubbles had gone screaming to the core of her electrical system.

She shook herself and tried to maintain concentration. The demon would find her at any moment.

Sure, she knew she was going to be the next witch to have her trial. Only moments ago she'd been assuming and hoping it would come soon. But this was ridiculous.

Fate took an awful lot of blame from the coven, and Paige felt obliged to lay one more complaint at her feet. *Crappy timing, lady. But you won't throw me off.*

As the flood of awareness ebbed and receded from her body, she actually felt even more charged up than before. Her time had come to stand for her coven in their war with evil, and the notion only ratcheted up her will to charge in.

The fighting part, that she could handle. Hell, it was what she had been *made* for.

But the other part of the prophecy pattern? That was the only thing that could spoil her righteous battle. A man showing up to kill her buzz.

Her head shook slightly of its own volition. No way. She'd

be damned if she was going to fall in love like the other witches before her. Shank a few demons here and there, face off with a dark witch or two, sure. No problem. No sweat.

But go weepy-eyed over some Y-chromosomer? *Hmph. I don't think so.*

A resounding shudder snapped her out of her daze. The golden wood of the gazebo shimmied as the beast gave up its sneak attack and slammed against the other side. Trying to flush her out? Not sure if she was inside, underneath?

The demon hit the structure again, and a dried length of ivy vine fell, feathering against Paige's cheek on its way down. Still, she didn't move.

She eased in one gentle inhalation through her lips. She was quiet. Calm yet tense. Her breath eased back out just as silently.

The beast had given up its attempts to rattle her, but despite the lack of sound she sensed it was rounding the gazebo to face her head-on.

With a motion so slick even a creature as highly sensitive as this one wouldn't hear, she glided the dagger from the sheath belted to her waist. Custom-made and teeming with her coven's magic, the blade was meant for one thing only. To end demons.

And when the creature sprang—believing it was still the hunter—she got her chance to put the weapon to use. Long, sinewy arms spread wide before her, as if the towering gray beast would enfold her in a death-hug.

Its flesh shimmered beneath the gazebo's lamplight, an iridescence from the acid slicked over its pale skin. This was the same breed of demon the guys had faced on their wild night out. They'd warned the witches that the creatures' saliva was also corrosive.

Despite her abilities, Paige couldn't heal herself. She needed to stay clear of the caustic liquid. She saw the fiend's stare flick to her dagger, glowing brightly with the special blue of the coven's magic.

The creature sucked in a mangled breath. It knew who—or what—she was.

Then the demon made a nauseating sound, coughing up phlegm as if simultaneously suffering from the flu, allergies, and pulmonary edema. The beast drew back its head, preparing to launch the lugie, just as the moon escaped from the quicksilver clouds.

Paige stared down her adversary, never taking her eyes from the creature's. The orbs were black as night, runny with excretions, and though deep-set, she was close enough to see they bulged with some sort of superficial vessels.

When the demon reared back a second time, its liquid catapult ready, she curled her lip with derision. "Tag," she growled, "you're it."

As the uber-spitball came flying, she dodged, ducking to the side. Apart from incredible strength, Paige had another unique attribute. When she decided to move…she *moved*.

Before the acidic mucus even landed on the gazebo behind her, she had flashed to stand on the other side of the demon. She took a moment to enjoy the comical rotation of its slimy gray head—back and forth, back and forth—as it searched for her.

Then with a leap and an upward thrust, she buried the dagger in the posterior curve of its skull. What luck, she thought with a sardonic sense of approval. She'd found a nice soft spot.

A cloud of particles erupted, but again, she withdrew herself from the immediate vicinity. In a flash, she was fifteen feet away, and in plenty of time to keep her white-blonde hair from turning gray. Ash-gray.

"There's another one."

Paige whirled, dagger raised. A guy was standing approximately five feet away from her. He was tall with an athletic build, light colored hair. A breath of familiarity passed over her.

How long had he been there? Had he actually seen the demon?

Better yet, how had he managed to sneak up on her?

Eyes narrowed, Paige tucked her dagger back into its leather cradle. She moved closer, and her surprise and confusion vanished, recognition sliding into their place. She'd seen this guy before, and the memory wasn't pleasant.

The last time she'd met up with him, he'd grabbed her arm, asked her name, and had come across as far too possessive for her tastes. Now, by sheer chance, he'd stumbled across her again?

Nah. No coincidence there.

"What are you doing here?" She flung her hand up to indicate the huge, antique style clock. "It's after four in the morning."

"Exactly. An odd time to visit City Market. I was curious to see what you planned to do down here."

"What…are you following me?" She shook her head, stunned by his apparent lack of shame and bemused by his foolishness. *You picked the wrong girl, buddy.*

"I saw you rush out of the house."

Paige's very molecules stopped their subcellular activity. She was rigid, her voice low and dangerous. "What house?"

He quirked a single brow, as if to imply she should already know the answer. "The yellow one."

Closing in so quickly her hair fluttered against her cheeks, Paige clenched the front of his dark shirt and jerked him forward. Just close enough to catch a hint of his clean, woodsy scent.

With her face bare inches from his, she warned, "You stay away from there. Stay away from me."

She was tempted to back up her menacing tone with magic, give the creep a good scare. But as much as she wanted to, she couldn't risk some stranger learning about the coven or that she was a witch. Especially this freak-ass stalker man.

He might have seen her stick a blade into the demon's head just now. He'd even told her there was "another one," but surely he didn't know she was tracking monsters. How could he?

"I have friends who are cops," she said, hoping to back him off by ordinary means. Since she really shouldn't burn his eyebrows off with the fire she could throw from her hands, a talent that came naturally to her and her sisters.

Instead of easing away or looking the least bit concerned, he simply quirked up one side of his mouth and smiled at her.

This guy had to be unbalanced.

"The other one is getting away." He jerked his head toward the line of roofs.

Shocked, Paige turned in time to see a gangly and all-too-familiar body type leaping from the locally famous cookie store to a souvenir shop next door. In under three seconds, the demon was on the corner, staring at the street below as if plotting its escape route.

Turning back to the man still gripped in her clutches, Paige curled her upper lip and made a decidedly unfriendly noise in her throat. Decision time. Haul the guy down to The Barracks, the metro police headquarters, where Cole and Trevor could sort him out. Or option two, let him go and chase the fiend.

After a quick mental rundown and comparison of danger

ratios, she released his shirt. The demon was a greater threat to the populace than one man. Even if he was cracked.

Anyway, he wasn't getting off scot-free. "You made a mistake following me. I told you the night I saw you at the bar to keep your distance."

"Paige—" he began.

She pressed a hand to his mouth, and still she could tell he smiled beneath her palm. So she crushed a little harder. "Your stalking days are over, asshole. So smile while you can."

In one flowing streak of movement, she reached around to his back pocket, and then moved to the other after she found the first empty. She was rewarded on the second try, and slipped out the one thing she'd need to make sure he didn't get away without repercussions.

With his driver's license in hand, she dropped the wallet and blasted off in pursuit of the monster, the one bouncing across the rooftops like a mutant Mary Poppins. As she'd anticipated, the beast leaped down to land on the asphalt of an intersecting street and lurched its way from the City Market.

Paige turned on her turbo boost, opting to enjoy herself once again. She'd catch the demon as well as take care of a human annoyance, bagging two problems in one night. Make that three, she mused, recalling her previous kill.

Grinning as she ran, she pictured what the stalker's expression must have looked like when she'd left him standing there. How she'd love to see his face.

That persistent smile was probably gone, and he was likely at a loss as to how she'd picked his pocket and...*poof!*...just disappeared. And all in the time it took him to blink.

Okay, maybe to blink *twice*.

Either way, Paige had come out on top, and he sure wasn't following her anymore. *Take that, suckerrrrr.* She pictured him again. *Let's see you catch me now.*

2

Paige slowly descended the wide mahogany staircase to the grand hall, where she was met by the muted sound of multiple conversations carrying from the kitchen. Despite only a couple hours sleep after her return from the city, she was wide awake, semi-energized, and excessively hungry.

The last was not an uncommon state for her, considering her activity level burned at least three times as many calories as the average person. And last night she'd doubled the level of exertion that was normal even for her.

In jeans and a sleeveless white t-shirt, she trudged barefoot across the cool slate floor, telling herself she didn't need to sleep in anyway. A perk of her excessive strength was also stamina that never seemed to lag.

That's why she'd gone ahead and gotten out of bed. Her rising had nothing to do with the way her mind had been racing for the past thirty minutes. Nothing at all to do with the fact her trial had finally come calling.

Or the fact that her thoughts kept returning to the guy who'd followed her downtown. He was clearly suffering some social deficiencies, might even be a predator of women. So why had he popped into her head again and again?

Probably her subconscious reminding her a stalker was on the loose, and that she needed to bring him to the attention of the authorities. Yeah, and she'd do just that.

As soon as she ate.

A grayish-brown body streaked past her ankles, causing Paige to chuckle at her feline mini-me. Tiger Lily rushed ahead, sidestepping and ignoring Hayden's playful Daisy when the other cat swatted at her tail in an attempt to stir mischief.

Like Paige, Tiger didn't have time for play, especially when food was involved.

Raking a hand through her short hair, she worked up a smile as she entered the kitchen. "Morning."

"Well, good morning." Willyn half-turned to greet Paige, her hand on a mug that sat beneath a stream of coffee. The coven's healer was a caffeine junkie, along with most of the women. "We didn't expect you up so early. Anna told us you had a late night."

Shuffling like a zombie, Paige went to the silver and black coffee machine to get her own hit. She might have a bottomless source of energy, but even she needed her java fix.

A soft laugh pulled her attention to the far end of the room, where Anna's brother, Quinn, sat with a smiling Kylie on his lap. The youngest witch tossed a wealth of golden hair over one shoulder and whispered in her boyfriend's ear.

For the past year, their relationship had been tumultuous to say the least, and Paige was happy to see them both finally at peace with each other. But that didn't mean she was done giving them a hard time.

"Hey, why don't you two take that somewhere else?" She hiked a brow when they both glanced over. "People are trying to eat here, you know."

In response, Kylie took Quinn's chin in hand and turned his face to hers. Then she gave him a thorough kiss.

Paige faced the counter again, but not before she allowed a sly grin to creep out. As she selected a coffee pod titled Dark

Magic—*ha ha*—she glanced to Anna who was sitting at the crescent-shaped island in the center of the kitchen. "Sorry if I woke you when I came home."

Anna set aside her morning crossword. "From the top floor? No, I didn't hear you."

"Then how did you know..." Paige broke off. "Duh. Never mind." The coven's leader was also clairvoyant. "I guess you saw some of what happened downtown."

One of Anna's shoulders lifted. "I got a sense."

"Hmm." Paige stirred her drink, staring into the undiluted black. Anna was cryptic like that, only revealing what she gleaned from her visions if absolutely necessary. Her gift wasn't always clear, and she hesitated to share all, possibly affecting future actions or outcomes in the wrong way.

Sometimes her ability could be quite practical, though. When Paige and the other women had followed a whisper of magic to the island off the Georgia coastline, they'd found rooms at the St. Germaine mansion already made up for each of them. Their individual chambers had been styled to perfectly suit their tastes and personalities.

But even Anna couldn't always predict or understand their enemies. The Amara.

"The demons last night weren't showing themselves to people, at least not like the ones the guys encountered on their night out." Paige blew on her steaming coffee. "I think they were hunting for people to take back to Ronja."

The leader of the Amara was one cruel and vengeful witch. She'd walked the earth for over a thousand years, graced by immortality in exchange for her loyalty to Bastraal while the demon had been trapped in the underworld.

Her goal, and that of all of the Amara, was to resurrect the demon permanently. So far, he'd managed his way back into this realm, but he wasn't finished yet. For Bastraal to truly enjoy life on earth, to wreak the carnage he planned, he had to be in human form.

All he had to do was choose a man and steal the unlucky soul's body for eternity.

Paige didn't want to imagine what actually happened to the victim's soul, his spirit. Where did it go? Was it forever trapped in its former shell alongside a heinous beast?

She shook off the terrible image and returned to her recounting of events in City Market. "I'm not positive, but if those demons last night wanted to kill someone, I don't see why they would wait until so few people were out. They could easily have attacked earlier, taken out a few wandering drunks or a college kid walking home alone. No one would have been the wiser. Not until it was too late."

Moving to stand next to Anna, Paige rested her arm on the back of a wrought-iron barstool. "My guess is the Amara are back in the business of providing bodies for demons, the kind who can move around among people unnoticed once they have a human skin."

She leveled a cool gaze on her friend. "They're amassing troops."

"A demon army." Anna nodded. "The prophecy is coming to a head, so I can't say a move like that would be unexpected. Ronja wants to win, and we already know she's not above breaking any rules set down for the prophecy or twisting any circumstance to her favor."

"Yeah." Paige lifted her eyes, dancing her attention to the others gathered in the room. "But that doesn't mean we won't try and stop her."

Willyn's husband Dare was present, as were Hayden, the coven's ghost-whisperer, and her boyfriend Trevor. He was one half of the pair of police detectives aligned with the coven.

Cole, the other half, had just walked in with Claudia. Meeting the stare of the flame-haired witch, Paige decided to deliver her news. "My trial has started."

"Wait. Hold that thought," Claudia said, thrusting out a flattened palm like a professor shushing an errant student. "The others are on their way down. Save it for everyone."

Paige pursed her lips. "Fine, but I don't see the big deal. It's not like it's a surprise. The candidate pool had gotten pretty shallow." She shared a look with Anna. "But I'll wait. That way I won't have to repeat everything to the rest of the crew. This place is becoming its own little village."

She sent a sidelong glance to the others, but no one was crass enough to imply the village would probably be gaining another man soon. Paige wasn't going to let it happen, and no one could convince her she had to, or needed to.

She'd spent her whole life without a partner and had been as fulfilled and successful as the average person. And in her experience, men usually caused just the opposite of happiness.

She would allow that Fate had chosen well for her friends, or the gods and goddesses, whoever actually ran this magic show she was involved in. Still—she filled her lungs as anxiety spiked—no *way* was she letting some deified fortune-teller do the choosing for her.

Like a fairy godmother, Mrs. Attinger, the estate housekeeper, breezed into the kitchen with an aqua-blue glass vase filled with white flowers blooming on tall and straight green stems. Paige realized the arrangement was to honor her time of challenge.

Anna must have seen a lot through her psychic abilities, and she'd let Mrs. Attinger know to make preparations. The blue vase represented Paige's color, since few flowers came in that particular shade. "They're beautiful Mrs. A. I love gladiolus."

The spry woman with her hair in a short silver cap set the vase in the center of the kitchen island. "I learned their plural is gladioli, though I've never heard anyone call them that." She cocked her head and studied Paige. "They symbolize strength of character, so I felt they were appropriate."

The older woman's eyes positively glistened as she added the last, and Paige wanted to hug her. She settled instead for a choked up, "Thanks."

Mrs. Attinger winked, a sign that she knew what was in Paige's heart. And that the tough, stoic soldier didn't often give herself over to emotional displays.

Well, assuming anger and all its forms didn't count.

She was enjoying the silkiness of a white petal when Viv and Shauni strolled through the door. However, these two were sans their male counterparts. Viv's boyfriend Nick had his pub to see to, and Michael, Shauni's fiancé and center of the great bachelor party debacle, was at his veterinary clinic in town tending to his animal patients.

Behind them, Lucia entered with her trademark hip-roll and a happy-to-watch-her-roll Ethan trailing close behind. The demon hunter who'd joined their little club was still mesmerized by his Spanish witch.

With everyone gathered, Paige recapped her interlude with the two demons, and discussions were waged about Ronja's intent and whether or not the coven should up their efforts to locate and destroy portals created by the Amara. As long as the inter-dimensional doorways existed, demons would continue to cross over.

When the debate finally began to die down, Paige delivered the rest of the story, including the strange rush in her bloodstream, heralding the start of her challenge. She paused and took a bracing breath before wrapping up with the last piece of drama. The creep.

She notched her chin to Cole and Trevor. "There's something else. A guy I want you two to check out for me."

"A guy?" Now Kylie was on her feet, deserting Quinn's cozy lap. The college coed, on hiatus from school to help save the world, was more excited about a new male presence than the previous mention of monsters prowling downtown.

Lucia and Claudia also stepped closer, faces alight with curiosity. Paige pulled her mouth to one side in a sour expression. *Typical.*

"It's not what you're all thinking, so get those stars out of your eyes." She shot down a few other hopeful looks before pulling the confiscated driver's license from the pocket of her jeans. She held it up and spoke to Cole and Trevor again, the homicide detectives with access to background checks and rap sheets. "I seem to have a stalker."

Trevor's face turned to stone.

Cole's brow creased. "Um…a stalker?" Rubbing his chin with the back of his knuckles, he edged closer to Claudia and cleared his throat. "What makes you think so?"

Paige studied the pair. Was it her imagination, or did they both seem nervous? "It's the same guy that grabbed me that time at the nightclub. Apparently he's been watching me, all but admitted to following me from the yellow house last night."

"Following you?" Ethan shot a glance to Quinn before swallowing audibly. "He told you that?"

Lucia crossed her arms. "What's the matter with you?" she asked Ethan. Paige wasn't the only one picking up on the odd behavior the men in the room were demonstrating.

And only the men.

"Wait a minute." Now she paid closer attention to the shifting eyes, sudden coughs, and lowered heads, all subconscious tells. The stench of collusion rolled right over her. "Just what do you guys know about him?"

Quinn took Kylie's hand and tried to pull her toward the far door. "Maybe we should take it elsewhere like she asked."

Kylie held steady, tugging him back. "Hold it right there."

"Dare?" Willyn looked up to her husband.

He winced before saying, "He asked us about Paige the night of Michael's bachelor party. We didn't think it would take him so long to follow up."

"You saw him that night?" Paige was stunned.

"And we thought he'd come out here to the island," Trevor tossed in, avoiding a direct answer to her question. "He seemed like the kind of guy to be more direct."

"Oh, he was direct, all right." Paige set her cup on the gray granite island with a *thunk!* "After he got done being creepy."

"*Corazon.*" Lucia spoke low to Ethan before shaking her head with a *tsk-tsk-tsk*. "Why didn't you tell me?"

"Why didn't any of you tell any of us?" Hayden had both hands planted on her hips, glaring up at Trevor.

"Like Dare said, we thought the guy would come straight out here." Cole looked pained, and for good reason, considering the stink-eye he was receiving from Claudia. "When he didn't and time started to pass…"

"He saved Michael's life the night of the bachelor party," Quinn blurted.

"What?" Shauni's green eyes flew wide.

"He was almost demon road-kill," Trevor added with an enthusiastic nod. "But Chris got him out of the way. He helped us with the injured students too." The tall blonde cop turned serious eyes on Hayden. "He only asked for one thing in return."

"But why didn't you just tell us all this?" Kylie asked Quinn, holding out her hands.

Quinn's gaze gradually lifted, but not to Kylie. He and every other man turned to stare at Paige.

"Oh." Kylie grimaced as she studied Paige's clenched fists and wide-set stance. "There is that."

Paige worked her jaw muscles, searching for the right balance of accusation and disappointment to fill her words. "So you just gave this guy our address and offered me up as some male-bonding sacrifice?"

Then, fearing she would say something hurtful that she might regret later, she reminded herself how much she cared about all the people gathered here, the men and the women. To keep her mouth shut, she snatched up her cup again for a long, hot gulp.

She was usually the composed and stoic one, but the news, this revelation, had shaken her to the bone. Not because the men kept the truth from her and the coven, that was only worthy of a little irritation. And good fodder for future guilt trips.

What bothered her, what had her head shot full of buzzing anxiety, was if the guys already knew the jerk from last night, if they'd already accepted him...*Shit. Just shit.* Then maybe he was—

"He's a good guy," Dare said, inserting the very conclusion Paige didn't want to come to. "Really," he added with sincerity, speaking as much to Willyn as to Paige.

At least she didn't have to hand out reprimands herself. The witches would take care of that for her.

Having been raised as an only child, Paige had often come to the same shocking and warming realization since her arrival in Savannah.

It was good to have sisters.

But even they secretly rooted for her to find a match. Just as they had.

She'd said before the pool had gotten shallow? Understatement. Because Anna was the only single fish still flopping around with Paige, and she had always accepted the foibles of the prophecy. Including the love scenarios that were part and parcel.

"Doesn't matter." Paige licked the scalding coffee from her lips and held up the license as if offering state's evidence. "You guys just participated in some erroneous male bonding. But it's not your fault. Only a female could pick up on the vibes that I did."

She clucked her mouth and concluded, "He's a freak."

"I'm on Paige's side with this one." Kylie spoke up, surprising them all. The youngest witch was the most optimistic romantic among them. "If he's such a great guy, why didn't he approach her instead of just," she shivered with revulsion, "watch her from afar?"

"Good question," Claudia said.

Paige felt a surge of cheer at the female support. She'd expected her sister-witches to be in favor of any man who happened to show up during her trial. Even though they were all neck-deep in love and glad for it, they knew Paige was disinclined to follow suit.

She didn't want a man in her life. And she sure didn't need one.

Especially a stalker.

Resolved to simply make her usual morning smoothie and forget about this guy—this Chris Decker, according to his driver's license—Paige blew out a breath laden with frustration and took another sip of coffee.

A robotic buzz came from Quinn's front pocket, and he pulled out his cell phone to check the screen. Though he tried to hide his reaction, Paige caught the mild shock as it flitted over his face.

"What is it?" she asked, her tone warning him not to dodge the question.

"A text from Joseph." Quinn's shoulders rose and fell with the depth of his sigh. "He says, 'Heads up.'"

Paige's fingers strangled the stem of her cup. "Why?"

Then the doorbell chimed.

"Talk about timing," Anna mused, directing a pointed stare at Paige and her iron grip. "But please, mind the porcelain."

"Is he..." Paige felt her brows clash together to form one line of oh-hell-no. "You've got to be kidding me." Without another word, she put down the mug—gently—but shoved away from the counter and strode out of the kitchen. Strident steps took her through the grand hall and into the foyer.

Careful not to unhinge the massive slab of oak, she jerked one side of the double doors open. And found herself staring into the face of her most recent nemesis.

A moment of astonishment registered in his expression before his lips turned up in a grin. "Good to see you again, Paige. I believe you have something of mine."

"How the hell did you get here?" Ignoring his outstretched hand, she peered over his wide shoulders and down the forest trail. No sign of the golf cart.

"Joseph taxied me out here on the boat. He offered me a lift to the house too, but I decided to walk the trail, get a look at the island."

"Hmph." Another colluder. Joseph could have given a little more warning.

Though Quinn had just received the text, Paige's visitor was already on her doorstep. He didn't even look winded.

Paige glared at him, the trespasser, but all he did was stand there, patience and humor rolling off his shoulders.

Taking in his confident stance and well-muscled arms, she reminded herself that he was a Ranger. At least, he had been. His dark blonde hair was a bit longer now, definitely not regulation, so maybe he'd been discharged.

Regardless, in his line of work, he'd probably gotten used to overcoming a wide range of obstacles and was accustomed to getting his way in all things. Professional *and* personal.

But he'd never dealt with her before, and she wasn't the kind of girl to be swayed by his lean-machine physique or pure green eyes. In her mind, a charming smile like his was a bright red flag.

Narrowing her eyes, she held up the license. "This what you mean?"

"Yeah." He reached out as if to take back his property, but Paige tossed it in the air instead, forcing him to back up a step to make the catch. When he did, she took the opportunity to snarl at him one last time. "Now screw off."

Then she slammed the door in his face.

3

Chris waited outside on the gray stone steps and tried to decide how to proceed. He was already out here on the island, and Paige was well aware of his presence. Aware? What a soft sell. She was fuming.

Well, he wasn't going to just leave, not now. He'd been looking for her for far too long. And at last, he'd found her.

He'd been stationed at Hunter Army Airfield for several years, and even though it was one of only three Ranger battalions in the country he still felt the hand of providence at work. Savannah was where he'd finished his military career, and the same city was where he'd stumbled across Paige.

Luck? He didn't think so.

Last summer he'd gotten his first glimpse of her, just as she'd been leaving a nightclub with some of her friends. Too shocked to believe it was really her, Chris had let her leave, believing she'd be easy to locate now that he knew she was local.

Not true. He hadn't found a scrap of evidence she even existed. No registry anywhere, no phone or address listing. Hell, not even a social site. He'd had absolutely no lead on her whereabouts, until the night he'd spotted Dare, Trevor, and Quinn, the men he'd seen with her at the club.

Of course, when he'd come across the guys in town again, he'd refused to let them out of his sight. Not until they told him where she was.

They'd done so, if a bit reluctantly, in exchange for his timely yet unwanted help.

After another couple of weeks spent on Paige Reilley reconnaissance, Chris had a better idea of what she was doing here.

And that she might finally be ready to use the gifts she'd been given.

Before he could knock or ring the doorbell again, the tall panel swung inward to reveal a petite blonde with welcoming eyes. "You must be Chris. Please, come in." She stepped aside. "Paige was just a little…surprised to see you, but I'm sure we can get this straightened out."

So his interest in Paige—and her vexation with him—wasn't exactly a secret. Nodding acceptance, he crossed the threshold. "Thanks."

"I'm Willyn, one of Paige's…friends."

"You mean one of the witches."

"Uh…" she stammered, and then chose not to say anything at all, closing the door and leading him silently into the home's interior. The place was impressive, and very old, far surpassing the description of "mansion," as Joseph had referred to it.

They walked through a massive main room with a ceiling that soared up two floors. Rich, antique woodwork gleamed in the formal wainscoting and banisters on the stairs. Traditional furnishings and artwork mingled side-by-side with modern pieces.

All of it was a far cry from his Spartan existence for the past six years. Or for even longer if he thought about it. His life in the military had been more stable than all the years before it combined, and considering the short but frequent deployments that comparison said a lot.

He'd kept pushing forward, though, knowing one day things would change, and he'd finally be able to settle down, stop looking over his shoulder. But if that day was going to come, he had to keep his eye on the goal.

And that goal was Paige.

Now that he was out of the Army, and now that he'd found her, he finally had a chance for a normal life. And if given the opportunity, Chris knew he'd succeed.

So with no envy or resentment, he was able to appreciate the Waterford bowl as well as the Harrington table the crystal sat upon. His nomadic upbringing had introduced him to many fine things, and he planned to have an elegant home of his own.

Chris stayed with Willyn until they entered a large kitchen, replete with masonry to rival any castle in the old country. Then she veered off to take a seat at a smoky-colored granite island in the shape of a half-moon.

Chris recognized the man next to her and inclined his head. "Dare."

"Chris," the male witch returned with a nod. His head swiveled with a careful slide of his gaze, and Chris followed his line of sight to discover Paige clutching the glass jar of a blender. She looked as if she might launch it at his head.

"I have to talk to you," he said quickly. "Explain about following you. It's not what you think." He hoped to quell her fury by starting off with her main concern. Having taken the time to review his actions and how he'd approached her in the streets, he understood why she wanted to toss him out, or better yet, have him arrested. "I'm not a stalker."

She raised one delicately-arched brow, clearly conveying her doubt. "Your presence says otherwise."

"I'm not. I swear. At least, not like you probably imagine."

Casting an aggravated glance to the other people gathered

in the room, of which there were many, Paige shook her head and said, "I guess you're invited in." She narrowed her eyes first at Willyn and then at a woman with long brown hair who also sat at the curved island.

Her gaze was still averted when he heard her hiss, "So spit out whatever you feel you just *have* to tell me."

The men in the room he'd already met, but several of the women were giving him guarded or outright hostile looks, and his attempt at a genial smile faltered under their inspection.

He returned his attention to the woman who practically bristled with irritation. All because of him. "I'd rather speak to you in private."

"One," she snapped out. "You don't make the rules here." She put the jar into the base of the blender and screwed it in. "Two. I don't keep secrets from my friends." Rotating her upper body, she used her eyes to stab at Dare and the other males. "Unlike *some* people."

Still ignoring Chris, she went to the refrigerator and took out eggs, what looked like coconut milk, and a couple of items from a vegetable drawer. With her back to him, she began loading the blender. Finally, she spoke again. "You obviously know about the demons in this city, since you pointed one out to me last night."

"Yes."

"And that we're witches," Willyn supplied helpfully with a grin.

At least one of them was friendly. Chris had faced terrorist groups less intimidating than this all-female coven.

Paige whirled around. "So you think you should be involved, is that it? Well if that's the case, you can stop thinking. I don't know why you latched on to me or why you've been tracking me, but you've got five minutes to say what you came here to say."

Before he could open his mouth, she speared a finger in his direction. "And to be clear, I don't care about your Special Ops training. I have skills of my own. Ranger or not, this is not your war."

"Fine." He shrugged, and almost smiled when his acceptance seemed to throw her off balance. But he tamped the response down, because she seemed to get really pissed when he smiled at her. And he needed to get on her good side. Which…he had yet to witness.

Patience, he counseled himself and decided he couldn't hold anything against her until he explained himself. By all accounts, he had been following her around. Not revealing his presence. Generally being sneaky.

Okay, so technically, he'd stalked her.

With the admission in mind, he studied Trevor and Cole to see if the two cops were still as amiable toward him as they'd been after his assistance during the bachelor party. As far as he could tell, they still had his back, and once he explained why he was here he felt sure Paige and her friends would understand.

And if she only knew what he was risking by being here. She assumed he was just a guy who'd spotted an attractive woman and wouldn't take no for an answer, but the truth was far more complicated. He wasn't supposed to be within sight of her, but not because of her objections.

Locating Paige, speaking to her, any contact at all—had been forbidden. *He's going to be furious if he finds out. Better to get it done first. Report later.*

Taking note of the protein powder she scooped into the blender, Chris put aside the bad taste of betrayal in his mouth and sidled a few steps in her direction. "That's looks good. Could you make me one while you're at it?"

He bent to rub the grayish-brown tabby cat nudging at his leg. Cute little thing, and persistent. "Or I could cook," he offered, looking to the others.

Paige stilled and glanced over her shoulder. "Seriously?" Then her eyes darkened as she looked down. "Tiger, get away from him."

He patted his stomach. "I didn't have time to make my usual frittata."

With a major eye roll, she gave him her back again. "Whatever. Your five minutes are counting down, so waste them however you want."

Settling in to wait, Chris crossed his arms over his chest. "Don't worry. I'll use the time wisely."

With a grunt, Paige proceeded to double up on the ice, raw eggs, coconut milk, protein powder, banana, strawberries, and some green produce he couldn't identify.

"I know my veggies, but what's that prickly green—"

She showed her interest by hitting the grind button.

So he remained silent while the loud motor churned and the blades chewed the mix into a lumpy brown concoction. Taking advantage, though, he observed the play of muscles in her tight arms—bared by her sleeveless white shirt—and continued to watch as she poured the mixture into two large glasses.

She seemed plenty fit and strong, and that was good. She'd need to be.

Slinging out an arm, she offered him his smoothie.

Chris accepted and said, "Thanks, princess."

The atmosphere went stone-cold calm. Paige froze mid-motion, and the whole room stilled. Silence reigned as everyone stared.

At last, Paige ground out, "What. Did you. Just call me?"

"Princess," Chris replied, not at all concerned about her

mounting fury. He had a flash-bang in his arsenal.

And he knew when to pull the pin.

"That's what I used to call you. We all did." He sipped the awful-looking smoothie and tasted berry. "When you were little."

~~~

Closing the library doors firmly behind her, Paige pivoted and faced Chris. She felt completely wild and emotional in the face of his tranquil demeanor, so she brushed past him and moved to take a seat at one of the long desks.

Normally, she preferred to face adversaries on equal footing, but now…she just needed to sit. Dragging her eyes up to him, she scanned his face for any resemblance to a memory she might have stored. None came forth. "Who are you?" Her voice was whisper-thin and shaky, but for once she let her pride take a back seat to distress.

"I come from the same people as you do."

"We're related?"

He shook his head. "No. We're not family, if that's what you mean. But the people we lived with were all brought together due to certain…similarities."

The vast library with its ceiling-high bookcases was usually a place of peace, soothing with its serious and dark colors. But she could find no trace of serenity at the moment. Not with this unwelcome visitor becoming something more than an easily brushed aside pest.

He was hurling pieces of a forgotten life at her feet. "We were part of the same commune when we were kids," he said. "A haven for people who were different, people possessing unusual talents."

"You mean magic?" she asked, eyeing him more cautiously

all of a sudden.

"Yeah." Chris came over and leaned against the desk, not crowding her, exactly, but making himself comfortable, as if he expected to be here for the long haul.

But Paige didn't have the energy to dredge up any resentment. Her system was still buzzing with shock. "I left there so long ago. I was young, four or five, so I don't remember much of it. Most of what I know are just stories my aunt and uncle told me."

She studied his face, noticing how the set of his hard jaw contrasted with the kindness in his gaze. He couldn't be much older than she was. "How do you remember me?"

His hands gripped the edge of the wood, work-worn hands, hard and strong. "I was a little older, and I've kept in touch with a few others." Now those grass-green eyes shadowed over. "Though there aren't many of us left."

"Left? What happened?" Paige couldn't stem her interest in the information he possessed, even while rationality started to tap her on the shoulder, telling her she shouldn't ask about those days.

Her entire life she'd tried to pretend they'd never happened, because their very existence filled her with questions. Questions no one had ever answered.

The Ranger tilted his blonde head to the side. "You don't know? I thought your aunt and uncle would have at least told you that much. About what happened to your family."

My family. The word was akin to knives scraping over raw nerves, and Paige's jaw clamped down involuntarily.

Too late, she realized she should have listened to her logical inner voice, because suddenly an old and uninvited friend showed up. A roiling, fiery ball of hurt and rage she thought she'd finally destroyed. Here it was trying to resurface, burning her from the inside out.

Growing up, she'd been consumed with confusion and sadness. Then, over time, the emotions coalesced into something stronger, an overwhelming and uncontainable ferocity. There were years of her adolescence when even her aunt and uncle had backed away from her with caution.

Those days shamed her still.

It was bad enough when the average person had anger management issues, but when someone had an awful temper as well as the strength to fling manhole covers around like Frisbees?

Paige grimaced at the reminder and the cost of those windows she'd had to pay for.

After that fiasco, she'd wisely learned to self-isolate, at least until she'd graduated high school and had gotten away from the inherent teenage stressors. Once out alone in the big, bad world, what else should she have done with all her energy and rage…but join the Army?

So that's what she'd done, and channeling her vexation into a real and deserving enemy had helped. So had growing up some. Not only had she been useful in the Army, but serving had provided an outlet for her fury—all the hurt that evolved into hate.

She'd gained physical conditioning, strictly regimented training, and hard-earned self-control. But now, with this man shoving her one great loss into her face, all of that simply dissipated.

Her discipline eroded as she considered Chris's question. "Yeah. Sure." Her voice lashed like a whip. "I know what happened. My mother died."

She stood quickly, her legs shoving the chair away as she did. "And after she was gone, my father couldn't handle raising a kid on his own. So he dumped me with his half-sister and her husband. He got rid of me."

Chris started to speak, but then, seeming to rethink his words, he pressed his mouth closed. He stood fully, looked her in the eye. "There's more to the story than that, and I think you have the right to know all of it."

"How can there be more? My aunt and uncle always told me—"

"What they were instructed to tell you. What they swore they would make you believe, for your own good." He lifted a hand as if to touch her arm, but Paige jerked out of his reach.

"Who the hell do you think you are? Do you really expect me to just take the word of some stranger over the people I've loved and trusted my whole life? My aunt and uncle raised me when no one else could be bothered." She took another step backward, suddenly afraid of what he might reveal about her past.

But why? She didn't know him. She had no reason to believe him.

Yet she couldn't make him leave. Not yet. A sneaking curiosity urged her to hear him out.

Truthfully, she'd often wondered why the accounts of her early childhood had always been so limited. She'd had doubts when her aunt and uncle had explained about her parents, because they'd both used such similar phrases and expressions.

As if repeating them by rote.

A breath trembled out through Paige's lips as she and Chris stared at each other. He was letting her make her own decision, waiting for her next words. Patiently.

"So what?" she asked at last. "If you lived in the commune, then are you a witch too?"

"That's one name, I guess." He visibly relaxed but still stood straight and tall, his shoulders held back with self-assurance. "I'm not really one for titles."

Again she took her time before speaking, using the extended silence to exert some control. The guy didn't come across as cocky, but Paige could tell he was used to wielding a certain amount of authority.

"You know about the demons," she began, "but what else do you know?" Maybe she was stalling, avoiding any further discussion of her mother's death or her father's betrayal, but she would be the one to drive this conversation. She would set the pace.

Given the option, she preferred to have her world shattered in small increments.

"I only know pieces, what I could extrapolate from the guys' conversations the night of the bachelor party."

"The night you saved Michael's life and earned brownie points." She groused internally at the debt she was forced to acknowledge. Michael was like a brother to her. All the men were.

Lucky for them too, after the stunt they'd pulled by keeping Chris a secret.

If he picked up on her lingering resentment, his impassive attitude didn't show it. "You and your friends," he began, "sorry, your *coven*, are waging a battle against another witch named Ronja who controls demons." He scratched his chest through the dark blue fabric of his t-shirt. "That's the gist, anyway."

"Close enough." Paige was a little glad he didn't know everything. That he didn't have the upper hand in all things having to do with her life. "The point is I don't have the time for any side drama." She scoffed. "I have my *destiny* to contend with."

"Actually, that's why I'm here."

Her heart struck out in one hard pump, like a fist driving into the interior side of her sternum. Surely he didn't mean…

But how could he even know about that part of the challenge?

"You're destined to complete a task. It's why I had to find you." One long stride brought him within a foot of Paige, but she didn't retreat, simply caught her breath. He was a big guy, daunting when he needed to be.

But he was so earnest as he hovered over her. "I came to help you."

Paige released the breath in a rush. "Help me do what?"

"Seek justice for what was done to you." His eyes darted to the side, his nostrils flared. "And to me."

"I don't know what you're talking about." Holding her ground, Paige firmed her mouth and demanded, "Justice for what?"

"My parents were murdered, Paige." He held her gaze, daring her to do the same. Then he sent a quake through her already upturned world. "And so was your mother."

4

Ronja sipped her Oolong tea and inhaled the sweet, flavorful fragrance. Breakfast was one of her favorite times of the day, when she sat in the sunroom and partook of a light repast much like any wealthy lady of the manor. For her, the mornings were a form of playacting, a sinister deception in the guise of delicate china, healthy fruit and grain, and even the cheerfulness of the room.

The entire production was the antithesis of who she truly was.

Here was the one place in her home she allowed bright décor. Chairs of light-toned wood were cushioned with gold, in tune with Ronja's lovely hair. A wall of windows allowed sunlight to filter in, though every other room of the remodeled Southern plantation eschewed the yellow rays as if allergic.

The only harshness came in the form of a large light fixture hanging above the table. The aged brass was better suited to a dungeon with its thick vertical bars encaging wax candles. But she enjoyed that one austere piece, a single dark spot amongst the bright.

The muffin with a pat of butter was halfway to her mouth when a hooded figure glided into the sunny room with a feather-soft tread. Searenn, the Droehk. A woman whose tattoos constituted a second skin but enabled her to wrangle demons with an iron hand. Just as her long line of forebears had done.

"You have something to report?" Ronja asked, concealing her annoyance. This was her private time. Like a mother with too many children, she required space away from her followers.

"The two demons I sent out last night didn't return." The scratchy voice conveyed no fear, though Ronja suspected even Searenn dreaded reporting failure to the witch who ruled her.

"And the humans they would have brought back?" Wrath sparked within Ronja, and she allowed the flash to show in her eyes.

Searenn simply shook her head.

Ronja set down the pastry, her desire for the melting butter momentarily sidetracked by the bitter taste of disappointment. Once, she would have lashed out at the Droehk, verbally and physically, but now she sipped her tea and attempted to find control.

The last time she'd acted out of anger alone, she'd made tactical mistakes. After killing the young golden-haired coven witch, that Kylie girl, Ronja had been sure of her victory, so she and her brethren had launched an assault on the witches' very home, their safe territory, the sainted island.

And had promptly been delivered a resounding and humiliating defeat. Plus, that little bitch had somehow revived herself, ensuring the coven circle remained intact. And the coven magic still at full strength.

Searenn still stood waiting in silence, so Ronja put her out of her misery. "Relax, Searenn. The witches wouldn't be paying closer attention to the city if I hadn't drawn their attention by opening so many portals." And opening the last one in a public place only to have the men—the men!—chase down the monsters who'd come through the gateway.

Ronja's head snapped up. Had she just admitted making a mistake? Had she taken responsibility? In front of an underling?

To rectify the slip and recover her status, Ronja nailed the woman in place with a cold glare. "Pull back your hood and let me see your eyes when I'm speaking to you." The Droehk had one weakness, one shame—her mismatched eyes.

When Searenn did as commanded, Ronja met the one-black-and-one-blue gaze. "We still need human bodies. The demon berserkers are mighty but can't conceal themselves in society." She gave a false smile, more threatening than any word she might utter. "You know what that means?"

"Yes. More people." Searenn reached for her hood, then hesitated, waiting for permission.

More concerned with her cooling breakfast than punishing the woman, Ronja flicked a dismissive hand. "Make it happen."

As the Droehk exited the sunroom, another entered in her place. An essence seeped into the room, glacially cold, encompassing the entire area. The presence settled itself around Ronja.

Her master had come. And he required her attention.

You were too soft on her. Without corporeal form, the powerful demon could only communicate with Ronja's mind, just as he'd done for a thousand years. But now that he existed on this plane instead of in the nether world, his mental voice was stronger, deeper, and more menacing.

As the heavy bass vibrated through her, reminding her of his might, Ronja bit down on her tongue. She knew better than to offer excuses or arguments, having learned the foolishness of disrespecting Bastraal long ago.

I demand the army you swore to deliver. Too long have we

planned for this time of prophecy, yet the coven witches are proving to be a problem. A ribbon of cold encircled Ronja's neck. *After you assured me they would not.*

She opened her mouth, but pain lanced into her chest before she could reply. Bastraal reached inside of her to clench and twist the heart that would not stop beating. Not by any mortal means.

Your arrogance has already cost you, and therefore has cost me. If I am sent back to the darkness, Ronja, make no mistake. A frozen vise clamped harder on her pulsing organ. *You will go with me.*

Ronja licked her lips, nervous, experiencing a kind of agony she rarely received from the demon. Usually, the pain he gave her led to pleasure. She spoke through quivering lips. "I've always served you, Bastraal, and I always will."

Yes.

"I'll take care of it. You will have your army." When his cruel hold on her heart lessened, Ronja ventured, "I would ask one thing in return."

Silence exploded in her head. Had she angered him again? He wouldn't kill her. He needed her.

But he could do other things. Terrible things, not of this world.

The chill of a non-human appendage wrapped around her waist. A caress? A warning?

Still, she must speak. Only one other person was lodged inside her soul, alongside her master. The very reason she'd sought comfort from the demon's awful power in the first place.

She'd traded her soul for immortality, but only after the devastation of losing him.

"My brother." She almost simpered, so desperate was she to be reunited, fully, with her twin. "Please, I implore you, though I have nothing more to offer in return, please bring him back to me. Give him to me."

The pressure on her side increased, and she pulled in a breath expectantly. Then the cold eased from around her body, but not before stroking up her back, over her shoulder, and across her cheek.

Bastraal's voice didn't echo inside her mind, but she felt his blessing and acceptance.

Her hope was a sudden fire fueled with accelerant. "I won't let you down. I promise."

I know. The last was a telepathic whisper, but still she heard the underlying threat.

As the demon eased away from her, leaving her alone again in the sunny room with her strawberries and muffins, Ronja's respiration slowed and gradually returned to normal.

Her terror lingered, but Bastraal must have been satisfied by her answer. Her promise, a continuation of the oath she'd sworn so long ago.

But she had to act quickly, lest he return to convince her more thoroughly.

"Searenn!" She called for the Droehk, sure she would be answered immediately.

Apparently, her shout had aroused concern in others, for Scarlett and Tyr accompanied the hooded woman this time.

Ronja focused on Searenn. "Go rub those hideous markings on your flesh and bring me the bodies I need."

"Yes, Ronja." Searenn started to step out of the room but stopped when Scarlett put a hand on her arm.

"We're sending out more demons?" The red-haired witch was Ronja's female lover and cherished confidante, trusted only second to Tyr.

"Something like that." Ronja's plan was still whirling, still forming in her villainous mind.

"When?" Scarlett asked.

"Now. Today." Ronja stood and wrenched closed the curtains, no longer enjoying the happy light nor her food. "Find out what's happening in Savannah. I want to strategize, consider logistics."

"I'm sure we can find something to suit. A crowd or gathering?" Scarlett fingered the cuff of her peach silk shirt and rubbed the pearlescent button as she gave a fierce grin. "It is Savannah after all."

Tyr made a grunting noise. He moved to retrieve the silver pot and top off Ronja's tea, add two sugars, just as she preferred. He was always the one to try and soothe her.

"What do you say, Tyr?" Ronja eyed his naked arms and decided to engage in a post-breakfast distraction.

Tyr's lids fell to half-mast, his deep voice rumbled. "The city is always busy. There will be plenty of cattle to choose from."

~~~

"My mother was murdered?" With every word Paige uttered, her expression grew a shade darker, more menacing. "How? Who did it?"

The library was a vast, quiet cavern, and her voiced echoed off the thousands of books. Chris could see she was stunned, shaken to the core, though she tried valiantly to pretend otherwise. "We never knew for sure, but—"

"What?" She swiped a hand through short, jagged bangs of the lightest blonde. Her eyes zeroed in on him.

And he had absolutely no business noticing how blue they were. Tropical waters under full sun.

He shook himself. "But there's a chance we can find out." Focusing on the dire topic under discussion, Chris ushered the untimely and inappropriate thoughts out of his head.

"Who's we?" Then she pressed both palms straight out as if shoving an invisible wall. "No. Stop talking." Putting a hand on her hip, she swung around and walked away. "Just give me a minute."

Marching to the long bank of French-paned windows, she stared out at the sunny day.

Chris wondered what she saw out there that might calm her or provide focus, but she gave no clue. She didn't speak. This island of the coven's was filled with natural beauty, its wild glory preserved, and he hoped the view helped settle her anguish.

He hated delivering news that was taking the life, the past she'd known, and rewriting a much uglier version. But she needed to know. And he needed her help.

She wasn't the only one who deserved vengeance.

After a few minutes, she spoke, but her gaze still pierced the glass panes. "How do I know you are who you say you are?"

Despite the question, Chris could tell she believed him, or her body wouldn't be as relaxed as it was. She'd have already tried to escort him out, or worse.

This new, adult Paige seemed to have a violent streak.

"When we were kids, your favorite thing to do was gather flowers and make long necklaces by looping blooms through stems. Your favorite was the Rocky Mountain iris, a deep purple." He laughed. "Or as you used to say, puh-pell."

His walk down sentimental lane got nothing from her. Instead, she glared at him. "Is my father alive?"

He started, taken aback by her line of thought. "He was gone from the commune when they attacked." Chris curled his fingers, tightening until his joints tingled.

Then he gave her the first misdirection. "Last I heard, he

was alive."

Paige's shoulders drooped. Then her laughter rang out, short and caustic. "What does it say about him that for a moment I wished for a different answer?" She turned to face him again, leaning against the windowsill. "What does it say about me?"

Standing in front of her and choosing the right reply, and the safest one, was so much harder than Chris had ever imagined. He wasn't comfortable revealing only half-truths, but if he told her everything, she'd kick him straight out the door. And slam it again, he was sure.

He avoided by posing a question of his own. "Do you hate him that much?"

Those pretty eyes of hers narrowed. "It's not about hate. I just might have been relieved to know he didn't desert me on purpose. That throwing me away wasn't a fucking *choice*."

She swiped her hand through the air and made a sound of disgust. "Never mind him. Tell me what happened. You said 'they attacked.' Who did?"

"Again, I don't know for sure, but I came to you hoping we could find out. Together." Tread easily, he told himself. "I said before that you have a destiny, you were prophesied to be the one who—"

Chris halted mid-sentence when she covered her face with both hands and started laughing. *What the hell?* Was she still suffering from shock?

Because he found nothing humorous about what he'd revealed. Paige was meant to carry out revenge, and according to his source, she was the only one who could.

Then again, he'd been living with the knowledge for years, ever since the seer had deemed him old enough to know the truth, about the attack, Paige, and what would be required of this beautiful, angry woman.

And the part he was meant to play as well.

He shifted and took up a stance, calling forth as much patience as he possessed. With Paige, he was apparently going to need it.

Finally, she dropped her hands, looked at him again, and shook her head. "I'd rather you go back to being a mental-case stalker. *That* I could handle. But all of this? All at once?"

Standing swiftly, she began to pace in front of the windows, intersecting sunbeams as she moved. "Do you have any idea what my coven is already dealing with? I just started my trial. This morning, right before you bumped into me."

"Your trial?"

Her expression morphed from haunted to disgusted with a swiftness he couldn't figure out. She looked at him as if he'd grown horns.

Then she fell back into what seemed to be her go-to state. Pissed off. "You know about Ronja and the demons. Well, what'd you think? My coven and I aren't just here to sit around and look pretty. We have a demon to vanquish, and not just one of those baby ones you boys dealt with during the bachelor party."

Did Chris detect a little man-hate beneath her very obvious derision? Or was he the only object of her animosity?

"There are nine of us. We each get to have a go and try to pass some mystical test. And..." Here she faltered, pressing her mouth into a tight bud. What had she decided to leave out of her explanation?

"Anyway," she continued, "after my trial, only Anna is left. We're almost finished, so I do not have time for another destiny. And, God forbid," she barked out a laugh again, "definitely not another prophecy."

"What can I tell you?" His voice was deadpan. "This sort of thing happens in our circles."

"See? Right there's the problem." She jabbed a finger in his direction. "I never had circles before, and then I was brought here." She spread her arms to encompass the grand library, the estate beyond the walls. "And I became part of the coven. Which I accepted. Just like I accepted Iraq and all the lovely shit I saw there."

Chris jolted at the reminder. He hadn't known until the night he'd seen her at the club that she'd served in the military, and that fact drove home more clearly than anything else that she had changed. She was no longer the little girl that he remembered. Sweet and playful—

"Fuck this!" She kicked a chair.

Oh, yeah. Little Paige Bennett was no more.

Strike that. Paige *Reilley*. She'd taken on the last name of the aunt and uncle who'd raised her. For her protection.

Chris studied her, hands on her waist and a stare that would cut down most men. All of this was coming to a head, and he couldn't blame her.

Maybe he should back off. Save the rest for another time. He'd waited most of his life to see her again. What harm could another day or so do?

"Look. This is a lot to take in."

"Yeah. It is." She glanced up before rolling her shoulders and walking back toward him. "I'm good. Sorry for the emotional display. Now tell me everything."

"You sure you want to—"

"Yep." She gave a single sharp nod.

He didn't believe she was as "good" as she'd claimed, but he still hadn't gained her cooperation or her commitment. So he pushed on. "There's not much to tell about that day. I was with a small group of people who'd gone to town. A young married couple with a boy my age. We were friends, so they let me go along with Todd." Damn, he hated remembering.

"With their group."

Chris blinked, willing away the gruesome images that always bombarded him when he let himself go back there. When he recalled the day his life changed forever.

"There was an older woman who accompanied us, a seer." He met Paige's hard stare. "Your father went as well. And you."

"So we lived because we went shopping." She pressed her lips together.

"When we returned to the community—it was out in the country and isolated—we found the others." He tidied the tale quickly and with no specific detail. "They were all dead."

He didn't describe the carnage, the awful things that magic could do to a body, or the stench that was left behind. The smell his child-self had thought was barbecue, charred and sickly sweet.

"Why were they killed?" she pressed.

"The older woman who was with us that day, she has answers for you." Chris dodged her query. Even a witch as tough as Paige could only take so much in one day. He'd already dumped a lot on her, and he could well imagine the weight.

He'd carried it alone for years.

Still, from what he gleaned about her character, this new Paige, he believed she could handle it. That she'd make herself deal.

Yes, he'd looked into her the past couple of weeks, watched when she'd come to the mainland, and he'd been pleased to see the steely fortitude she possessed, the pride with which she held herself.

But her anger ran deep. That was no surprise, but he'd do what he could to keep her focus elsewhere, and on anything other than her father.

He pictured the wheels spinning furiously in her head, so

he tried to slow them down a little. "I've searched for you for a long time, Paige, but only because I'm supposed to help you."

"You said that before. But why you? This is all crazy talk." She eased closer, but with no malice lingering in her body language, only confusion. "And why would you *want* to help me? You hardly know me at all."

But I've never stopped thinking about you. "My parents were home that day. They were murdered." *Ripped apart.* "Just like your mother."

Letting loose a sigh, Paige angled her head and seemed almost brittle, as if one more blow might do in her in. "I still have so many questions."

"I know." He wanted to take her hand, like he had so often when they'd been young, but this warrior standing before him now wouldn't take kindly to an uninvited touch.

So he stood tall and resumed his own stalwart persona. It was something she would respect. "We can help each other."

"My trial—"

"Here." He pulled a piece of paper from his pocket, and before she could object he shoved the scrap into her front pocket. He'd prepared the note with his phone number and current address. Just in case.

"Take the time you need." He offered the slightest of smiles. "I'll be waiting."

Before she could respond, the library doors burst inward. The witch with reddish-brown hair, the one called Hayden, barged in with a hard determination in her eyes. "Sorry to interrupt, but we've got trouble downtown."

"The Amara?" Paige stepped past him, their personal drama forgotten for the moment.

"It's got to be, based on what the officer who called Trevor and Cole was describing. But the Amara have never attacked in broad daylight before." Hayden waved her hand for Paige to follow. "Quinn's gone to ready the boat, and Joseph's on his way back with the other one. I knew you'd want to be with the first team." She backed out and hurried down the corridor.

Paige followed before quickly overtaking the other woman to rush ahead.

Chris took only a second to decide his next course of action. He could be useful, more than these people realized, and he needed to earn some of Paige's trust. So what the hell?

He fell into a jog, intent on staying apace with Ms. Speedy up there. In fact, if he had his way, he wouldn't let her out of his sight.

He'd go along and he'd help Paige, and by extension her friends, whether they asked for it or not. He just needed to make sure he was on that first boat.

Whether he was active duty or not was irrelevant, certain credos stuck. And in his world, Rangers lead the way.

5

Paige launched herself from the SUV as soon it screeched to a stop on River Street. The day was sunny and warm, typical early-autumn weather. Hayden, Claudia, and Anna disembarked the car as well, leaving Joseph to drive off in search of a parking space.

River Street was usually semi-chaotic, and tourist season ran long into the fall. Street vendors and entertainers, booths featuring arts and crafts, and the regular throng of visitors who came out to enjoy the city, even when the heat was on full blast.

Anna spoke to someone, drawing Paige's attention, and after a side-glance she scrunched her lips into a bow of irritation. Because despite her arguments, *he* had come along as well.

Chris, with all his well-honed muscles rippling under his blue shirt, eyes cool as they surveyed for any immediate threat. He was channeling full-on Ranger, slipping into his training like armor that had been modified just for him.

But even Special Operations didn't train for the shit demons could hand out. Or witches, for that matter.

Chris had alluded to having abilities of his own, but other than his killer smile, she had yet to witness any.

An unmarked cruiser pulled up with Trevor and Cole inside. They edged up to the curb, their official capacity providing the luxury of parking anywhere that necessity—or emergency—required. The flashing light on their roof whooped a final siren's cry and stopped strobing its bright red.

Anna and Chris were still conversing, but the coven leader spared Paige a quick glance, a look too full of meaning, as if Anna knew something about the man that she didn't.

So Paige hurried toward Trevor and Cole, ignoring the overbearing soldier who'd forced his way into her life. She tensed with the reminder. Chris had all the finesse of a battering ram.

But she had *real* problems to deal with today. He would just have to wait until she had time to spare for him and his outrageous stories.

Trevor was scowling at the two-way he held, listening to its transmission. Finally, the towering mountain of a cop cursed beneath his breath.

"What's wrong?" Paige demanded, striding up to him. "Isn't this the right place?" She indicated the margarita bar on which they'd descended. Raucous sounds and screams spilled through the doors to the sidewalk outside.

Trevor's frown deepened. "This is it, but now we've got a disturbance on the bridge too. Uniforms are en route to check it out."

Paige turned and shaded her brow to block the sun's late-morning glare. Cars were piled up on the Talmadge, the cable-stayed bridge that led over the river and toward South Carolina.

A loud clatter brought her around to see a uniformed cop staggering out of the bar. His head dripped blood. "It's bad in there," he said, making it a few steps before his knees buckled. Paige grabbed his arm and stopped him from crumpling to the cobblestones.

"You the only uniform here?" Cole asked, helping her move the younger cop to the side.

"No." The man shook his head and winced, just as Hayden rushed over with the scarf she'd been wearing. She balled it up and pressed it to the top of his bleeding skull.

He nodded his thanks and explained, "My partner's still in there. I caught a glass to the side of the head." He tried to smile. "At least it wasn't a beer bottle."

Paige met the stares of Trevor and Cole and motioned for them to step away with her. She pointedly passed over Chris to quietly address the other three women who'd accompanied her here. "Could still be the Amara," she said.

"They've got multiple bags of tricks," Claudia agreed, twirling her red hair into a tight bun, her final preparation for action. Anna and Hayden were equally prepared for any eventuality, both in durable pants.

With the supernatural war coming to a head, each of the witches stood at the ready twenty-four-seven. Comfort clothing had become the norm.

Jerking the bar door open Paige tossed over her shoulder, "Then let's see what Ronja and her minions have got for us today."

When she marched inside, she found a melee unlike any she'd witnessed before. Her hand had been easing toward her dagger, but she paused as she processed the pandemonium.

She dealt in battle—on every front of her life—but the scene greeting her now chilled her through and through, as if her blood had been flushed with one of the icy concoctions behind the bar. The drink mixes whirled in what looked like candy-colored washing machines.

But there weren't enough margaritas in the world to inspire this rampant blood thirst, this...*savagery.*

"Oh, my God." Chris came up beside her, his face telling of

his revulsion as well. She was certain he'd seen his own share of human-fueled devastation, and even the hardened soldier was appalled by the butchery on display.

One man held another against the bar, wielding a broken margarita glass. From the look of his opponent's face, the jagged shard had already been put to use. Across the room, two other men were grappling, both bloody and messy.

And these were only two examples. Throughout the bar, the basest, most ruthless aspects of human nature were on display.

Chris grabbed her arm, as if he thought to hold her back. And what? Protect her?

While his touch, his closeness, did spur her out of her shock, a small, petty part of her refused to let him be the first to wade into the fray. *This is for me to take care of.*

The commencement of her trial was not an ideal time for her to have to deal with him, let alone the baggage he was dredging up. Added to that, something about his take-charge demeanor made her competitive nature rise up.

But she'd psychoanalyze that later.

She ripped free of Chris's hold and focused on a huge man who'd just tossed a high-top table to the side. He was in pursuit of another man, and now he raised two meaty fists high above the bald guy whose attention was elsewhere.

The bigger man's arms bulged with brute strength as he aimed straight down toward baldy's cervical vertebrae. Paige knew the strike could cause severe damage.

And she couldn't let that happen. The effects might be life-altering, for both of them, hospital for one and prison for the other. And neither of them deserved that.

The problem was, these weren't just two assholes who'd gotten into a bar fight.

No, more insidious things were at work here. The reek of

noxious magic was rolling over her, betraying the Amara's presence.

With a leap too fast for anyone to see, she landed between the two men as the muscular guy's fists fell. She stopped the blow cold. "You don't want to do that." She stared into eyes glazed over with mindless fury.

"Get out of my way before I bend you over my knee and break your back too!"

So that *had* been his intention. Instead of trying to reason with someone so clearly bespelled, Paige employed some brute force of her own, twisting his arm behind his back and upward to the point of pain. "The cops are here now, so you might want to calm down."

"But he wants to take her from me. I won't let him!"

The maniacal bear in her arms still struggled, against her force as well as common sense, but his words lit a match in Paige's brain. A flame of comprehension. All these men were fighting over a woman, the *same* woman.

She was certain now that the Amara were behind the violence running rampant in the margarita bar. She just had to find the bitch who'd caused the free-for-all. Preferably before Claudia did.

As she hauled the giant of a man across the room to the door, Paige cast an apprehensive look back at the ongoing bedlam. She was fast and strong, but there were a lot of people in here.

A swift tide of relief rolled in when she saw Cole and Trevor intervening in the worst fights. She had to give Chris his due as well, since he was putting his brawn to good use. Like her, he'd picked the more dangerous combatant in one particularly nasty fight and was now ushering the man to the open door.

Another couple of cops rushed in past him, and then, to

Paige's great relief, Dare and Willyn followed close in their wake. The second boat had left St. Germaine Island only minutes behind the first, so thankfully, another wave of riot control had arrived.

Dare could help counteract mental influence, particularly the vile kind that had been exerted on these innocent people. They'd only come to see the pretty margarita machines and have a taste. Then the fun had turned into a blood-soaked brawl.

That's where Willyn came in, with her ability to subtly heal a few of the worst injuries.

When a police officer took custody of the man in Paige's arms, she made another quick survey of the room. This time, she knew what to look for. The bar was easy to scan, long and narrow with the leg of its L-shape kicking off in the front.

She didn't spot the face and figure she was sure hid among the chaos, so instead she focused on the one area that *didn't* have any disruption. The one place a troublemaker could stand clear of her own creation.

Two men tumbled over a chair together, locked in an angry embrace. Their absence gave Paige a new line of sight.

And there she stood. Valentina. Amara member and succubus extraordinaire.

In short—a real bitch.

The brunette had not a hair out of place, but stood with one hip cocked as she enjoyed the show. She must have influenced all the men here, making them each want her so badly they were ready to kill to claim her.

Paige started making her way to the back when a thought occurred. Forget the possible arrests that would be made today, these poor guys would have to contend with wives and girlfriends who'd watched as their men went crazy over another woman. And all the poor people had only wanted was a little vacay.

Now Paige had one more reason to disfigure the smarmy Valentina's perfect little nose.

A scream drew the succubus's attention suddenly, and when she turned her head she caught sight of Paige. The woman had few magical talents, and was well aware that Paige would wipe the sticky floor with her face, so she should have shown signs of fear.

But all Valentina did was kick up a cocky smile and wiggle her fingers, like one member of the ladies' cotillion to another. With a flourish and hair-toss, she turned on her heel, tossed something to the floor, and dashed into a dark hallway. She was going for a back exit.

Paige grinned and pushed her way through the tangle of bodies, mindless zombies intent on inflicting damage to one another. Damn Valentina for causing this mess. *Her ass is mine.*

The door was closing behind the woman, but Paige had seen where'd she'd disappeared. Did she actually think she could get away? Silly little succubus.

The worst of the fighting was over and, with more police there to break things up, Paige planned to make catching the Amara floozy her personal mission.

Until she saw a young man, college-aged at best, scramble across the dirty floor to pick up an object near the wall. Paige caught the glint of steel and recognized the item he clutched inside his bloody, busted knuckles.

Her fists clenched and her plans changed. No more chasing the succ-u-bitch.

Valentina had thrown down a knife, and Paige cursed her for playing dirty. She'd known there was no way Paige would walk past a scuffle involving a deadly weapon.

The college boy was out of his mind, but his sunny blonde

hair and pressed pants didn't give the impression he had much experience with blades. Not so for the older, rougher opponent he faced. That man was the proverbial back-alley cautionary tale.

"Come on, pretty." The man curled his fingers, taunting his younger opponent and urging him closer. Not only was he in a denim vest with what looked like a biker-gang insignia on the back, but those bending fingers of his revealed dark marks on the knuckles. Prison tats.

And the college boy was too wired by Valentina to know what he was getting into.

The biker feinted an abrupt forward move, causing sunny-hair to swipe out with the knife. When the kid's arm swung in the wrong direction, the biker charged, gripping his opponent in a crushing embrace before lifting him and slamming him into the wall.

Paige should have made it in time to prevent the first blow, but her foot slipped in what looked like grape margarita, a purple slushy-like mixture that made her hydroplane to the side.

Superspeed did have the occasional pitfall.

Regaining her balance, she got there in time to reach around and take the knife while simultaneously arm-wrapping the biker's throat. With her light but effective choke hold in place, she warned, "Let go of the kid, and calm down."

Again, she threatened law enforcement, only this guy actually responded as she'd hoped. Maybe the power of Valentina's charm was fading, or maybe—and more likely— the biker had a healthier and more deep-seated aversion to the cops.

He nodded his head, a gray braid wiggling like a snake on his back, and patted Paige's forearm urgently as if tapping out of a wrestling match. Still cautious, she released him, but without further quarrel he went on his way.

Chris showed up then to escort the disarmed and befuddled younger man to the front. The violent mood was calming, and many of the people involved looked dazed, coming out of their stupors and wondering what had just happened. What they had just done.

Paige sidled up to Anna and Claudia before taking the latter's elbow in hand. "Your favorite succubus was here. She caused all of this."

Claudia's mouth tightened. "When are you guys going to let me put her down?"

Gifted with the ability to sense an object's past, Claudia had been cast into a haze of suspicion while first falling in love with Cole. She'd picked up on another woman's presence in his life, including his house. And his bedroom.

But Cole had been innocent and completely unaware of Valentina's visits. The succubus had cast her wicked spell just to cause Claudia pain and to distract her from the Amara's real motive. Bringing the demon Bastraal into this world.

Claudia had actually been the one to allow his entry, but in a twist of Fate, she'd only done what she'd been meant to do all along. Still, she'd experienced a foul and unsettling completion of her trial. And her hatred of Valentina had yet to dissipate.

Chris joined them then, walking up to Paige and offering a smile of approval. "You move like a Super Short fired from a Winchester."

Hmph. Like I need his endorsement. The compliment was a lame attempt to connect with her, since she'd know he was referencing one of the fastest bullet-weapon combos in the world.

"I thought you said you knew me?" Paige intended to keep up her guard. She preferred a barrier of hostility between them.

"Just an observation, princess."

Oh, now *that* made her feel pretty hostile. "Unless you want to end up looking worse than these bloody pulps," she hooked a thumb at a man going out on a stretcher, "then don't ever..." she got in his face, "ever...call me that again."

She couldn't believe he'd used the ridiculous nickname. It was bad enough he knew things about her, about her childhood. Things even *she* didn't know.

His knowledge put her at a disadvantage, and she was still unsure how best to move forward with him. She needed to know the truth about her past, and how much of this alternate destiny crap he'd mentioned was for real.

But she didn't have to get all friendly with him. In fact, the sooner he learned to keep the required distance, the better.

She was about to ask him if he wanted to go somewhere for a more civil and less emotional discussion when Trevor leaned inside the door and waved to get her attention.

She and Chris exited the almost-empty bar that was now in shambles. But the whirling margarita mixers continued to spin round and round, their cheerful colors out of place in the muck and devastation.

Trevor and Cole were waiting on the sidewalk and started for their car as soon as Paige and the others came outside. "We need you to come with us, Paige, and maybe Dare."

"He's still inside." Hayden stepped out into the sunlight. "He's helping change some minds." Her gaze locked meaningfully on Trevor as he paused mid-act of climbing behind the wheel. "Of some of the arresting cops," she clarified.

Paige was glad. Maybe the innocent people would be let off with a pass. As for the cost of the damages...probably not.

"Well then, tell him to hurry. We need him on the bridge."

Trevor's face was set, his jaw tense.

And his good-natured partner didn't look much better. "Chris, you come with us too," Cole said. With an apologetic look to Paige, he added. "The more muscle the better."

Paige stifled the instinctive objection that sprang to her tongue. She'd just shut up for now. If Cole was asking for the Ranger, she'd trust his judgment.

But she'd keep her eye on Chris. Because she didn't trust *him*.

Anna lightly pushed her shoulder. "Go on. We'll finish up here. If you need us, we'll catch up."

"All right." Paige made haste for the cop car. Once settled into the back, she studiously avoided the middle of the seat. Chris's bulk already took up half the space.

She scrunched against the door on her side and stared out the window, determined not to even brush knees with him. Childish, maybe, but he buzzed with an undercurrent that unsettled her.

They had a link, one from long ago, but there was also another sense of connection between them. One that sprang from shared similarities and experiences, a take-charge no excuses attitude.

He reminded her…of *herself*. And the parallel was a bit disturbing.

He was efficient, skilled, and trained to be lethal. He also had magic and, apparently, an unyielding sense of duty to those in need. He'd helped the guys at the bachelor party, and hadn't hesitated when things had gone awry this morning, jumping in to give yet more assistance.

At the moment, his profile was rigid with determination, but she couldn't help thinking of the grin he'd been wearing when she'd confronted him on the front steps this morning. For Special Ops, he sure did seem laid back.

Paige leaned one elbow against the door and tugged her mouth into a frown. That was the one major difference between them, and for some reason it bugged her. He smiled more than she did.

A lot more.

She jerked against the door when Trevor gunned the car out into traffic. Then Cole reached over to turn on the siren.

Chris leaned forward to ask, "What's going on now?"

The two detectives up front shared a quick glance before Cole looked over his shoulder. "We've got jumpers on the bridge."

Now Paige eased forward too. "A jumper?"

"No. You heard me right the first time." Cole's expression was troubled, his eyes full of fear. "There are more than one."

6

"Multiple jumpers?" Paige asked, and Chris could hear the incredulity in her voice. Then the suspicion. "The Amara again." She slapped a palm against the beige leather seat. "What are they doing now?"

"Causing trouble," Cole grumbled from the front. "Because they can."

"Or maybe they're getting daring as the trials come closer to the end." Trevor pulled the wheel to one side and sped up the ramp that would take them to the bridge. "And they don't mind sacrificing a few people to make their point."

Chris was too new to this whole situation to really speculate, but he was tired of waiting for Paige to fill him in. "You said that woman, the succubus, ran from you," he said, hoping to pry her gaze from the car window. "She didn't seem to want to attack you. What about the island? Maybe they drew you all out so they could—"

Paige's grunt cut him off. "They already tried that." She faced forward with a smile that could have cut glass. "I doubt they'll try again."

Though she was addressing him, she refused to meet his eyes. With his lips seamed, Chris studied the stubborn woman. He'd given her a valid reason for seeking her out, and he had information that was crucial to her future.

So why the blatant disdain? Besides, he was helping her

and her friends. He understood that his news had been a shock and that she probably needed time to adjust, but he didn't understand the rudeness.

Maybe it had to do with this trial she kept mentioning. He needed to learn more about that. Certain aspects of the coven's trouble with this witch, Ronja, and the demons he knew about.

But a prophecy? When Paige had thrown that out, Chris had bitten down on his own surly response.

Because as far as he was concerned, her other duty, her other destiny, had to come first.

Still, she was putting great effort into making sure he understood that she wanted nothing to do with him. And Paige Reilley didn't seem like the kind of woman to waste time or energy on superficial fronts and fake attitudes.

So that meant she just didn't like him. At all.

Averting his gaze, he looked out his own side window. Better than staring at her white-blonde hair and being distracted by her angelic looks.

Those looks conflicted sharply with her personality, like a Venus fly trap, pretty on the outside and alluring from a distance. But she'd chomp down on his head if he got too close.

He'd told her about the time he'd spent searching for her but had held back the full reason. She had an obligation, that was true, and his priority was to see that she fulfilled her duty.

But Chris had his own reasons for wanting to see her again. Curiosity and yearning had always clung to him, vines that had grown slowly over the years, wrapping him up in an inescapable knot of need.

The need to know Paige again, after an entire life of wondering about her.

But damned if he would tell her about the picture he

had, the one with worn spots on the edges from excessive handling.

She wasn't the bright and cheerful little girl anymore, and the coldness she showed him destroyed a little piece of the dream Chris had always carried with him. Hope froze beneath her arctic stare and splintered into a thousand pieces when she spoke so dismissively to him.

No, Paige hadn't recognized him, hadn't remembered him.

And she sure hadn't been glad to see him.

As the cruiser approached the foot of the gridlocked bridge, the light flashed on the dash and the siren emitted the occasional get-out-of-the-way *whoop*! Once they got closer to a barricade of slanted police cars, parked to hold gawkers at bay, Trevor pulled over and they all piled out.

To say it was windy up here would be a gross understatement. Exposed to the elements and with no barrier of any kind, the suspension cables moaned and thrummed as gusts whipped across the river.

Chris fell in step behind the two detectives and heard a low murmur of both fascination and concern rolling through the gathered onlookers.

"Wait here," Trevor instructed, while he and Cole joined a couple of cops clustered in front of one the police cars. They clearly knew the other officers, and they all fell into a quick exchange of information.

After a moment, Trevor and Cole returned, their faces grim. "Three jumpers," Cole summed up, then turned to Paige. "By all accounts, they appear to be sleepwalking."

"Sleepwalking," Chris parroted. Not a question or an observation. He was growing more and more confused with each new development.

Mysticism and strange powers were not a new concept for him. He'd long accepted what most would deem impossible.

But he'd never come across such a public display of magic. First the bar and now this? The Amara didn't seem to care how many people witnessed their displays.

He hazarded another glance at Paige. Did she and her sister witches deal with this craziness all the time? No wonder she'd balked at the additional stressors he'd dumped on her.

The space between her brows was puckered, her lips in a flat line. She didn't question the fact that the people were dozing as they stood atop the guardrails at the side of the bridge. Instead, she was covertly scanning the crowd.

She was circumspect, but Chris caught the measured movement of her gaze from one face to another. Who was she looking for?

As if in answer, she muttered, "If she's here, I don't see her."

"Who?" Chris asked, feeling like he should have spent his time having an Intel briefing this morning instead of taking the time for a smoothie.

"Beth," Trevor said. "She's a mare, as in nightmare. Her abilities include influencing people while they sleep."

Apparently the Amara had quite the collection of mythical beings. Chris had already had two brushes with demons and then the succubus.

"I didn't know she could actually put people to sleep, though. When she got to Willyn and Tadd, they were both already asleep." Paige was studying the crowd behind her now, and not as secretly as before.

"Maybe someone is helping her?" Cole had joined in to inspect the walk-ups pressed at the perimeter of the scene. Other people had their heads craned out their car windows or stood impatiently beside idling vehicles that couldn't go anywhere.

"Either Ronja or Scarlett could pull it off." Paige huffed, shook her head, and looked past Cole to the concrete guardrail where the three innocent civilians swayed, waiting to be forced to their deaths. "We have to be ready. The Amara are getting too unpredictable, and at this point I wouldn't be surprised if they actually made these people jump."

Paige put a knuckle to her mouth in thought before jerking it away again. "But why? What do they have to gain?"

"Hell if I know. Retribution on us?" Cole blew out a frustrated breath and kept scanning the masses for a familiar face.

"We need to get closer," Chris muttered, surprising himself.

"There's a crisis intervention officer in place." Trevor indicated a small African American female with cropped hair. She looked like she was trying to get the man and two women on the ledge of the bridge to talk to her.

Chris studied the man's profile. *Hell, she can't get them to talk. They aren't even awake.* The cruelty of what was happening to those people struck home for him. The coven had signed up for a war and, as of this morning, apparently so had he.

But those three out there on a ledge? They hadn't. As far as he was concerned, this mind control was just another form of terrorism.

He picked up on the sound of crying and followed the pitiful whimpers to a small boy, maybe three, who was being held by another policewoman. He struggled to be set free, tiny arms reaching out toward the side of the bridge. "Mommy," Chris heard between hiccups.

And that was just about all he could take.

"Paige and I will flank," he announced, staring straight into her bright blue eyes. "She'll take one side of the jumpers, I'll take the other." He then focused on Cole and Trevor. "You two position yourselves behind them and be ready to catch if a body comes flying back. We may have to jerk them away from the ledge."

The men nodded agreement, just as Paige said, "Hey," with a flick of her hand against her thigh. "I've got this." Then she glanced to her friends. "*We've* got this." She crossed her arms.

Chris met her mulish posture with his own. And when his arms crossed, they were much bigger. "I've dealt with more than a few crisis situations, Paige."

Lowering her voice, she focused all of her irritation on him. "You might be used to commanding other people, but don't swagger in here and screw things up. I don't care what you've seen over there. This is not what you're used to."

Without waiting for his reply, she wound through the crowd and made her way to the spot where the cops held the line. The next thing Chris saw was a white blur, the color of the shirt she wore, and Paige was suddenly beyond the jumpers and on their far side.

Once in place, she tossed Chris a narrow-eyed look. *Did she just snarl at me?*

But he just gave a nod in return and tried not to smile. Because furious or not, she was going along with his plan.

Why did that small acquiescence please him?

Returning his full attention to the three in peril, he waited. Minutes dragged by, and occasionally he and Paige shared an anxious glance at each other. Trevor and Cole remained close as well, both visibly restless and agitated.

They all watched as the intervention officer attempted to get a response from the trio perched on top of the concrete guardrails. None of them spoke or even moved very much, but all it would take was one large step and off the side they would plummet. One hundred and eighty-five feet to the Army-green water below.

Chris's brow popped up a few beads of sweat every time the woman in the middle leaned out toward the water. But like a weeble-wobble, she always came back.

He wasn't the strongest of magic practitioners, but he did have his talents. As the three ill-fated people teetered over certain death, he stood ready, focused on the targets, eyes never straying.

So he detected the coil of muscle beneath the fabric of the man's pants before anyone else. A mere breath before Paige vaulted between the officers manning posts on her side. Because she'd seen the motion too.

Chris was also already moving when the female intervention cop called out, "No!"

Like three marionettes on the same string, the jumpers bent their knees ever so slightly, the telltale sign that they were about to leap. Chris vaulted over the police barrier on his side, rushing in to grab the one closest to him, the man.

Like a stream of light, he was there, his arm wrapping around the man's thighs, encircling and clamping down to wrench the weight of the jumper's body backward. To stop the forward momentum, he had to give it all he had, and the hard pull in the opposite direction sent the guy flying.

Back toward Trevor and Cole, just as he'd told them to expect. He was sure they were there ready to play catch; at least, he hoped so. Because Chris had already moved on to the woman in the middle.

Paige was a split-second behind him.

Despite their speed, the woman's feet had left the rail. She'd been in the center and was farther away from both Chris and Paige. She'd already thrown herself forward, out over nothing but air.

Chris's entire body seemed to seize up as he gave an extra push with his legs, flung himself over the concrete guard, and managed to catch the hem of her long denim skirt. His fingers curled into the tough fabric, and he had a split-second to pray the waistband wasn't elastic.

Her weight yanked against the skirt, pulling Chris's hand, and the small obstruction to her flight barely slowed her momentum. The slice of time was incremental, but it was enough.

And then Paige was there.

With both hands, she clasped the woman's lower leg and ankle, a solid grip that would never yield.

With both of them putting their strength into it, Paige and Chris were able to stop the woman's plunge and lessen the impact when she swung like a pendulum down and back into the side of the bridge.

She might have a few bruises and scratches to her face, but she would live. And she would hold her baby boy again.

Together, he and Paige pulled the woman up as carefully as possible. She was blinking as if she had sand under her lids, and babbling unintelligible gibberish. Once her feet were safely on the bridge, the woman's eyes opened wide and she sucked in a breath. "Where am I?" she asked, and Chris could tell the mare's magic had abated.

He looked to find the petite crisis officer tending to the other female who'd tried to jump. She too was waking up. And the man.

And what about the murmur in the crowd? There was a new undertone, one of speculation and awe. Chris heard a woman say, "Did you see that?" Maybe she was talking about the close call, but he doubted it.

Trevor, Cole, and the entire coven clan would have a hard time getting the events of the day back into the bag. The cat wasn't just out, it had jumped the fence and caught a bus to Oh, Shitville.

The crisis officer let paramedics step in to deliver care and, leaving them to their work, she homed in on Chris and Paige.

As she strode toward them, he wondered whether they were about to be reprimanded or thanked.

"That was amazing," she expelled on a breath, velvety brown eyes still wide from the tragedy that had been averted. "I'm so grateful you were both here. And I just don't know how you did it."

Her mouth clamped together as she looked between them. She rubbed her eyes, and Chris feared the worst. Then she laughed. "Stress'll do crazy things to you." Her serious expression softened and became truly appreciative. "All I know is you saved them when I couldn't."

Chris wanted to tell her there was nothing she could have done, that her crisis training hadn't failed her. But he'd been raised with some of the same tenets that the witches lived by now.

And number one on the list was don't reveal secrets to the non-magics, even when they'd seen something they shouldn't have. Deny, deny, deny.

It was amazing how often that actually worked. Most people who witnessed something fantastic could convince themselves they'd imagined the whole thing. Others simply didn't mention what they'd seen, because they didn't want to be viewed as flighty or nutty.

But with a crowd this big and camera phones? Who knew?

The officer patted him on the elbow. "If you'll stick around for a few minutes, I'll need your names for the report. We can handle all the follow up later." After another elfin smile, she walked away.

"Should we stay like she asked?" Chris was itching to move, to get away now that the Amara's scheme had been derailed.

"No way." Paige pulled her head to one side, indicating he should accompany her. She maneuvered through the police and out into the concealment of the crowd. Heading straight for Trevor and Cole's cruiser, she kept her head down and kept her bead on the car.

"We can walk," Chris volunteered when they came to a stop behind the vehicle.

"Yeah. That's what I was thinking."

Just then, Cole called her name, so Paige halted. His grim countenance and hurried step told them the trouble wasn't over yet.

"We've got two more incidents coming in that sound like Ronja and her thugs."

"Where?" Paige skipped straight to the practicalities, demanding her next assignment. Chris had to hand it to her; she was a soldier through and through.

Eyes stern, Cole said, "Reports of a wolf in Forsythe Park. So far, a pet dog has been killed, and animal control is en route." He pulled car keys from his pocket. "But we all know he'll never be caught by humans."

"He?" Chris butted in, still picking up tidbits as he went.

"Ross," Paige explained. "He's a shifter."

"Been a while since I came across one of those." Chris glanced up at the sky, remembering his envy of the girl who could fly far and free whenever she'd wanted to. "But then, the ones I knew weren't enemies."

"What else?" Paige pressed, ignoring what he'd shared.

"It's like they're all leaving calling cards." Cole's statement jerked Chris back to the conversation. "Strange red mists rolling in near Factor's Walk." He expelled a breath and gazed across the river, back toward downtown. Then he shocked Chris by pulling a bag of candy from his pocket and tossing a few back. "It must be Scarlett."

Cole held the bag out to Chris, but he shook his head. The detective's cravings must be for sugar, but right now Chris only wanted one thing. He needed Paige to look at him. To listen.

He'd been trying, subtly, to make her accept that he was comfortable with this world. The one where supernatural creatures existed. She, however, didn't seem interested in his past.

It's your past too. But he would let her do what she had to. Like she'd said, this was her war.

Chris had known people like her before, other military, who were always keeping everyone at arm's length. No attachment meant no worries.

But being alone wasn't always safe, and some of those he'd known had eventually broken from the self-inflicted torture. Internalizing pain didn't get rid of the anguish. It only allowed it to stay locked inside the gut, in the mind, where it ate away at the soul. Breaking down exterior strength from the inside out.

Chris hoped Paige didn't destroy herself that way. And him along with her.

Pacing a couple of steps away, Paige ran a hand through her hair. Then once again. "All right." She turned back to them. "I can hit the park first. Meanwhile, get in touch with Anna, and see if she can head to Factor's Walk. I'll catch up to her and help with Scarlett as soon as I can."

"No." Chris spoke evenly, but she jerked her head toward him as if he'd shouted. "I'll take the park. The wolf. Trevor can give me a ride, and that frees you up to go confront Scarlett."

"You can't handle—"

"I can." Chris frowned. Was it possible she hadn't noticed before, during all the turmoil and fast-action? Well, she'd catch up to the truth soon enough. Whether she wanted to or not.

With his piece said, he simply turned and marched through the lines of cars still stranded atop the bridge. Yes, he told himself, it would all catch up.

7

Sirens blared outside the windows, but Ian Keller kept his attention on the man in the black robes. The judge was about to rule in his clients' favor, so he wasn't about to risk offending him now.

The gavel rapped against wood to announce the ruling, and a mere ten seconds later a stunned Mr. Martinez took Ian's hand in his own and shook vigorously. Tears of exultation brimmed in his eyes. "Thank you. Thank you." He released his grip to allow his wife to step in and hug Ian tightly.

His outer appearance and cool demeanor often deterred such displays of affection, but the kind older couple paid no mind to the neat Tallia business suit or Ian's composed expression. They knew him better than that.

"We have our house back?" Mrs. Martinez asked, her hands now clasping Ian's.

"Yes. Free and clear." He waited as her sobs rose and were quickly brought under control again. "I'm just sorry this ever happened to you. The bank will provide full restitution for the months you had to rent the apartment, the mortgage for that time period will be waived, and," this was the kicker that made Ian smile, "you'll receive damages for the anguish they caused you."

The couple had been wrongly foreclosed on and had missed out on the settlement made last year by some of the country's larger banks, since the financial institution the couple used had not been included in the lawsuit. The outcome today—if Ian said so himself—was a much better deal anyway.

And Ian couldn't be happier. These were the moments that made his job worthwhile, despite the perpetual lawyer jokes and the real life lawyers who made the jokes seem tame in comparison to truth.

Some might assume Ian was a cold-hearted man, one only in pursuit of high-esteem and the almighty dollar. As a lawyer, he surely had no compunction or morals, right?

The notion caused Ian to flash to a particular face. He didn't know why Anna St. Germaine popped into his head out of the blue, but his resulting frown caused Mrs. Martinez to pat his hand. "You work too hard. You must come by tonight for a celebration dinner."

"I'm afraid I have—"

"No, no, Ian." Mr. Martinez threw his weight behind his wife's demand. "Not this time. You should join us." His arm stole around his wife's shoulders. "We don't eat until late anyway."

Recognizing a corner when he was backed into one, Ian chuckled. "All right. You win this time. I'll see you around eight?"

"Perfect." Mrs. Martinez leaned in to whisper, "I'll make *frijoles negros* for you." With a wink she nodded to her husband and the pair turned to leave.

As the couple ambled down the center aisle of the courtroom, Ian gathered his briefcase and files. He'd head back to the office, check in with his secretary, and barring any crises needing his immediate attention, he'd make time to grab a quick lunch.

Mrs. Martinez knew him well enough to have made an on-point remark. He did work too hard.

With a satisfied grin on his face, he passed the shining wooden benches and was careful not to meet the eyes of the bankers or their legal team. None of them were pleased with the ruling, and he didn't want to come across as smug.

But handing it to those jackasses had been pure and shining pleasure.

Outside his footsteps fell to polished marble, clopping lightly in a way that always made him think of justice prevailing. When Ian was a boy, he'd been so impressed by his few visits to the courthouse with his father, and the sound of dress shoes against stone flooring reminded him why he'd become a lawyer in the first place.

He believed in the system, and that even with its flaws, the law provided protection for the majority of citizens. The Martinez family had deserved safeguard against predatory financial institutions, and their case was clearly one resulting from malfeasance.

He just wished all of his decisions were as simple and sound. All of his clients so pleased.

Stopping for a drink at the stainless steel water fountain, he let his musings drift to another client. One he was not as sure of.

Ronja, the woman he'd helped win rights to an isolated and seemingly low-value piece of land. Aside from its historical aspects—including a structure that by all reports still stood after decades of neglect—the property seemed worthless. Still, Ronja had coveted the house and acreage, claiming to be the rightful owner and providing documentation to back up the assertion.

So why did Ian have the crawling and relentless feeling that he'd made a mistake? That in this particular case, he'd been on the wrong end of righteousness?

Perhaps it had been the unsolicited visit and advice from

one Anna St. Germaine. A female who by all accounts appeared to have class and quality embedded in her very bones, yet spoke easily of lunatic-fringe conspiracies. Magic? Evil?

Ian chuffed dismissively and continued down the wide corridor, letting the resounding claps of his footsteps restore faith in himself and the world. If he had chosen poorly when he'd accepted Ronja's case, then he'd done so with the best of intents. Besides, the matter was long put to bed by now.

From here forward, he'd follow his instincts and have nothing more to do with her. If she came calling again, he'd refer her to other representation.

Looking forward to a real lunch for a change, Ian lifted his watch to discern how long he had before his next meeting. But when his hand rose, he didn't see the wide-faced dive watch, the one he always wore in case of sudden urges to take off in his boat and submerge in the Atlantic. In fact, the hand before him was not even his own.

Gone were the long, tanned fingers he knew, having been replaced with a paler version of a child's hand. The small fingers gripped a wooden sword, left-handed. Ian was dominant in the right.

He shook his head at the absurdity. That the first thing he'd noticed in this hallucination was his switch to southpaw.

He was no longer himself, and was far, far removed from the classic halls of the Chatham County Courthouse. He was outdoors now, and snow—thick, white, crystalline snow—covered everything for miles.

Though Ian's consciousness rejected what he felt and saw, the tiny body he possessed carried on unperturbed, hacking the little sword at anything he passed—tree, rock, piles of drift. And all Ian could do was travel inside the foreign receptacle.

What the hell is this? Am I dreaming? No. No! He'd just been in a courtroom contemplating whether to have a Jo Burg style burger or fried fish sandwich. Now he was stuck somewhere in the Arctic.

His mind revolted, and flashes of color blotched his vision as panic catapulted to the forefront. This wasn't possible. *This kind of thing is not possible.* He told himself to pull out, to close his eyes and open them again. He'd be back in Savannah, he was sure.

I have to be. God, help me. The boy's hand lifted again to strike down a rebellious sapling sticking its head from the snow, and as he did, Ian focused his mental energy on his watch. He hoped some sort of talisman might bring him home.

Silver rim, black face.

The vision wavered.

Three smaller gauges in the center for depth and time period.

"Ian?"

Yes. Almost there!

A woman was calling his name. *His* name.

"Ian, are you okay?" He felt a shudder in his shoulder. He was being shaken.

The scene changed so swiftly he imagined a *pop!* as the imaginary snow globe burst to release him back into his own world, his own time. And—*whew*—his own body.

Afraid to move, even to lower the wrist that sported his watch, Ian slid his gaze to the woman beside him. "Jules." An estate attorney he knew and respected. Her kind eyes searched his face, proving her to be the cautionary mother she was.

"You should sit down." She gestured to a line of wooden chairs against the wall. "I called your name three times before you snapped out of it. Are you dizzy?" Then her face collapsed into a sly grin. "Elated at your victory over the money-grubbers?"

At the mention of his case, Ian let the awful and inexplicable experience fade to the background. "I guess my thoughts drifted and got stuck somewhere." Giving her his best bolstering I'm-just-fine smile, he finally lowered his arm. "Actually, I was thinking about lunch."

"Well, I'd invite myself along, but I've got to pick up Leo." She rolled her eyes. "Apparently, he's a biter."

"Good thing he's got a lawyer for a mother then." Ian forced a low laugh, hoping his pretend good humor fooled her. He was off-balance by whatever mind-travel he'd just encountered and didn't want to be fussed over.

"Tell me about it." She chuckled before hurrying away with a dashed off wave but called back to him without looking, "Go get something to eat."

Once she'd passed through the security station and pushed out the front doors, Ian let his guard down. But he considered her admonition, and found that he agreed with her.

Obviously, he was suffering from a physical ailment. The condition was affecting his over-burdened mind. So he'd go so far as to actually sit down in the restaurant and eat his lunch on-site.

Then, and only then, he'd head to the office and get back to work.

~~~

With the morning hours quickly leaning closer to the lunchtime rush, Bay Street was tightly packed and moving at a sluggish crawl. In such a crush, even the police lights Cole had going did little to clear the way. Finally, he and Paige made it to Factor's Walk and caught a break in the traffic.

Cole made a hard left into a brick drive that circled back toward the main street. He nodded as another car pulled in behind them and told her, "Go."

Paige didn't waste any time. In a leap she was out of the car to search for Scarlett. She didn't see the witch but evidence of her proximity was everywhere. A thick and unnatural red mist rolled over the grass, its tendrils climbing up the sides of massive live oaks.

On the drive over, her worried mind had traveled back and forth between two main topics. One was her concern over Scarlett and why the witch was setting off her colorful bomb of magic downtown. When it came down to it, she had no idea what any of the Amara were up to today, but their actions were highly suspect.

The second thing plaguing her was Chris. Rather, the reality that she wouldn't have made it to the second jumper in time if he hadn't gotten there first.

Paige was grateful he'd been there to intervene. He'd helped save that woman's life as well as the male jumper he'd rescued. But how had he done it? Paige had barely made it in time herself.

Her gaze couldn't penetrate the fog still roiling around her, so she dispelled all thoughts of Chris, as they were proving to be a distraction. She continued a forward creep, unsure where the Amara's second in command was located, and whether or not Scarlett was alone.

The Amara members rarely were.

Across the lawn, Paige detected a slight discoloration in the fog. The rubied hue was denser, more concentrated, and grew larger upon her approach. A few more strides and the aberration became more visible. The imperfect sphere glowed a vibrant cherry-red. It throbbed as if fed by a pulse.

This was Scarlett's signature. The color of danger.

The witch was here, all right, and she appeared to be holding her poisonous haze in check, keeping it close and controlled. So why was she downtown, and what was she doing?

The fog had been reported, easily detected by human eyes. If she'd shot a bright flare into the sky, she couldn't have announced her presence any more clearly.

Scarlett had to have known who would answer her signal. So she was lost in the haze, just lying in wait. She had to have known one of the coven would respond.

"Message received," Paige said to the swirling crimson vapors. "And here I am." Step by step she stalked her way through thick, opaque mists. This end of Factor's Walk terminated in a small park enclosed by wrought iron fencing, Bay Street to one side and an overlook of the river opposite.

Soon she detected a yellow glow from over her head and glanced up to find she was beneath the Old Harbor Light. The metal of the tall post was light green, covered by the hard-earned patina from decades of exposure.

Huge ship anchors lay scattered around the area like a set of pick-up jacks left forgotten by a giant child. And amongst the anchors and trees, Paige now noticed several other shapes sprawled across the grass.

People. Dead or unconscious, she couldn't tell, but Scarlett's noxious gas had apparently served a purpose after all.

"Scarlett!" Paige yelled into the smothering fog. She would allow no more time for deadly games.

In answer, a gust of air moved to clear away the magic haze. The witch was revealed, her lithe form leaning against one of the massive anchors. Scarlett observed Paige with a ghoulish grin on her perfectly made up face.

Today her outfit consisted of fitted black pants and knee-high boots to match. Her peach-hued, ruffled shirt clashed with the deeper crimson of her hair. Any other time, Paige would have pointed out the fashion oversight just for the spite of it, but there were more urgent matters at the moment.

Motioning at the fallen citizens, Paige angled her head in warning. "You'd better hope they aren't dead."

Scarlett's thin, arching brows rose as one. "Ooh. I'm to be threatened by the great and powerful Paige, am I?" She lifted her chin and looked down her nose, appraising her opponent. "I see someone's come into her trial."

So the bitch wasn't going to make this easy. Deciding to see for herself if the people were alive or dead, Paige knelt next to the prone figure closest to her. After pressing two fingers to the woman's neck, she was relieved to find a pulse.

Employing her gift of speed, Paige then rose and shot over to Scarlett. Moving in close and quick, she was darkly pleased to see a flicker of fear in the woman's eyes. "What did you do to them?" she demanded, taking advantage of the red witch's unease.

"Don't worry. They should wake up. Eventually." Scarlett touched her curls, a sign of her never-failing vanity. "I was just bored." She gave a faux pout. "Can't a girl have a little fun now and then?"

"Today was about more than fun." Paige inched nearer, ready to choke the witch or dodge her poisonous red vapors, whichever came first. "You and the other Amara scum caused all this trouble for a reason."

Now Paige let her scathing stare rove up and down Scarlett's ridiculously prissy outfit. She filled her eyes with as much disdain as she could muster. "You wanted us here for a reason. So talk."

Scarlett's countenance hardened, her lip curled. "Why? You seem to have all the answers."

Paige would have replied, but caught sight of movement behind a nearby tree trunk. Was this another of the Amara's traps?

The last time she and her friends had been taken by surprise, they'd come close to choking to death, poisoned by the red fumes. They'd also lost a few weapons that day in the woods, allowing the Amara to get a sample of the coven's unique magic.

Today, she'd keep her head up, eyes forward.

As she scanned the perimeter for more evidence of movement, she felt a sly grin trying to force its way to her lips. So Scarlett wanted to bait the coven witch? She wanted to test Paige?

She returned her stare to the powdered and primped woman in front of her. If they were planning to spring something on her, then Scarlett and whoever was hiding out there had better be ready to bring it.

Paige had been waiting for her challenge, for a chance to take the lead. And if there was one thing that she knew how to do, it was fight.

Shauni had her animals, Viv her telekinesis, and Kylie her lightning. Willyn healed bodies, just as Hayden helped spirits, and Lucia found what was lost. Claudia could see the past and Anna the future, but while each of her sisters had their own brand of spice, none of them could make quite the same claim as Paige.

She had been *born* to kick some ass.

Riding on a potent mix of adrenaline and confidence, she performed a super-fast flick of one of Scarlett's curls. She chuckled at the flash of outrage on the redhead's face.

"Like you said, Scarlett, it's my turn for a trial." Paige crossed her arms. "And since you don't know me very well," she continued, all the while glaring at her foe, "I'll give you a heads up."

She leaned in to snarl, "I don't intend to fail."

Scarlett lifted a careless hand and pretended indifference. "Save the speeches and bravado. This is me you're talking to, not Ronja."

But still, she took a step away from the anchor she'd been leaning against, also putting some distance between herself and Paige. "Between you and me, I think we can admit that every witch in your coven is going to face and win her challenge."

If the witch's eyes had been slick with devilish intent before, they now grew bitter and hard. "You all *have* to succeed if we're ever going to get to the real prize."

The crimson cloud around Scarlett intensified as her emotions heightened, and her magic intensified. "Anna." She spat the name as if it tasted bad in her mouth. "She's the one we *really* want a piece of. Any good villain will tell you that pain and suffering are much more enjoyable when they last," she smacked her lips, "until the very end."

A warning was on Paige's tongue, but the red witch's demeanor took another unexpected turn. Scarlett shrugged and smiled as if she hadn't just threatened the coven's leader. "So you see, I'm certain you'll succeed in your challenge. In fact, I hope you do. You're the only one of your coven that has any backbone. Any…fire." She nodded. "I can respect that."

"You'll respect my fist when it slams into you and my fingers puncture all four chambers of your heart."

Scarlett laughed, low and thick. "See?" She pointed a finger at Paige and twirled it in a small circle. "Fire."

"Well, *I* may have to survive until the last trial." Paige mimicked the witch's gesture with the finger-twirl. "But you don't." She was poised to strike, ready to kill. And judging by the spreading red fog, so was Scarlett.

The two women of magic glared at each other, neither giving an inch.

Suddenly the screech of tires drew their attention. Paige groaned when Chris bounded from the patrol car with Trevor at the wheel. They must have wrapped things up with the shifter.

Returning her gaze to Scarlett and her noxious fumes, Paige called out loudly, "Stay back, Chris."

He didn't respond, but the sound of his steps across the grass pinpointed his position to Paige's rear right side. He was holding steady this time, letting her take command.

Finally, she thought, with no small amount of resentment. But while Chris wasn't causing Paige any trouble, he'd surely drawn Scarlett's full attention.

The red-haired mage held her magic at a low boil as she studied Chris. With shrewd eyes, she inspected him as if he were a strange insect. "Don't I know you?"

Paige heard nothing from Chris, and the air grew brittle with confused tension as Scarlett's eyes darted between her and the Ranger. The witch seemed contemplative, unsure how to proceed.

Only seconds before, Paige would have been happy to dust the woman and heave her corpse over the trees and into the river. But now she felt a prickling sense of caution, as if her inner witch was trying to tell her something.

Did Scarlett actually recognize Chris? And if so, why? How?

But the red witch appeared to make an abrupt decision, and not the one Paige would have expected. "We're leaving," Scarlett said to her mysterious cohort still obscured by the tree.

In response, Valentina stepped out from behind the oak. She wore a bemused expression on her face, but was obviously deferring to Scarlett.

"You're not going anywhere." Paige took a menacing step to intercept the witch when she made a move to leave.

Scarlett was back to playing it cool, tousling her hair and mocking Paige with a laugh. "We've done what we came for." She lifted her hands but not to emit any more of the mist. Sending forth a power she rarely displayed, the witch lifted two of the unconscious people from the lawn and levitated their bodies high into the air. They floated up, up, above the Old Harbor Light, almost thirty feet above the ground.

With a pucker of her lips, Scarlett sent an imaginary kiss to Paige and said, "Catch." Then she let the people drop.

Paige locked her focus onto the person nearest her and dashed in the woman's direction. Her attention was split between the female and a man who was also falling.

No time. There was no time. She couldn't catch them both!

A streak of color blasted by Paige, the movement so fast it rustled the ends of her hair.

With her mouth hanging wide, she struggled to make sense of what she'd just seen. What she was still seeing. Chris was now beneath the falling man, strong arms open and ready to catch the weight.

Remembering the body plummeting toward her as well, Paige eyeballed the woman's form and cradled her in a firm yet gentle catch. Softly, she laid her on the grass.

With the woman safe, Paige turned her still-astonished gaze back to Chris. He too deposited his catch on the ground, and stood again.

He displayed no signs of muscle strain or injury at all. Any ordinary person would show something, some after-effect of having caught the weight of a crashing body with only their arms.

But Chris seemed fine. Perfectly. Fine.

So many emotions rushed through Paige that she couldn't put a name to any of them. But the breath that poured from her was a release of anxiety. And relief.

She was relieved, because she wouldn't have made it to the falling man in time.

She was anxious because Chris had.

The Ranger, the man who'd pushed his way into her life and her trial, had just blasted by her at the speed of light before demonstrating the strength of a mythological demigod.

Chris had even more in common with her than she'd realized. He shared the very gifts that had always made Paige feel special. Unique. Invulnerable.

In addition to all the other things she found so annoying about him, he also possessed the kind of speed and strength that was so much a part of her identity.

In the space of a few seconds, with one amazing feat, Chris had become a whole new person to Paige. A new problem.

Was her heart fluttering?

Connections. Damn all these connections. The Ranger was weaving a web of obligations and emotional bonds, and Paige was beginning to feel trapped.

The woman near her feet moaned, causing Paige to remember the others lying on the lawn as well as the witch who'd poisoned them. She turned to find the rest of the area deserted except for the other bodies still on the ground.

One of them coughed and began to rouse. They didn't seem to be at death's door. In fact, Paige realized as she moved to another man on the lawn, they were apparently on the way to recovery.

She heard sirens in the distance, response to the medical emergency called in by Cole or Trevor. The two detectives could explain what they'd found in the park, but Paige didn't need to be here when EMS arrived.

Neither did Chris.

She met his stare and motioned with her thumb. "We need to get out of here." She pressed her lips into a tight line. "Guess I don't have to ask if you can keep up with me."

"No." His head gave a slight tilt forward. "How do you feel about that?"

After a moment, she brushed past him and mumbled, "I'll let you know."

8

Paige sank into the reassuring softness of the green velvet couch. The single piece of furniture had become symbolic for her, a sign that she had returned to a safe haven, to the island mansion that was somehow as cozy as any wooded cottage, despite the soaring ceiling and expansive rooms.

The mood in the grand hall was somber as the witches straggled in and flopped unceremoniously onto chairs or sofas. The blank expressions weren't due to fatigue; if Paige had to guess, she'd say they were simply shell-shocked.

Because she sure was.

"The Amara have upped the stakes." Viv gave voice to what was on everyone's mind, the cause of the deflated morale. She wasn't wearing her black glasses, part of her physicist look, and without them, the fear in her eyes was apparent.

"We barely kept things under control," Lucia said. "There was too much happening in too many places."

Had that been the purpose of the Amara's staggered assaults on the city? To keep the witches busy, harassed? Or had there been more to their games?

"So what did they gain from today?" Paige asked, allowing her head to rest against the back of the couch. "Scarlett said she'd done what she'd needed to do, but I can't believe she knocked people out with her gas and drew attention to herself just so she could have a conversation with one of us."

A stray strand of hair tickled her cheek, but when she brushed it back, she found Tiger's tail instead. "Hey, girl." She could use a little feline booster right now.

"When I showed up at the Walk," she continued, "Scarlett didn't run or attack. She was just waiting. And it's not like she told me anything of great importance." Paige grumbled beneath her breath. "Her little red fog was a diversionary tactic if I ever saw one."

Claudia folded her long legs beneath her in one of the fancy chairs Paige liked to think of as "Louis-somethings." "So if it was a diversion," the flame-haired woman said when her feet were tucked in, "then what were they steering us away from?"

"Have you heard from Cole?" Hayden asked Claudia, who shook her head and gave her cell phone another worried look. Hayden sighed. "Trevor hasn't called or texted either."

"Lots of paperwork for them to fill out," Kylie suggested, an effort to make the two women worry less about their boyfriends. She still surprised Paige at times, when her youthful face and mature personality clashed. As they did now.

"I just hope no one makes too much of the strange occurrences." Willyn strode from the base of the stairs, having just returned from checking on her son Tadd. "Dare offered to stick around in case anyone needed their minds changed, but Cole and Trevor said they'd handle it." She flopped down in one of the royalty-inspired chairs. "But I don't think they felt right about planting ideas in the minds of their coworkers."

"I can understand that," Paige said, leaning forward on the sofa to rest her elbows on her knees. "At what point do we draw the line? We've tried to hide the paranormal activity in Savannah—"

"To protect the people," Shauni interjected. "So no one gets frightened by what's happening with the Amara and Bastraal."

"But when does our protection become too invasive?" Suddenly restless, Paige rose from the couch and went to the fireplace, turning to face the other women. "Even when it comes to magic and monsters, people need the truth if they're going to stand on their own and defend themselves. I know I want the ability to protect myself and those I care about. Everyone should have that right."

"What are you suggesting?" Hayden asked. "That we should start telling people what's really going on?"

"No." Paige leaned against the rocks of the fireplace wall. "But if someone is targeted by the Amara or is inadvertently involved, maybe we shouldn't lie to them either."

The room fell silent, and Paige shifted, studying the floor. The slate had seen countless years of wear. Yet still, the stone endured, as had the St. Germaine home, the island, its family…and the prophecy.

"You're right." Shauni's voice broke through the hush. "I should have learned my lesson from before, from my trial. I thought I had to protect the animals, but they ended up helping me." She fingered the end of her raven braid. "I didn't give them enough credit."

"Another day like today, and people will know something's happening in the city, whether we want them to or not," Kylie said.

"It's growing beyond us." Anna finally added her opinion, and all eyes turned to the woman who'd inherited this grand estate, along with the duty to see the prophecy to fulfillment. Anna was the only one of The Nine who'd always known her destiny.

Paige wasn't sure if that foreknowledge was a blessing or

a curse. Would it have changed her own decisions? What might she have done differently if she'd been aware of the prophecy and the role she would play? Would she have risked her safety by joining the Army?

She might have turned out differently, might have self-protected and ended up making herself more fragile. Less useful to her coven sisters.

She glanced at each in turn, remembering their hard-fought trials. Each woman had come to the prophecy with a history, but second-guessing the past never proved beneficial, only frustrating, since nothing could be undone.

No matter the devastation or loss, the only choice was to press onward. To live with what you'd been given.

But now someone else was making Paige take another look at her history and how it had really come to be. Chris had brought new information into her life, new questions, new obligations.

According to him, she had an alternate destiny that had to be addressed. But anything that could influence her now, also had to be put forth to her coven. "I never got a chance to tell you what Chris wants from me," she said abruptly, drawing every eye. "And it might affect us all."

She gave them a quick rundown of who Chris really was and that he claimed he'd come to help her. Then, after a bracing breath, she told them the rest. When she added the part about her mother's murder, her friends each displayed a level of sympathy.

But knowing Paige, understanding how she would feel about a great show of emotion, they kept their condolences brief.

"Oh, Paige," Hayden said.

"Yeah." Paige nodded, numbness stealing over her as she once again let herself take in the full impact of what Chris had told her. Had it only been this morning?

As a soldier, she'd known days and nights in the desert without food or rest, and even they hadn't felt as long as today suddenly did.

"And of course you want to avenge your mother," Viv offered, her matter-of-fact tone a balm to Paige's ragged nerves. Direct and to the point, that was Viv's way, her scientific side coming out.

The businesslike observation and conclusion were exactly what Paige needed. "Yes," she replied. "I do. I've grieved for her over the years, but knowing that she was deliberately taken from me, that someone…*hurt* her…" She curled her fists, unable to express the aching rage the knowledge caused her.

In addition to mourning her mother, she now had to deal with her own vivid imagination, and the pictures that wouldn't stay out of her head. Flashing, gruesome pictures of her mother running, screaming, suffering.

And finally, lying on the ground with flat, dead eyes.

But even these images were conjured from blurry memories, guesses as to what her mother had actually looked like. She was a few years younger than Chris, so, unlike him, she couldn't remember much.

Paige barely recalled her mother's blonde hair, and even that could be her wishful thinking, a result of looking at herself in the mirror for so long, and wondering.

She didn't have a single picture of her mother, another thing she'd always hated her father for. His half-sister, the aunt who'd raised Paige, couldn't be faulted for not having pictures of a woman she barely knew and who'd lived far away.

But Paige's father could have damn well left a photo behind, one single memory for his daughter to carry with her.

The cruel-hearted bastard hadn't even given her that.

"You have to find out what happened," Lucia said, bringing Paige out of her dark thoughts and back to the eight women looking at her with concern and anger. Yes, her sisters were furious. Not at Paige, but *for* her.

Especially Lucia, who'd been raised by a substitute mother herself. Her wealthy parents had been too busy jet-setting to care about little Lucia, and the Spanish woman was actually standing with hands on her hips, her brown eyes stormy with indignation.

For some reason, her friend's outrage was bolstering. Paige had never lacked for confidence, that was for sure, but the morning's unsettling news had affected her sense of direction, her internal compass.

But leave it to Lucia, the relic hunter, to know where she should go.

Paige glanced from one face to another, and wondered why she'd ever had any doubts. These women had been there, stalwart and unfailing, when every other witch had stood for the coven.

Even with her strength, speed—and stubbornness—Paige was going to receive their support too. And there wasn't a damn thing she could do about it.

Thank goodness.

She found herself rubbing her arms where goose bumps had risen. The huge house of stone could get a little drafty, but Paige suspected there was more to the sudden chill. She was coming down from a roller coaster of a day, and in a very real emotional sense, she was crashing.

As if by magic, Mrs. Attinger appeared behind Kylie's chair. She held a tray of snacks in her hands and came to set it on a table near Paige. "Eat," she instructed.

Then the kindly older woman moved to the hearth and struck a match to the already laid logs and kindling. She started a fire. For Paige.

Feeling more grounded, more like herself, Paige smiled her thanks and rubbed her hands before the growing flames. Then she filled the women in on the rest of the story, including Chris's last big reveal.

"So he's as fast and strong as you?" Kylie said with a suggestive grin. "Maybe even stronger and faster?"

"*Pffft*. You can get those crazy ideas out of your head." Paige shot back an evil grin of her own. "No one's faster than me."

She didn't mention the other notions likely floating in the younger woman's romantic mind, particularly the opinion that Paige had finally met her match. Chris was her male equivalent and someone she probably couldn't body-slam if the urge took hold.

And she positively denied the creeping pleasure that imagery brought her.

She was saved from delving further into a discussion of Chris's attributes by the arrival of Cole and Trevor. The detectives both wore stern expressions, though, and Paige was suddenly even more grateful for the fire and the warmth it delivered.

"We all got played," Trevor said, moving to Hayden and taking her in his arms when she stood to greet him.

Cole joined Claudia, standing next to her chair. He met her eyes for a moment of shared angst before he told the others, "By the time we got to The Barracks, the chaos we ran around trying to stop today had already been forgotten."

"What do you mean?" Paige asked. "Did something else happen?" The only thing that would supersede a crisis was an even bigger one.

"The station was flooded with missing person reports." Trevor cast a side-glance to his partner. "And Cole and I got two new cases. They've been classified as homicides, but…"

"It's like nothing we've ever seen. Nothing anyone has." Cole took Claudia's hand. To comfort her, or himself? Raking a hand through his dark-brown hair, he continued. "The bodies were dry and shriveled, brown. The M.E. is still working on them, but he says they're desiccated."

"Bone dry," Trevor added. "But both were fully dressed and had IDs, so making identifications and placing them at their last known whereabouts was fairly easy."

"The thing is," Cole finished, "both of them were last seen alive this morning."

Viv gripped the handrails of her chair. "You said they were already brown? What could drain bodily fluids so quickly?"

"Nothing natural." Quinn had come downstairs, likely hearing the male voices and the ardent conversation. He directed his attention to the detectives. "What about the missing people? Do you think the same thing could have happened to them?"

"No one's been found." Trevor's tone betrayed his defeat. "Yet."

"Maybe they're alive," Hayden said, looking up hopefully at Trevor. "The Amara's taken people before."

"Yeah. To give their bodies to demons." Paige surged away from the wall. "Okay. This clinches it. I know what I said before, but forget the stuff Chris dumped on me. We've got bigger problems to deal with. The Amara's gone wild and turned completely unpredictable. Now we have more kidnappings…" She could feel herself amping up and didn't care for the desperation seeping into her voice.

"I can try to locate the missing people." Lucia held up a hand to get Paige's attention. "But we probably know who took them."

"And Ronja may have created a blocking spell to keep us from finding them. The way she did before," Claudia said.

"With Kylie."

Lucia could usually locate anything lost or hidden. Or anyone. But when the Amara had taken Kylie, Ronja had combined her magic with Bastraal's to blind Lucia, and even Anna, to the younger witch's location.

"Once they're possessed by demons, Lucia can't find them anyway," Ethan said. Paige was pacing, so churned up inside that she'd missed that Lucia's demonologist boyfriend had joined the group in the grand hall.

Lucia nodded at him. "Once beasts are in the bodies, the people technically aren't lost anymore. The demons become the controlling essence."

"So what are you guys saying?" Paige spread her hands, instinctively moving closer to Anna. "You think I should follow up on this other thing with Chris and just forget about what I need to do here? I hardly think my challenge includes abandoning my coven."

"You aren't doing any such thing." Willyn gave her a "mom" look, and Paige felt the burn of embarrassment. She was overreacting, but the first day of her trial had brought too many surprises. And failures.

She'd done all she could do—logically, she understood that reality—but people had died on her watch.

She took in Trevor's and Cole's shadowed expressions, their clenched jaws. The losses had been on their watch too.

As if sensing her inner struggle, Anna looked straight into Paige's eyes, demanding her full attention. "You've seen a different war, one like none of us have experienced. I'm sure things didn't always go according to plan."

"No." Paige crossed her arms. "Hardly."

"So," Anna said, "what did you do when things went wrong? How did you make decisions? Prioritize?"

Paige felt the stiffness enter her spine, the determination

fill her voice. "People first. Mission always." When Anna raised a brow, she clarified, "Save and defend who you can but complete the op. The mission."

"And what is your mission now?"

Paige was being prodded, but her disciplined side told her she likely needed it. Even a soldier like her had to get a kick in the butt on occasion.

Anna was great at giving advice in a way suited to each individual, so she was brooking no bullshit from the coven's warrior.

Paige nodded, her eyes locked onto Anna's of royal blue. "My trial."

"Chris's arrival is rather timely, don't you think? He was literally there when your trial began. No matter what that means for you and him on a personal level, you have to consider what he brings to your challenge and how he might help you."

"But a whole other destiny, Anna? It just seems too far fetched."

At last Anna decided to sit, lowering herself leisurely to the green couch. "What if it's not another one?"

"Huh?"

"What if they're one and the same?"

Paige mentally recoiled, her mind linking several fragmented pieces into one disjointed whole. The coven prophecy and her role in it, the justice she should seek for her mother and the others, Chris and his obligation to help her do that, and finally, his being part of her coven destiny.

If it all rolled into one sick threesome to include Chris, Paige, and that trickster known as Fate, then she had an idea what the outcome was supposed to be. And she didn't have to be psychic like Anna to know she didn't want any of it.

No man for her, no romance or interdependency. She

couldn't stand the idea.

Which meant no Chris.

But without him, she didn't know where to start or how to proceed. If avenging her mother was part of her coven trial, she had no choice but to follow her pre-ordained path. And in her heart—which was already so often filled with anger and distrust—she wanted to find whoever had destroyed her young, happy life.

And she wanted to make them pay.

So that meant she had to push her way through the unpleasantness if she intended to get to the victory. Besides, if it weren't difficult, it wouldn't be a challenge.

Reaching into her pocket, Paige found the paper she still had tucked away. She looked at the number and address written on the scrap. Feeling the weight of the decision she'd made, she closed her eyes and sighed.

She knew what she had to do.

9

Chris added a quick swirl of olive oil to the pan heating on the stove. His garlic and onions were already diced and ready to be sautéed, so while he waited for the oil to bubble, he'd start halving the cherry tomatoes. The water for the pasta he'd start in about ten minutes, after the chicken was partially cooked.

He took a huge whiff of the fresh basil and oregano and smiled. This was where he found relaxation.

There was little to be said about his apartment as far as comfort. His dining area consisted of a card table with two folding chairs, but they were quick to clean, and portable, the one requirement he had of furniture, going back almost as far as he could remember.

Because growing up, the less they had to carry around, the easier it was for them to get lost again. To merge into society and simply vanish.

But he had a permanent place now, even if it wasn't much.

He sprayed the tomatoes with veggie cleaner and rinsed with water, a necessity his fellow Rangers had enjoyed needling him about to no end. Whatever Chris might lack in other domestic areas, he made up for when it came to cooking.

And when his buddies had been stuffing their faces, they hadn't made any complaints.

When Chris invited friends over to watch a game, his guests ate real food alongside the junk. He found prepping a familiar dish as soothing as experimenting with new recipes or trying his hand at invention.

More than once he'd considered how his hobby developed. The truth was food was easily left behind and could be replaced as often as need be. It was no wonder he'd found enjoyment in the bright colors of fresh fruits and vegetables, the aroma of a steak sizzling on the grill.

These pleasures could be found anywhere, so they were always available.

He'd never had to worry about having to cram food into his well-worn backpack in the middle of the night.

As Chris added the garlic and onion to the hot oil, he was both surprised and irritated by the knock on his door. The day he'd had would go down in the books, and after confronting Paige, breaking up bar fights, and saving more than one person from falling to their death, he was so hungry even his bones felt hollow.

He didn't want to put off his dinner for a minute longer than absolutely necessary. He trudged down the short hallway and summoned as much hospitality as he could muster, unsure who'd be searching him out. The guys were gearing up for deployment, he knew, so they'd have no spare time for visiting.

When he opened the door wide and found Paige on his doorstep, the annoyance riding his shoulders all but floated away. She wore jeans and a black leather jacket that set off her light hair.

With her arms covered, he could no longer appreciate the toned and sexy shoulders, but the new look was just as edgy, befitting the woman who wore it.

He was about to ask her in when she beat him to the punch

with a dose of her usual charm and grace. "Why didn't you tell me about your abilities?" Her eyes accused even as she looked past him, as if scoping his home for hidden enemies. "Or did you just forget to mention that you're like me?"

A soft chuff that might have been laughter erupted from Chris's throat. He shook his head and said, "Come in," backing up to make way for her entry. When she stood rooted to one spot, he added, "I've got something on the stove," and left her to find her way by herself.

The thump of the closing door told him she'd come in. Once he had the burner turned off and the pan safely to the side, he turned to find her watching him.

"So?" she asked, eyes like blazing turquoise flames.

"I'd already dumped a lot on you this morning. I planned to save a little something for another time, but then you and your friends got the call…"

"And we both got busy trying to keep people alive." She nodded and the expression on her face seemed to be giving him a pass. Before she frowned. "So I guess this makes us equals."

"Uh…thanks?" Chris heard his own mockery.

She raised a shoulder then let it fall limp. "Come on. You know what I mean."

After a long, probing stare, he decided to let it go. Because oddly enough, he knew exactly what she meant.

It was a rare thing to meet another with his particular gifts, and knowing he didn't have to explain anything, try to hide what he really was, or—and this was the worst part—be careful not to hurt anyone, was more of a relief than he'd expected.

He'd always been aware of Paige's power, but seeing it up close, seeing her in action, not only was it a thing of beauty, but it made Chris feel a little less alone in the world.

Especially since so many of their kind had been eradicated.

"Something to drink?" he asked to break the tension, but she only held out a hand to wave aside the offer.

"I came here to give you an answer," she said, "but you probably already knew I would agree to work with you."

"I hoped you'd come around. But if you didn't, I was just going to keep trying to convince you."

Oblivious to his comment, she barreled on. "Listen, I'll look into whatever you and I are supposed to do together, but, full disclosure, if the coven has a problem—"

"You have to go. I understand."

A slow nod, an unspoken agreement, and then her eyes turned quizzical. "Did you know who I was that night, when we bumped into each other at the club?"

"The night you threatened to knock me out if I didn't let go of your arm? Yeah, I was pretty sure when I saw you, but positive when I heard your name."

"How did you recognize me?"

Unwilling to destroy this semi-pleasant conversation with more of the bad old days, Chris sidestepped and said, "I was pretty surprised by you, that you were so..." He wisely decided to forego any adjectives. "Well, let's just say you've changed."

"Yeah," she dead-panned, "life will do that sometimes."

The reminder of her childhood gave Chris a good reason to face the refrigerator. He held a beer out around the door, but again she refused with a head-shake.

He, however, was having one. Her mention of how life had affected her caused red-hot guilt to flash in his gut. There were things she had yet to hear, things he had failed to tell her, but he believed the omission was for the best.

Paige's path had been laid for her on the day she was born, and it was Chris's duty to make sure she found her way through the twists and turns. No matter what or who tried to steer her off course.

If he told her the rest right now, though, she'd probably walk away from him as well as from her destiny. So for the time being, Chris would keep the lie going.

No, not a lie. He preferred to think of it as an intentional oversight. One he would correct when the time was right, when Paige trusted him more.

But at this rate, he thought, popping the cap of the bottle, he wasn't optimistic about that being any time soon.

She deserved the truth, and she would have it. Just not tonight.

Chris was divided, torn between two separate loyalties, but he had one critical goal in this lifetime, and he was bound to see it through. To stand with Paige, whether she liked it or not.

If for no other reason, he owed it to his dead parents.

Paige shuffled, moving her weight from one foot to the other. "I had to tell my coven everything, about our parents and this other…pursuit."

"The hunt," he corrected. "For the murderers of our people."

"Like I told you, my trial just began, so I had to make sure I was doing the right thing by helping you." She stiffened her back. "As important as what you want me to do is, I have to put the coven prophecy first."

"You hungry?" Chris asked. "I can make double."

She looked at him as if he'd lost his mind. "What? No. I'm good."

He would leave the tomatoes alone then, focus on her instead. "This trial, how does all that work? What do you have to do?" He thought of sitting but chose to remain standing, as eye-to-eye with his new partner as he could get.

Paige was tall, but he still had a good six inches on her. He wondered how she viewed him, now that she knew what he could do. Would his abilities make him attractive to her? Or an adversary?

"That's part of the challenge," she told him, relaxing only marginally. "I have no idea what I have to do to completely and unequivocally pass the trial. I'll only know when I succeed."

"How will you know?"

"My amulet." She fingered the silver piece hanging from her neck. "It will…uh…tell me."

Chris gulped the mouthful of beer down his throat. "Really. That I'd like to see." Following up on a strong and sudden urge, he moved nearer and reached out.

She stepped back just as quickly.

"I only wanted to get a closer look." He met her cool, blue eyes. "At the necklace, I mean."

"I thought you were going to, I don't know, hug me or something."

Chris laughed, and eased back, giving her space. She'd been skittish at the mere idea of him touching her? What was that about?

And why did he feel like he'd just lost out on something?

"So listen, I'll work with you." She folded her arms and gave him a hard stare. "But you need to understand one thing about me. I don't do controlling very well." She lifted her chin to convey unflagging self-assurance. To make sure he saw it within her. "So no more stunts like on the bridge when you started barking out orders. I don't report to you."

"And you should know that I don't do edicts very well." Chris set his bottle down on the card table so hard it wobbled from the impact. "If we're going to be partners, then let's act like it. *Neither* of us is under anyone's command anymore."

Chris saw a pot shot and took it. "Don't forget." He added

extra emphasis when he said, "We're equals."

If eyes could grow colder and more heated at the same time, hers did now. She zipped over to face off with him, up close and personal. "Are you going to be a problem for me? I came here to agree with you, but here you are provoking me again."

"Hell, Paige. I only have to breathe to make you mad." Sipping his beer slowly and with a belligerent eye on her, he tried to swallow some of his vexation along with the brew. But his next comment was still somewhat hostile. "You know, there are people you can talk to for that."

"Don't worry about my personal issues." She'd been standing on her toes to get in his face—the little badass—but now she lowered to the floor. "I have my own anger management methods."

"Do you?"

"Yeah." She retreated to her corner again. "I usually just stay away from people who piss me off."

Chris held out his hands. "But you're stuck with me for a while, so I'll just have to make a list of what pisses you off and try to avoid them. Actually, the stuff that doesn't make you angry would probably be shorter."

Chris saw her jaw move as she ground her teeth. This attitude of hers was non-stop.

But he sensed an undertone of skittishness lurking beneath the toughness. "What is it about me that rubs you the wrong way? Is it because I surveilled you?"

"Surveillance? That's the word we're using now?" She stuck her hands in the pockets of her jacket.

Her chilly demeanor had returned in full. If cold fronts were named like hurricanes, the most bitter of them would be called Paige. "Then what is it?" he asked. "You act as if you're afraid of me."

Chris could actually see the pride roll up her back to flare in her eyes. "Afraid?" She laughed scornfully. "Okay, out of respect for our new partnership, I'll just tell you there are some elements of my trial that I might dislike. I might be… cautious about them, but I am definitely not afraid."

"What does your trial have to do with me?"

"Exactly."

Chris literally scratched his head. "You want to explain in a little more detail? You know, talk slow for those of us who can't read minds."

"No. I've said all I'm going to. It's a subject best left alone, and as far as you're concerned, the only thing we need to worry about is finding who killed the people we loved." The set of her mouth told him the topic was closed, and locked securely. At least for the night.

"What's our first step?" she asked instead. "Since you're the one in the know, I defer to you. On this only." She smiled at him, but it was so brittle it would snap under any more pressure.

Chris relented. He wouldn't pursue the subject now, but he would follow up later. He wanted to know what she was so worried about. She faced off with other witches without blinking an eye, had been ready to chase down the succubus, and toyed with demons late at night without concern for her own safety.

But there was an element to her trial that she feared, and Chris would find out what it was.

He assured himself it was simply because of their connection and that they now had to work together. His concern for her welfare had nothing to do with his softer memories of her, or the startling warmth that spread through him whenever he saw her face.

Even when it was scowling at him.

"The older woman I told you about, the seer, we should go talk to her," he said. "There are things she'll only tell you, and only at the right time."

"Well hell." Paige clucked her tongue. "I guess the time doesn't get any more cherry than this. "Do we have to go far to find her?"

"She's a couple of hours south."

"I'll pick you up at eight." She only had to take a few strides down the hall to reach the door.

"I can come by the yellow house instead."

Her hand paused on the knob. He saw her sigh, and as she looked back at him he caught the second half of her eye-roll. "Fine. Whatever," she said.

She exited on that note without a glance back or any of the little niceties most people would have used. And she sure didn't offer a feminine little "Bye-bye" when she left.

She just slammed the door.

Chris laughed, a rumble low in his belly, and shook his head. Paige was prickly as hell. And he liked her for it.

But with plans made for tomorrow, he had to make sure everything was a go on the other end.

His cell phone lay on top of the table that served as dining table and desk. The dual-purpose setup again reminding him of a lifetime of nomadic patterns and changes of residence.

Always trying to stay one step ahead of those who might have been tracking him. Tracking *them*.

He picked up the cell and dialed a number. The old woman's crackly voice picked up right away.

"I need to see you tomorrow," he said, getting straight to the reason for his call. But she likely knew what he was about anyway. She'd probably sensed he would reach out to her before he'd known himself.

"In the morning?" he asked, then paused, as if he couldn't

believe he was finally able to say what he was about to say. "I found Paige. I'm bringing her to you."

The sound of rushing breath came through the receiver. So maybe he'd surprised her after all. "Does anyone else know you've found her?" she asked in a whisper.

"No."

"Good." A raspy cough, and then, "Keep it that way."

10

Savannah and St. Augustine were like first cousin cities, similar backgrounds but different faces. Paige could see the Spanish influence in the domed buildings the color of sand, and in streets and boulevards with names like San Marco, San Carlos, and, of course, Ponce de Leon.

But she and Chris hadn't driven over two hours south to find the Fountain of Youth. They'd come to piece together an old mystery, to bridge their past to the now, and to start their search for those who used magic to kill.

She could tell he'd taken this route before and knew the area well. He'd been on the lookout for a place to park, but still she was jarred when he veered sharply into a spot made vacant by a departing minivan. "It's a short walk from here," he explained.

Paige nodded and disembarked. She was intently curious about the woman they'd come to see and knew little about Matilda Flannery other than that she'd been one of the fortunate few to evade the massacre in the commune that day, the one that had taken both of Chris's parents along with Paige's mother.

Thanks to Chris and a long drive with nothing but time to talk, she was also aware of Matilda's ability. Like Anna, the woman had a sixth sense and often "knew" things others didn't.

As she and Chris walked over cobblestone streets, Paige took the opportunity to covertly study the man she'd been thrown together with. Today his easy grin and laid-back attitude had resurfaced, as if their dispute from the night before had never happened.

But underneath the easy-going facade, she detected a core of steel. He was a man who stayed on task, kept his focus, and didn't let frivolous distractions sway his motivation. And of all the similarities they shared, his drive and tunnel vision were traits she could appreciate.

Dropping her gaze to veil the inspection with her lashes, she admired the fiercely toned physique and play of muscles beneath his clothes when he moved. Arms, back, legs, not a piece of his body could ever be called weak.

The gods had created him to be powerful, and it looked like Chris had worked hard to make the most of that gift. Every muscle was cut, not a trace of softness anywhere, and Paige had seen firsthand how swiftly he could move, putting all that strength to good use.

Chris was the ultimate super-soldier.

Yet his jeans, dark gray t-shirt, and ball cap added a touch of rugged boy-next-door. The more charming aspects of his personality kept catching her off guard. Like now, as she slipped in another peek at that tear in his back left pocket.

And the firm curve underneath.

Chris was amiable, all right, but today he walked with a purpose, never deviating to take in the sights or start up a meaningless conversation with locals or tourists. He wasn't rude, not at all. He was simply…focused.

Still stealing glimpses of him—the dark blonde hair peeking from beneath the cap's rim, long, strong legs moving almost silently despite the scruff of denim—she considered the reasons for his involvement in all of this.

After leaving his place last night, she'd had time to re-inspect the situation. And to look at things—especially herself—as they might appear from his point of view.

She didn't really care for what she'd seen.

Every time he'd tried to explain things to her, all she'd done was slap him in the face with her own troubles, her own commitments. She'd tried to eject him from her presence, and her life.

He didn't seem like the kind of guy to put up with any nonsense, and now, as she studied his no-nonsense stride and straight-ahead demeanor, she wondered how he'd maintained any patience with her at all. Paige had to give him props. Because with her he'd been a freakin' saint.

A pang of regret clutched in her chest, right above the stab of guilt. She had been a terror to deal with, and if what he said was true, he'd dealt with his own fair share of pain.

Chris was an orphan after losing both of his parents, and he'd searched for Paige for years in an effort to avenge their deaths. But when he'd finally found her, she'd welcomed him like a nest of territorial hornets.

She sighed and continued her trudge through the hot-and-humid-as-hell streets, hoping she got some clear answers today, if not from Chris, then maybe from his friend. Matilda, the seer.

It'd be nice if Chris also learned something new. Paige admired his dedication to what he called "justice," and she wondered if she'd have held it together as well. After all this time, he still diligently waited for Paige to deliver her fated vengeance.

For both of them.

When it came to coven business, she might still be territorial, but since she'd learned of his powers, she'd been more willing to accept him as an ally.

But her interest in him in other ways had shot through the roof. Exactly what she hadn't wanted. Not now, not during her trial.

This time, when she stole one final look at Chris, her stomach went all nice and buttery. Damn it. She didn't need that little burst of lust she'd just felt.

Chris was a great looking guy with a heart-crushing smile. She'd be stupid, or blind, not to notice. But with all the other links between them, and the timing—the awful timing—she just didn't want to acknowledge any level of sexual chemistry.

Not a single throb in her chest or swirl in her belly. Nope. *Nada*. Nothing. Not a blip on her libido's radar, even when she looked into those green, green eyes.

Crap! She gave a mental shove to the invasive images, keeping in step with Chris as he led her past two huge, square columns of stacked stones. The materials had been whitewashed by time, but the fortifications stood tall and strong. Just like him.

"Down here," he said, notching his chin slightly to indicate the side street filled with shops. The cobbles persisted here as well, speaking of the neighborhood's age.

Paige imagined what types of businesses or homes had once lived inside the dwellings and felt certain they hadn't been painted the happy pastels that greeted her in modern St. Augustine.

Finally, Chris stopped in front of a narrow building, canary yellow with a powder blue door. A wide window displayed an array of colorful sun catchers.

Paige wondered again what type of person Matilda was. Chris had shared little, saying only that she was older and "knew things."

And that she would only share certain details with Paige.

A cheery bell announced their entrance when they pushed

through the door, drawing the notice of a thirtyish woman with a brown cap of short hair and a whole lotta' rings in her ears. "Welcome. Feel free to look around," she said from behind a counter.

As Chris went to speak with the clerk, presumably to ask for Matilda, Paige did as suggested. She looked around. Pottery in shades of taupe and cerulean, hand blown vases in clear gemstone shades, and other bright ornamentation covered tables and shelves. The walls also held an eclectic mix of paintings and pieces, clearly made by a variety of artisans.

So Matilda ran an art store.

"Paige." Chris called her name softly, so she turned to find him beckoning to her. "This way."

He followed the clerk, and Paige followed him, careful not to bump any of the fragile pieces she passed. In the back of the store, they came to a door. The clerk produced a set of keys and opened the lock. Then she held back, indicating with a palm that they should go ahead without her.

They entered into a short corridor, and when the door lock clicked into place behind them, Paige hiked a single brow in question.

Chris only shook his head. He strode to a door at the other end of the hall. This entry was painted a deep blue, where the previous one had been the clean white of the store's shelves. He knocked lightly.

Paige felt as if she were in a transitional space, as if the hallway traveled from one world to the next. When the new door creaked open to reveal what lay inside, her instincts were confirmed.

The back room was aglow, filled with blue and red candles in clear glass containers. As her eyes adjusted to the dim light, Paige detected a bare amount of furniture, and heavy drapery closed securely over the windows.

No sunlight filtered into this little cave, not like it had in the store. Did the woman spend her whole day burrowed into this room? If so, why? Clearly she relished beautiful things, like the artwork in the gallery out front.

As if she knew she was in Paige's thoughts, the woman in question popped her head from behind the open door. Her flowing hair was a combination of silver and white streaks, a natural style no salon could ever mimic. She wore a black peasant blouse that Anna would simply adore, but in lieu of the coven leader's favored jeans, Matilda had paired the top with a black broom skirt.

"You're a witch." The words flew from Paige's mouth almost as if they'd developed wings all by themselves. If the statement had been blunt, Matilda didn't seem to mind. She laughed boldly, never taking her peanut-brown eyes off of Paige.

"I've wondered how you'd turn out," the older woman said. "It's glad I am that your pain has sharpened you, like the sword you're meant to be."

Wow. Nothing like jumping feet first into weirdness. But Paige kind of liked the sword analogy.

"Sit. Sit. I've made some tea." Matilda waved Paige to one of the four chairs situated around an oval table of rosewood, dark and gleaming. Tarot cards were half-spread across the surface, near a chair that had been pulled out, and what looked like one of Anna's gazing balls perched dead center of the table.

Either this lady was a walking stereotype of a witch-slash-fortune teller, or she worked very hard to give that impression.

As soon as the notion occurred, Paige knocked it back down. Matilda wasn't putting on an act for anyone, or why the two locked doors where none would see?

Was she an exceedingly private person?

Or was she afraid of something?

Upon closer inspection, Paige noticed drawings etched—not painted, but *etched*—into the walls. She didn't recognize the symbols, but they reminded her of Quinn's runes. As a magickal language expert, he often used the signs for spells.

And sometimes to cast protective wards.

Sympathy and a sense of injustice rushed through Paige. She was horrified for anyone who felt the need to hide away in such a claustrophobic space.

She wanted to ask Matilda who she was hiding from, but she didn't know her that well yet. Too much boldness and the older woman might clam up.

Supposedly, she'd held onto the information she had for over twenty years. If Paige raised any doubt or alarm, the witch just might decide to wait a bit longer.

So she'd have to continue to let Chris set the example. For once, Paige would stay quiet and simply observe. Besides, this was his show.

Matilda patted Chris's shoulder all the while as they walked over to the table, and then she grabbed him for a quick hug. "This is so exciting. I can't believe you finally did it. Little Christian."

Paige turned her head ever so slowly to look up at Chris. The slight smile on her lips was appropriately smug, and she made sure to tease him with her eyes. Little Christian? How sweet. How cute.

She'd have to be sure to use that one in the future.

With a quelling frown for Paige, he sat in the chair between her and Matilda. Paige was on the far end of the oval from the other woman but watched with interest when she gathered the Tarot cards into a neat deck and reached to set them aside on a bookshelf.

"You aren't going to use those to tell…" *our future*? Paige almost said, but chose to go with, "to tell us what we need to know?"

"Oh, no." Matilda lifted a teapot, replete with tiny purple flowers, and filled three matching cups. "I don't have to search for what you need, Paige Linen."

The use of her middle name felt like a familiar yet uninvited thump to Paige's gut. She kept forgetting that this woman had known her as a child, as had Chris. Again, she felt at a disadvantage.

And the discomfort only doubled when Chris sent her a mocking grin of his own. This Matilda knew too many names.

"No," Matilda continued, "no cards today. You see, I sought all I could back then." She scooped a teaspoon of brownish sugar into her tea before her gaze traveled upward. She seemed to stare at something beyond the room in which they sat, perhaps beyond the time in which they now lived.

"It's organic," the older witch said, jerking her attention back to Paige and passing her the sugar bowl. "Raw. So's the cream."

Hoping to spur more pertinent dialogue, Paige accepted some of each before handing them to Chris. He passed on both, and addressed their hostess. "I know what you have to say is for Paige, but I'd like to hear also."

"Of course, you must stay." Matilda gently placed her hand on Chris's forearm. She blessed him with a warm and loving smile, and Paige suddenly ached, wishing she'd known this strange but motherly woman as she'd grown up. At the very least, she wished she could remember her.

Then those soft brown eyes flicked to Paige and back to Chris as Matilda told him, "You are privy to all now. You're her guardian."

Paige spat a mouthful of tea across the dark wood. "Um… sorry." She looked down and used her napkin to dab at the droplets covering the table.

She muttered to herself, ignoring Chris when he began to help with his own paper square. *What kind of little girl was I? One whose middle name came from a fabric? The kind who needed a man to have her back?*

She looked up again and faked a smile. *Well, not anymore.*

"Matilda," she began in an even and respectful tone, "I really need to know whatever it is you want to tell me. I've agreed to work with Chris, but I was under the impression you knew something that could help us find the person who killed our parents."

Matilda nodded, her face turning grim, as if she dreaded sharing what she knew she must. The candles all flickered at once, drew down to their wicks, and then resurged with a great flash.

The older woman waved her fingers. "Apologies. This all makes me a bit emotional."

Chris patted her hand. "Take your time."

A tiny nod and Matilda seemed to shore herself up. She concentrated on Paige.

And Paige's spine chilled from top to bottom.

"When we returned from town that day, everyone had been killed," Matilda intoned, her voice as somber as the tale. "Not a soul left alive, not even the children. Especially not the children."

She swallowed and drew a breath, then she skipped ahead, avoiding any gory specifics. "After the shock wore off enough to allow me to think straight, I did my best to block out the horror and read the scene for any lingering information. Seeing backward is more difficult for me than seeing forward, but I was so upset, so agitated, that my emotions opened doors I'd never been through before."

When the woman paused, Paige picked up her teacup

again, just for something to hold. Something warm. "Go ahead. Please."

"I didn't see any faces, but I picked up on two very strong and distinctive signatures. One was a practitioner of magic, very good at it too. But the other," Matilda shut her eyes and hunched her shoulders as if defending herself from the memory, "that one was filled with darkness, a kind of power rarely found in this world, and never for very long."

"What?" Paige didn't understand. Two signatures? A rare power? "What do you mean?"

"Too strong, nature won't allow it to exist for any length of time." Matilda raised pools of light brown to stare into Paige. "That depth of evil would swallow the world if it were allowed free rein."

A cool breeze passed over Paige's nape. "This dark person, or thing, did it kill the people there?"

"I believe both of the beings who came that day took lives, but I can't tell you specifically who killed whom. I'm sorry."

"You've already told me most of this," Chris interjected. "What is it that you saved all this time for Paige?"

"As I listened to the death and destruction crying around me that day," Matilda lifted her face and closed her eyes, "the wind suddenly rushed through me, and it whispered."

Now the candle flames leapt high into the air, beating back the shadows that would press in if given the chance. The tiny room began to vibrate, as if the very air surged with electricity.

Paige glanced around. Another presence, a power, had entered the space.

Matilda's eyes jolted open, and a sound hissed through her bared teeth. "*Angramana.*"

Chris pried the old witch's fingers from where they gripped the edge of the table. "Matilda." He rubbed the thin white skin on the back of her hand. "What is it?"

Her body shook, as if she was struggling against an internal force. As if something inside of her fought for release. She took deep, heaving breaths while Chris held her hands.

Gradually her jaw relaxed, the shaking and the snarling stopped. Matilda forced her tongue through her teeth twice, smacking and licking as if fighting a bitter taste. Finally, she picked up her tea and drank it all down.

Exhaling with a *whuff*, she said, "Some words have power. Therefore, they must remain quiet, unspoken." She looked to Chris. "I couldn't risk releasing this name until she was here to receive it."

Paige didn't like the sound of that. Exactly what had she just received? *Angramana*. "Is there more?"

Matilda shook her head, and as Paige watched, the woman changed. Her skin tightened almost imperceptibly and grew the slightest bit more rosy in hue. She suddenly looked fifteen years younger.

A debt of gratitude bloomed within Paige. Matilda had carried a terrible weight for so long, all so she could deliver that one evil word to the person destined to pick it up and do... *something* with it.

If Paige had her way, it would be some damned bloody justice.

"I'm so sorry for what you've been through." She leaned forward, hoping the earnestness she felt came through. She wasn't very good at the touchy stuff.

There was someone else she owed an apology, so she'd camouflage it with this moment. She shifted to Chris. "And you. I'm sorry you lost your parents."

Sitting back again, she clasped her hands in her lap. *And that I lost mine.*

But she didn't say it.

Matilda nodded, gave a soft smile. Then she put the flat of her palm to the table. "Now. They came that day searching for the prophesied child, the one with strength and speed handed down by the spirits. Both of you will be in danger once you start your search. If you stir things up," she twirled a finger in the air, "the dark ones will sense it."

"And you've released the name." Chris held his head high, but his shoulders were tense. With anger for past wrongs? With concern for Matilda, for all of them?

"Yes. It's begun, and you must be careful." The older witch gently moved her long silver hair from the front of one shoulder to the back. "But you have one thing in your favor. Those who came that day never knew if they searched for a boy or a girl. They went to every commune, every gathering place with magical people, and they struck down every child of the right age and right abilities."

Paige stiffened. "They attacked more than one place?"

Matilda didn't answer the question, but said instead, "Now, at last, you'll make them pay." Her laugh was a true cackle this time. "Just like Oedipus, the killer has wrought his own misfortune by the wrongs committed against the two of you. By seeking to kill this one child, they set their own foul destiny in motion."

An insistent static was in the sublevels of Paige's brain. How many children had been murdered?

She was distracted when the woman's aged finger pointed at her insistently. "Paige, you are the one meant to avenge our people, and your parents." The finger wagged between Chris and Paige. "The two of you must make it happen."

With a swift droop of her shoulders, the woman's eyes became downcast, along with her buoyant mood. "I saw a prophecy years before, when Chris was small, and you, Paige, but a baby."

Her eyes grew sad, bewildered. "I knew you would right a terrible wrong and destroy the killer of children. But I never knew they would come looking for you. I didn't put the pieces together. That is my cross to bear. If I'd seen everything back then, the others might have been saved. And the ones like you."

"There were more like us?" Paige asked, the idea so unexpected that she turned to Chris.

"Oh, yes. Several were at the commune." Matilda put a hand to her mouth. "But they killed them all, even the little ones who had no magic at all."

The connection snapped into place then, and Paige felt sick to her stomach. "Are you saying…"

"But they don't know who you are." The witch's whisper was rapid and hoarse, filled with urgency. "We all protected you, Paige. We kept your presence, your survival a secret. And running, hiding like we've all done, this has made them lose the scent."

"We'll make sure they pick it up again." Chris's voice was threaded with steel, with resolve. "I *want* them to find me now."

Paige would have agreed with him, but she was still reeling. "Those people came and destroyed our community and others. How many others?"

Her head swam with the terrible knowledge. "They were looking for this one gifted child and killed innocent people, kids who had nothing to do with any of this."

Chris turned to her, compassion morphing his features, softening his green eyes. "Paige—"

She stopped him with a raised palm. "So what you're saying is the people at the commune, all those children, Chris's parents, and…my mother…" Paige stopped, swallowing the burn of acid climbing in her throat.

She considered herself a strong woman, but something deep inside her faltered, "They all died because of me."

11

Ian didn't know where he was. Even as a wash of familiarity filled him, as he smelled the unmistakable scent of summer grass and blooming *Kusymre,* he felt disjointed, disconnected from himself.

And how did he even know what to call the flowers?

Taking in his surroundings, he blinked as if the world would somehow come not only into focus but also into recognition. He—Ian Keller—didn't know this place with its scents and sounds. But an obscure, previously slumbering part of him did.

Staring into the icy-blue sky, he felt a thrill of anticipation. Summer was finally here, the season of the midnight sun. And how in hell did he know such specifics?

There could only be one answer, he thought as the clouds parted, as the sun made him blind.

He had been here before.

The frigid winds in the presence of colorful blooms told him just how far north he was, and the visceral sensations made this vision all too real. Recalling his experience in the courthouse, he identified with his true self and understood that he was having another…episode.

With no better idea how to categorize what was happening to him, he chalked it all up to a mental break of some kind. Wild fantasies spawned from the rambling ideas of a mad woman.

That had to be it.

But just as he knew who he was in the present, the environment he now visited tugged at emotions he couldn't deny. Poignant and fresh, they filled him with longing. But for what, he couldn't say.

A giggle startled him as a girl ran past him with her arms spread wide. Long, golden tresses spilled down her back and bounced as she did, with childish abandon. She leapt into the air as if attempting to take off and fly away, across the deep and haunting blue of the fjord.

Halting her erratic jumps into the air, she abruptly switched to spinning in circles to entertain herself. Her arms were still thrown outward, as if she would grab the whole world and make it hers.

Robust warmth and tenderness made Ian's chest sting, his throat swell. This small person, this child of light, was terribly important to him. He was connected to her in ways that were indescribable. Bonded for eternity.

He brightened at the idea of joining in with her revelry, but a woman's voice rang out, carrying across the meadow with that special mixture of love and authority that spoke of motherhood. "Vanir!"

Ian ran cold. Why did he feel the urge to respond to that name? And where had he heard it before?

But the next name that echoed to him, and to the yellow-haired girl who frolicked so gaily, destroyed all the warmth and tenderness he'd felt before. "Ronja!"

The pretty spring day started to whirl around Ian. Nausea sprang to his gut.

"Vanir!"

He clutched his stomach with both hands.

"Ronja!"

He clamped his eyes shut. And opened them.

With his fingers still tight against his abdomen, Ian scanned the room in which he found himself. No more flowers. No more blue sky.

And no more little…*sister.*

The severely organized space he'd returned to was far more comforting than the gorgeous spring day had been. He'd come back to the haven of his office and was seated behind his desk. Dark teak, straight lines, stylish, and most importantly, modern.

Thank all that's holy.

He'd managed to pull out of that alien place, and though he'd felt a connection, he simply did not belong in that place or with those people. Not anymore.

A knock on the door had him jumping to his feet, so quickly that he scraped the top of his thighs against the underside of the desk. "Yes?" he answered, patting at his face as he waited for the door to open. He felt flushed.

"Mr. Keller…" His office manager trailed off when she got a good look at him. "Are you feeling all right? You look…ill."

She'd wanted to say terrible, he'd bet. Because that's exactly how he felt. And had he actually fallen asleep at work? He'd never done anything remotely like that before.

What was going on with him? And was it going to stop?

Ian wasn't the kind of man who let situations rule him. Just the opposite, any challenge that presented itself was firmly taken in hand and dealt with in whatever way he deemed necessary.

"Actually, I don't feel well." He looked at Ms. Dillon in her trim and tidy suit. "Anything crucial come up while I was… napping?" He offered a tired smile.

"Nothing that can't wait until tomorrow." Her intense focus told him she thought he would do well to get some recoup time.

"Message received, Ms. Dillon." He stood, sure she could field any issues that might arise in his absence. "I think I'll take the rest of the day off."

~~~

Paige and Chris had met with the others upon their return, bringing them up to speed on their search. In exchange, they'd listened to the latest regarding the missing and murdered people downtown.

But there wasn't much for anyone to tell.

Thus far, there had been no word, no more leads for Cole and Trevor to pursue, and hardly any evidence left behind. The detectives had asked for the best criminalist the city had to work on the forensics, but even he'd found nothing.

As if all trace evidence had been "magically" erased.

The M.E. was also flummoxed as to what could have caused the bodies to dry out to such extremes. Cole and Trevor were walking a fence that Paige and the other witches had balanced on more than once.

How much should they share with the medical examiner? And if they told him anything at all, how quickly would he recommend psych evals for them both?

It's our job to handle the Amara, anyway. Paige nodded to herself and prepared to get to work. If completing her challenge had anything to do with the strange term Matilda had hissed at them, then she and Chris would get right on it.

By the time they'd gotten to the island and provided an update to the others, the sun had begun its westward disappearing act. So as she and Chris entered the library, they found Anna and Claudia turning on several desk lamps for those who would be researching.

"Just giving you some light," Claudia said before coming to Paige, taking one look at her face, and then nodding. "We'll leave you to it, but if you need us…"

"I'll send up a fireball." Paige hadn't been quick enough to mask her troubled mind, but Claudia only touched her shoulder as she walked past and out the doors.

Anna followed silently. Her friends must have sensed her need for space, as perceptive as Chris had been on the drive back from St. Augustine. He'd been quiet the entire time, casting only the occasional searching glance her way.

Even now, as she struggled against the dull ache in her mind, he let her stew in her own silence, her own troubled thoughts.

Until another emotion broke the surface, and she lowered her head, pinching the bridge of her nose. She hated showing even a hint of the pain inside of her, but she did momentarily.

Chris noticed. And he was clearly done waiting for her to internalize what she'd found out.

"It's not your fault," he said bluntly. "No more than it is mine or Matilda's."

"They didn't come to the commune because they were looking for you."

"Sure they did. They killed all the children, those who had our abilities and those who didn't. If we'd been there, they would have killed us too." He stepped closer to her and gripped her arm, not harshly, but not gently either. "They wiped everyone out because they could. It's as simple as that."

Raking hands through her hair, Paige wished she could accept what he was saying. She'd been trying to convince herself that she was blameless since they'd left the art shop.

His hand on her arm eased off, but he moved in, spoke softly to her in a way far too familiar for her comfort. "I know you just found out about all this, but take it from someone who's been fighting the very same guilt for years. We were kids. There's nothing we could have done."

"Yeah," she said, but without much conviction.

"But we can do something now." His tone had turned fierce, touching a place inside Paige that built up her anger, helped smother the remorse. She wondered if he did it on purpose, if he understood her better than she'd given him credit for.

"If you're anything like me," he continued, "and I know you are, then you won't like hearing this. But you're a victim too. Just like our parents and the others who were killed, like the people they left behind. Like me. It took me a while to come to that conclusion, but unfortunately, you don't have the same amount of time."

"I know. You're right. This is just all new to me." Paige forced the shame leave her, let intensity take its place. Rage was a much greater motivator than guilt. "I don't want to screw this up. Our one chance to set things right."

She flinched slightly, but Chris didn't seem to notice. Neither had he responded to how easily she'd said, "our chance." She no longer saw him as a complete outsider.

And that worried her.

"We won't screw it up." Surveying the rows of books, Chris edged away from her to run his finger down a navy blue spine. "But I have to admit, this might be harder than I thought. All we have to go on is that name, or word, that Matilda gave us. Hell," he laughed but without any mirth, "we don't even know how to spell it."

"Quinn can help us with that, and if it's a demon, then Ethan may be able to find it faster than us." Paige was all business again, as if the unwelcome idea of Chris as anything other than a pushy stranger had never entered her head.

"We have the best human resources around for this kind of thing," she said. "It's as if, well, as if some all-knowing gods and goddesses brought us all together for a reason." Paige marveled she didn't choke on sarcasm so thick.

"Have you considered that this witch, Ronja, that she could be the person we're looking for?" Chris asked.

"Maybe. But attacking all those people herself just doesn't seem like Ronja's style." Paige wasn't convinced. As cruel as the immortal witch was, the massacre Chris had described—however briefly—sounded like the work of henchmen.

"And the murders at the commune don't have anything to do with the coven prophecy," she said. "Otherwise, all of us would be destined to seek revenge. Not just me."

"Do the other women come from families of witches or those who practice magic?"

Paige considered, and when she smiled broadly, he asked, "What's so funny?"

"You asking about their families being witches." Paige chuckled. "I was just picturing General Worthington on a broomstick."

"Who?"

"Never mind." She went to peruse her own shelf of books, but the imagery of Kylie's father had lifted her spirits.

Chris's idea had merit, though. If she and her sisters hadn't been raised among people who practiced, it wasn't surprising that no one had ever talked about mystical destinies. Anna and Quinn were the only ones who'd always known what they were meant to do.

Just then, Quinn tapped the open door as he walked in with Ethan right behind him. "Did someone order two devilishly handsome geniuses?"

Paige scoffed but was glad for the extra help, and for the attempt at humor. "Go easy, Quinn, or we won't be able to read through all the horseshit piling up."

Looking just like his sister Anna, Quinn grinned, his blue

eyes overflowing with mischief. "I'll try not to let it get too deep."

He was correct on one count, though. The guys were intelligent and well-versed in topics that Paige needed to know more about.

Quinn was the greatest bibliophile in a house of readers, and he knew the stacks almost by heart. He was also a whiz when it came to languages, both ancient and occult.

Ethan had spent his life studying and hunting demons and other dark entities, so he also knew his way around strange phenomena and names. Most of the myths he'd tracked down had turned out to be not-so-mythical at all, but real stories, with real monsters.

The two men would be lending a hand to Chris and Paige as they followed up on the lead provided by Matilda. All they had to go on was the one word.

Ethan crossed the large room and stopped in front of the section Paige knew contained periodicals and books on esoteric beings. "Now tell me this name. That we're looking for."

Paige and Chris shared an aggrieved glance, neither wanting to test vocalization of the awful sound that had rushed from Matilda like a death wheeze. Instead, Paige approached Ethan and handed him a piece of paper. She'd written the best phonetic expression of the word she and Chris had been able to come up with. "We aren't sure of the spelling," she said. "Do you recognize it?"

Ethan took the paper and before Paige thought to caution him, he sounded out the scribbles. "An-gra-ma-na."

Paige stood stock-still, waiting for the walls to shake or winds to form within the library. But nothing happened. A breath escaped her, followed by a light laugh.

Movement to her side made her turn to find Chris. He too

had a look of relief on his face. "At least we know some people can say it."

"Yeah," Paige agreed. "But you and I probably shouldn't test that theory yet."

Even though they'd survived the first utterance, when Ethan started saying the word over and over again as if tasting it for possible recognition, Paige couldn't help cringing every time.

"Sounds like it might be Zoroastrian. It seems familiar." Ethan looked high above his head and after a moment, went to retrieve the rolling stepladder used to access the higher tier of shelves. After rolling the ladder around, he climbed up and located a thick black volume, the spine at least three inches in width.

"Heads up," he warned, and dropped the book to Paige. Faded and worn, the tome appeared ancient, with tears in the cover that revealed a stiff backing beneath.

Paige placed the book on one of the desks, letting Chris step in to catch the next volume Ethan deemed pertinent. Before she knew it the table was covered by piles of thick and heavy tomes. Quinn and Chris were even now separating the stacks into four sets.

"Maybe we should call in reinforcements," Paige said, only half-jokingly. Of course, the other women had offered, but Paige promised to let them know if they were needed.

Scowling at the massive amount of reading material Ethan had chosen, Quinn rubbed his chin. "We should keep it a tight group, so nothing is overlooked. But, we will need coffee. Full pots, not just the pods and machine the girls love so much."

"Think we could rustle up some food too?"

Chris looked so hopeful Paige momentarily forgot about the daunting task before them and laughed. "You're the only person I've ever seen who eats as much as I do."

He edged over to her and squeezed her arm as if testing her muscles. "You and I use up more fuel than most with our physical exertions."

Maybe it was the warm rumble of his voice or the teasing in his smile, or the fact he'd hammered her with those green eyes while saying "physical exertions." Whatever the case, Chris's hand sent a shock of heat from where he grasped her arm that flowed to her chest and then down to her belly where it circled pleasantly.

"Right. Food." She'd been reduced to caveman-speak.

Carefully, she tugged herself free so her brain would return to functionality. She tried to make the move seem normal and not the scared-rabbit reaction it actually was.

She'd been with men, of course she had. She was a healthy, make that a *supremely healthy* woman in her twenties, and sex wasn't a bad form of recreation. She'd always chosen wisely, though, and had never, ever let complex emotion or simple lust dictate who she took to bed.

But the exquisite ache resulting from Chris's touch left Paige stunned and a little bit shaken. Not surprising, since up until this very second she'd been relegating him to the off-limits category.

Especially since she would be spending so much time with him during her trial.

Just when she thought she was free, Chris let his hand slide down to hers. He held on firmly. "Paige," he whispered.

She was fixated on his hand and how he was holding hers in place. With any other man, she could toss the grip aside as easily as blowing a piece of lint.

But not with Chris.

Even though he wasn't exerting his strength, she could sense it just beneath the surface. Like her, he was always buzzing with untapped ferocity.

She'd never believed there was a man in this world who could be her physical equal, but Chris was more than able to meet her toe to toe. In any arena.

And the mental images she conjured gave her a secret thrill.

She registered then that he'd grown silent and, with his skin still against hers, Paige lifted her face and locked her eyes with his. She was amazed by the true green, like that of a tropical forest.

She felt herself drifting as she let herself see him, really see him, for the first time. Not as an intruder or a link to her past, but as a man.

The intimacy of the moment shocked through her, the pure and unadulterated energy of two people who had a connection. Truer than their joined history and deeper than physical, the surge was a force she'd never felt before. And one she couldn't deny.

The library, the other people nearby, all the books and problems faded as she marveled at what she'd discovered. She gazed up at him, his hand still holding hers, and the entire world simply fell away.

12

Chris sensed a shift between them, and from the way his balance wavered, he'd swear a bomb had detonated nearby.

Paige's lips parted with a whisper of a sigh, and he wasn't sure she realized. Where his hand had been flat in hers, he now traveled upward to curl his fingers around her wrist.

Her skin was velvet, her fine bones felt fragile in his hand. But he knew the impression was deceptive.

This woman had been forged of steel.

Like shattering glass, the image of small, sweet Paige from childhood broke into a thousand pieces and reformed into the solid vision before him. And he finally allowed himself to accept that they were one and the same.

Strong yet graceful in her way, loyal to a fault but distrusting of so many things. The delicate woman he'd always expected to find didn't exist. In her place was a fierce, volatile, and independent witch.

Whose beauty struck his heart like hammer to anvil.

"Ahem." Male throat-clearing followed. As if in a mental sludge, Chris and Paige both looked up to see Quinn hovering with a speculative and mischievous half-grin in place. "I asked if you wanted anything particular to eat," he said slowly, as if Chris were addled.

Truth be told, he felt a bit foggy and was still trying to come to grips with whatever had just passed between him and Paige. "Anything is fine."

"I'll go." Paige ripped her arm away as if suddenly realizing Chris carried a contagion. She didn't offer excuses to any of the men as she hurried—not jogging, but almost—to the double wooden doors to disappear into the dark corridor.

That was the second time she'd freaked out over the idea of Chris touching her.

With a churning in his gut, he turned a deadly stare to Quinn and Ethan. His voice was low but demanding. "What happened to her? Did someone hurt her?"

He must have come across as particularly fierce, because Ethan went so far as to raise his hands. "Whoa. What are you talking about?"

"Paige. She jumps every time I get close to her." He crossed his arms, channeling tension to his thighs. He jittered his right leg, just barely, the way he did whenever he was about to explode and needed to bleed off some extra juice. "She doesn't act that way around any of you guys. Is it because she knows all of you better?"

"Well..." Quinn began but appeared to have second thoughts about spilling.

"I thought we'd worked everything out, but if I so much as brush against her, she acts like I hit her with a cattle prod." Chris dropped his hands to his side again, shook his fingers. "Does she think I'll hurt her?" He was talking to himself now.

"Not in the way you're thinking," Ethan said. "And maybe not hurt so much as...make her do something she doesn't want to do."

"I wouldn't. Even with all of this." He indicated the stacks of books. "I talked her into searching for the killers from the commune, but I didn't force her."

"It's not like that." Quinn blew out a breath and walked closer to Ethan, speaking in a cloaked voice. "She wouldn't want us telling you this, but your arrival, now, during her trial, has got her a little on edge."

Chris arched a brow. "A little?"

"Yeah, well she's usually kind of grumpy but…" Ethan took a pause. "Just so you know, you aren't the first one of us to hear this and think it's crazy."

Chris performed a hurry-up motion with his hand.

"Every one of the witches meets a man during her challenge and falls in love." Quinn spit the sentence out as if he couldn't get rid of it fast enough.

With both Quinn and Ethan looking at him expectantly, Chris held himself completely still as he considered this final piece of the puzzle and how it made so many others click together. "So that's what she thinks I'll make her do? Fall in love?"

"Yeah." Ethan looked back toward the door, checking to make sure they were still alone.

Couldn't have Paige flashing in to catch the boys gossiping. About her.

Chris remembered how nervous the guys were when he'd helped them the night they were all downtown. How they'd been so worried about telling him where to find Paige. Finally, he understood why.

"I take it she doesn't want this," he said.

"Not at all." Quinn actually gave Chris a look of sympathy. "If it makes you feel any better, most of the witches fought it and even laughed at the idea. So did we." He shrugged and smiled the goofy smile of a man who'd fallen hard. "But look at us now."

"Well, that explains all the men." Chris shook his head decisively. "But no thanks. I'm not here for anything like that. Paige and I are in agreement on this one." *Aren't we?* Because something different had just surged between them.

Ethan guffawed at Chris's denial before reining in his outburst and sharing a grin with Quinn.

"Just give it time," Quinn said. Then he flinched. "Oh, I hear voices." Like a school kid afraid he'd be busted by the principal, he went back to his desk and started rifling through a book.

Ethan did likewise.

Still stunned by their secret admission, Chris gradually turned his head and watched as Paige and the housekeeper strolled into the room, both carrying trays. Mrs. Attinger held coffee and its fixings while Paige hefted the food.

She pitched him a discreet glance, and to cover the numbness still swelling his head, Chris said, "The coffee smells good." He tried not to look at Quinn or Ethan but made his way to the table near the doors where the two women were setting up refreshments.

When they were finished, Mrs. Attinger offered Chris a tall black mug. And then she winked.

He accepted the cup and filled it with the rich caffeine-laced drug he needed so badly at the moment. Surely the sweet older woman hadn't meant…nah. She was just being polite. But Chris was afraid he'd view everything through a different lens now.

The one colored by Paige's rejection of him as a man. And all because she was afraid she'd fall for him?

How had his righteous pursuit of justice been turned into an awkward tap dance around sentimentality? His epic drama into a romantic comedy?

He felt a stare burning into him, and when he shifted he found Paige frowning at him. "Are you done?" She head-tilted toward the coffee tray he was still standing over. His cup was full, but he was unmoving, blocking the way.

"Yeah. Yeah." He stepped far back. "Go ahead."

With the intent to lose himself in a book for a while, immerse himself in the research that *had* been the evening's goal, Chris beelined for the wide table he'd chosen as a work space. He grabbed the nearest book and delved in.

Though his mind bounced occasionally to Paige and her refusal of something he'd never even offered, he found himself getting caught up in tales of ancient practices that accompanied various religious sects. Some were fascinating, others gruesome.

From her side of the room—several desks over from Chris, which was now suspect to him—Paige called, "Ethan, can you take a look at this?"

Chris wanted to see what she'd found. Whether she liked it or not, he was still supposed to stay close to her, help her find the answers they both sought, and watch over her.

So far, he'd been her guardian in name only, and he wondered if Matilda had gotten that part of her vision right. Paige wasn't the kind of person who needed a body guard, and she sure didn't seem to want one.

He rolled his chair to her table. The book she had open appeared to be a relatively recent production. The pages were crisp and white, the words clearly inked. "You mentioned Zoroastrianism. This mentions something similar to what Matilda said, but I'm not sure."

She sat back in her chair so Ethan could read over her shoulder. "Yes."

Chris was following along from his more distant position, but he was the first to notice what she meant. "I see it. Look how *angra* is a separate word."

He paused, giving Ethan time to catch up to where his mind was going, but Paige's rapid nod told him she was way ahead of him. "Maybe we made a mistake by running two different things together. If we separate them, we can revise our search for *angra* and *mana*."

Chris snapped his fingers. "I think I've seen that somewhere but didn't make the connection."

He located the word *angra* and tapped his finger to the ink. "Look. Here it stands alone. What if the second part of what we're looking for, *mana*, is also a word by itself?"

"Good thinking." Ethan leaned forward, essentially placing his upper body between Chris and Paige, and became absorbed in reading what Paige had found. "Now this is important. This *Angra Mainyu* is a Zoroastrian legend. It refers to the ultimate source of darkness, destruction, and death."

Paige linked her fingers over her stomach. "Of course it does."

Chris grinned at her dry wit.

"You've got a good idea, and now that I think about it, the second part is probably spelled with an h." Ethan took the piece of paper and scratched through the original spelling. In its place he wrote *Angra Manah*.

A memory clicked for Chris. "Now I'm certain I've seen the second part." He rolled his chair back to the table where he'd been working alone. "In here."

Ethan moved to peer around him, so Paige rose and came to Chris's opposite side. He sensed her regarding the book intently, an older, handwritten text of Persian myths.

At last, he stopped on a page with a picture of a strange-looking figure. The creature's head was only a skull, but the shape of the bone and curling horns that were attached made him think of a ram. "Aka Manah," he read aloud. "Another demon. His name means 'manah made evil,' with 'manah' referring to the mind."

"The mind made evil," Paige said dryly. "Perfect."

Chris rolled back so he could look up at the two of them.

He also saw that Quinn had come closer to listen in.

After crossing her arms with just a hint of attitude, Paige said, "So we've got the ultimate source of darkness and the mind made evil. I can just imagine what we'll find at the end of our search."

But her flippancy didn't disguise the anger in her tone. Chris wondered what she was thinking, and if, like him, she was imagining the attack on the commune, picturing what might have been done to their parents.

He'd seen the remnants of the butchery firsthand but couldn't say for sure what had caused it. Still, digging into these stories, some of them awful, did nothing to alleviate the horror of what he *was* able to recall.

"We should keep looking," he said, and as he'd hoped, the announcement brought Paige's attention back to the books, their research, and the dimly lit atmosphere of the library.

All of which were better than the brutal, violent place their imaginations could take them.

"Okay," Quinn said suddenly. "So now we're looking for the new spelling. Two words." He clucked his mouth and returned to the computer he visited every time he thought a new phrase needed a good Internet search.

Chris flipped to the index of his own book while Paige and Ethan both made themselves useful with similar pursuits. After a few minutes, a discovery was made, and this time, it was Ethan who spoke out. "I've got it."

"Well, I'm glad someone does." Quinn whirled on his stool to face them. "I can find the words individually, but I don't see them being used together."

"I'm not surprised." Ethan's dark brows clashed. He looked disturbed. "There isn't much here either. I found the words we're looking for but only a single reference with them combined, and that's in connection to an obscure and relatively unknown ceremony. And I quote, 'that shall not be described here in discouragement of any further exploration by the reader.'"

Paige made a disdainful sound. "Seems to me that would only inspire more curiosity."

"Maybe in today's torture-porn society." Chris swiveled his chair to face Ethan. "But that book was written when?"

Ethan studied the first few pages. "1953."

"See? A gentler time." Chris tried to catch Paige's eye, but she looked quickly away.

"Do you at least have a name for the ceremony? Or religion?" Quinn sat at the ready, eager to perform another electronic hunt for information.

Ethan nodded and flipped to where his hand was holding his spot in the text. "The syntax sounds even older than Zoroastrianism, which was founded around the seventh century BCE."

The demonologist frowned. "*Jin deva*. Old Sanskrit, I believe." He cast his gaze to the side in thought as if retrieving what he needed from the depths of his memory. "The translation basically means to conquer evil qualities or evil personification."

"That doesn't sound so bad." Paige's eyes flicked to Chris. She sat stiffly, arms folded again. "But if we're dealing with a force this ancient, pre-Persian even, then why would it focus on finding me, the so-called gifted child? I'm fast and strong, sure, but that isn't what makes me able to fight demons. The coven magic does that, and all of the witches have that power."

She stood and paced slowly, fingers worrying her bottom lip. "What or who am I supposed to destroy? Something this big," she held her arms out and then dropped them to her sides, "just doesn't fit into my challenge. I can't see it being the killer of children just because it was afraid of what one child might do as an adult."

Chris agreed with her but could provide no answers. "I wish we had more specifics. And don't forget, there was another person there that day. The one with magic."

"Do we really think one of them has something to do with my trial?"

"Why else would I find you now? Bring you all of this now?" As soon as he made the statement, his neck crawled with discomfort. He wondered if Paige was thinking about his possible role as her romantic hookup.

He really needed more time with the other guys to find out more about this element of the trials. Ethan had said it might sound crazy? Yeah. Try certifiable.

"Yes!" Quinn exclaimed, cutting into Chris's musing on insanity related to female covens.

Then after a moment of reading the computer screen, Quinn reversed his apparent cheer and said, "Damn."

"What's wrong?" Paige flashed to his side.

"There's a book with more details, good stuff, and it's for sale." Quinn pivoted a one-eighty on his stool to speak to all of them. "You can't just order it, though. It has to go through certain channels."

He grabbed his cell phone off the desk and was already dialing. "But I have connections. It just so happens I have a thing for old books."

Ethan grunted. "That's putting it mildly."

Quinn greeted someone named Vince and fell into a quiet conversation. Paige, meanwhile, meandered back to stand next to Ethan. They waited for quite a while, each in their own safe and separate areas.

Chris felt sure his agitation was second only to Paige's, since she took turns picking at a thumbnail, leaning against the nearest table, and standing once again to cross her arms and fidget her legs.

Chris saw her sigh when the phone call finally came to an end.

"It's a done deal." Quinn's smile was wide and proud. "Vince specializes in the occult. He has a store here in Savannah, but the book won't be delivered for a few days."

"A few days." Paige parroted tonelessly.

"So we're on hold until then." Chris closed the book that was still open on his desk and ran his fingers over the raised lettering on front. "I'll help you put all of these back."

A stone seemed lodged in Chris's gut, one that was slowly sinking. At first he couldn't identify where the disquiet was coming from. If there was nothing to be done, why did he feel so uneasy all of a sudden?

As he stood with his arms loaded down with books, he glanced aside to see Paige doing the same. With that mulish set of her chin.

And Chris understood his surprising discontentment.

If they had to wait a few days to take the next step, then he'd have no reason to come to the island. No reason to spend time with the coven or the men here.

And no reason to see Paige.

But surely that was just the guardian in him, worrying over the one he was supposed to protect. Chris had no interest in Paige the female, the witch who was supposed to find love. No interest at all.

So then why, he wondered as he rubbed his gut, did that damn stone suddenly feel like a boulder?

13

Two painfully long and eventless days later, Paige twirled a green bow around her finger, completely slacking off from her bag-filling duties. She had to chuckle, though, as she glanced around the long, high table. Here sat nine powerful witches entrusted with the duty of defending the world from evil…all stuffing bird seed into little net-like pouches.

Regardless of whether or not rice was an issue, Shauni liked the idea of giving the birds, her friends, a treat on her upcoming wedding day.

Tapping her nails on the black top of the table, some sort of chemically resistant material, Paige considered the oddity of her surroundings. The dining room had long ago been converted into a makeshift science lab, and she still got a kick out of stirring up white sage or dragon's blood while a genuine Renoir looked down on her from the wall.

When laughter rang out, she raised her eyes to study Anna. The head witch was enjoying herself immensely and was crowded at the far end with Shauni, Willyn, and Hayden. Paige often thought of these four as the elders of the coven, not because of actual age but their level of composure.

Next in line came Lucia on one side with Viv and Claudia opposite. This slightly less-serious trio chatted and laughed like coeds, their fingers busily packing pouches and tying them off with the emerald-hued ribbon.

Paige cast a look to her right and grunted to herself. If the pattern stayed true, then she and Kylie were down here together, at the very bottom of the dignity spectrum.

As Kylie reached for another pile of bags, she caught Paige's expression. "What's that look for?"

Paige shrugged. "Nothing, just thinking."

Kylie gave her another minute of blissful silence, but then she leaned closer. "You know what makes Chris really hot?"

With a sigh, Paige studied the younger woman from the corner of her eye. "I was wondering how long it would take you."

"No one is surprised you were matched up with a physical man, all muscle and," here Kylie winked, "wicked good looks. I mean, it's not like your guy was ever going to be an accountant."

"Chris has a business degree," Paige said, her voice flatter than a pancake. "He let that slip on our trip to St. Augustine." She was giving her best impression of a woman who couldn't care less, but everything Kylie was saying made her inner female sit up and listen.

"Oh." Kylie was unperturbed. "Good, he has even more dimensions. But that's not what I was getting at."

"Then please get to it and get over it," Paige said, reminding herself not to crush the seeds in her palm. She'd just *known* all this matrimonial girl stuff would push one of her friends over the romantic ledge.

"Yes, get to the point, Kylie." Claudia was watching them now, her eyes hooded and critical. And then a devious smile broke over her face. "I want to know if you think the same as I do. That Chris's rugged I-have-a-gun-and-have-used-it personality is so well balanced by how laid back and easy going he is." She put a hand to her heart and sighed. "And he has such sweet green eyes when he smiles."

Paige pointed a finger at the history professor who dressed like a model. "If this is some sort of set up, let me know now, so I can go take a smoke break."

"You don't smoke," Hayden chided.

"Well, I think I'm about to start." Paige slanted a narrow stare to Kylie. "And Chris is not my guy. Even if I was interested in that sort of thing, he is way too domineering for me."

Kylie stared back, never blinking. "I think he's just the take-charge type."

"He's over-protective."

"He's a guardian," Viv chimed in, adjusting her glasses.

"Ugh." Paige slapped the table. "Guardian my ass. And he's not even that good looking."

"Oh, Paige," Anna said with a smirk. "Now you're just lying."

"I give up." Paige knew when she was outnumbered and decided to stop arguing, to not give them any more rope to hang her with.

And she made it an entire minute and a half before saying, "I know I've never explained it all to you guys, but I just like being alone. It's what I know, and it feels more secure."

"It's a false security, though." Viv wore a sage expression. "I should know, Paige. I never thought I could give up control, because I didn't think I wanted to. But I was wrong."

"But that's you, Viv. And I'm happy for you and Nick." Feeling crowded now, Paige stood and edged to stand with her body framed by the window. "Look, I don't want to hurt anybody's feelings. I know how these little pep talks usually start turning the tide right about now."

She shook her head adamantly. "But it's just not for me."

She wouldn't say the word *love*. Such a simple expression for a multitude of complicated hopes, fears, joys.

"All I'll say is this." Lucia dangled a little baggie of birdseed between two fingers. "You deserve to be happy. We all do." She pinned Paige with understanding eyes. "Even those of us who believe we don't."

The sentiment struck too close for Paige, so she gave a nod before staring out the window, away from all those sympathetic faces. It's not like she was dying or anything. Hell, she just wasn't ready for a commitment. Especially one so fragile, with passion, romance, tenderness—things that could fall apart with the snap of her fingers.

If the strongest of relationships, that of parent and child, could go off the skids so easily, why did anyone think a flimsy male-female union would be any stronger?

This is all just so ridiculous. Who would have ever thought the fate of the world would literally hang on whether or not Paige had a boyfriend?

She'd known her time was coming, and now all she could do was get through to the end without falling for Chris. The perfect man—according to her coven.

"I just prefer my independence." Her tone was even more solid than the slate floor beneath her feet, but she wasn't sure who she was trying to convince.

"Just as long as your freedom isn't a disguise for loneliness." Hayden spoke softly, the antithesis of Paige's hard-nosed attitude. But she knew her ghost-whispering friend only wanted her to be happy. They all did.

But I am happy. If she didn't count every other hour of the day when she studied a person too suspiciously, barked out her distrust, or generally pissed on everybody else's sunshine.

But how was one guy supposed to change what was so much a part of her makeup? Despite all the romance movies and Anna's historical love stories, Paige knew the world didn't work that way.

Once a heart had been completely wrecked, it took a lifetime to reconstruct. Certainly more than the span of weeks that most of the trials had lasted.

But maybe that's just the beginning. Journey instead of destination, and all that frou-frou crap. "Whew. Okay." Paige walked in a tight circle, as if she could spin her wandering ideas back into a tiny, controllable ball.

She so did not need to be imagining traveling down life's road with Chris.

"Let's get back to wedding talk," she pleaded, facing what felt like a jury of her peers. "Someone please tell me about centerpieces or boutonnieres or anything to deflect the spotlight off of me and back onto the bride. The one who actually wants the fairy tale."

With a grimace, she met Shauni's green eyes. "No offense."

"None taken." Shauni smiled and fluttered her lashes. "That's just how you roll."

"Touché." Paige took her seat again and got back to the critical task of seed-bagging.

"All right." Shauni took up the challenge of wedding topics. "I've been thinking. We should each have something of our signature color as part of our dresses."

Paige perked up, but not in a good way. "We're wearing dresses? What happened to a small, intimate ceremony? Eight bridesmaids does not sound simple."

"You won't be standing up front, and you can wear whatever you want. I just thought it would be nice to have outfits in your magically-appointed color. Or accessories?" Shauni looked to Paige, and then her face fell. "I guess it was a silly idea."

Lucia, Claudia, and Kylie all sent Paige withering glares. But without need, because she already felt terrible. She backpedaled. "No, Shauni. It's a great idea. You know me. I can wear a dress. It's just…rare."

And she'd wear a burlap sack if it would give her sweet sister the radiant smile she'd been wearing before.

Shauni bounced in her seat, the Kylie-esque move ensuring Paige that the bliss was back. "Yay!" She winked at Paige. "You can make it sexy if you want."

"Not too sexy," Willyn said. "Somewhere mid-way between Lucia and me would be ideal."

"Hey," Lucia objected, "why am I at the other end of the sexy-range from you? What are you trying to say?"

Willyn was unabashed. "Do you remember the black dress you wore that time? The one where the boots covered almost as much as—"

"Oh, yeah," Lucia drew out the last word while smiling dreamily. She gazed into the air as if remembering. "I should wear that for Ethan."

"In bed maybe," Paige said, trying to get into the festive mood. But inside, all the talk of love and forever after was making her queasy.

Normally, she'd be as into it as the other women, only tossing in the occasional snarky remark. But this was a different time and different circumstances. Her trial had finally shown up.

And so had Chris.

So far he seemed to be as on-task as she was. Aside from that moment in the library the other night, he'd never given the slightest hint he was interested in her that way.

He and Paige were of the same mind, with the same goal. Revenge.

Others might debate the proper word—justice, vengeance, or payback—but she wasn't one for semantics. And she wasn't ashamed to say that she wanted revenge. Cold, ruthless, and unapologetic. Just her style.

If Chris continued in the same vein, they'd be just fine working as partners. No talk of chemistry or kisses. No hearts and flowers.

Paige was just ready to get on with the hunt. That's the only reason she was restless, eager for word that the book Quinn had ordered had arrived.

She definitely wasn't looking forward to seeing Chris again. Of course not.

She choked on a laugh and drew looks from the other girls. Then she widened her smile just for them.

"No men!" Kylie cried suddenly, leaping to stand in front of Shauni and shield her as if she were a sacred and protected goddess.

Paige cocked her head to look back and found Quinn. Mouth quirked, he shook his head as if to say *crazy females*.

"I'm not the groom," he pointed out to Kylie. "And even if I were Michael, it's not like Shauni's in a white dress."

"Still," Kylie complained, pouting at him. "This is private girl time for girl talk."

"Okay, I'll only be a minute." He eased over and wrapped an arm around her waist, tugged her slowly to his chest, and planted a sweet, lingering kiss on her lips. "I just need to update Paige."

Paige sat up straighter. "About what? The book?" Or Chris. She really was going stir-crazy just sitting around the mansion like this.

"Vince just called and said the shipment will be in tomorrow. We can pick it up late afternoon, after the delivery arrives." Quinn held up his hands and started to back away, wide-eyed innocence all for Kylie's sake. "Now, I'm outta' here."

Finally, Paige thought, something for her to work on. She'd remembered the other women having restless moments during their challenges. She'd never understood why they couldn't just be patient and wait for whatever danger or riddle would come next. But now she did.

Her muscles felt rigid from inaction, and so did her unquiet mind.

Tomorrow she'd be able to get back at it, though, and true to her word, she would let Chris know. He was equally invested in tracking down those who'd killed their loved ones, and he would want to be there when she picked up the book.

He deserved to have the first look with her and, oddly enough, she wanted him by her side when she cracked the spine. Just one more night to get through, and then they might have some answers.

~~~

Jerking the pillow from beneath her head, Paige mashed it onto her face and yelled into the downy fluff. Was this night ever going to end?

She couldn't get to sleep because her mind wouldn't stop working. For whatever reason, she was anxious and restless. She couldn't stop thinking about…well, everything. Her challenge, her past, and…*him*.

Why had her friends gone and put so many ideas into her head? Wasn't their established pattern pressure enough? It didn't soothe Paige at all to know her sisters were so solidly in Chris's corner, as if their union was a foregone conclusion.

And that Paige might as well just suck it up and carry out her preordained duty.

Right. Let's see anyone make that stick. She knew about duty, and honor, and obligation. She'd made her oath to support and defend.

But nowhere had there been mention of that meddling

bitch called Fate.

And as if the turmoil inside of her wasn't enough to contend with, there was the mini-spa taking place right next to her knee.

Exasperated, she sat up and glared.

She never truly comprehended how long a cat's bath could take until one of the fur balls was doing the smack-lick-shake routine on her bed. Tiger Lily was grooming herself as if preparing to meet the Queen of England.

Paige slapped the mattress a few times. "Tiger. Enough."

Even in the shadows and moonlight, she could make out the what's-your-problem stare the cat was giving her. Then, with an annoyed exhalation, Tiger studied her right rear leg as if debating whether she'd addressed that particular body part.

"Aren't you clean yet?"

Paige guessed not when *sluuup-sluuup-sluuup* recommenced.

Throwing back the covers, she rolled out of the bed and onto the hardwood floor. There was no way she would get any rest, and Tiger's nocturnal bathing habits couldn't shoulder all the blame.

She wished she'd truly understood what to expect from the emotional upheaval that would accompany her trial. She wished her friends could have given better warning.

But then, none of them could guess what the next woman would face, or what she'd have to deal with. The personal aspects of the challenges varied from witch to witch. Prophecy altered the agony to suit each individual.

And Paige couldn't unwrap her head from the questions and uncertainties that plagued her. Of all the troubles keeping her awake, the one foremost in her mind was a bit surprising.

It had to do with a man. Just not Chris.

So maybe the basis of her issues didn't have to do with men in general, or the particular problems inherent in their species. She'd always distrusted males more than females, but now, faced with new information that turned everything around…she pondered her lifelong discontent.

And it kept tracing back to one thing—one person.

Paige was afraid she'd wear a groove in the floor with her pacing, and apparently she wasn't the only one. Her jerky movements drew Tiger Lily's attention from her bath. As if tuning in to her human's agitation, the cat walked to the corner of the bed and perched like a watchful sentinel.

Paige gave the feline a scratch behind her ear, the one that was missing a small chunk from one of her pre-spaying battles. She'd seemed to get a kick out of teasing the toms. And then tearing into them when they thought to pin her to the ground with a bite on her neck.

"My Tiger," Paige whispered in a voice reserved for her longtime friend. "How appropriate that we were brought together." Two females who didn't simply give as good as they got. But gave it *better*.

Like all the cats in the house, Tiger Lily boasted a botanical name, another confirmation that the women of the coven had been meant to unite. Along with Sassafras, Ivy, and all the others, the felines pretty much ruled the estate.

But they gave honorary four-legged status to Shauni's dog, Skid, likely accepting him because he too could see demons. Because he protected all within the household. Just as the cats did.

Paige gave a few more scratches and, once Tiger was purring again, she padded on bare feet to the cherry wood chest of drawers. There she flicked on a small lamp, and the utilitarian brushed steel gave off just enough glow for what she needed.

Her room was the only one that didn't scream of color and style, unless the lack thereof spoke for itself. Everything was practical, dark gray bedding, eggshell-paint on the walls, and only a few personal effects to add any depth. Or to prove anyone lived there at all.

A picture sat beside the lamp, a framed photo of Paige's aunt and uncle, the only family she'd ever claimed. Meg and Troy with lush Hawaiian mountains in the background. Their one big vacation.

Having raised two children of their own, they'd taken Paige in at the age of five, and had done so without a qualm. At least, that's how they'd always made her feel.

Their love over the years had been bright, cheerful, and unconditional. They'd done their best to fill the gaping hole left by the loss of her parents.

Meg was her father's older half-sister, his only sibling. For most of Paige's life, the woman had filled the role of mother.

Meg's position in Paige's heart remained unaltered, but alongside the warmth she felt for her aunt and uncle, she now discovered a void. A hollow spot where the memory of her real mother had always been.

The images she'd carried had changed, decaying into an awful truth of murder and violence. Her mother hadn't simply died. She'd been killed, and Paige believed her death had been horrific. The fact that Chris so studiously avoided describing the scene at the commune that day only worsened what she'd conjured in her mind.

Paige plucked her phone from the charger on the nightstand and scrolled through her short list of contacts—mostly the coven women and their guys—until she saw the word "Home." It might be past midnight here, but it was two hours earlier in Montana.

A booming male voice answered after only two rings.

"Who's calling all the way from Savannah, Georgia?" She smiled into the white LED glow, grateful to hear her uncle's usual off-base humor.

"Hey, Uncle Troy. It's me. I just wanted to check in and see how you guys are doing out there. Getting any snow?"

The two of them chatted about trivial things for a while, and before she even had to ask, her uncle seemed to pick up on her distraction. "Hey, kid, you want me to get Meg for you?"

"Yeah. I need to talk to her about something."

A murmur of voices, muffled and quick, and her aunt came on the line. Like the high country where Paige had grown up, her aunt was beautiful, enduring, and nothing to mess around with. She was exactly what Paige needed right now.

"Hey, hun. Troy said you sound like something's wrong?"

Paige could feel the stress leeching from her body, but at the same time, she dreaded bringing up her father and his absence from her life. Meg had lost her brother too and still suffered her own grief.

Paige said, "I need to ask you about my father." She heard her aunt's intake of breath. "And I need you to tell me the truth," she continued. "The real truth."

Instead of hedging or pretending ignorance, Meg simply asked, "How much do you know?"

"That my mother was murdered." Paige waited.

"I'm afraid we can't tell you much more than that, because your father didn't tell us, not when he…brought you to us." Meg's voice grew thin with sorrow. "That was the last time I saw or spoke to him."

"Do you know why he left me?" Paige suspected, but Meg and Troy were her one link to the past that hadn't changed. They were still solid and unyielding. If they'd lied to her when she was younger, she knew without a doubt they'd had good reason.

But now she had to know why.

"I've told you your whole life how much Matthew loves you, but I saw as you got older that the assurances didn't hold much water for you. Not when he wasn't here to tell you himself." Meg sighed. "Your father only told us that you were in great danger, and he had to leave you with us for protection."

"So I wouldn't be found."

"That's right."

Paige pinched her lips together as the old resentment rose inside of her. "But he couldn't call. Not ever. Not once, even on my birthdays?"

"No, he couldn't." Meg's tone was both persuasive and strong. "Your father loves you Paige, so much he cut off all ties to save your life. He told us very powerful and magical people were looking for you, and he—"

"Magical?" Paige stuttered for a moment before getting her tongue to work around the shock. "So you knew all along?"

"We did. I'm sorry. It was to protect you."

Paige suddenly recalled all the times her aunt and uncle had shrugged when Paige lifted the car to help change a tire or told her she shouldn't try out for sports no matter how badly she wanted to. That she should take up solitary activities to expend her energy.

Now she felt stupid. Of course they'd known about the magic. How could they not when they'd raised a female Hercules? They'd always told her she was exactly as she was meant to be but never gave her any explanations.

What were they supposed to say? You're a witch and you're being hunted by one of the greatest evils known to man? That would have gone over well, especially with the angry, questioning kid Paige had been.

"Okay. What else?" she asked Meg. "You started to say something."

"Your father left us a book of spells to protect the home and your whereabouts, as an extra measure. When you went off to join the military, we did what we could."

Paige smiled up into the moonbeams slanting through her window. "The sachets. I always wondered why you were so worried about my underwear smelling good."

Meg chuckled but then turned serious. "I take it you're asking about all of this because something's happened? Is it your father? Has he contacted you?"

Paige hated to dispel the hope she heard in her aunt's voice. "No. But someone else has. Someone who was there that day, when everyone was killed."

"Is it that man who called looking for you? We never told him anything."

Paige clenched the phone. Who had called? Could it have been Chris? He knew about her aunt and uncle and had said he'd looked for her.

"Oh, Paige," Meg pleaded. "Don't get involved, whatever it is. Please, just stay out of it."

"I can't," she said, but she didn't elaborate. "But you know I can take care of myself." She tried to inject humor into her voice, to make her aunt feel better. So she'd worry less.

"Is this person…can you trust them?"

Paige pictured Chris and his easy grin, determined focus, and strength to match her own. Though he only demonstrated the power when he needed it to save other people's lives. "Yes. I think I can."

"All right." Meg groused a little and made Paige laugh.

"Hey, Aunt Meg. Now that I know everything that *you* know, I can tell you what's really going on down here."

"Are you still living with that friend? The one who put you

up in her apartment?"

Paige cringed. Her aunt and uncle weren't the only ones who'd lied to protect loved ones. "Actually, I'm on an island."

Chuckling to herself, she recalled those early memories, impressions she'd formed on the first day she'd met her sisters. Then that drizzly evening when they'd all crossed the ocean waters to a flat piece of land just bursting with secrets they'd yet to learn.

Sitting on the edge of her bed, Paige reached out to pet Tiger. The cat took the overture as permission to start bathing again.

With a shake of her head, Paige fluffed her pillows and leaned back against her headboard. When she spoke again to Meg, she was smiling. "Just wait 'til I tell you about these women I met."

14

The place wasn't quite the occult store Chris had imagined. Instead of dark walls and long shadowed aisles filled with musty books, the appropriately named "Third Eye" seemed more like a meeting of Tuscan cafe and ancient Asian herb shop, with soft music that was decidedly middle-Eastern.

A bar was situated on the left with a busily working barista. A gleaming amber countertop stretched down the length of the wall before it was interrupted by a gap to allow workers to come and go. From there on, the counter fronted a wall of glass jars filled with various herbs and homeopathic ingredients.

Eyeing the abrupt switch from coffee to ginseng, Chris wondered if the store had any unique cooking herbs. He was always on the lookout for different flavors.

Paige also surveyed the assortment when she joined him. "I never even knew this was here," she said. "Interesting place."

The front section held tables for those wanting to enjoy their beverages or…treatment? But as Chris's gaze traveled farther back, he finally discovered the book stacks he'd anticipated. Not only were there library-type shelves on the ground floor, but a set of steep metal stairs against the back wall led upward to a loft area with more reading material.

Quinn and Kylie now strolled up to the herb counter, presumably asking for Vince, the store's owner and purveyor of unusual books. Chris made the best of the delay, taking time to browse.

And moving away from Paige before she caught him sneaking glances at her. Today her shirt was a passionate red, and as any good psychologist would tell you, the shade made Chris think of...well, *passionate* pursuits.

The exact sort of things he'd been thinking about the last two days, ever since Quinn and Ethan had let him know he was on Paige's radar as a potential—or not so potential—mate. The more he considered her denial of him, the more he pictured her in a romantic sense.

Paige might be as tough and sturdy as the Savannah tabby that covered the streets, but she was still a female. The most amazing and intriguing woman he'd ever come across.

To redirect his mind, he moved to a display of tarot cards. They reminded him of Matilda, and he realized he should call her and see how she was feeling. Better, was his suspicion, since she'd unloaded the horrible and toxic words that had plagued her spirit for so long.

The expression and its connection to the obscure ritual they'd read about was the very reason Chris and Paige were so eager to get their hands on the new book. He only hoped the information it contained led them closer to a resolution, a clearer idea of exactly what or who they were looking for.

All these foreign words and antiquated rituals just went around in circles. Old magic, dark entities, and the ability to unleash terrible power. This still didn't point them to the person—or people—who'd killed his parents.

What did this ceremony—*Jin deva*, as Ethan had explained—what did any of it have to do with Paige and her current challenge? Because Chris had come to firmly believe the search for the gifted child had something to do with the coven prophecy.

Right now, though, he couldn't see the connection. Unless...

His deep musing must have shown on his face, because Paige did an extraordinary thing. She touched him. After her reaction in the library and what Quinn and Ethan had told him, he was stunned to see the openness in her expression.

With her hand on his arm, she perused his face. "What are you thinking?"

"About you?" He didn't mean for it to sound like a question, but it did.

She pulled in a breath as if steeling herself. How hard was it for her to even consider him as something other than her friend, or her so-called guardian. Matilda apparently hadn't had a clear psychic picture of the woman Paige would become.

But he would stand guard, all right, silently if need be. Yet always at the ready. Paige neither needed nor wanted a defender, and Chris kept telling himself that shouldn't scrape at his pride.

Paige could take care of herself and he should be glad of that. She'd had years of training, just like him, and there was good reason for her to feel safe and independent. But part of him was growing to resent the tough-as-nails aspect of her personality.

Would it kill her to lean on him? Just a little?

"Don't worry," he told her. "I was only trying to make sense of how all of this *angra manah* stuff relates to you and your coven."

"What do you mean, 'don't worry?'"

"Nothing," he dodged. "I just wish we knew more, or that I could have done something to prepare, to become more knowledgeable." He shrugged. "But all in due time, I guess."

Paige's Caribbean ocean eyes turned thoughtful. "I know

what you mean. I had a talk with my aunt last night, about that very thing." Her hand, those long and capable yet lovely fingers trailed over a boxed set of cards and accompanying book titled "The World of Tarot."

Then she faced him. "The secrecy, the things my family kept from me. We had a heart-to-heart, and I understand why she and my uncle kept the hard reality from me. Too much for a kid to bear." She huffed. "I just wish they'd told me before now. I'm an adult, have been for some time. I should be informed about anything that affects me and my safety."

She frowned suddenly, as if realizing she'd said more than she'd meant to. Then she picked up the box and muttered, "Hayden would like these."

With her head angled down, Paige's profile was striking, so delicate and flawless. Chris let his gaze travel down, to the carved biceps and leanly curved back. Every muscle in her body was honed to perfection, and he couldn't stop staring at her.

He didn't particularly want to. She possessed such rare beauty, yet her looks hid so much resolve, and an impossible strength.

Again she ran her finger across the brightly hued box. Then the stroking finger became part of a fist. "Meg said she and Uncle Troy thought it was best for me to not know the truth, and I think they believed that with all their hearts. They only tried to take care of me. Unlike my father, who just ran."

At the mention of her father, Chris tensed up, but in an effort to cover his reaction he simply nodded and began to walk toward the bookshelves. There he could pretend to browse the titles while his brain clicked and turned.

He was beginning to understand Paige, this complicated and prickly woman, but she was also starting to reveal a soft underbelly. Even the strongest had a weak spot.

He couldn't stomach the thought of striking her where it would hurt the most. Not after all she'd been through. But the time had come to tell her what he'd been keeping to himself, even if his admission proved fatal to the fragile relationship they were building.

She'd trailed along with him to the shelves and was perusing the books. A random title caught her notice, and she pulled it out for closer inspection. But her mind was still churning over her father. "Regardless of the danger, he could have sent me a damn post card. He could have..."

Paige shoved the book back into its spot and mumbled, "I would have taken anything from him, one crumb of affection. And I would have been grateful." Her gaze met his, and he saw the battle within, the duel between rejection and fury.

"But not anymore," she whispered.

Chris averted his face and feigned interest in the books, a weak attempt to hide the shame and guilt spreading from his center. He couldn't be held responsible for the past and what had happened to him, his parents, or to Paige.

But he could damn well affect what happened to her now.

Her well being had to come first, and if Chris's honesty cost him the woman he was coming to care about, then he would have to accept it. All of this, whatever happened, was supposedly meant to be.

"I don't want to be angry all the time, you know." Her voice tightened, as if she was having to force the words out. "It's just, the shadows are always there. I meet a new person, and I wonder, are they kind and honorable like my aunt and uncle? Or temperamental like me?" She worked up a fierce scowl. "Or are they like my father? Totally unreliable."

Chris drew a slow, tight breath. She really detested her dad.

So he definitely had to tell her. He had to set things straight. But now was not the time, and this sweet-smelling bookstore was not the place. He could, however, be honest about something else.

"I like you just the way you are, Paige, temper, distrust, and all. There's a reason you had to learn to be strong, to be on the lookout for traitors and those who would do you harm."

When she continued to scowl at the books, he tried for a joking tone. "And it's kind of nice having a partner who isn't as fragile as everyone else. Especially girls."

When her expression sharpened, he knew he'd scored a hit.

"Nice try." She pursed her lips, but then rolled her eyes. No irrational anger or explosive outburst.

Chris smiled, watching her as she returned the book to its slot and shoved her hands in her pockets. He'd spent years keeping an eye out for any girl who might look like Paige, any woman who might have the same blonde hair as the little girl he'd known, the friend he'd been torn away from.

But the woman he was discovering wasn't all butterflies and sunshine. Her main components were harder, more durable. But even these parts were tempered by a softness few got a chance to see.

He'd seen her tender side with that scrappy little cat of hers, as well as with the women of the coven and the men they'd each brought into the circle. He admired her for loyalty to those she cared about, to whatever cause she'd committed to. And he was touched by the gentleness she so rarely revealed.

The rarity of her sweetness made it all the more valuable.

Paige had plenty of amazing characteristics, traits she simply didn't give herself enough credit for possessing.

She had her back to him now, so he studied her more casually, charmed by the way the tips of her pale hair tickled her red shirt. Just a touch of soft against the bold, a contrast so symbolic of who she was.

He began to reach for her—

But Kylie chose that moment to appear at the end of the aisle. "We got the book, and Quinn's checking out now."

"I'm paying," Paige answered, already moving toward the front of the store where the register was located.

"But Quinn—" Kylie tried to object.

"No. Claudia bought the watch that started her trial, and I can contribute to mine too. I'm not going to just let the St. Germaine estate foot my bill." Disappearing around the end of the shelving unit, Paige hurried off to make her wishes known to Quinn.

Chris could pretty much guess who would win that debate. Paige was both self-reliant and stubborn, two traits that often went hand in hand.

But his jaw clenched as he imagined the reason. She believed she did best by herself, and for herself, a side effect of the earth-shattering rejection she'd suffered.

A place in Chris's chest ached again for the little girl that once was, the heartbroken teenager waiting for a call on her sweet sixteen, and the woman who'd signed up for the Army, never knowing how proud her father might have been.

Kylie swooped up beside him then and hooked her arm through his. "I've decided to like you. You aren't creepy after all." She beamed at Chris and he remembered Quinn calling her his sunshine girl. He could see why.

"I'm glad to hear it?" He cocked a brow and was amused by her responding smirk, overflowing with mischief.

Why did he feel like an invisible tag had just been clipped to his ear? That he'd somehow been designated to a certain herd? Or maybe a coven?

"I'm glad to say it. You had me worried in the beginning." She lowered her voice as they drew closer to the register, where Quinn was scowling at the back of Paige's head as she forked over her cash. "Even I couldn't approve of a stalker."

A short, guttural laugh shot out of Chris, drawing Paige's annoyed attention. She was the only female he'd ever seen who could look sexy with a wrinkle between her brows.

With the transaction complete, the four of them converged on the exit and entered onto streets lit with the preternatural glow of dusk, of the gloaming. Late afternoon had given way to twilight, and Oglethorpe Avenue was cast in a pale bluish-purple.

The main thoroughfare would lead them to any number of restaurants, pubs, or coffee shops, but Chris had something else in mind. A lively atmosphere, but one where he and Paige could have a talk.

He only hoped she was amenable to the idea. "I think I'll get a drink before we dive into that book." He pointed to the large package in Paige's hands, wrapped in plain brown paper. "You guys in?"

"Yeah," Quinn said.

Paige nodded. "Sure."

"There's a place—" Quinn started.

"Quinn," Kylie said sweetly, "don't forget you were going to help me this afternoon, before it gets too dark."

"With what?" Quinn cast a confused look to his girlfriend, who looked like she wanted to kick him. "Oh. Right."

A few steps away, Paige hadn't noticed the byplay, but Chris had both seen and understood. Kylie was trying to give him some time alone with Paige, and he was suddenly extra glad the animated blonde didn't find him creepy anymore.

He was oddly encouraged by the younger woman's vote of confidence. She was apparently all in favor of him getting to know Paige better, or at the very least, being her friend. Her guardian.

He smiled when Paige turned back to them, but when she looked as if she might change her mind, he quickly notched his chin down the street, toward a brewery he favored. "It's not far."

She glanced at Kylie and Quinn. "You sure you can't spare a half hour?"

Quinn shook his head a little too vigorously.

"Okay," Paige said. "We'll come out later, but not too late."

"Great. See you then." Kylie offered them a bright smile before pulling Quinn in the other direction.

Finally leaving Chris with Paige all to himself.

Chris could handle almost any situation; his training and strength made sure of that. But as he glanced at Paige and began to walk with her, he suddenly felt very nervous.

The truth was always supposed to be the best alternative, but in this situation, it might be devastating.

Damn it all, he was actually afraid, because what he had to say would hurt Paige all over again. And if she reacted the way he thought she might, he wouldn't be around to help her get through the pain. He wouldn't be able to console her, or convince her that he was still on her side. She might very well refuse to speak to him again.

Please let me handle this the right way.

Because he wanted to be there for Paige, to help her, to fight beside her, and to defend her.

He wanted it more than anything.

After ten minutes of quiet yet quick walking, they came to one of Chris's favorite hangouts and, as he held the door for Paige, a wealth of scents rolled out from inside, full of familiarity and nostalgia. He and his friends had seen the bottoms of many, many bottles in this place.

The brick building was several stories high and had stood in this very spot since its early days in 1904. It had opened as a distilling company but had lasted barely more than a decade before business fell off in the twenties, beaten down by the stampede of prohibitionists curing the country of all their liquor-based ills.

Since then, the stalwart structure had served as a pharmacy, deli, and soda fountain, and had only recently been returned to its distillery roots. But the roaring spirit that ensured the survival of socialized alcohol consumption seemed alive and well as they pushed inside.

Paige spoke to the hostess who then led them to a high-top table they were lucky to get, because the place was packed. As they slid onto their chairs, Chris asked her, "Have you ever been here?"

"No." She took a leisurely look around. "But I wish I had." She shrugged one shoulder. "I consider myself a beer connoisseur, but we usually go to Nick's."

Exposed brick lined the walls, and wooden pillars stood throughout, supporting a second floor high above. A bar that stretched the length of the room—a very long room—was decked out with a multitude of taps. A variety of commercial shapes advertised the brands dispensed from each spigot.

"You can't beat the beer options, but take my advice." He motioned his head to indicate the woman in jeans and black tank top scurrying around. "Have your order ready when the server gets here. If we let one go, we might not see another again for a while."

"Roger that." She set to studying the menu on the table, and then the specials written in colored chalk on a hanging black board. "I don't recognize half of these."

"I can't help you there. I'm a man of habit."

"So what are you having?"

"The Belgian Dark."

She wrinkled her nose. "I'll pass. Guess I'll try the Czech Pilsner." She set the menu down. "Besides, there's no such thing as a *bad* beer."

When a waitress stopped at their table, Chris quickly relayed their order. Then she was gone again, weaving her way through the lower tables where people dined.

"Good idea coming here. I like it." Paige set the large book on the table between them. "And a drink might help before the next round of mind-numbing research. Quinn loves the stuff, could bury his head in the library for days. Not me. I need the occasional injection of action."

Her hand tapped on the brown paper of the book's wrapping, and then she hooked a finger under the fold, ready to rip her way inside.

Chris put his hand over hers. "Wait. I need to tell you something first."

"About what?" Her gaze flicked over his face, but she didn't pull her hand from his.

"It's not about the book, but it's important. Something you need to know." He was grateful when their beers arrived to interrupt. He lifted his for a bolstering slug, the cool droplets on the tall glass feeling particularly cold against his palm.

"So?" Paige prodded once the waitress was out of earshot. "What is it?"

Chris forced himself to meet her searching stare head-on. "Remember when you asked me how I recognized you that night at the club?"

She nodded.

"I had a pretty good idea what you would look like as an adult." He gestured to encompass her. "I expected the white-blonde hair. The eyes."

"Okaaay." She gave him a *So what?* look and drank her Pilsner.

"Well, I didn't just have memories of you to go by. I actually—" Chris cleared his throat, wondering if he would seem like a stalker once again. "I had a picture of you, one

I've carried with me for a long time."

"Uh...okay. I don't know if that's sweet or just weird." Her head swiveled slowly, incomprehension furrowing her brow. "But how did you get it? You found it and kept it or something?"

Better spit it out and deal with whatever came next. "I took it from your father."

Paige's thumb stopped running up and down the side of her glass. She grew cagey, as if she knew he was about to drop a bomb. "You mean, when we were kids?"

Chris stiffened his back, he took another drink. "I know you don't understand why your father left you, why he never sent so much as a card. I can promise you, Paige, he only wanted to make sure you were safe."

"What are you talking about? You can't possibly know what my father's motivations were."

"But I do know. I know your father very well." He didn't mean to sound so harsh and was grateful for the loud buzz of conversation that filled the huge brewery. "He wouldn't allow anyone to take chances with you or go near you. Not even me, even though I was the one designated to help you, to protect you."

Chris locked onto Paige's confused eyes. "I know him,"—inside he yelled *incoming!*—"because your father raised me."

"What?" Her expression was blank, revealing nothing. Setting her Pilsner down softly, she squinted as if trying to decipher a confusing dialect.

But slowly, understanding dawned and her face tightened, her voice pitched. ""Raised you? He *raised* you? As in he took care of you?"

Chris nodded, refusing to run for cover, even though her wrath was a tempest brewing on the horizon, soon to roll over them both. "You lived with him and he brought you up like…like…his own fucking child?"

"Yes." Chris kept calm, knowing he had no choice but to ride out the storm.

"So, he gave me away, but he kept you? And this whole time…" She pounded the table, so hard the heavy wooden top tilted toward her. "This whole time you kept that from me!"

Chris made a grab for the beers, stopping their precarious slide as customers turned to stare. "I know I should have told you—"

"You're damn right you should have." The snarl she'd given him that night in the City Market was back. She wrenched her beer from his hand and emptied the mug. Slamming it down with a clatter, she shoved away from the high top. "I should have never let you worm your way in. I should have listened to my instincts."

"Sit down, Paige. Let's talk this out."

"Why would I? You're nothing but a liar. So you and my father…no wait." She held out her hands and laughed scornfully. "You and *your* father…can both just go to hell!"

She grabbed the book, gave him a glower, and stalked past him, leaving nothing but a cloud of fury behind to choke him.

Momentarily stunned and unsure how to proceed, Chris kept his hands on the table to hold it steady. He stared straight ahead.

Sure, he'd seen her anger building but had stupidly thought she'd stick around and lambaste him for a while, maybe even calm down eventually and demand an explanation.

But she'd done none of that. She'd never gotten past the shock of learning that Chris had a place in her father's life. The very one that had been taken from her.

Her anger—her insult and pain—had been even greater

than he'd expected.

I should have said more. I should have made her listen. But why would she when in her eyes he was deceitful and, as she'd said, a liar?

Raking a hand down his face, he continued to beat himself up, wondering what he could have done, or should have done, differently. Not that it mattered now.

Because Paige was gone.

She was probably well on her way back to the island, leaving him and everything they shared—the good and the bad—in her rear view mirror.

As seconds passed, Chris would swear he could feel the distance between them growing. He was still attached to her, and sensed an imaginary wire pulling, tugging, threatening to snap.

To break forever.

To hell with that. Standing abruptly, he pulled several bills from his wallet and threw them onto the table.

He had to catch her. There was more he had to say.

Wheeling around, he set off in pursuit, sure Paige would do her best to shake him. But that was just too bad for her, because he was the one man in the world who'd been created to keep up.

So he'd find her. He'd catch her and make her listen.

Most of his life he'd wondered about Paige, and the last decade he'd been actively searching for her. At last, he'd found her and had come to know the real woman instead of the fantasy.

He liked this Paige better, with all of her rage and insolence, the flashing eyes, and pretty mouth that just couldn't stay shut. He liked the fire that lived within her, and her thirst for vengeance, as strong as his own.

It was as if she'd been made for him.

So maybe Fate *had* brought them together for more than one reason. Maybe he was supposed to view her as more than an ally.

Whatever was or wasn't meant to happen between them, he'd finally found her after a lifetime of searching.

And he wasn't about to just let her go.

15

I should have known. I should have known. Paige repeated her mantra of self-recrimination as she marched down the sidewalk, intent on getting as far away from Chris as possible. But she knew the only chance of that was if he chose not to follow.

And suddenly she despised his lightning-fast speed. She hated having anything in common with him—magic, the military, but *especially* the link to her father.

Damn Chris. Damn him and his manipulative ways!

First he'd had the audacity to put her under surveillance, then once he'd coerced his way onto the island, he'd gotten closer to her. He'd used their similarities and joined past to make her listen to him.

He'd used their shared tragedy to gain her trust.

So this wasn't just about the jealousy she could now add to the feelings of rejection. It was more than the sting to her pride to know her father had chosen another child over her.

Chris hadn't just lied; he'd betrayed her in the worst way. And he'd made her look like a fool in addition to everything else.

All this time, he'd kept silent, hiding the one thing Paige should have been told from the start. She thought back to the day he'd first come to the island. During their discussion in the library, she'd made her feelings about her father very clear.

Still, Chris had never said a word.

Paige had one open wound, one thing she'd been unable to overcome after all these years. Her father's desertion and the inherent distrust his abandonment had created in her. How many people had she pushed away out of fear? To protect her pride?

But Chris had played it cool, all smiles and charm, pretending to be on her side. To be her guardian. Ha!

And then, just when there'd been a glimmer in her mind, the tiniest inclination that Chris might become more to her than a friend, he'd dropped his great deceit in her lap.

Her father's absence from her life still affected her self-confidence, and now she had to find out that Chris was... what? Her semi-adopted brother? Sick. Sick. Sick and warped!

The selfish little apple hadn't fallen far from her father's twisted tree.

All the hate she'd felt for her...her...*paternal donor* over the years had now come crushing back in like a vindictive tide. Not only had Chris shocked her, made her feel foolish, but he'd made her loathe her father all over again.

Paige slowed her hard, jarring steps and glanced around. She'd been motivated by such powerful indignation that her pace had increased with every passing second. And because of her upset, she'd let herself go blind to the world around her.

Cars passed by quickly, people meandered. She was still on Liberty Street, and a quick look to her left revealed Chippewa Square two blocks over.

She had to take a moment to calm her breathing. Her hands were shaking so hard she feared her bones would clank against each other.

And the blurriness of her eyes, surely that was from the

madness, the pure insanity brought on by Chris's treachery. No tears would dare flood from her, not for him. That would mean she'd begun to care, that she'd let him find his way into her heart.

Paige Reilley was too smart, too stubborn for that.

Messy emotions were the very reasons she steered clear of entanglements. If she ever let herself care for a man, he would then have the power to hurt her. And she'd suffered enough desertion and dejection to last the rest of her days.

She let her anger renew itself, a much more reliable emotion than pain. But fury? Rage? Violence? Oh, yeah. She knew just what to do with those.

Shaking her fists at her sides, she let a growl escape, uncaring that passersby stopped to give her strange looks.

The reality of Chris's admission was still sinking in. He'd been raised by her father? What kind of sick bullshit game was he playing with her?

Chris hadn't just lied to her; in essence, he'd stolen her childhood, her fatherly guidance. And after all of that, he'd hunted her down to demand that she seek justice? Well, she was the one destined for vengeance, and she didn't need any guardian. She didn't need him.

She was her own champion, always had been.

With a dark curl of spitefulness in her chest, she clutched the package in her hands, felt the brown paper crinkle beneath her fingers. She had the book. It was hers by right, and Chris could just go screw himself.

He'd signed his expulsion papers. He was out of the club.

And she would *not* feel remorse over cutting him out of their joint mission. He'd played her like some naive girl, and even if she hadn't fallen because of his charms, she'd let herself trust him because of a couple of childhood stories.

Hmph. Stories. Told by Chris the liar.

Had she ever even made flower necklaces? Had she really liked *puh-pell* irises best? Even those borrowed peeks into her lost childhood could be false as far as she knew.

She shook her head and barreled onward. The Chris she'd come to know just didn't seem that cruel, that cold.

Sniffing when her eyes burned again, she pinched the bridge of her nose to crush the weak sensation. She'd begun to think better of him, to respect him. Hell, she liked having him around.

How could she have stared so deeply into those pure green eyes and not see him for what he was?

She crushed her eyes closed, to hold out the memory. Because even now, even after his devastating revelation, she still thought of his particular shade of green as warm and assuring.

And her instincts still told her she could believe in him. That he truly did care.

A few more pounding steps and her outrage began to fade. His choices had been misguided, but most of the time they'd been on the same track, of a like mind. They both wanted justice.

He was on her side, damn it!

She refused to think about the fact that Chris had lost his parents, and that he too had been left alone. She would *not* care that he'd spent his childhood on the run, while Paige had slept in the same warm, safe bed every night.

No, no. This couldn't be her conscience sneaking up her, not when she deserved a good, blustering rant.

She absolutely wouldn't allow herself to think of him as an orphan. And she wouldn't picture him as a little boy with a tear-streaked face who'd seen the remains of his slaughtered parents. A child Matilda had once called little Christian.

She stopped again and clamped her arms around the book,

crushing it to her chest. The misery spreading inside her was relentless.

What if her father was a good man after all? One who'd taken in a lonely, traumatized boy because somebody had to? Or maybe he had ulterior motives for keeping Chris with him.

Paige couldn't say, but honestly, one scenario was as likely as the other. Bastard or savior, she had no idea. Because right or wrong, for selfish reasons or righteous ones, she'd never been allowed to know her father.

Finally coming closer to Chippewa Square, she was surprised to see it so empty on this balmy night. But she welcomed the privacy. The shadowy park would be a good place to lick her wounds, and to weigh her pride against her humanity, to see which would win out.

Many years had passed since her last real tantrum, and as the cool wind kissed her face she was embarrassed to feel the heat of the residual anger in her cheeks.

Chris had thrown some serious stuff at her, but she'd been reactionary, overly sensitive, and now she needed to take a good hard look at the underlying cause.

This wasn't just about her father. Chris was still a fairly new presence in her life, and she hadn't known him for very long.

Yet no other man had ever caused this kind of emotional blowback.

Wishing suddenly for the consolation of her sisters, Paige drew deep cleansing breaths, as Hayden would have her do, and tried to clear her head.

She wound though the brick-paved paths of the square until she sank onto one of the wooden benches. It had a view of the huge bronze statue of General James Oglethorpe, the founder of Savannah.

Savannah. The city where Paige and her sisters had

discovered their destinies. And a place that still needed their protection.

So suck it up. She didn't have the luxury of whining over hurt feelings. Too many people depended on her and the coven, so for their sakes, for her sisters, she'd get her emotions back under control.

Calmer now, she absorbed the gentle clicking of leaves as they brushed against each other, the crisp scent of approaching fall, and the ease of sitting quietly in the shadows. Night was Paige's friend, the darkness a consolation.

As she sat in the shadows, stared at the pattern on the ground created by moonlight through the leaves, she allowed herself to admit her weakness. She acknowledged that she could be hurt.

And maybe this reflection was what she had to do for her trial. Paige the strong, Paige the quick, had to confess her fears. Or even admit that she actually had any.

"Paige!" Chris's voice broke into her reverie, and despite the goodwill she'd just been feeling toward him, the cut in his tone made her bristle.

He marched to where she was still seated on the bench and towered over her, fuming. She could hear his heaving breaths.

Wait a minute. He's the one who's mad?

She looked up at him, one brow raised in disbelief. "Now is not a good time. I was just about to—"

"Be quiet." He glared at her, eyes hard and glittering in the dark.

Paige actually sucked in a stunned breath. She'd never seen him angry before. No matter the situation, he'd always managed those charming smiles.

But he sure wasn't smiling now. He was glowering at her like a Drill Sergeant about to ream her one good time.

So, naturally, Paige leapt to her feet, her stance all but

shouting of defiance. "Excuse me?" Her tone was belligerent.

"You heard me. I'm talking now." He advanced on her, and Paige barely—just barely—kept herself from retreating. Boy, was he pissed off.

He leaned toward her. "I've been dancing around your bad attitude since I met you, playing nice, being patient and considerate. And tonight, I was trying to come clean with you and admit what I'd done."

"A little late," she sniped.

"Maybe so, but considering what a pain in the ass you've been since the first moment we laid eyes on each other, I think you owe me a little latitude."

In a move that stunned her, he turned and stalked away. Had he chased her down just to bitch at her and then turn his back? *Oooh.* She gritted her teeth. "Don't you—"

But he flashed a U-turn and was on top of her so quickly she jerked her head back in shock.

She kept forgetting he could do that.

"Don't what?" he seethed. "I was only trying to walk it off. I've been trying to for blocks, but instead of cooling off I got angrier with every step." He held out his hands, frustration rolling from him in tense, vibrating waves. "Not everybody is out to get you, Paige. Not me and especially not your father."

"Then why lie? You were dishonest with me and that's the worst thing you could have done." She turned to the side, tearing her gaze away from Chris and looking instead to the safety of the huge trees.

The beauty of the park couldn't soothe her, though. She shook her head. "You're a liar. And just when I was starting to—"

"To what, Paige?"

"To not…dislike you so much."

Chris stayed where he was but crossed his massive arms

over his chest. "And that's interesting isn't it? Since you don't have any reason to dislike me, not anymore."

"Until tonight," she threw back, unwilling to become the villain.

"No, no. Even before tonight, you've been skittish around me, acting like you don't want to be in the same room." He dropped his arms and took a few casual steps her way. "And you definitely don't like it when I touch you."

Paige refused to meet his eyes. She remained mute.

"It's your trial, isn't it?" he pressed. "It's the whole scary falling in love thing you can't get past, right?"

She whirled on him. "What?"

"You know what I mean. The guys filled me in on the coven pattern, the inescapable matchmaking game." He thumped a hand off of his chest. "And I'm the only eligible bachelor around."

Paige pulled air in through her nostrils, like a bull about to charge. "The guys, the guys. It's always the guys giving you whatever you ask for without any consideration of me, or what I want. Why don't you talk to me instead of them?"

Now he threw out both arms and yelled, "I tried!" Reining in his temper, he moved closer to her, speaking with less volume. "You always shut me out or shut me down."

"No." She was stoic, stubborn. "You've had plenty of time to tell me that you…" She choked on the words, unable to say that he'd been *raised* by her father. That he'd belonged, when she hadn't. "You should have told me you knew him. That should have been the first thing you said."

"Clearly." Sarcasm dripped. "Your reaction now tells me I was right to give it some time, to get to know you and earn just a hint of trust before I told you all of it. But I can see now there would never have been a good time. You blame me, fault me, no matter what. But I lost everything that day,

Paige."

"So did I. The only difference is that I didn't take anything that was yours. He was my father! Why did he want you instead of me?"

"It wasn't like that." Chris heaved a sigh. "You have no idea how hard it was, on both of us."

"No," she snapped. "I don't."

A thought both horrible and uplifting occurred to Paige. "Did he send you here? To find me?"

"No. He ordered me never to try and find you." Chris glanced to the side. "That's another reason I didn't say anything." His eyes grew harsh. "You aren't the only one I've been keeping secrets from."

"I just don't understand. If things were so bad, why did he keep you? Weren't you in danger?"

"I didn't have any other family to go to. And, yeah," he scoffed. "It was dangerous. We were always running, and your father sent every bit of magical knowledge he came across to your aunt and uncle to help protect you. Every special ingredient or rare find went to you, to improve cloaking spells. And in exchange, he and I had to run. We had to keep moving."

Chris let his weariness show all of a sudden, his broad shoulders slumping as if he'd finally given up. "I don't tell you this to make you feel guilty, Paige, but you need to understand…"

He waved a hand and began to turn away.

"What?" she whispered.

He kept his gaze on the huge statue. He wouldn't look at her. "You aren't the only one who lost something or who had to make sacrifices."

Slowly this time, he pivoted, and started to leave. Had he had enough? Had she finally pushed him away?

A hole opened up inside Paige. She didn't want him to leave. She didn't want to not know him anymore. *Oh, no.*

Her tongue felt swollen and dry, her chest too tight to possibly draw oxygen. But Chris was still walking. He'd said what he needed to say, and she'd blasted him for it.

"Wait." The word was a rasp of air passing her lips.

He was still going.

"Wait." She swallowed. From a place she hardly ever—*ever*—visited within herself, Paige extracted some humbleness and remorse. She opened her mouth, and tensed her entire body. "Please!"

Chris stopped, and she wondered if he knew how hard it was for her to summon that one awful word. Next to an apology, it was the most foreign expression to her tongue.

Channeling courage, she walked up to him but stopped while still a few feet behind him. She spoke to his back. "I don't know how I was supposed to…what I should say to what you told me."

Conflicting shame and agony enveloped her, crushed her with invisible arms. "I still don't know."

"You could have at least stayed and talked to me, railed at me if you needed to." He eased around slowly, easily, as if she were the one about to bolt instead of him. "I promise you, no matter what has happened in the past, all I ever wanted was to be there for you."

He cocked his head. "Well, until I actually met you and received your warm welcome."

"I—"

He moved forward, in that special way of theirs, and was suddenly close, so close to her. He pressed his hand to her lips, like she had the night he'd followed her, only his touch was gentle. "But no matter what you believe, no matter how confused you are by all of this, understand one thing."

He slipped his fingers away, caressing her lips and then her jawline until his hand was resting on the side of her neck. "I would never...*never* hurt you. In fact, I always felt just the opposite. I ached for you and your loss. I wondered and worried...what ever happened to little Paige?"

He stared into her eyes but removed his hand. "I always wanted to find you." He looked down. "And this sounds ridiculous now that I know you." His grin made her legs weak when he tilted his head and told her, "I wanted to make sure you were safe. And if you weren't," he laughed low and deep, "I always imagined rescuing you."

Paige's heart stuttered and almost stopped. No man had ever said anything like that to her before. Not remotely. She simply wasn't the rescue type. No distress for this damsel.

Yet the yearning in his voice touched her, sparking a flame she'd tried to deny. As the emotion ignited within, she felt a desire more fierce, more fearless than she'd ever been.

And much more demanding.

"I wondered about you, and where you were," Chris continued. "Your father finally told me where you'd grown up, but only after you'd moved on and joined the Army."

He stroked the side of her neck. "I had so many questions about you, Paige. I wondered if you were afraid of your powers or in complete control of them. Then, when we were both older, and I learned of your destiny, *our destiny*, I was more determined than ever to find you. Even though he forbade it."

"My father forbade it?"

Chris nodded. "I told you. He did nothing to risk your life. He feared my coming to you, even to help, might lead them to wherever you were, the ones who hunted you."

Paige roiled inside, unsure of anything anymore. Had she detested her father all this time for no reason? Was her distrust of others unfounded?

If so, just how was she supposed to react to Chris?

"I never stopped thinking about you," he said. "But I never planned on this." He waved his hand between the two of them. "This thing we have between us. I never saw you that way."

Paige's heart sunk.

"That is…" His voice softened. "Until recently."

All she could see was the pure, perfect green as his gaze held steady on hers. His male scent teased her and the heat from his corded muscles radiated, enveloping her as surely as an embrace.

As the two of them stood beneath the shelter of towering oaks, they met each other as equals, not only in magic but as a man and a woman. They studied each other openly, honestly.

Paige's heart spun and her head was fuzzy. Her belly pooled with a warmth so sweet and full of yearning she truly didn't recognize it.

"I want to kiss you," Chris said, his deep voice so near she could feel it. "But I think you might punch me."

Her mouth opened but no words came out. He'd been teasing her, yet she could tell he was serious.

What would she do if he angled his firm lips over hers? If he delved inside, pushing, searching for her, as he always seemed to be doing?

Would she resist? Would her ingrained resistance cause her to hit back with anger or denial?

These were her usual reactions to any unwanted advances, whether by men or the vagaries life so often threw at her.

But Chris was different, and even she had to admit that now. So should she let his gorgeous mouth take like no other man ever had? Could she risk it?

"I didn't expect to feel this way about you." He released a

ragged sigh and stepped back. "But there you go."

"There you go," she echoed in a frail, uncertain tone, realizing the moment had passed.

"You and I still have work to do. That is, if you think you still can." The eyes that had been so heated seconds ago were now blank, lifeless, as if Chris had forced away any inappropriate feelings for her.

The hardened soldier was back. Ready to report for duty.

Paige recognized the cold retreat, the withdrawal. She, in fact, had perfected the move.

Coughing to clear her throat and the lump that had lodged there, she eased back as well. "Right. I can handle it."

Then she lifted the book still in her hand. "What you and I feel doesn't matter." Her words caught him off guard and he scowled. "Our goal remains the same," she explained, "and we don't get to take a break due to whatever personal conflicts we have."

Or personal attractions. She held herself still as the statue behind her, waiting to hear his response.

Chris set his jaw. "Agreed. We still owe justice to those who were killed. That's all we need to focus on."

Inclining her head, Paige mustered the bravery to reveal one final frailty. "But if it's all right with you, I'd rather leave the research until tomorrow. I don't think I'm ready for whatever we're going to find inside this book."

"I understand." In a gesture that surprised her, he held out his hand, and smiled. "Then why don't we walk to my apartment? I'll cook, and we can talk."

A cozy dinner for two, while she was this wound up? "No. I don't think that's a good idea."

He angled his head. "Then call for a ride, and I'll stay with you until someone gets here."

"I'll be fine by myself."

Chris looked to the heavens. "Don't I know it." He dropped the offered hand.

And Paige channeled her fighter's attitude. "Fine. We'll call a ride and then drop you off at your apartment. But I should go back to the island. I need some time to process all of this, everything you've told me."

"Sure." But he didn't look happy about it.

"This situation, my trial, it's all become far more complicated than I ever thought it would." Paige held the book out and studied the brown wrapper. "I have to focus on my goal."

"With no additional complications," Chris said.

"That's right." Paige met his stare and refused to waiver. "No more complications."

16

Ian stood in the circular drive transfixed, taking in the vision of the grand, plantation-style house with the moon floating over one corner of the roof. Dusk was but a remnant in the air, the night having stolen in to claim dominance.

The Southern grace and pure, clean white simply didn't align with the image he held of the woman who resided here. His client, the mysterious Ronja.

If he were discovering one thing about himself, though, it was that his pre-conceived notions of late had been pretty off-target. His concept of his own identity was now riddled with questions, so how could he presume to know who Ronja was?

As a lawyer, he'd always had to make connections where none existed. He was used to working around missing pieces, but the problem he faced now was entirely different.

He had too many parts to put together, and they seemed to form more than one picture.

More than one life.

Might as well see if she can offer an explanation. He made his way up the steps, where even the front door was painted white. As he stood there, it opened in silent invitation.

A step forward, and then he halted, assessing the black-haired man standing just beyond the threshold. Ian hadn't seen him from outside, and now that he did, he felt the ferocious expression the man wore was anything but gracious.

He entered gradually, shot the cuffs of his shirt out of habit, and gave the man an impenetrable look of his own. "Ronja should be expecting me."

If he'd intended to bring the man down a notch, the plan was unsuccessful. "This way," the hawk-eyed man said without a glimmer of respect.

If Ian didn't know any better, he'd say the man was downright adversarial. He couldn't fathom the reason for his animosity, as they'd never set eyes on each other before this moment.

As per the norm for houses of this age, the main hallway ran front to back shotgun style. Ian followed the man halfway down before they veered into a dining room. And if he felt he hadn't known the real Ronja before, the macabre space in which he found himself confirmed that assessment.

The walls were a deep and somehow unsettling red, paintings on the wall might kindly be referred to as a violent impressionism, and if he could believe his eyes, the intricate chandelier was constructed of bones.

The woman he'd come to confront sat at the head of a long black table, and with the ossiferous lighting fixture set to dim, his hostess was cast in an unearthly luminescence. The robe she wore was the color of blood and shimmered with satin reflections.

"I can't tell you how happy I am that you've come." Ronja motioned her hand to indicate an offer to sit.

While she seemed genuinely pleased, and he detected no underlying threat, Ian couldn't shake the feeling a mouse might have just before it went for the cheese. And had its neck snapped for the trouble.

"As I said on the phone, this isn't a business meeting." Ian made his intentions clear and pulled out a chair to sit. His posture remained rigid. "In fact, I'm not sure how to begin."

He could not have been more surprised when Ronja reached across the table and took his hand in hers. "You don't have to say a word. You never have to explain anything to me. You and I go back much farther than even language itself."

A current he couldn't identify ran from her body into his, causing his blood to feel hotter, his flesh more sensitive. Normally comfortable in his business suits, Ian felt as if the fine fabric now chafed every point of contact.

So he reacted as instinct commanded, pulling free of her harrowing touch. "You clearly understand what's happening to me more than I do." Opting to reveal as little as possible, he opened the way for her to fill in the gaps. "Would you care to explain what you mean when you say we 'go back'?"

Instead of acting offended, the golden-haired woman gave him a smile, much like a patronizing adult to a child. "I can see that you've tapped in to your experiences from a past life."

Her eyes, the exact mixture of blue and gray as his own, were hypnotic as she gazed at him, into him. "Ian, you must know that you and I are connected, that we are family." This time, when she slid her hand across the gleaming black surface, she pressed her pointing finger tip-to-tip with his. "Or should I call you…Vanir?"

The jolt of electricity surged into his hand and startled Ian so severely that he jerked away, scraping his chair over the dark hardwood. He stood, and in an expenditure of his unease, he shoved the chair back up under the table. "I don't know what you want from me or what you've done to cause…" He held a hand out to the side of his skull. "All of *this*."

Striding to the far end of the room, he did his damnedest to hide how unsettled he was. "Somehow you've planted these images, these false memories in my head." He fixed his stare on the hollow center of the fireplace. The empty spot was scorched, black, conveying cold instead of warmth.

Finding his emotional balance once again, Ian turned a flat stare toward Ronja. "What was it, some sort of hypnosis or subliminal suggestion?" He laughed, but only to contain his disquiet.

He didn't want to believe his experiences were anything else. And he didn't want her to know he feared them. "Whatever you did, it worked. Very well."

"Vanir," she addressed him in a plaintive voice.

"Don't call me that!" The name was too reminiscent of the vision he'd had, the one with the maternal voice that he still couldn't get out of his head. She had been his mother, but was not his mother. At least, not the woman he'd known the past thirty-four years.

He wheeled around and barked at her, "I am not Vanir."

Finally, the serene mask slipped and the true Ronja revealed herself. It was only a moment, but enough for Ian to glimpse the depths of her wickedness. "I see you need more time," she said, the adulation now missing from her voice.

She was still playing it cool, but Ian could tell she was not used to being denied anything. And for whatever reason, she wanted him. But why? To pretend to be her brother?

"I don't need time. I need you to stop whatever you're doing."

"I'm not doing anything." The woman's tittering laugh was strained, as if forced. "Except waiting." She tapped her fingernail on the table. "Waiting for you to remember who you are."

With a tug on his jacket sleeve, Ian faced her fully and stared her down. "I think it's best you find new representation. You obviously had more in mind than a simple real estate transaction when you sought me out."

Now her laughter was real, full and rich. "But that's the beauty of it. I found you purely by chance, just another sign that we are meant to be reunited. After a thousand years apart."

She stood and edged around the corner of the table. "After you were taken from me." Her face contorted into rage so swiftly Ian felt a stab of fear. "After you were murdered by those self-righteous holy men...I *mourned* you." She thrust a fist against her stomach. "I almost died from grief."

Slipping her arms around her waist, she began to speak more softly. "And I would have allowed myself to sink into that death if not for...another who came to me, who offered even greater power than I'd been naturally blessed with. He rescued me, dragged me back from the edge, and gave me purpose."

Pressing a finger to her lips, she breathed in through her nose. "But it is too soon for that. You won't believe."

"I don't believe in any of it, and I want you to stop whatever you're doing to me." He wanted to test her, to see how she would react if he dropped a certain...name. "I should have listened to Anna St. Germaine when she tried to warn me."

"Do not mention her to me!" The command that erupted from Ronja shook the morbid chandelier and pushed Ian two steps backward. "Do not associate with her! She is not worthy of your attention!"

Jesus. What was that? Her raised voice had carried the force of a strong wind, and the very real cascade of moving air forced Ian to reanalyze his hard-nosed beliefs.

His mind flashed back to the blue light in Anna's palm, the one she'd shown him in an attempt to convince him that magic was real.

And that evil was as well, especially that of the murderous woman he now faced. What was Ronja supposed to be, a witch? And had she just claimed to have been alive for more than a millennium?

No, she was right. He didn't believe. There was no way he could accept what she was saying. His fact-based lawyer mentality wouldn't bend, wouldn't crack enough to allow such insane ideas to enter.

But there was no denying the gale of untamed wind still circling the room.

And he was alone here, with a power he couldn't define by any logical means or…hell, even natural.

Then he thought of the black-haired man who'd met him at the door, the one with bloodlust so apparent in his hate-filled stare. He was probably still lurking nearby, just waiting to rip out Ian's spleen.

Not only was there danger in this antiquated house, but Ian could tell he would accomplish nothing this night. In fact, he had more questions now than answers.

He was beginning to suspect he'd made a terrible mistake. That he'd somehow chosen the wrong side, without even realizing there was a division.

"I don't know what you are or what's going on between you and Ms. St. Germaine, but you can both leave me the hell out of it. I don't know you." He paused and wondered if he dared tell her the truth.

Then he did. "I have a feeling I don't want to know you."

Her mouth twisted with barely contained fury, so he began easing toward the door. Right now, he actually hoped she continued to see him as her long-lost brother. Her delusions might be the only things that kept him alive.

He needed to get out of this rotten place. How had he not picked up on the stench of decay when he'd first entered? Because now the odor was overwhelming, and becoming stronger by the second.

Ronja was no good, just as Anna had warned him. He kept walking, gradually, so as not to trigger any further attack.

But if this crazy woman truly felt he was connected to her, that they were siblings, then Ian would probably be seeing her again.

So he needed to be prepared.

With a final cautionary glance at Ronja, he slipped around the door jamb and into the hallway. She didn't pursue him, so he took the opportunity to head for the exit.

Without a glance back—but listening for the cruel-looking man's footsteps—Ian walked in a fast clip to the front door, outside to the porch, and toward his car. Once safely ensconced, he hit the locks.

The engine revved and the tires spun, and then the car shot down the long unpaved road lined on both sides by huge menacing oaks. The dangling moss seemed to shiver as Ian roared past.

He'd managed to step into something he hadn't seen and definitely didn't understand, couldn't even comprehend. In his rear view mirror, the white plantation home grew smaller and smaller.

But even with the increasing distance, he didn't feel any safer.

~~~

Ronja flung the door open, bouncing the wood off of a newly-plastered and painted wall. Furious and aghast at Ian's refusal, she stomped down the stairs into the cellar.

After purchasing the house, she'd had the subterranean level carved from the ground and mystically reinforced against the water table that so pervaded the Low Country. She'd had need of a concrete-walled basement, a dungeon in which to house the occasional human entertainment.

But more than that, she had to have the pit.

As she hurried through the main room, clean despite previous splatters of blood and gore, she sidestepped a drain in the floor and burst through the roughly-hewn hole in the wall. The entrance to an even more primitive chamber.

Here the walls and ground were of dirt, hard-packed earth that contained itself. In the center of the room was a gaping hole, the pit. Though Bastraal had already crossed over to this realm, Ronja had left her altar intact.

The crudely shaped stone construction had been created by her own loving hands. The mortar was made of sand, shells, and blood. Expensive and raw gems were set within the mixture, along with rune stones and bones.

Human sacrifice made dark magic stronger, and the suffering that had gone into this work of art was legend.

She no longer needed the altar to commune with Bastraal, but craving the familiarity, she'd come here to demand her demon master's attention.

"You promised me!" The dirt room drank in the sound of her outrage, the earth swallowed the impact of her bare foot as it stomped.

Tempting Bastraal's wrath was a reckless thing, but Ronja was distressed beyond caution or care. What did it matter if her master punished her? What did it matter if she was successful and defeated the coven, if she found Bastraal a human vessel?

Dominating a world without her brother was worthless to Ronja. Now that she'd found Vanir, she realized how bereft she'd been without him.

When the glacial presence that was Bastraal blasted into the chamber, Ronja felt the first trickle of concern. But still, her temper ran hot, enough to counter the first wave of the demon's cold.

"You told me I would have my brother again," she accused the air. Bastraal had entered this world, but only his spirit, his cruel black soul. He still did not have a body for her to see.

But, oh, did she feel his freezing wrath.

"You promised me!" She rushed on with her verbal assault, paying no heed to the increasing friction on her skin, the scrape of the beast's essence over her hand as she made a fist, or her lips as they twisted with fury. "A thousand years I've served you, and I only ever asked for one thing in return!"

Without thinking through her actions, Ronja lashed out at Bastraal with her magic.

And in return, the mighty demon struck back.

In one swift blow, he skewered her with frozen pikes, lifting her body and nailing it to the wall behind her. At last Ronja awoke from her anger-induced haze.

And realized her mistake.

Bastraal's terrifying power rolled over her, through her, cutting her like a thousand blades until she cried out. Another stab, another scream, and finally she clamped her lips shut to stifle the sound.

Only whimpers escaped her now, but still he continued his barbaric form of discipline. When it seemed as if he would never relent, Ronja opened her trembling lips. "Forgive me," she implored, as wave after wave of pain descended.

The hits began to slow, though they didn't let up completely. Still, she sensed a change in Bastraal, and she recognized the redirection of his pent up emotion.

He'd shifted from anger to arousal.

Ronja's pride had been brought low, so without a word of protest, she acknowledged her master's triumph. And her own submission.

Once again, the demon would make her his conquest. He

would claim victory in every way, physically, magically, and mentally.

As the spikes of his invisible form held her against the cold dirt, Bastraal eased closer, surrounding her with his essence.

As he communicated with her mind, a part of him brushed her cheek, as if he were whispering in her ear. His telepathy was filled with both consolation and reprimand.

He still cherished her, but he would not tolerate insubordination.

The freezing cold of his limbs ripped away the fabric of her dress, baring her white skin and full breasts. An icy tendril snaked down her cleavage to skate across her exposed stomach. Then the rest of her clothing was torn asunder.

Bastraal was no longer puncturing her with his power, not as he had before. But as he held her against the dank cellar wall, the demon pierced her body one final time, yet much more intimately.

Ronja cried out as the frozen hardness filled her. Even she couldn't imagine what form he possessed. What would his shape look like if she could see him?

Ronja pictured the human body he'd taken for himself centuries earlier, the tall, intimidating man with hair and eyes as dark as the stolen heart that had beat in his chest.

In a mercurial shift, Ronja too changed her feelings, allowing rapture and narcissism to warm her veins even as the cold length of Bastraal held her pinned. She was still his one and only, and so she would let him take her, in any form he chose.

The sensation of Bastraal began to pound into her, and as he did, his mind whispered to hers. *You will have your brother again, your precious Vanir. He will stand beside you long into the coming reign of darkness.*

This I swear.

"Yes!" Ronja cried, as her fear and frustration receded, pushed aside by sinful desire.

Bastraal changed his tempo then, moving in a more sensual and teasing dance. Pain and promise coalesced into pleasure, the unique blend only the demon could bring.

As Bastraal's invisible form continued to punish her, his low voice reverberated in the depths of her mind.

He swore again that he would give her Vanir. He swore on his very existence.

"I'm yours, Bastraal. Ever yours." Ronja let the many arms of her demon lover hold her; she gloried in his ravishment, and even loved the sweet pain he wasn't quite finished giving her.

When one final time, he made promises concerning her twin, Ronja let her head fall back and imagined the world of chaos they would all create together. She, Scarlett, and Tyr.

Bastraal.

And…Vanir.

With this rapturous vision in her mind, Ronja gave a final scream. And as pain and climax twisted into one cruel sensation, she shattered.

17

Paige was still thinking about the kiss that never happened when she opened the front door the following evening and ushered Chris in. They'd decided on the sanctuary of the island for the evening's activities, since opening the book might expose them to more than information. Better to take that risk in a mansion guarded by a coven and their combined magic.

The aroma of baking bread carried through the grand hall, and she could tell when he lifted his nose to sniff that Chris's appetite was going full bore. "Hmm. You gotta' love Mrs. Attinger," he said.

Paige gave a grunt of agreement. "She always seems to know when we need a pick-me-up. I swear, she's more psychic than Anna."

They made their way through the house, coming to a halt only when Viv poked her head out the kitchen door. "Spaghetti with herb bread," she told Chris without having to be asked, further proof that Paige's friends had all but taken Chris into the fold. They'd all adopted him.

"Hmm." Chris lifted his head and closed his eyes. "Rosemary, thyme, and…marjoram."

"A chef's nose and a warrior's body." A blush threatened Paige's cheeks when she realized what she'd said, so she cleared her throat and added, "I guess I don't have to ask if you mind having dinner first."

His lips turned up at the corners. "We do need our energy."

"A man after my own heart." And again, she wished she could take back her words. Too much had passed between them last night, and ever since, her head had been crowded by a whole new stockpile of images.

Pictures and fantasies that involved Chris, and possibilities she'd never allowed herself to consider.

But as swiftly as she started feeling more amiable toward him, she remembered that he was much closer to her father than she'd ever been. And vice versa.

Her emotional shields shot into place.

It didn't matter how much he explained or how viable the rationale was. Paige still felt left out, and unwanted.

Chris stepped in front of her then, stopping her with a hand on her shoulder. And despite her fluctuating irritation, when she came face to face with his easy-going smile and paradise green-eyes, her foolish heart just flipped.

"Let's just put everything behind us, okay? I can let it all be bygones if you can."

She forced herself to look away from the brilliant green depths, scraping her gaze over mahogany walls instead. "Believe it or not, I've been trying to do that. I've tried to understand why my father did what he did."

She bit her bottom lip. "And to understand why you kept it all from me."

"I hope you listened last night, when I told you I never wanted you to be hurt."

"I did." She worked up a smile to smooth things over, but her gut still clutched with conflicted emotions. "I may have to work at it for a while, but I think I can get over it. I know you were trying to do right, by me and by him."

She didn't say "my father" again, because the phrase felt

strange now. She didn't have a grip on what the words meant to her, what they should mean, especially after all she'd discovered.

She might one day come to forgive the man, but she doubted she'd ever forget what her young life had been like without him in it.

Chris was still studying her, and all she could do was stare back. His jaw was firm and strong, yet softened by the play of blonde hair just touching the tops of his ears or falling over his brow.

And now that she was looking at him full on, her gaze was drawn to his mouth.

The almost kiss.

She might be able to forgive and forget where her father was concerned, but how could she forget the moment that had passed between her and Chris? They'd shared a magnetism—so intense—that had come very close to pulling them into each other's arms.

Even after they'd been yelling at each other.

Chris was still staring, and Paige's face grew even hotter. So in lieu of anything better to say, she inclined her head toward the kitchen, broaching a topic that was safe between them. One on which they always agreed. "Let's eat."

The hardy meal would be exactly what she needed, and judging by Chris's satisfied smile, he felt the same. As soon as they entered the kitchen, he fell into a discussion with Mrs. Attinger about herbs, leaving Paige a few moments to find her balance.

And to forget about kissing.

Apparently oblivious to her lurid line of thought, Chris seemed to enjoy himself at dinner, laughing often and indulging in the easy banter that was second nature for him.

It wasn't until coffee and dessert that Paige decided to

bring Chris up to speed on the unhappy subject of missing people and deformed bodies. She took turns with the others, filling him in on Cole and Trevor's long hours at work, and the frustration they endured knowing who was likely responsible yet unable to share their hunches with the rest of the police force.

"So your suspicion was correct," Chris said to Lucia. "You can't locate the people who've gone missing."

"No." Lucia cast her brown eyes to Anna. "None of us can see them in any way, which only confirms that they've been taken by the Amara."

"They're being blocked," Chris surmised. "Like you said they probably would be." His expression was grave as he stared into his black coffee. "There's been no progress on the murders either, then?"

"No." Now it was Claudia who answered. She'd moved to the breakfast area to sip her cappuccino while holding her cat, Ashbi, in her lap. The stately tom always seemed to hold himself so regally, even as his cautious feline eyes scanned the room.

Other cats were in the kitchen too. Viv's orange Kiko sat in a corner by himself, grousing at any other cat who came near. Tiger was sitting under Chris's stool, and Paige suspected he'd been slipping her nibbles of "human food."

Meanwhile, Willyn's sweet Snowball was busy cleaning Daisy's head, and Hayden's tortoiseshell was purring as she received her bath. Sassafras was admiring herself in the reflection of the stove, the act so reminiscent of Kylie that Paige almost laughed despite the now somber atmosphere.

The only ones missing were Iris, Cuileann, and Ivy, belonging to Lucia, Shauni, and Anna respectively.

Actually, Paige thought, they never saw too much of Ivy. Much like her mistress, the sleek black feline had mysterious ways.

Even when they appeared to be at ease, the coven cats were ever on guard, protecting the witches while the witches protected Savannah and its innocent and unaware citizens.

Only this time the coven's line of defense had been broken, and Paige was haunted by the deaths that had occurred during her trial. Others had been where she was now, and both Viv and Hayden had seen innocents killed during their challenges.

But Paige still took her failure to heart. She remained silent throughout the rest of the meal, rising only to help when the others began to shift and stand, loading the dishwasher and preparing for the next phase of dark discussions.

They still had to investigate the book.

The post-dinner cleanup was quick and quiet, with everyone pitching in and making Mrs. Attinger take a break. When everything had been set to rights, however, Anna sent a questioning glance to Paige.

"So where should we do this?" Paige asked, her eyes roving to encompass all of her friends. Quinn, Ethan, and Dare were the only men present tonight other than Chris.

Cole and Trevor were burning up the ground in search of whatever or whoever was responsible for the bizarre murders downtown, while Nick and Michael were busy finishing out or starting up a day or night at the office.

Quinn stepped up with a suggestion. "We'll go start a fire in the study. There's a cold front blowing in off the ocean tonight." He began to move then stopped to stare at Ethan. He hiked his brows. "When I said we..."

"Oh, yeah. I'm on it." Ethan winked at Paige and strolled off with Quinn. The two could be heard arguing as they went. Old college friends reunited to help the coven.

Not long after, Paige and the others followed. Like the

majority of the mansion, the sizable study was trimmed in deep mahogany, but the walls here were papered with silk, a dove gray threaded with gold designs.

Comfort was the first word that came to mind whenever she entered the majestic room. A lavish Bessarabian rug stretched to the fireplace appointed with brass detailing. Even a tough girl like her could appreciate the soothing effects of splendor, and she was pleased by Quinn's choice.

Paige and Chris took front and center on the nickel-toned couch, and she placed the book on the ebony coffee table. Gone were the books that were normally on display, as were the knickknacks and antique medical tools in their glass case.

The table was large, but even against its width and breadth, the package before Paige pulsed with presence. Claudia handed her a pair of scissors to cut the paper, and after a second of hesitation, she divested the book of its wrapper.

Soon Paige was staring at a pine green cover with silver embossing, much too lovely to contain anything dreadful.

But then she opened to a random page. A single glimpse of an image made her slam the book closed.

She clasped her hands together, one thumb anxiously circling a joint on the other hand. "I've seen a lot of horrible things, during war time and here as well. But this, I…"

When she didn't finish, Chris said, "I have too, but this is different." He scanned the faces around them, each expressing various levels of concern or trepidation. "This cuts close. These things might have been done to Paige's mother. And my parents."

"We understand." Hayden's voice was gentle, conveying her trademark compassion. "If the two of you need to do this alone, we can go."

"No." Paige almost spit the word out, so she softened her tone and added, "I want you all here. If this is connected to my trial, it affects all of you too. I'm the eighth of us. No turning tail, not when we're almost finished. We're in this together, for better or worse."

Paige put both hands on the book, mentally preparing herself for more of the horror it might contain. Clearing his throat, Chris said, "Take your time." He repositioned his arm so that his shoulder rested lightly against hers, the final bolstering that she needed.

Foregoing a repeat of her previous jump to the middle of the volume, she waded in slowly, as if a monster might leap at her from behind each page.

The date of publication was mid-eighteenth century, but the copies of hand-drawn illustrations had been sketched long before then. Nothing had ever shaken Paige like the finely detailed pictures.

Comparing war to Hell was nothing new. The nightmare-inducing reality she'd actually witnessed overseas far surpassed any imagined version of Hades in a book.

Chris had likely dealt with his fair share of horror as well.

But the graphic sketches in this large volume depicted such hideous imagery, such inhumanity, she had to force herself to look. Finally, she came to a drawing of a woman, and for whatever reason, Paige saw her mother.

Unable to go on, she closed her eyes and a memory solidified. Blonde hair, a woman staring down at her with a world of love in her eyes. And then a slideshow of what Paige had seen on those pages superimposed on her mother's body.

A hand gripped hers and, as if sensing her distress, Chris took the book from her. "I'll take over from here."

Flipping to the back, he opted to forego any more needless revulsion and went directly to the J heading in the index. Paige watched as his finger trailed down, presumably searching for the ritual's name. *Jin deva.*

She clasped her fingers together into a tight ball, trying to control the tremors in her hands.

"There are a couple of listings," he said, thumbing his way back to a chapter title with a foreign word Paige didn't recognize. "This chapter seems to cover the details of the ceremony known as Jin deva." He quoted, "'A perilous rite undertaken by the rare individual assigning more value to the potential endowment of unbridled strength than to his very life.'"

Paige leaned closer to Chris, stealing a glimpse of the pages he was reading. "I guess if one wants to conquer evil personified the ritual would have to be dangerous. Otherwise, anyone might try."

"Remember not to take things too literally," Ethan warned. "First of all, the meaning has been translated from Sanskrit, but even more than that, these types of occult practices are often given misleading names."

Paige released a sigh and looked to the young flames of the newly-built fire. She let the dancing fire mesmerize her. "You're right. I shouldn't take anything for granted." She inclined her head, indicating the open book that Chris still supported on his knee. "Go ahead."

"I'll summarize," he said, before skimming several paragraphs in silence. At last, he explained what he'd read. "Apparently the ritual itself is the risky part, seven days enduring very specific levels of pain intended to…open spiritual pathways and allow reception."

Hayden rubbed her arms and stepped closer to the fire. "Reception of what, exactly?"

In reply, Chris lowered his head and read some more. "The person also undergoes food and light deprivation for extended periods, to harden and prepare his body for what it must endure. The only nourishment he receives is blood."

"They drink blood, endure torture?" Kylie asked with a shiver. She and Quinn sat on a piano bench in front of the black baby grand. They both wore expressions of concern, and Kylie gripped his hand. "Why would anyone voluntarily put themselves through that?"

"I have no idea." Chris's expression was tight and tense, as if he was mentally braced to feel the pain vicariously. "This is pure torture," he said. "I don't know how anyone could survive this. "Knives." He grimaced. "Hooks."

Paige shivered, but when she noticed Chris's fingers gripping the book, so tightly that his fingertips were white, she decided it was her turn again. Her time to carry the burden.

She tapped the back of his hand and eased the heavy tome onto her own lap.

Then, feeling tainted, she relocated it to the table once again. "I'll check the other page number listed in the index. Do you remember what it was?" Chris reeled off a number and she went in search.

The intent of the next portion of the book was to explain the results of the ritual, if the person survived to reap the reward. Paige read intently and heard her own sharp intake of breath. "Holy hell."

"What?" Anna asked, just as everyone else seemed to lean in a bit more. They were all abruptly on edge.

"The conquering of evil, it's…Ethan you were right." Paige picked up the book, now weightless as her adrenaline surged. "The ceremony invites certain forces into the person's body while simultaneously preparing it for the power."

Paige sought Anna's eyes, hoping the coven leader's calm and serenity would be a balm to the terror rushing through her. "The rite enables a person—if they live—to harness the strength and abilities of malignant spirits, any that have been destroyed or banished."

"Banished?" Willyn twined her hands through Dare's, holding onto him for support. "Like demons?"

Paige hissed air through her teeth. "Demons, fiends, evil entities. You name it. That's why the process is so dangerous. The participant of Jin Deva is essentially an open house for any pissed off monster that wants to take another shot at the world that killed it off."

"And by taking all of this in, the person transforms." Ethan put his hands on his hips and stood with legs at shoulder-width. "I've never heard of anything like this before. One human with multiple demonic possessions, yet he is able to control them? Use them for his own demands?"

"It must be rare," Paige said. Her gaze traveled from page to page, raking through sentences furiously. She frowned as she read. "There's more."

"Let's hear it," Chris said, his voice flat.

Paige studied him and took note of his posture and corded neck. He had to be going through the same gamut of emotions as she was. Every new clue they found led to more horrible imaginings.

Unlike her, though, Chris had actually seen the aftermath of the commune attack. He had a full visual, a real comprehension of what a person could do if they survived the ritual. If they lived to receive the power of evil.

Paige tried to imagine it, a collection of demons and other terrible creatures sucked back into the world, into one person. Surely this creature, if created, would rival even the mighty Bastraal.

Paige grew cold as she considered the possibility.

And again, Chris was there, his hand on her back, urging her to continue. He gave her the support she needed, and reminded her of the courage she possessed.

"Okay," she said and expelled a breath. "This person, the vessel as it reads here, can only sustain this amount of power for a short period of time. He has to control all the beings inside of him, each battling to come to the front of the line." She started turning pages. "It can last approximately one cycle of the moon, depending on the vessel's strength and stamina."

"A whole month?" Lucia was aghast. "*Dios*, the damage that could be done."

"There's an example of one who supposedly took form in Yuzhou, a province of ancient China." Paige flipped faster now. She had to learn more of this impending monstrosity. The depictions of violence that had forced her to close the book before now greeted her again, in all their gory splendor.

She'd thought she'd found her fortitude, but the gruesome depictions all began to blur. Evisceration, amputation, blood, carnage…*Oh, God*…children.

"There was a…town or village." She couldn't form sentences, too caught up and appalled by what she was seeing. The drawings were of the damage left by one of these beasts.

"I need to—"

"Paige." Chris said her name, the stern sound cutting into the shell she suddenly felt enclosed inside. Her head was buzzing. Her chest felt constricted.

Her mother. All she could think of was the fuzzy, incomplete image she had from so long ago. The idea of her mother was all she had, but she loved her, with or without a face to put with the tender emotions. "What happened to you?"

Had she said the words out loud? Had she?

Hands were on her shoulders, lifting her from the couch. And then they were on her upper arms, steering her, forcing her to move. Instinct told her it was Chris, and for the first time in years, she let someone else take control of her, let a man guide her when she didn't know the way.

But nothing could protect her from the heartbreak that was swelling up inside. The nature of her mother's death hit with destructive clarity.

What did they do to you?

The revelations from the past two weeks piled up on her all at once. Everything she'd thought she'd known about her past, and her life, was gone. It was as if the person she'd always believed she was now never existed.

The atmosphere darkened, and she pulled herself from the stupor long enough to see she was being walked down the hallway. Chris's strong arm was around her waist, helping her, supporting her.

"I'm good," she said, pushing at him to release her. "I'm just going to take a walk. Get some air."

"Paige—" he began, but she turned and stared deep into his eyes. "Chris, please. I can deal with this on my own. I'll be fine." She hardened her features, hoping to hold her riotous emotions at bay. "Just let me go."

18

Chris watched Paige until she turned the corner at a swift pace. He was still debating what to do. She'd insisted that she be left alone, and that she'd be fine. But he'd seen the eclipse in her eyes, the complete disappearance of her usual strength, as pain and horror rolled in to dominate.

Chris looked again down the empty corridor and made his decision. Maybe she could handle it all by herself, but the fact was, she didn't have to. So no, he wouldn't just let her go.

He had a vague idea how the mansion was laid out but was unfamiliar with the rear section of the estate. Taking a guess, he veered to the right, down a dark hallway until he saw two doors with French panes, and then out onto a patio of gray stone.

The night air was cold, as Quinn had predicted, and manicured shrubs which were normally green now hunched like a low black wall in the shadowed gardens. Chris started in Paige's direction, but she shook her head.

"You didn't need to follow me." Her voice was hoarse, and she couldn't seem to stand still, as if waves of energy and her tumultuous emotions were all vying for release.

Chris had done the right thing by coming after her. Though he'd also been affected by the horrific ritual and the beast it could create, his own fear and disgust had to take a backseat.

As he watched the strongest woman he'd ever known come

undone.

For a moment, she ignored him, and then she simply stared, inspecting him as if deciding what to do. "What happened to our parents, Chris?"

She wiped a hand over her mouth, looked out into the dark gardens, and then, in a move that shocked him, she walked to him. She took his hand. "What did that thing do to the other people, and to all those children?"

Her eyes were wild when she looked up at him. "They must have been so scared."

He stroked her hair, hoping to help her calm down. She didn't seem to notice. "We can't be sure of anything," he said softly.

"Oh, yes, we can. We know for a fact that those two people, whoever or whatever they were, came looking for me and murdered everyone who crossed their path."

"You aren't blaming yourself—"

"I know!" Now she tried to pull away, but for once, Chris imposed his will over hers. He would not let her go through this by herself.

This was a misery they both shared, and he'd take a larger portion of the agony if he could. If she'd only let him.

"I..." she stammered, "I just don't know who I am anymore. Being defined by anger, I got used to that. Hate for my father is what always drove me, made me feel I had to be the best, and that I had to do it alone. But even my anger at him may have been misplaced."

She took his other hand so that they were joined in a continual loop. He felt her sadness and despair completing the circuit, flowing through him as well.

She bit her lip. "I can't have a crisis of conscience now. I need my hate more than ever."

"No, you don't." He tried to cup her cheek but she wouldn't

let him.

"I don't need to be coddled." That crinkle of obstinacy formed on her brow. "Don't try to slay my dragons for me, Chris. You'll only make me weak."

Not likely. But still he said, "I won't stand in front of you, Paige. I have more respect for you than that." He met her hard stare with his own. "But I'll damn well stand beside you. I'll guard your blind side and watch your six, because none of us are meant to do it all alone."

He wrapped his hand around her neck, ignored her when she tried to balk. "None of us. Not even you."

The rigidity left her body in a rush, as if floodgates had been opened to release pressure. Her eyes were bruised with uncertainty now, no longer tight with anger.

She eased herself away, but still clung to one hand. "I just want to do the right thing."

Chris saw the resemblance now, the similarities in her determined face and her need to make wise decisions. To fight the evil, even at her own expense. "I can't tell you how many times I heard Matthew say the same thing."

He felt her jolt when he used her father's name. "Paige," he began, but instead of shunning him, she met his eyes.

"It's okay. I don't hate you for the time you had with him. That would be unfair." Her hair was a halo in the starlight, when she let her head fall forward. "It just hurts to hear you speak of him with such familiarity, such closeness. When he's nothing but a stranger to me."

"As wrong as it was, as unfair as this has been for *both of us*, the fact remains that you and I are alike. We were both formed by adversity." Chris cupped her cheek now, and she didn't resist. "You're a warrior, Paige. The best." He stroked her hair. "Because you've already slain so many dragons."

He wanted to kiss her, to bury her uncertainties beneath all the intensity he felt for her. But she was too vulnerable now. And he had yet to admit how deeply that intensity ran.

But his personal feelings wouldn't affect his duty. He would guard her, and whether she liked it or not, he would protect her.

Part of him wished they didn't have destiny to contend with, that Paige didn't have to seek justice. Especially against such powerful and dangerous enemies. His desire to seek vengeance was suddenly butting heads with a more pressing need.

The need to keep Paige safe.

He felt her give a little, her powerful body simply falling against him. He rubbed her back, slow circles meant to comfort. "You know you can cry if you need to, Paige. It doesn't mean you're weak. Just human."

Her hand loosened its grip on his, and her arms slipped up to cling to his shoulders. "I never cry."

Now why didn't that surprise him? "I know it's been a rough day, hell, a lot of rough days since I first came out here and dumped all this grief on you."

She tilted her head to the side and lifted one shoulder.

"But if you think you're up to it, I have something I'd like to give you."

"I'm up to it, but first..." After a long searching pause in which she perused his face, she started speaking again, her words coming out in a rush. "I've had too many questions to deal with, too many things I thought I was sure of that turned out to be false."

As her arms snaked tentatively around his neck, she continued to stare up at him. She blew out, and then sucked in a breath. "I don't want to have to guess about anything else. I'm sick of wondering."

"Okay." He barely got the word out before her arms were

tightening around him and she was lifting up on her tip-toes.

When her chest pressed against him, and her warmth infused him, Chris simply accepted the flow of her magic. Her force was so powerful, so vitalizing, he was sure he could exist on her energy alone.

He was stunned by how much her nearness affected him. And instead of brushing him off, she was soft and receptive. She was opening up to him.

With her lips a whisper away from his, Paige was still holding on as if both of their lives depended on this unbroken connection. But she'd stopped moving, hesitation in the hitch of her breath.

So Chris took over and locked his hands onto her lean waist, excited by the fact he could hold her as tightly as he wanted. That she wouldn't break beneath his strength.

Lowering his head softly, cautiously, he tested her mouth with his own. Her taste was pure and warm, heat surging and scorching into him, though their lips barely touched.

The moment was too precious to mar with anything more than this gentle communion, so he held his raging desire in check. Brushing his mouth lightly over hers, he applied the softest pressure, the slowest glide of his tongue over hers.

With a small moan, Paige relaxed into him, her tight, sculpted form all but melting beneath his touch. Then, sighing with what sounded like regret, she pulled back from the kiss and lowered her forehead to his chest.

She hugged him more gently and nestled in. "Thank you."

He didn't know if she was thanking him for the kiss or for not pushing her any further. But he was happy to gather her in his arms, to simply be. Just him and Paige.

After a moment she raised her head, squared her shoulders, and took a step backward. "Now. Do you have any more surprises for me? Any secrets?"

"Uh..." Chris was bemused by the swift change.

She crossed her hands over each other before flinging them wide. "Anything else whatsoever that you haven't told me?"

"Well," he recalled his gift, "only one thing." He hoped what he had for her would cause more joy than grief. Seeing Paige suffer was a bullet to the chest.

"Hmm? Oh, that's right," she said. "You were going to give me something."

Reaching to his back pocket, he extracted his wallet and opened it up. The picture was in the same spot it had been since the day he'd snatched it from Matthew. Sure the wallets had changed over the years, from a boy's to a man's, but the priority placement of the photo never had.

Neither had his daily ritual of taking out the picture and staring at the faces imprinted there. That's why the edges were so worn.

"I've kept this with me, waiting for the day I'd finally find this little girl again." Chris was suddenly overcome. "And now that I have, you're so much more than I expected."

"Just not as sweet?" she asked wryly, pretending disinterest in what he had in his hand.

"Sweet is a subjective assessment." Swallowing the nervousness, he pulled out the picture and handed it to her. "And you still are. It's just balanced now by your other side. "

She diverted her attention to the photo, and when her eyes clasped onto the images they grew wide. She lifted it higher, up to the moonlight.

The look of pure joy on her face told Chris he'd done the right thing and had timed the delivery perfectly.

"My parents." There was the barest amount of uncertainty in Paige's awed statement. "That's my mother holding me, isn't it?"

Chris nodded silently.

Still studying the photo, Paige's eyes misted with fresh emotion. "My aunt and uncle didn't have any pictures of her." She blinked and inhaled a shaky breath. Then her piercing blue gaze swung to Chris. "I look like her."

"You do." He stepped in and lifted her chin. "You have her eyes."

Paige leaned into him as together they turned their attention to the likenesses of the happy young family. "My father I recognize from my aunt's old photo albums, and me because, well, it's me. But my mother…" Her fascinated litany trailed off as she clasped the snapshot close to her heart.

Then again she held it at arm's length. It seemed she couldn't stop looking at her new treasure. "Oh, Chris," she said, and he thought she might cry after all. "You're right."

Paige released a shaky breath. "I do have her eyes."

~~~

Ian was still in his building well after darkness had fallen. Everyone else had departed for their homes hours ago, including Ms. Dillon. But he was still there, going over problems in his mind. And after a day of evaluating his options, he'd finally come to a conclusion.

Opening the drawer that held random business cards, he pulled out the organizer and flipped through the plastic sheets until he found the card he needed. His visit to Ronja's the day before had left him reeling and unable to decipher fact from delusion. He still had no rational explanation for the things he'd seen but was ready to make headway toward some real answers.

First, he had to know the sort of people he was dealing with.

Leaning back in his chair, he dialed the number on the card

and waited through several rings. He was sent to voicemail. "Damn." With a swipe of his thumb, he ended the connection. He wasn't of a mind to leave a message.

Setting the cell phone on top of his ruthlessly clean desk, he scanned the glass-enclosed shelves and law books kept inside to remain free from dust. Across from him were the client chairs he'd selected himself, modern and sleek. Beyond them the walls were painted a stately and subdued beige with only the requisite amount of art.

Rubbing his jaw, he paused and considered how to proceed. Ian was a man of logic and law. He didn't believe in magic.

He'd never encountered anyone quite like Ronja, or heard wild claims like she'd made, so he wasn't quite ready to entertain the possibility of supernatural forces.

Or, he scoffed to himself, reincarnation.

That didn't mean he wasn't wary of the bizarre woman and her intentions. Maybe Anna St. Germaine had been onto something and Ronja did have bigger plans, murderous plans. But for whom? And why?

And what did that hunk of land out in the sticks have to do with it?

Well, whatever the case, he wasn't going to be a part of it, neither as accomplice nor victim. He hadn't had a vision since his meeting with Ronja, but he felt the need to prepare himself with as much information as possible. In case the episodes continued to occur.

Ian was accustomed to the gray areas of the legal system, but at the end of the day, he always relied on facts. He knew that any case was made stronger by irrefutable proof.

So even in his strange dealings with Ronja, he refused to go any further on circumstantial evidence. Not when his sanity was at stake.

The phone vibrating across his desk made him jerk in

response, but he quickly picked it up. The incoming call was from the number he'd just dialed.

"Ian Keller," he said in way of a greeting.

"Mr. Keller," the man on the other end said with a pant to his voice. "Sorry I missed your call, I was in a bit of a…tight spot."

Ian didn't ask because he didn't want to know. Don Jacobson was a P.I. he'd used in the past, and despite the man's flippant attitude and haggard appearance, he was a dogged investigator. Blessed with the capability to conform to more facets of society than the average person even knew existed, Jacobson was the one to go to when answers were in order.

And Ian desperately needed some answers. Preferably with photographic proof. "Thank you for getting back to me. I have a job, if you're interested."

"I'm always interested," Don replied. "Outline it for me."

That was another reason Ian appreciated the man, his ability to speak without wasted and worthless words. "There's a woman I need investigated."

"I'm listening."

"A client crossed some professional boundaries. I want to know exactly what she's up to."

"What kind of tracking are we talking about?"

"Physical. I doubt there will be anything on the books, aboveboard or otherwise. She covers her bases, but I believe she might be involved in other activities." Ian pictured the bones dangling over their heads at the dining table. "Don't get too close. Just keep an eye on her or any of her associates. They could be dangerous."

"This some sort of gang or organized crime?" Don asked.

"To be honest, I don't know what she is." He rattled off Ronja's name and address along with any other pertinent details that would help Don get a line on her.

"Fine. I'm wrapping up a job now, so I can get started on this first thing tomorrow."

"Be cautious with this one." Ian was starting to feel a creeping sense of dread. "She and her friends have ways of learning things. Just be sure to keep a safe distance."

"You got it. I'm circumspect."

"Thanks, Don. I'll transfer a payment as soon as we hang up." Ian's gaze fell again to the chairs on the other side of his desk. A memory surfaced, and he got another idea. "Don, I'm going to double that payment."

Ian narrowed his eyes, deciding to gather facts from both ends. A faster method of closing in on the truth. "There's someone else I want you to look into."

19

Paige woke to purple-gray twilight angling across her ceiling. After an all-nighter of research into dark things and torturous rituals, she'd slept through the day and almost into the following night.

She heard optimistic birds outside that didn't seem to realize evening was fast approaching. And she felt a rumbling purr against her thigh, followed by the stretch and quiver of a long, post-nap stretch that was pure feline.

Her hand slid down to find the long, thin belly she knew was exposed. Tiger Lily's happy purr grew even stronger. "We had us quite a nap, my little tough girl." Paige yawned and performed a stretch of her own.

Then she froze, her eyes popping open as she remembered her overnight—and then some—house guest. She and Chris had stayed the rest of the night to pour over the entire hideous book, searching for anything that might be another clue. Dawn had grown bold and bright before they'd each crept up to bed with Chris going to one of the few rooms not spoken for by the other witches.

Though they'd shared a look at the top of the stairs, each had gone their separate way. If he'd felt anything like she had, his head and heart must have been overflowing with perplexing new ideas. Notions that had been unthinkable a scant week before.

Paige curled on her side and gave her cat a tickle under the chin. She was conflicted about having Chris around now, thrilled at the thought of seeing him. Yet terrified of where their new relationship might lead.

Paige couldn't shake the feeling that they'd inched across an invisible line. She was experiencing, saying, and doing things that were so not a part of her normal repertoire. Again the sensation stole over her, the feeling that she didn't quite recognize herself anymore.

She threw back the covers and emerged from her cozy spot in the bed. A quick shower and she was ready to head down to face the approaching evening. As well as her guest.

She just needed a hit of coffee and a smoothie and she'd be fine. It didn't matter that she was rising late, she still wanted her routine. Some aspects of her life needed to remain unchanged.

Then maybe she could convince herself that *she* hadn't changed. That she hadn't let her passion override her common sense last night.

And that she wasn't falling for the hot blonde Ranger.

Deciding to give herself a pass this one time, Paige told herself she was just long overdue for some male companionship. And just this once, she'd chalk her swooning female routine up to mid-trial jitters.

She pressed a finger to her lips as she opened her bedroom door. But she sure had enjoyed that kiss. Their impromptu hookup had been hotter and more meaningful, not in spite of its sweetness—but because of it.

The way he'd lingered over her lips, breathing her in like a delicacy. And never before in her life had Paige felt delicate. The experience was new to her, and not entirely unpleasant.

With the burning memory still in mind, she hurried downstairs to find everyone crowded into the grand hall.

With each trial another male was added to the mix, so "crowded" wasn't an overstatement. Her odd and mystical coven family just kept getting larger.

Nick was with Viv on the green couch, for once away from his pub for the night. Michael had shown up too, and was close to Shauni, while Dare, Quinn, and Ethan were with their own girlfriends.

Cole and Trevor were the only non-residents conspicuously absent.

And that had Paige worried.

She heard Chris's voice booming from inside the kitchen. And then Mrs. Attinger's tinkling laugh. The charming Ranger, doing his thing.

But the idea didn't rub her the wrong way like it would have in the beginning. She no longer saw Chris's smile as a red flag, or his laughing green eyes as camouflage for sinister ulterior motives.

He was just Chris, plain and direct. And sweet.

Just like he was last night.

"Glad you finally decided to join us, sleeping beauty." Claudia's teasing snapped Paige out of her fantasies.

But despite the light tone and interior design magazine on her lap, the shadows in Claudia's eyes betrayed her worry.

Paige crossed to her chair. "Have you heard from Cole?"

"Nothing since this afternoon. And nothing on the missing persons or the strange deaths." She supplied the last bit without needing to be asked. Having completed her challenge two trials ahead of Paige, Claudia knew how important every detail could be.

None of the witches could ever tell where a trial would lead, where the prophecy would take them. Kidnappings and murder were important any day of the week, but when connected to the Amara…the crimes usually meant even more complications, more danger.

Paige pondered what monster could possibly have killed those people, sucked them dry and left them behind like late autumn leaves. Dry, broken, dead.

Sure, it was probably a demon, but what was the purpose? To taunt the coven? Terrorize the city?

With no resolution rising to the forefront of her muddled brain, Paige nodded to Claudia and turned toward the kitchen, still intent on her caffeine-smoothie duo.

Just then, Chris stepped out, his phone pressed to his ear.

With a chin-notch in way of acknowledgment, she went into the kitchen and straight for a coffee cup.

Mrs. Attinger was buzzing around, but no dinner preparations were in sight. "It's a fend for yourself sandwich night," the older woman said, still wiping the counter without a single glance over her shoulder.

Paige chuckled, wondering how the woman knew it was her. "Thanks, Mrs. A. I hope I didn't mess up your schedule."

"Mess up?" Rotating her silver-capped head, the housekeeper gave her a wink. "You just gave me an excuse to take the night off from cooking. Besides, Chris took care of most of the food requests."

"He did?"

"Hmm." Mrs. Attinger narrowed her eyes at Paige. "Don't underestimate the value of a man who can cook."

"Well…I…"

"And I've put some new flowers out," the housekeeper said, as if she hadn't just given Chris a huge plug. "Now I'm off to make some tea in my own kitchen."

"Thanks, Mrs. A." Paige shook her head as the older lady exited to head for the house she shared with her husband on the back section of the estate.

A new bunch of flowers sat on the counter, cheery white

daisies in a vase of turquoise. The arrangement was a reminder that every soul on the island was backing Paige one hundred percent.

After a quick sniff of the sweet flowers, she went straight to the machine and started making her coffee. She might try the pod titled "Wake-up Call," since she felt like she was getting one of her own.

With her father, her destiny, her trial, and…Chris.

"Hey." The man on her mind spoke as he came from behind to startle her. "I haven't been up long either," he said, sliding his mug onto the granite counter. "So I'll get in line for another cup."

Paige pretended she wasn't unsettled and that her heart wasn't about to fly away from being so close to him. All of a sudden he was like a new man to her. "Yeah. It's been a while since I pulled an all-nighter."

As the machine purred and streamed hot coffee into the waiting cup, she leaned against the counter and frowned. "I'm just sorry we didn't come up with anything else. Nothing to guide us in the right direction."

"In any direction at all." Chris seemed as perturbed as she was by the dead-end they'd come to. "What was the point of figuring out the meaning of Angra Manah and then finding the specs of the ritual if it didn't give us another clue?"

"Maybe we learned something, but just don't realize it yet."

"I hope you're right."

Enjoying a companionable silence, they finished making their coffees. Then, in a domestic move that was absolutely foreign to her, Paige offered to make Chris a smoothie. "I'll be making one for myself, so it's no big deal," she said, brushing off the strange mix of emotions she felt by simply offering.

Excitement and annoyance both fought to have her on their side, because she liked the idea of doing something so simple for him. She just didn't like the fact that she liked it.

After her usual food-gathering routine, she handed him the completed masterpiece of brown sludge. "So, is everything okay?"

He looked over the rim of his glass, licked his lips. "What do you mean?"

"The phone call you were on. You looked bothered."

"Oh, well, someone's pushing me for an answer I can't give them yet."

"Hmm." She hoped refraining from asking would prod him to tell her the rest.

It did.

"About a job." He edged past her to stare out the window. "A friend of a friend is interested in hiring me. I'd like to get into business and put my degree to use, but I told him I can't commit to anything yet."

Doing her best to pretend indifference—doing her best to actually be indifferent—Paige lightened her voice. "Where's the job?"

"Phoenix."

She almost choked, and then coughed to cover her reaction. "Nice warm weather," she managed. And all the way across the country.

She'd always wanted to settle in the South. Gardening season was longer, and she wanted a huge yard of her own one day. Now that Anna had inspired her, maybe a greenhouse too.

But why should she care if Chris went so far away? They'd only shared one kiss, and a small one at that.

She slid her stare his way, covertly. She bit her bottom lip.

Oh, who was she kidding? Chris had opened a door inside of her that she'd kept firmly nailed shut for years. Turns out, she rather liked what she'd found behind it—a romantic heart she'd never even known belonged to her.

True, it was rusty from disuse, but now that Chris had started tinkering with it, Paige was curious to see how adept he really was. Could he repair what had lain untouched for so long?

"Paige!" Shauni burst into the room, causing Paige to jerk and spill hot coffee on her hand. "You're never going to believe who just called and left you a message."

At Paige's questioning look, she said, "Jack."

Paige set her cup aside. "Jack? Jack of the Amara? That one?"

"Yes. She wants you to meet her downtown." Shauni dodged her gaze to Chris and back again. "But she said you had to bring Chris."

Paige's flesh ran cool as she turned to Chris. What was Jack doing? There could be no good reason she wanted to meet him, unless she was curious about a man who shared the speed and strength that she and Paige had.

But still, the vicious little female had never reached out directly to her before.

Unless it was with a balled up fist to the face.

Paige clicked her tongue. "So, Chris. Did I mention there was another one of us, someone as fast and strong as we are?"

"No." He dragged the word out, still nursing his smoothie. "You must have missed that part. I always thought most of us had been killed."

A chill crawled over Paige's skin. "You're right. I haven't even thought of Jack. She's part of the Amara, so I guess, in my mind, she's just one of the bad guys. I never really pictured her as a child or considered her age."

"Is she about our age?"

"Close enough."

"How long has she been with their group?" Chris asked. "Do

you think she survived because she had Ronja's protection?"

"I couldn't begin to guess." Feeling the need for extra caffeine, Paige promptly decided to make her drink a double. And she'd put it in a travel cup. "Why don't we go ask her?"

~~~

They stopped in front of the huge house, a dilapidated Victorian that looked like it had once been an elegant ivory but had dirtied to a patchwork of peeling paint and grime. By all appearances, the place was empty and void of life.

The back of Chris's neck prickled with unease as he opened his senses. He didn't have magic in the way Paige and the other witches did, but he had a righteous sixth sense that had rarely steered him wrong.

No one else had accompanied him and Paige, at least, not up to the front door. Shauni and Michael had been purposely left behind on the island, with Paige brooking no argument from them. "It's two days before your wedding," she told the couple. "There's no way we're risking a black eye to go with the white dress. Even I respect the wedding day."

Chris had been surprised to hear her flout her disinterest in marital bliss so openly. But they'd been in a rush to travel to the mainland and get to the abandoned house on time. This Jack person had also left a menacing threat as part of her message, implying someone would suffer if Paige and Chris didn't meet her by the appointed hour.

Was it a trap? Probably.

But could they risk an innocent's life? He sent a sidelong glance to Paige, took in the stone-cold determination she wore like a mantle. Hell no, they wouldn't take the risk. Not now, not ever.

Chris treaded quietly over the cracked upheaval that had

once been a sidewalk. "This is the place?" They climbed the steps carefully, avoiding rotten boards as they went.

"The address matches." Paige pulled the outer screen door open with a squeak, revealing another door of wood with a glass oval inset. Amazingly, the glass appeared whole and undamaged. The rest of the old house hadn't fared as well.

Paige looked behind her, to the car parked down the street. She inclined her head subtly, letting the others waiting know that she and Chris were going ahead. They were stepping inside a dilapidated house to meet up with an established and dangerous enemy who might or might not be alone.

Yeah, Chris thought as he eased in after her, no problem with that plan.

Inside dust had taken over like a replicating virus. His shoe actually dragged and left tracks in the muck. "Wonder why this place is empty? In this area, property gets snatched up and rehabbed."

Paige glanced aside. "Ronja probably owns it, keeping it this way for whatever reason. A future safe house? Place to take kidnap victims? Who knows?"

At her somber words, Chris stopped cold, noticing dark stains on the floorboards of what had likely been a parlor. Dried and dingy brown, they were probably old. But his gut told him the marks were from blood.

And his hatred for these thugs intensified.

"Up here," a female voice called out suddenly from above, the tone half humor, half demand. Chris guessed this would be the infamous Jack, and she was expecting them to climb to the second floor.

Paige took the lead on the staircase, leaving him to do as he'd promised. To watch her six. There were only the two of them in a cramped space with no light. Even with their enhanced agility and strength, the setup was a disaster in the making.

At the top, they came to a hallway, and a shadow on the dusty floor gave away the woman's presence. Chris turned to see her silhouette in the doorway of a front room, backlighted by an outside lamp. She beckoned them her way.

"Be ready," Paige whispered.

"Always am."

The room turned out to be a master suite with two areas separated by a partial wall. Wallpaper, a light color he couldn't make out, was torn and peeling with large strips hanging down to the floor. A petite woman with black hair and a rock star-biker hybrid sense of style stood next to the grimy windows.

"I can't believe the two of you actually followed instructions and came alone," she said.

Chris couldn't tell if she was impressed or amazed by their recklessness.

Truth be told, he wasn't sure either.

With the room only half-lit by exterior street light, he felt as much as saw her dark eyes tracking up and down his body. Assessing? Judging?

"So you're the other one." There was a sneer in her tone.

"Why did you want to see us, Jack?" Paige stood in a fighting stance, ready to leap into attack or defense. "Are you finally reconsidering your bad choices? You know Ronja is only loyal to herself."

The wiry woman named Jack spread her hands. "There are so few of us special ones, and I wanted to get a good look…" she eyed Chris, "at *him*." After a slow, insulting perusal, she licked her lips. "Mm-mm-mm. Too bad you went to the sugar-side. 'Cause I bet you fuck fast and hard."

Paige made a move as if to rush her, but Chris stilled her with a hand on her shoulder. When he felt her expel the breath she'd been holding, he let go.

"I also wanted to tell you both something," Jack said. "Face to face. It's only fitting." The leather of her jacket creaked as she crossed her arms, thin silver chains dangled. "Since you almost got me killed."

"Well, if that's your problem, let me help." Paige took a step forward. "I'd be happy to kill you outright."

Jack sneered and jutted her chin out. "They came for me when I was a kid, you know. They thought I was you." She jabbed a finger at Paige. Then she made air quotes and added, "The gifted child."

Chris's heart kicked into overdrive, and suddenly, the last thing he wanted was for Paige to thrash this person before they got some answers. "Wait. Who came for you?" he demanded. "What did they look like? How did you survive?"

"Survive—" Jack burst into laughter. "You guys really are dense, aren't you? Don't you know?" When neither Chris nor Paige responded, she clapped her hands with one loud *pop*! "This is priceless. You have no idea. But then again, they didn't figure out their part either. They convinced themselves it couldn't be you."

Jack fixed Paige with a look so suddenly full of hatred that Chris almost stepped in front of her. "But I knew the first time we fought. They killed so many like us, so many kids. They swore the chances of you being the one were almost non-existent."

"Who?" Paige yelled. "Who killed the children and…" She drew in a ragged breath. "And everyone else? Why didn't they kill you?"

"Tyr put his hands on me and saw that I was meant to be one of Ronja's seven women. That I would serve her in the Amara. You know, he has that see the future thing going on like your head bitch. He must have sensed…" She wiggled her finger dramatically. "My dark side."

"Tyr," Paige gasped. "He was part of it? So does that mean Ronja—"

"Ah-ah." Jack waved a finger, clearly enjoying teasing Paige. "You'll find out soon enough."

The fierce looking female studied Chris, shook her head, and then clapped her hands again. A tall disheveled woman and a man with bleached, buzz-cut hair slunk out of the shadows from the connected room.

And the anxiety ramped up when Chris saw they were dragging a woman between them.

"Paige," he said in a low voice.

"Carson is a wild fighter," she replied, understanding he was asking what to expect from the new entries, "and Ross is the shifter."

Behind the two newcomers, another person shuffled forth in slow, lazy steps. The body type suggested female, but she was wearing a gray hooded sweatshirt to hide her face.

"And Searenn. A Droehk," Paige told him, her voice dripping contempt. "Be careful with her. She controls demons."

"Yes, I do." A gravelly voice came from the hooded woman. As soon as the words left her mouth, she held up a hand and started chanting in a strange dialect. Her palm glowed amber.

"Shit." Paige thrust her hands out and sent a gust of wind toward the window, bursting the glass outward, the previously agreed upon signal to the others waiting in the car. A sign that they needed backup.

They'd been almost certain this would be a trap of some kind, but they'd played along anyway for the reason now standing before them. The victim Jack had hinted at.

Chris tensed. The involvement of the woman changed everything. Innocent civilians always did.

He eyed the shifter. The tall woman looked at Paige. And Paige held ready, her attention split between Jack and the woman in the hoodie.

Then the semi-calm state of the people in the room exploded all at once. Jack leapt and Paige moved to intercept her, leaving Chris to choose his own target.

He decided to go for the shifter, and Ross let go of his captive to throw his arms out to his sides. Where they promptly became the arms of a bear, complete with sharp, lethal claws.

Good thing Chris was fast. He ducked the first two swipes, and swooped in to pummel the guy's abs. He kept dodging blows to deliver his own, and when he sensed his opponent growing winded, he drove a kick into his right knee that quickly brought him down.

This is easier than I expected. Taking advantage of the shifter's incapacitated state, Chris turned to search for the other woman, Carson, and the female she was still holding hostage.

But both women were gone.

He searched hurriedly, because they couldn't have gotten far. After his first pass, he zeroed in on them. They were huddled in the corner, disguised by shadows.

A bite on his calf brought a roar of rage from Chris. He jerked free, skin ripping, and whirled to find Ross still on the floor, but the shifter's upper half had fully morphed.

At the sight of the bear-man, the woman broke out of her silent stupor and started to shriek.

Glancing over, he saw Paige and Jack taking turns driving their fists into each other. She was still occupied and couldn't break away, so he'd have to deal with the other three. At least until Paige put Jack down.

With the burning agony of torn flesh streaking up his leg,

Chris focused all of his energy, his rage, and his strength. And he turned it all toward Ross.

The shifter must have seen the bloodlust in Chris's eyes, must have recognized exactly what his opponent was about to unload on his sorry ass. Because in a sudden act of true cowardice, Ross began to shrink, to pull in on himself.

And with a rush of air, the shifter became a rat. He changed so quickly, the atmosphere actually crackled and popped from the reduction of mass.

As the rodent scurried between Chris's feet, Jack went skidding across the floor on her face. Paige still stood upright, but she was panting heavily.

She tossed him a quick grin, but then looked past him into the other room. Her features contorted. "Searenn!"

Chris looked and saw…he wasn't sure what he was seeing, but the amber glow had expanded from Searenn's hand and now encompassed a long, distorted shape. The body was similar to a cheetah standing on its hind legs, but the skin, if it could be called such, was corded and ridged, like bare muscles without any fascia or flesh.

The fibers were thick and ropy, a shade of brown like the light the Droehk had held in her palm. So now he knew… she'd been summoning a demon. And the one she'd pulled from the dark depths was one ugly bastard.

He understood the panic and fury he'd seen in Paige's face, that he'd heard in her voice as she yelled Searenn's name. The monster had been called forth for a vile reason, and as he watched, the thing's jaws widened.

The creature's mouth was round, and as the hole grew bigger, Chris saw three razor-like teeth at angles to each other. Their bite would create a Y-incision, an injury he'd seen before. From common blood-sucking leeches.

He broke from his disgusted daze but not before the

demon clamped its revolting mouth around the captive woman's shoulder. Her scream was like nothing Chris had ever heard, and he moved to intervene without thought for his own safety. He had to get that creature off of the woman.

Searenn actually bolted to the side, leaving the one named Carson to hold the victim for the creature's attack. But then Paige flashed in front of Chris and tackled Carson. The Amara woman let loose a surprised yell and rolled across the floor, desperately trying to avoid Paige's blows.

He heard other voices then: Anna, Willyn, and the Spanish roll that belonged to Lucia. But he was too involved to yell out to them, too busy trying to grab onto the demon.

Finally, he was able to wrap both hands around its throat and pull back, but hardly an inch was gained. The strands comprising its body might look like muscles, but in reality, they were closer to steel cables.

The sucking sound coming from the demon's mouth and throat was obscene, and as Chris traded off punching its head and pulling at its torso, the woman's skin started to change. Her flesh began to wrinkle, morphing from healthy pink to a morbid and unnatural brown.

An awful truth hit Chris like a sledgehammer to his gut. This creature had killed those other people, the ones who'd been found desiccated, dried out like jerky. The beast had sucked them dry.

No! Chris yelled internally. He would not allow this woman to perish right in front of him.

Channeling strength even he hadn't known existed within him, Chris locked one arm around the demon's throat and used his other hand to latch onto the front of its face. Curling his fingers inside the deadly mouth, Chris planted both of his legs and thrust backward with all he had.

Both he and the creature went staggering across the floor

to collide with the wall. Screeching in a high-pitched sound that made Chris's ears hurt, the beast opened its hungry mouth again and rotated its head in an attempt to bite him.

Suddenly Paige was there, with cerulean light shooting from her palms as she reached for the monster. She latched onto the back of its head, literally burying her fingers in its wiry flesh. Then her blue magic flowed freely, and the screaming leech turned to dust.

Collapsing against the wall and sliding to the floor, Chris knelt on one knee, the leg that hadn't been partially devoured by Ross's bear. "Thanks." His breath was harsh and shallow as the effects of the struggle swamped him. "That thing was strong."

Paige held out a hand and helped him to both feet. "We need to get you a weapon, one with the coven magic stored inside." She gave him a funny look. "If you're going to be around for a while, you need to be able to protect yourself from demons."

Before he could reply, stumbling footsteps had them both peering around the half-wall. Jack had rushed to the broken window and now had one foot perched on the sill, ready to jump out.

She took a moment to look at Paige, raising a finger to point. "They know who you are! They finally listened to me!" She swung her arm to Chris and snarled, "And you too. The ones that got away."

The brutish woman grinned, revealing bloody teeth within her ruined mouth. Paige had done a job on her. "The Daevo will be coming for you and your coven. You can't hide anymore!"

In a blur of black leather and black hair, she was gone, just as Dare barged into the room.

Paige whipped around to the others. "Where's Willyn?"

"Here!" Willyn cried from the stairs, and then the coven's healer was scooting past her husband.

"Are you hurt?"

"Not me." She gestured to Chris. "He's going to need you, but first, there's a woman in here. She was attacked by one of Searenn's monsters."

Paige pointed, so Willyn and Dare went to tend to the woman. Then she met Anna's stare. "It was the same kind of demon that left the bodies downtown."

Chris sidled up to join in. "They're like leeches, only worse." He moved his attention from Paige to Anna, and then Lucia as she strode up to listen. "Do you think there are more of them?"

Anna blew out an aggrieved breath. "There always are."

Lowering her head and staring at nothing in particular, Paige put her hands on her hips. "What did Jack say? The Daevo is coming?" She angled her head to the side to look at Chris. "She meant the Jin Deva, right?"

"Or something like it. She pretty much admitted that the Amara were the ones searching for us all this time. The Daevo," Chris whispered. They were so close to finding the murderers.

Then he fixed a stare on Paige. "But who do you think it is?"

Paige shook her head. "They're each as bad as the next, though Ronja is the most powerful, the one with the most to lose." She wiped at her chin, smearing red droplets. Her blood or Jack's?

"You were right," she said, gaze still on the dirty floor. She looked to Anna then. "You thought my two destinies were really just the same one." Her fist slammed against her thigh. "But the joke's still on me. Every time we've gone up against the Amara, I was probably standing right in front of my mother's killer. I never even knew."

Chris was churning with some of the same fury he saw in Paige. "We'll kill them all if we have to. One way or another, we will avenge our parents. And the children."

Paige locked her aqua-blue eyes on his and opened her mouth as if to speak, but she paused when Dare stuck his head around the corner. "She's doing better but still needs a hospital."

Willyn came out, one arm supporting the woman who'd almost had the life sucked out of her. Literally.

"I'll call Trevor and Cole," Dare said. "They can pick her up and take it from there." The flat line of his mouth made it clear he despised what had been done to the poor woman. His anger burned right alongside everyone else's.

Chris suddenly felt the full weight of the coven's obligation, and for the first time, he let it become his as well. Completely.

He was no longer beholden only to Paige. He would lend her sisters anything they needed—his abilities, his knowledge, even his life.

Just as Dare, Michael, and all the other men did. Having feelings for one of these witches might come with enormous peril, but he knew now how valuable the final prize was.

He studied Paige as she watched Dare carrying the woman down the stairs, a scowl on her face and concern in her eyes.

There were layers and layers to this amazing woman, and each one he discovered made him want to stick around and learn more. To see what else she kept hidden beneath that fierce exterior.

A touch on his elbow brought Chris around to Willyn. "How about I take care of that leg?" she asked.

Chris briefly imagined how much it would help to have a hundred medics like this healing witch on the battlefield. Instant care and recovery. She knelt and put her hands around his knee, gradually making her way down to his foot, erasing all traces of injury as she did.

When Chris shook his ankle out and grinned at her, Willyn winked. "Thanks for being there." She patted his knee and then moved on to check out Paige. Who, of course, insisted she was fine.

As the others filed out of the room, Chris noticed Paige's leg jiggling, just like his did when he had energy to spare. When his power was zipping around inside of him like a live wire with no termination point. Despite the brawl—or more likely because of it—she was still amped up.

"You want to go back to the island?" he asked.

"Not really." Her mouth was tight.

"You want a drink?"

She shrugged. "I could do that, yeah. But I don't want to go to Nick's." At last, she glanced at him. "I don't want to talk to anyone. I'm not in the mood for questions or theories about the Amara and…"

"I get it," Chris said. "Believe me, I understand." He jerked his head for her to follow him. "Come on, then. I know a safe place."

20

An hour, just an hour, Paige told herself, so she could put aside all thoughts of murder and monsters and just take a short break. Funny that the person she most wanted to crack a bottle open with was the tall, kickass Ranger beside her. The very man she'd warned—more than once—to stay away from her.

Now, it seemed, he was becoming something of a habit, a source of consolation. Chris was the first person aside from her sisters who really understood her. He and she shared common values. And a common goal. Justice.

Or vengeance. To Paige, they were the same.

Only Chris could truly understand how she felt, so it was fitting that she take some time with him, not only to reflect on the confrontation with the Amara and what Jack had told them, but also to plan how to proceed. He was, after all, her partner.

The first glimmer of acceptance flared for Paige, and for a second she wondered if Fate might know what she was doing after all. But as soon as the troublesome idea struck, she averted her eyes from Chris's powerful build.

What was that expression about not making major life choices in the wake of tragedy or crisis? Paige was currently barreling through both, and was certainly in no mental state to be changing her mind. Not about her one great fear.

Falling for a man and giving him the ability to desert her, leaving her behind to wonder why.

She might now acknowledge her father's justification for abandoning her, but that didn't mean her self-assurance had just popped into place after the revelation, not when it came to matters of the heart.

Her inability to place faith in another for the long term was still intact, and she couldn't just re-wire herself. So as far as romance went, she was still a lost cause.

They'd been traversing the city streets, but now Chris stopped and indicated a set of concrete steps leading up to a single door.

Paige nodded. "Lead the way."

She realized how appropriate her words were as soon as they were inside and she got a good look at the clientele, at the framed pictures and plaques on the walls. "It's a Ranger bar."

Chris gave her an easy smile. "Owned by a former Ranger and one of the few places in town even Ronja might think twice about attacking."

Paige's laugh came from deep in her gut, and the release felt good.

Tonight could have gone very badly, and it was clear the Amara weren't underestimating the coven anymore. They'd come prepared for Paige and Chris and had packed a little extra firepower.

But even with the addition of Ross, Searenn, and her pet demon, the coven soldiers had been the ones left standing.

She and Chris made a good team.

She watched him raise a hand, greeting a group at a corner table then a couple more at the end of the bar. Sure, he was one of them, one of the brotherhood, but the response from the various men told her Chris was both liked and admired.

He eased along the front of the bar, stopping only long enough to say hello to a couple more friends and request two beers. Then he reached for Paige, as if he'd take her hand. But he dropped his arm instead.

Taking point, he headed out a single door in the back and climbed a set of stairs. Paige ascended as well, up to the top floor, where she discovered a deserted upper deck that was open to the night sky.

The weather was warmer again, with the previous night's cold having rushed farther inland. One of the few things quicker than Paige's temper was the swift-change weather in Savannah.

Chris led her to one of the wooden benches on the perimeter. Once seated, Paige took a long, cool drink of her beer and sighed.

After a few minutes of quiet reflection, Chris broke the silence. "So that was Jack."

Paige took another sip. "Joan Jett wannabe. But her bad attitude isn't nearly as charming."

"Yeah. She's pretty much your polar opposite."

When Paige crossed one leg over the other and eyed Chris, he clarified, "That's a compliment. She's your opposite both physically and morally. Small, dark, mean, where you're tall, fair, and...not as mean."

Paige laughed again, beginning to enjoy the light sensation of sharing humor with a man this way. Reality was starting to crash over her, adrenaline fading, and she realized she'd never let her guard completely down when it came to males. Not like she was now.

For once in her life, she could close her eyes, turn her back, and know without a doubt that he would be there. Chris would have her back—her six—in every possible way. A feeling she was entirely unused to.

"You've got a great smile," he told her, flashing one of his own charmers with a wink for good measure.

"Chris, are you flirting with me?" Paige was direct, maybe to a fault, but she liked to know exactly what she was dealing with. Like she'd told him last night before their kiss, she didn't want to guess anymore.

"Yes." Apparently, he'd taken her at her word and was giving her a dose of her own straight-forwardness. "I'm warming up to the idea of you as a woman."

Her arms stilled, the bottle halfway to her mouth. "Uh… when was I anything else?"

"You know what I mean. In my head, you've always been the little blondie trailing around behind me." He pulled his mouth to the side. "You always had a crush on me, you know."

"What was I, like four years old?" She sipped and smiled. "You're delusional. I doubt I was ever the type to follow a guy around."

"Only me," he said, eyes focusing on her in a way that made Paige suddenly feel weightless. And completely breathless. She'd gone light-headed like no amount of alcohol could ever make her, and a spot in her chest fluttered wildly.

She'd known attraction before, had been blessed with true-blue friends, but never had both been combined with the deeper, emotional connection that was developing with Chris.

She should say something, should stop staring at him, anything to cover the desire urging her to lean over and press her lips to his. "Need I remind you that I wasn't the one stalking somebody?"

Yeah, that was good, just enough banter to hide her breathy voice.

The sex-tingle currently zinging in her veins was probably a result of her post-battle charge, and maybe a little unspent witchy mojo. The fight with the Amara had hyped her up. She just needed an outlet for residual energy.

But it certainly didn't help to be kicking back beneath the stars with a man like Chris Decker. The packed out body, boyish grin, and rainforest eyes were a too-delicious combination.

Plus, he could move as fast as she did. Those arms could probably hold her good and tight when he was on top of her and...

Paige turned her beer up and drained it. Then she set the empty bottle on the bench. Between her and Chris. *Yeah, like that would keep us apart.*

"I'm going to need another one of these." Was that her voice? All thick and raspy with sex, sex, sex?

"I'll go down." She cringed. Could she have used a better choice of words? "I mean, I'll go downstairs and order us a couple more."

Paige feared her nervousness was clanging like an alarm. Had she ever gotten flustered over a guy before? She didn't think so.

But, man, the floaty sensation actually felt sort of nice. She still couldn't seem to catch her breath and her nerve endings were extra sensitive. Her skin was radiating like an oven, and she just felt...*tingly.* All over.

For Pete's sake, get a grip. She shook her head as she descended the wooden steps. What the hell kind of word was tingly?

Two beers and a big tip later and she still hadn't managed to steer her mind-movie to more wholesome images. Every good-looking man down in the bar was instantly compared to the one waiting for her up top.

Chris's hair was a deeper blonde than this guy, his jaw was firmer than that one's, his shoulders wider than everybody in the place. The litany of compliments to his physicality wouldn't stop, and they drove Paige right back up the stairs to the handsome devil that had invaded her mind.

She'd hoped to use the reprieve to get her head back in check. And her body. But since that hadn't worked, she used the return climb to formulate a new plan. She'd lead with a defensive maneuver, a topic sure to sink her libido.

"All right, enough play time." She plopped down and handed him his beer. "We need to talk about this Daevo character. But I think we both know what Jack meant."

The breath he released was heavy with aggrieved acceptance. "Yeah. She knows who it is, all right. Daevo sounds too much like the ritual, Jin Deva, for them not to be related."

"None of this makes any sense whatsoever. The Amara is already loaded. They've got Ronja and Scarlett, and all the others, Searenn, and their own damn demon. They've got Bastraal. Why would they need this, this…thing?" Paige trailed a finger after a cool drop as it rolled down the curved brown glass of the bottle she held.

"And if the Daevo is so powerful, why did they worry about killing you when you were just a child? Was this creature the one who murdered the others? Is it the evil power you're supposed to destroy?"

Paige creased her brow. "It has to be. But if the person we've been looking for has been my enemy all along, why all this mystery? What good did it do for you and me to waste time figuring it all out?"

"Because you wouldn't have known who you were really facing." Chris pointed his beer at her. "You only knew what Jack was talking about tonight, because you've been learning about the ritual and the monster it releases. Who we now know is the Daevo."

"I guess." Paige stared at the floor of the wooden deck. "I

still don't understand why they haven't tried harder to kill me, especially now that they know I'm the one destined to destroy them. Or it."

"You're destined to have revenge on the one who killed our parents and the children," Chris clarified. "That's not necessarily the Daevo. Another person was there that day and could still be the one we want."

"Okay then." The unanswered questions just kept circling back around on themselves, causing frustration to crackle just beneath Paige's surface. "But again, if that's true, why did we need to know anything about the Daevo?"

Mouth tight, and features sober, Chris held her gaze. "Maybe that's where your trial comes in. And your coven."

Paige considered what he meant, and the impact hit her dead-center. She covered her face with her hand. "Shit."

"Yep."

"But we still don't know who the two are, the Daevo and the one with magic." Her fingers squeezed involuntarily, so she eased off before she shattered glass and spewed beer all over the deck.

"They both have to be old enough to have attacked us over twenty years ago. That narrows down the Amara candidates, right?"

"Sure." Paige sat up straighter. "But then we're assuming it's someone we've met. Ronja might be keeping this person away from the action until the very end."

"A secret weapon for the final showdown. I'm betting the Amara will summon the beast if the coven lasts until the end. The final trial."

"Oh, we will make it. I promise you." Paige felt the first skitter of fear. Not for herself, but for her friend. The only remaining witch. "Anna will be called after me. She's the last one. We always knew she would be."

"And she's the strongest?" Chris asked.

"Yeah. Magically, she kicks ass. She was born into the craft, with knowledge of the prophecy, and parents who raised her to cultivate her power."

"So it's all or nothing for them, Paige. They'll be coming with everything they've got."

"And that's why they'll create the Daevo." Paige nodded, letting it all sink in. "I'm ready, though. No matter what."

With concern, she looked at him. "According to Jack, you're in their sights now too."

"Wouldn't be the first time I've been in the crosshairs."

Paige had been there a time or two herself, those moments in battle when your mind goes numb and you just know someone somewhere has got a bead on you. But she'd survived that war, and she'd sure as hell live through this one too.

So would Chris. She sipped again, studying him surreptitiously. He wasn't the only one who could act as guardian.

Paige developed a new strategy. She just hoped her tactic to keep Chris safe didn't backfire in other aspects. Proximity to the virile man could be a whole other kind of dangerous.

She held out a hand in a halting gesture. "Now, don't get too excited," she grinned, "but I think you should start staying out at the island."

She would swear his eyes blazed for a split-second, and then he studied her face as if searching for the clue to a riddle. At last, he said, "In which room?"

Oh, yeah. His stare was definitely getting hotter. "You will have your *own* room. The one you slept in last night," she told him firmly, hoping he couldn't sense the raw sexuality he'd stoked with that one look. And his voice, so rich and deep. His statement had been filled with innuendo that had flooded through her like heated quicksilver.

"Anna's a great hostess." His gaze was steady on hers.

"She is." Paige glanced upward, hoping to hide her ridiculously pleased expression. Was it crazy that the cool air seemed more alive all of a sudden, cleaner and sweeter? That the stars above possessed a brighter, more crystalline shimmer?

Her head fell back against the wood, exposing her neck to a silky trickle of wind.

She heard a soft scrape, a shift of body, and finally the soft clunk of a bottle being put aside. Paige felt a hand close over her own, just before Chris slid his grasp down, over her fingers. The sizzling friction should have created sparks. He took her beer away to set down alongside his.

Trembling now—*but I don't tremble*—she lowered her gaze from the midnight sky and its sparkling lights. She met Chris's eyes; she locked on. Starlight and shadow danced around him, revealing both strength and tenderness, like two sides of the same card.

He was going to kiss her. She felt the pull, that tug in the belly and flush of the lips. And Paige, the strongest of the coven, was powerless to stop it.

He touched her cheek, hard against soft, and she didn't *want* to stop it.

Her name was the softest breeze from his lips before they took hers with primal demand. His hand still rested beneath her jawline, his thumb on her pulse as their tongues clashed and teased.

The gentle caress and arousing kiss were captivating, erotic. Chris was killing her with his tenderness.

Greedily, she flicked the tip of her tongue, reaching for his, giving permission for more. And the kiss exploded, turning from sweet and seeking to an overwhelming need to feel him, taste him. She wanted to give herself over, to trust him with every facet of who she was, both physically and emotionally.

He was the only man she'd ever allowed to come so close, to see her so honestly.

The hard bench beneath them wasn't the ideal romantic spot, but when Chris pulled her to him and shifted her body so that she was sitting across his thighs, the heat between them overrode good sense and any concern for the environment.

As far as she could tell, they were on a bed of feathers.

Paige shoved the neck of his shirt to the side, spying her first glimpse of ink on one shoulder. The tantalizing preview only made her hotter. "Do you have a tattoo?

Lids lowered slightly, he slipped a hand around to her thigh. "Maybe.

Hmm. His lap was so *warm.* "Can I see it?

His voice was a deep vibration of promise. "Maybe."

But when she would have lifted the fabric for a better look, Chris dove in to nuzzle her neck. The things he did with his mouth tormented her, and then he skimmed up to her ear to torture some more.

Wrapping her arms around his shoulders, she pressed her chest against the hard breadth of his. The rigidity of his muscles fascinated her, and when his thick, sculpted arms wrapped around her, Paige knew she was lost.

She felt the length of him beneath her, and knew Chris was as far gone as she was.

A voice traveled up from the stairwell, the abrupt noise shocking Paige and giving her a start. The upper deck of the Ranger bar might have already been initiated in this way, but Paige still clung to the tiniest bit of decorum.

Afraid people would appear at any moment, she fought to pull herself back from the brink of abandon. She only hoped Chris would follow her lead.

Because if he kept holding onto her this way, kissing her so deeply, she would damn the surroundings and let him take anything he wanted. Right here. Right now.

With a groan, he tore his mouth from hers, breaths heavy and hands still resting on her hips. His fingers massaged gently, as if they weren't on board with the plan to let her go.

Paige just closed her eyes and enjoyed his lingering touch. She let a soft moan escape her lips.

Chris growled in response to the sound. "Now, you're going to have to stop that, or I won't be able to hold myself back." His tone was playful, but the grip he still had on her, the burning gaze, they told the real story.

He was as close to losing control as she was.

"I don't want to stop either." Paige let the confession fly out before careful consideration and quickly pushed away to stand, just in case he took it as an all-clear. "But…we aren't *that* secluded here."

"No." He stood too but grabbed his beer to finish it off in one long swallow. Staring past her to the dark corner of the deck, he exhaled slowly. "You still want me to stay out on the island?" He cocked his head then to look at her. "Do you trust me enough to be close at hand?"

Paige studied the face she was growing far too used to, and again her response flew before she could stop it. "Oddly enough," she said with wonder, "I do."

21

Candles burned in Ronja's boudoir, lighting the elegantly appointed walls and giving the room a romantic glow.

Or a sinister appearance, depending on one's perspective.

In contrast to the most ancient form of light, she sat reading a book on an electronic device that was lit from within.

How marvelous, she mused, the wonders of the modern world. Every century, every decade, over the past millennium had amazed her with each new invention. But this one, a slim piece of plastic able to hold hundreds of books? This was her favorite by far.

Except for indoor plumbing, she then reconsidered, with heated water. She pictured her long, soaking baths. Yes, that was still the best.

Still, she relished her quiet reading time, so it was with an air of annoyance that she snapped out, "Enter!" to whomever was tapping on her door with the intent to intrude.

The door opened hesitantly as Scarlett, Tyr, and Searenn all walked in.

Ronja flipped the cover closed on her reader. All three of them at once? She was abruptly set on edge.

"What is it?" she asked, unwilling to let them stall or hedge. Tyr and Scarlett shared a glance of apprehension, and rarely were those two of the same mind. Usually they engaged in a sort of sibling rivalry combined with jealousy. They were both her next-in-charge, and they were both her lovers.

And she fed them both her blood to extend their mortality.

Their mild competitiveness was understandable, and was the norm. So the united front they now presented was enough to give her pause. "Out with it." She stood, letting the precious device fall from her lap and onto the hardwood floor.

"There was someone following us tonight," Searenn said, taking the lead and displaying her ever-present yet oft foolish bravado. If she was about to reveal something that would spur Ronja's temper…well, the Nordic witch never believed in sparing the messenger.

"What do you mean? Who would follow you and why?" Ronja stood regally, looking slightly down her nose at her three minions, reminding them of her superior position. Not that she needed to. She could wipe all three of them from existence in a single swipe.

Have to save my power reserves for the good bitch. As she so lovingly referred to Anna St. Germaine.

Tyr stepped forward. "We turned the tables on him, tracked him to his office downtown."

With her arms crossed, Ronja dug her long and perfectly manicured nails deep into the area above her elbows. "That's still not an answer."

Tyr's black eyes flicked to the side. Never was he afraid. The man could stand pain like no one she'd ever come across, one of the reasons she'd plucked him from that Indian tribe so long ago. Native American, she reminded herself. As if she cared about these new politically correct notions.

And she didn't. The cries and complaints of humans never ceased to amaze her. Or to irritate. Humans were like buzzing, whining insects, and she had waited a very, very long time to begin their extermination.

With no way out of delivering the information, Tyr rolled his shoulders back, posture erect, and stated plainly, "The room assignment for the building indicated he went to the office of a Don Jacobson, a private investigator. We searched the web and found his picture."

"Get to the point." Ronja advanced, having had enough of her fearless lover behaving like a scared boy.

Tyr's jaw flexed along with his shoulders, tension rolling through his form from top to bottom. "He left his office, and we followed him to a pizza joint. Crappy, dark, out of the way."

Tyr met her eyes, so Ronja held her reprimand in check.

"He met a man there," Tyr said and swallowed. "Ian Keller."

The entire room froze in Ronja's mind, her peripheral vision icing over, turning white and opaque. Then with the sound of a gun discharging, the illusion cracked and fell to pieces.

But the cold stayed within her, part of her.

As always.

"Are you telling me that Ian hired this man? This…" Poisonous rage cramped her throat and tongue. "This private *investigator*?"

Scarlett finally spoke. "The man handed Ian a piece of paper, probably some report of what he'd seen." She tapped her toes on the floor. "What we've been doing…who *we've* been watching."

"The witches, you mean?" Ronja threw up her hands and spun, turning to her vanity and the antique oval mirror. She stared at her reflection, the agony of betrayal marring her beautiful face and eyes. The unjust pain of disloyalty. "How can my brother not know me? How can he turn against me?"

She wouldn't break the mirror this time. She had the one before, in a rage, and finding an adequate replacement had been difficult. Ronja didn't care for difficulties, from objects or people.

But particularly from those who were important to her, those she loved.

"So we send him a message, my brother." Patting her face, she admired the sharp cheekbones. "Pretty words and plain speaking haven't worked very well." She ran a hand over her corn-silk hair. "He simply needs to be woken up. That's all."

She faced the trio again, calmly, once more composed. "A demonstration of my power will force my brother to recall his own." She looked to Tyr. "And my demand for respect will summon his."

She let her head fall back as she sighed. "Vanir was once so proud, so magnificent. He was always a better person than I, but when times called for violence, he gave it blow for blow. He knew how to deal with those who dared cross him, and how to honor those who stood with him."

Now her voice grew sad. "He used to be my most valiant protector."

Ronja whipped her head around to stare at Searenn, Scarlett, and lastly, Tyr. "He will stand with me again. He simply needs to be reminded."

Running her hands down her silk robes, the color of witch-smoke, she held her head at a haughty angle. "We will send Ian a message through this man, this *human*," she spat, "who dared investigate me. Make the message clear."

The three of them nodded, and Searenn reached for the door handle.

"And," Ronja said, stilling their motion with a single word. "Make it brutal."

22

Chris had only attended a couple of weddings, but even he could spot true love when he saw it. Shauni and Michael were the definitive picture. Love, honor, and—we'll talk about it until a compromise is made—were practically etched into their glowing, smiling faces on a daily basis.

As he'd trekked the hallway to deliver a boutonniere, he'd overheard Michael's Southern "Mama" bawling in one of the back rooms of the church just before an older female voice said, "For pity's sake, Lanette, he's not going anywhere. He's just getting married."

And this second woman, Chris had since learned, was Michael's paternal grandmother, a country woman through and through, very practical, and superbly empathetic. She'd probably passed down the magic gene that enabled her grandson to see other people's auras.

Now, as the older woman scooted into one of the pews down front, Chris wondered what she saw in her grandson as he awaited his bride. But no extrasensory perception was needed to see that Michael was bursting with happiness.

And Shauni hadn't even revealed herself yet.

Appropriate wedding music played courtesy of a trio of musicians—pianist, flautist, and violinist—but contrary to tradition, the long line of bridesmaids and groomsmen were absent. The other witches were present, though, and decked out in their signature colors. They might not be in a line up front, but they were standing for Shauni in their special coven way.

Chris smiled, as he pictured Paige's face this morning, her slight blush as she appeared in the great room. His warrior had been flustered, almost nervous for him to see her in a dress.

He gripped the rounded edge of the wooden pew, glossy with its golden wood. The room grew warm. He absolutely couldn't draw a breath. Had he just thought of Paige as his warrior? *His.*

And was it the possessiveness that gave him a jolt, or the underlying meaning he'd subconsciously applied? So far, they'd only shared a couple of make-out sessions, but if he took an honest look at the situation, he and Paige had been paired up in a much broader sense.

They were partners in the most important of battles, and shared childhood memories both tender and bleak. So did he feel such a kinship with her, such a physical pull, due to their history and enforced companionship? Or was it something more?

His gaze sought her out, as if the answer would be found in the cut of the sexy dress she wore, ivory and turquoise in bold, asymmetric blocks of color. The design befitted her character, striking at first glance, but revealing an almost dangerous flair upon closer inspection.

The music changed then, and Chris ripped his eyes from Paige. She was turning to look down the aisle, to the front of the church, where the bride was about to make her debut.

And Chris was mildly embarrassed at the thought of her catching him staring. Wanting. Wondering bemusedly just what had happened to his grand plan.

Yes, he'd wanted to find Paige. Okay, he was hell-bent

on helping her seek revenge, for them both. This was their interlinking destiny. Add to that, she was a childhood friend, one he'd been curious about most of his life.

But the pursuits he was now imagining were the stuff of confirmed-bachelor nightmares. He'd stolidly avoided serious relationships, having no desire to bind himself to any one person or place.

But only because he'd had another goal in mind. Years had been devoted to seeking out Paige, so he could tell her who she was, what she had been born to do. Now that he had, his previous solitary and nomadic existence didn't hold as much appeal.

He'd yet to even think of leaving her behind. He didn't consider ending their acquaintance and redeeming his freedom. Just the opposite. For the first time in his life, he was considering staying put.

As he listened to the music swell inside the vestibule, Chris chanced another look at Paige. Her face was alight with joy for her friend, her soft lips parted, eyes glowing.

And like a flash of magic, Chris understood. Paige had become home to him. Maybe she always had been. The one place he'd continually searched for, where he could find comfort, peace, and at last, he could stop running.

The people around him stood, so Chris did as well. With everyone on their feet, awaiting the bride's entrance, he took the opportunity to scan the women who were so much a part of Paige's life, these sisters he was grateful she'd found, even if a little late.

Beside Paige stood Viv in a plum-hued dress, and next to her was Claudia in her own version of "peachy." Chris knew they each had an assigned magical color, but what he found intriguing was how complimentary the shades were to the witches.

Like Kylie wearing a color as sunny as her hair, and Anna in a serene blue, befitting her royal grace as well as her eyes. One row up from them, Lucia was decked out in gray, but with a vibrant red scarf over her shoulders. Next to her, Hayden boasted a pale pink that was just as gentle as her nature.

Dare stood next to Hayden, and beside him was his wife Willyn. She too had chosen to wear a shawl, since the ivory would be too much in a full dress, and only the bride wore white today.

Turning his head slightly, Chris spied the beautiful Shauni herself, resplendent in a straight, fitted gown and a wide ribbon of emerald green around her waist. A silver pendant rested above her feminine neckline, the colored stones reflecting each of the women of the coven.

These witches were seriously loyal to those necklaces. As loyal as they were to each other, and their men, who were all present and at the sides of their chosen witch. Chris felt a blast of pride to be counted among them now.

He was beginning to feel like one of the club. And their approval was yet another layer of security.

Turning slowly, he tracked Shauni and her father as they passed by. Her parents had flown in from Colorado for the ceremony with plans to return in a couple of days. Chris wondered how much her parents really understood about their daughter, her magic, and her affinity for furred and feathered creatures.

As he faced toward the altar, his eyes again found Paige, and he couldn't seem to stop admiring the lovely slope of her shoulders, or the way the tips of her impossibly light hair feathered across her skin. He had an irresistible urge to lift those strands and kiss her...*just there.*

The preacher began to intone to those gathered in the pews, the somber words encouraging Chris to cleanse his fantasies and return to a more pure, more chaste state of mind.

Then Paige turned her head to whisper to Viv, her lashes fluttering above carved cheekbones and plump, pink lips. And his darkest fantasies were suddenly justified.

His attraction wasn't simply a virile man observing a gorgeous woman. He also wanted to look into her ocean blue eyes and have her assess him, to know his worth.

He admired so much about Paige, from her looks to her fighting skills. She was endowed with a steadfastness of character that was more unique than blue tourmaline.

Chris grinned, and knew he was done for. Even his bad analogies involved gemstones the exact color of her eyes.

His leg started jittering, proof that he couldn't wait until after the wedding, and for the reception that would follow at the yellow house. Claire had gone all out, and a band would be set up out back, on a stage with a view of the bay.

He had a strong inclination to dance with Paige, to see how she reacted to soft music and soft words. Because there had been so much hardness between them.

A tug on his shirt had Chris turning to meet the golden-brown eyes of Sylvie, Joseph's girlfriend and former Amara member. Her expression was full of sincerity as she looked at him, no anger and hate like he'd been told she'd once possessed.

Today she was as relaxed and happy as any of the other wedding attendees, with perhaps a hint of teasing in her stare. "Maybe you should turn your attention to the nuptials," she whispered. "And the *preacher*." She raised a brow. "Before you burst into flames."

Chris started to laugh outright but stifled it before he interrupted Shauni and Michael's special day. Now he knew how blunt Sylvie could be. And how transparent he was as well.

When it came to Paige.

As Michael began offering his promises to Shauni, as he swore to stand beside her for better or worse, Chris's mind began to wander down an unknown path.

Sure, he'd been to a couple of weddings. And yeah, he could recognize true love.

He'd just never imagined wanting it for himself.

~~~

Paige was twitchy. There was simply no better description for how this day was making her feel. All the well-wishers, jubilant smiles, and fancy party clothes, they were causing a brand new and not-so-welcome reassessment of her life's designs.

Worse, every time she heard someone tell Shauni and Michael how perfect they were for each other, she found herself glancing around for Chris. And what the freak was up with that?

So at first she'd started tugging at her dress, sure the costly design was at fault for her uneasiness. Then she'd moved away from the receiving line leading up to the blissful couple and closer to the open bar, provided by Nick. A beer or two would set her to rights, even if they were disguised in the delicate frosted glasses.

As she edged to the side of the patio, looking outward and letting the breeze from the water cool her down, she sensed a tall and formidable presence come up behind her. She didn't have to look to know who it was.

"How are you holding up?" Chris asked, a thread of playfulness in his voice that gave his question new meaning.

"Interesting way of putting that. It's a wedding. A happy occasion?" She kept her attention fixed on the green river water. "Why would I need to hold up?"

"You tell me." He joined her on the edge of the pavers, since she'd made it clear she wasn't going to look at him. "You seem nervous. Don't you like Michael?"

The sound in her throat was far from ladylike. "You know I do. Why ask stupid questions?"

"Then what is it?" Again, his tone betrayed a hidden meaning. An intended query Paige wanted to avoid.

"Just not used to this dress. I don't have reason to wear heels very often. The coven's needed a lot of training and sparring." She hoped that killed his curiosity and the leading line of questions.

"You seem pretty skittish to me."

She snorted.

"And from what I hear, there's only one thing in this whole world that makes Paige Reilley jumpy."

"Don't," she started, but then stopped, afraid warning him off the topic would only give credence to his assumption. But was it an assumption?

Or was the whole lovey-dovey day just too much for her to handle? Because seriously, a wedding? Right in the middle of her challenge, and a couple of days after her crazed bout of tongue-tangling with the same Captain Hottie standing next to her.

Since he'd come to stay at the island, they'd maintained a certain amount of physical distance. But that hadn't stopped the energy from crackling between them. As if their magnetism had been reversed, they floated near each other but never got close enough to actually touch.

Whirling to face him full on, she tilted her head and worked up her brightest, most flirtatious smile. "The only thing that makes me nervous is thinking the bar might run out of Corona."

"Not Corona Light?" he asked.

Paige raised a scornful eyebrow. "Do you not know me at all?"

"Why don't we find out?" He removed the glass she'd been holding and handed it to a waiter whose arrival was perfectly-timed. "Dance with me. We'll see just how in sync we are."

"Whoa." She extracted the hand he'd taken in his own. "I don't dance."

Chris got that cocky look on his face, the one she'd detested at first but now made her melt and shiver all at the same time. No. No way was she pressing up against his body and rubbing all around under the guise of "dancing." She might be reckless, but not foolish.

She'd learned her lesson on the top deck of the Ranger bar.

"So you're afraid," he challenged, lifting his head just enough to convey the dare.

Paige tried to reach around him for her beer. "Nice try, but that won't work on me."

But before her fingers reached the glass, Chris had a hand on her waist, holding her still as he advanced on her. The move forward was slight, but Paige would swear the air temperature shot up several degrees.

His voice was dangerously low, and so close the timbre caressed Paige's cheek. "So it's only me you're afraid of." His finger slid its way down to her hips, leaving a tempting trail of heat in its wake. "Why is that?"

Paige was trapped, both physically and verbally frozen in place. Why did it feel like he could see straight into her secret and hidden places, where she kept all her fears locked up tight? Chris seemed to be the only man in the world who'd been given access.

And at this point, Paige wasn't sure who'd handed him her key. The meddling force she knew as Fate?

Or had she somehow opened herself up willingly?

"I…" she stammered.

"One dance, Paige. What could it hurt?" He gradually repositioned them, merging with other couples who were taking advantage of the music on this sunny September day. "I know you see your trial as a sentence to fall in love. And that's exactly what it would be for you, sentencing to hard time."

She shook her head, wondering why they were revisiting this topic.

"But I think you're stronger than that." He pulled her closer, held her tighter. "You make your own decisions, and if you really want to, you can stay single for the rest of your life."

He stunned her then by leaning forward, cupping her cheek as he pressed a solid but gentle kiss to her lips. His forest eyes reached into her, sending shockwaves of heat through her system as he dared her to deny what was between them. "You can say no, and you can make it stick." His thumb was teasing her chin. "If you're sure that's what you want."

Paige eased back, a breath away from Chris. How could she say what she wanted with this whirlwind of sensation inside of her, threatening to either carry her to the clouds or bury her for good? "You said this wasn't what you came here for. That you weren't looking for me as anything other than another soldier, an ally against those who'd wronged us."

"And I wasn't." Chris twirled her, making her head even dizzier. "Believe me, Paige, in my wildest dreams, I couldn't have imagined how you would affect me."

He stopped dancing abruptly, but his arms held her when she might have missed a step. "But I'm not resistant to change," he said. "Not when it's like this, when I know how good it could be. You shouldn't resist either."

"That's easy for you to say. You haven't had everything

you've ever known ripped up and replanted. I can't identify with anything anymore. I don't know who I am, so how can I jump into this with you? You can't even be sure who you'd be getting."

"Oh, I'm sure, princess." His smile, his entire body lightened up suddenly, as if he'd already gotten the answer he wanted. "Don't forget, I know you like nobody else does. My first memories of you are sweet and carefree. Laughter, running wild, but both of us knowing we were safe."

He released her and stepped away, leaving Paige more bereft than she had felt since she'd been a little girl, missing her mother. And her father. The comparison terrified her.

"We can have that freedom again, Paige." He took a step backward. "Maybe we were always meant to."

Easing away, Chris blended into the increasing crowd on the patio, and Paige found her hand reaching out to bring him back. So she snatched the traitorous limb to her chest.

Damn him. How much could one man mess with her head? She felt as if her self-image was under attack, or at least the stubborn side that had sworn to live alone. The hardness in her that kept telling her what a pitfall love could be.

And yet, another piece of her—the newer, burgeoning part of herself—had great faith in Chris, and knew he would never cause her harm. So if her trust in him was founded, was Paige actually under attack?

Or was Chris carrying out a rescue mission?

"No, no, no." She veered sharply to her right, back toward the bar. She wasn't a lush, but screw it. Today was a celebration and she wanted to quell her chaotic mind.

She'd just gotten her hands on a glass when Kylie bopped up next to her. "I saw you dancing with Chris," she cooed, waving away the bartender when he asked if she'd like a drink.

Together, Paige and the youngest of the coven made their

way through the outside gathering area and around to the side of the house. There they could take shelter under live oaks and swaying Spanish moss, because even in the fall Savannah sunshine was no joke.

"I'm surprised by you, Kylie." Paige sniffed.

"What? I've kept my mouth shut the whole time since Chris got here. Well, almost."

"That's what surprised me." Paige smirked when Kylie rolled her eyes and feigned insult.

"Well, today is symbolic, and I thought it was time someone finally spoke up. We've all been walking on eggshells being very careful not to mention the chance of romance between you and Chris."

Paige gave a her a look of disbelief. "You mean other than the bird seed mob assault?"

"Well, there was that. But we all just want you to be happy and to fulfill your role in the prophecy."

"I'm doing my part," Paige said, a roll of warning in her undertone.

"Yes, you've been formidable." Kylie patted her arm. "As usual. But I'm talking about the romance part, and you know it. Don't growl at me," she said when Paige started doing just that.

Unabashed, Kylie tossed long golden curls over her shoulder. "You and Chris have been knocking around pretending you aren't attracted to each other, and I've finally identified a certain similarity between you guys and me and Quinn."

"*Psht*. Hardly. You and Quinn were at each other for more than for a year. Talk about growling. Even Chris and I don't argue like that."

"No." Kylie gave her a flat, don't-BS-me stare. "You're practically poster children for Emily Post, and yes," she raised a finger to stop the retort Paige was forming, "I am old enough to know who that is." Then she leaned in in a conspiratorial way. "But the only people you're fooling are yourselves."

Paige swallowed, her throat suddenly dry despite the libation in her hand. "Apparently, Chris has decided he wants to make love not war."

Kylie's face brightened. "Really? That's awesome!" She quieted herself and glanced around to see if she'd drawn attention. "Then why do you look so…pouty?" She reared back. "I've never seen this look on you before. That could be a good sign."

"Sign of what?" Paige was the one offended now. *Pouty?*

"Of change. Only you can accept your destiny. All of it. Challenge, battles, mystery…and Chris."

"Gee, look who's a wise old mage," Paige teased, though truth be told, the younger woman was actually making her feel somewhat ashamed. As if she'd been throwing a silent tantrum that everyone else had known about all along.

But if one thing held true for each of the witches and their trials, it was that they'd each experienced a change of heart over the course of their challenge.

And what was the one thing Paige had always refused?

No. She wouldn't dwell on it. Not right now.

She studied the back yard of the home, and from her vantage point she could only see a section of the patio. But she had a clear view of Shauni and Michael, having their first dance together as husband and wife.

As if hearing her sister's internal argument, Shauni looked over Michael's shoulder to Paige. She offered the most content, most reassuring smile, and gave a slight nod.

Then she returned her gaze to Michael, looking up at him as if he were heaven itself.

Something inside Paige set off in a blazing sizzle, working its way through her with the brightness of a holiday sparkler. *I do want that. A true partner in life, and in love.*

All of Paige's friends had ended up happy, even though they had fought destiny just as fiercely as she was. So after seven successful trials and deliriously happy-ever-afters, why was she still stonewalling Chris?

Didn't she owe him a chance? Didn't she owe herself a chance? She sipped her beer, but more placidly now.

Maybe that sweet little girl she'd once been had been a better judge of character. Perhaps she'd had an open heart and willingness borne of charity.

If Paige wasn't certain she could believe in herself, and her faith in Chris was still too new to be sure of, then perhaps she should look further back, and deeper inside. Back to a time when innocence ruled over fear and doubt, instead of the other way around.

Maybe she should follow that little girl's lead.

23

Paige made it through the rest of the reception without further discussion of anything other than how nice the weather was and how beautiful Shauni looked, two things she thoroughly agreed with. The music and laughter continued to flow, and before she knew it Shauni was up on the stage in front of the band.

Taking note of the convergence of females, Paige immediately went still, like a deer hoping to blend with the environment. Then she slowly shrunk backward, losing herself in the crowd. It was time to toss the bouquet.

"Oh, no, you don't," Viv said, taking one of Paige's arms while Claudia swooped in on the other.

"You two don't really think you can force me to go anywhere, do you?" Paige asked with just enough haughtiness to make Claudia grit her teeth. "Maybe not the two of us alone." The history-professor with a penchant for new clothes tossed her head to suggest Paige look behind her.

She did, and found Kylie, Willyn, Lucia, Hayden, and even the usually above-all-that Anna standing behind her with mulish expressions. "You don't want to make a scene on Shauni's wedding day, now do you?" Anna asked, all guileless innocence.

Paige shot her what was known around these parts as the stink-eye. "You know I could take you all, so you're playing dirty." She shook off her would be escorts and lifted her head. "What happened to all of you staying out of my love life, or lack of it?"

"We got tired of waiting," Hayden said.

Willyn's laugh was a mischievous tinkle. "And Kylie talked us into it."

"Oh, for—" Viv gave Paige a light push forward. "It's just a bunch of flowers. You like flowers. And we'll all be there with you."

Paige felt a smile trying to creep out. "Yeah. You guys usually are."

Viv's face softened as she looked at her friend. "Aw."

"Like toe fungus," Paige added, only to feel a swift telekinetic kick in her butt, reminding her not to goad her sister witches. They all had their special talents.

"Fine, I'm going. But if you guys do anything funny or try to cheat the system, I will cry foul, no matter who sees."

"Cheat the system." Kylie snickered. "Look who's become melodramatic in her old age."

"Falling in love will do that to you," Anna said.

Paige choked on air, but she didn't look back. The words from Anna were too close to a clairvoyant confirmation than Paige cared to admit. And that's probably why the coven leader had put it out there. Front and center.

Where Paige couldn't step around it but had to face it head on.

Her feelings for Chris were complicated. They shared a lot of history for two people who'd only become reacquainted a short time ago. Just a handful of weeks. Even though the other women and the trials had left a pretty indelible pattern behind, Paige couldn't believe she—of all people—could start to care for someone that quickly.

I mean, we've barely even looked at each other that way. We only kissed because of raw emotional states the first time and alcohol the second. That wasn't exactly proof of soulmateship. And was that even a word?

Her wandering thoughts came to a cold stop when Shauni spoke to the assembled women. Paige looked around, recognizing most of the girls, a few from Michael's office and Nick's bar, a couple of other places in town where Shauni and Michael knew people.

They were all eager-eyed and tittering, ready for the "toss." Paige shook her head and frowned, wondering how she'd been pushed into this. She felt like a Rottweiler amongst a bunch of toy poodles begging for rhinestone collars.

One of these things is not like the others. She kicked up her mouth in a grin despite herself and turned to watch Shauni have her fun.

The next thing she saw was her friend's arm rearing back over her shoulder, and then the elegant bouquet of white roses and baby's breath—with a lovely green fern added per Paige's recommendation—began its arc through the air.

Paige had the space of a breath to frown, sensing the flight path was heading her way, and before she knew to duck and cover, the "ladies" in her closest proximity began jostling around her, pushing and shoving as if battling for a Super Bowl ring instead of a bunch of posies.

She held out her elbows to deter the more aggressive girls, but when squeals rose to a crescendo, she couldn't help her reaction. She looked up.

To see Shauni's roses falling straight toward her.

All the while, she'd mentally been making fun of these women, laughing at their bid for what was nothing but an old wives' tale. But as the flowers descended, Paige felt her heart clutch with anticipation, her breath hitch with excitement.

Her arms had been tight against her torso, her body

language a small rebellion. But now they rose up and formed a cradle, just in time to catch the symbol of impending marriage.

And hell, before she could help herself, Paige smiled.

But she didn't hold the flowers up and dance around in glee. One woman reached over as if the prize might bobble from Paige's grasp. But one look from the owner of said bouquet, and the almost-thief hurriedly retracted her claws.

Soon the only women surrounding Paige were those of her coven, and even Shauni stepped down to join them. As always, when they were all together, the air buzzed and hummed in response to their closeness. Their unity.

Paige shrugged at Shauni when that one said, "Ahem," with a pointed stare at the bouquet.

"You did that on purpose," Paige told her.

"I was never good at sports," Shauni argued. "Can't hit the side of a mountain with a tomato."

"Whatever," Paige said, borrowing a phrase from Kylie.

After much ribbing and teasing, she found herself alone again, when the band struck up another slow song and each of the witches paired up with her man.

Anna was dancing with Joe, one of the men who'd stepped in as father figure after Anna and Quinn's parents had died in an accident. The other was currently romancing his wife, and Paige had to hand it to Mr. Attinger. The old guy had some smooth moves.

When Chris sidled up to her, her lips curved into an amused bow of their own accord. She had a feeling she knew what he was going to say.

He opened with, "Nice catch."

Paige laughed and slid her eyes to peruse the fine figure he cut in the slacks and white shirt. The sleeves were now rolled up, revealing toned forearms.

She had a thing for forearms.

To avert her attention, she fingered a sprig of baby's breath in the bouquet. Then she caught Chris watching. "What?" she asked with a touch of sarcasm. "It's not like I jumped up and reached for the thing."

"No." He laughed. "Never you, Paige." His eyes turned her way and her stomach dropped. "But you did open your arms."

~~~

Tyr watched the man ambling down the street toward him and shook his head in disgust. He shouldn't even be here, doing the dirty work best assigned to grunts, but Ronja was in a bad place these days, a very bad place, more distraught than he'd ever seen her.

And all thanks to that coward who now possessed a remnant of her brother's soul. Ian Keller, a prim and fussy excuse for a man with his expensive suits and cultured speech patterns.

He was an idiot, and hardly up to the standards that any blood-relative of Ronja's should fulfill. Ian's refusal to accept the truth along with his place by his sister's side had thrown the once semi-controlled den of the Amara into utter chaos.

So now, apparently, it was up to Tyr to help set things straight.

That's why he was here, downtown, during the late hours when only saviors and scum were moving about. He'd come to ensure Ronja's orders were obeyed to the fullest. To make sure the message was delivered loud and clear…and that it was both ugly and memorable.

The man shuffled closer.

How could this nobody with a hardly-noticeable limp make a powerful witch like Ronja so miserable? Who did the little pig think he was? With his odd fisherman's hat and loose-fitting khakis.

Tyr burned from the insult. This man was hardly worthy of Ronja's attention.

But her brother... Tyr ground his teeth. The spineless Vanir he'd heard so much about—*for centuries*—he was the true culprit, for hiring this human to check into Ronja's activities.

But now his offensiveness would be repaid in kind. No, not in kind. The indignity to this man would be tenfold.

Tyr notched his head to Scarlett, telling her to ready her magic.

The man wanted to know what they were all about? Fair enough. He would soon comprehend more than he'd ever imagined or desired.

Now that he was closer to them, the man's height was apparent. Despite the limp, he would be a real adversary, for anyone other than the Amara.

With a quick jerk of his eyes, he assessed Tyr and Scarlett's placement on either side of the walk, but his canniness and observation skills weren't going to save him. Not tonight.

Tyr had insisted the red witch come along, to put their quarry out quick and quietly. Scarlett did so now, with a blow of her ruby-hued dust directed at the man's face. Don Jacobson, the nosy P.I., collapsed to the sidewalk without so much as a grunt.

Tyr then snapped a finger at Ross, Ronja's pet shifter. The man had little worth mentioning beyond muscle and shifting skills, so tonight he would serve as henchman. He hauled the unconscious Jacobson over his shoulder and swiftly deposited his body in the van parked at the curb.

Tyr took the wheel, and Scarlett rode shotgun.

Thirty minutes later, they were in one of the city's less-frequented parks. The surrounding neighborhoods couldn't be counted on for after-dark safety, so few pedestrians would be wandering by this time of night.

Tyr nudged the man with his leather-covered foot. He still dressed in the old ways as often as possible, so his chest was bare and his pants a soft suede, reminiscent of buckskin.

As for the pig lying unconscious at his feet, Tyr planned to revive another ancient custom. After all, he wanted this man's death to draw attention, to serve as a calling card for any and all who had taken a position, any position, that opposed Ronja.

"Wake up," Tyr said sharply, with no patience at all for the investigator. He saw when the man roused enough to comprehend his position. He took note when the pig realized his dangerous situation. And he was expecting the move when the man rolled and attempted to make his feet in a sprint for safety.

Tyr grabbed the back of his neckline and yanked, choking the P.I. and halting his escape in one swift motion. "Hold him up," he directed Ross, tossing the dazed man in the shifter's direction.

Ross gave Tyr a contemptuous glare, but was quickly brought to heel when Tyr stared him down in return.

No more would he allow these Amara underlings to question his place among the pack.

Tyr turned to Scarlett and felt a trill of satisfaction at the shadow of fear in her eyes as well. "Scarlett," he asked, "do you have the knife?"

She presented a long slim blade from the satchel slung across her body, and then the conceited woman actually took a tentative step…back.

Good. Even she should quiver.

For what Tyr was about to sentence upon this human was one of life's more grotesque punishments. Oh, whom was he kidding? It was torture, plain and simply...torture.

Many years had passed since Tyr had last exacted this type of revenge, but he still remembered the proper placement of the metal tip. Don eyeballed the knife, opening his mouth to scream when Tyr moved closer, but Scarlett wisely whispered another sparkle of red toward his face.

He promptly became mute, but otherwise was still fully functional.

Meaning he was still awake and would feel everything. But that was the meaning of this entire exercise. Those who discovered the P.I. would quail at the scene. They would have no doubt of what the man had suffered.

A sharp jab in the right spot and Tyr made his incision. Deep in his throat, the man made a guttural moan.

But the one long mewl was nothing compared to the noises he tried to push out when Tyr threaded two fingers into the incision. The P.I.'s body thrashed as those fingers twirled and searched.

Finally, Tyr latched onto what he wanted. He slowly looped a bit of the man's intestines around his fingers and, once secure...he pulled.

The man fainted then, causing Tyr to curse softly. "Wake him," he uttered. Scarlett and Ross worked together, finally forcing their victim from his blessed slumber only to throw him back into a nightmare.

Tyr gradually extracted more of the viscera, wet, rosy, and shiny in the park's lamplight. "The spike?" Tyr asked.

"Right here." Ross stepped up and readied a hammer and nail near the tree trunk they'd chosen for this purpose.

Holding the length of guts in his hand tightly, Tyr pressed it against the bark and told Ross, "Now."

The shifter drove the nail through the internal organ and into the wood, fastening the man's entrails securely.

"Ohh." Scarlett let the sound escape, revealing her weakness of stomach, a surprising revelation from such a wicked witch.

Tyr laughed, a low rumble of fury, satisfaction, and greed that threatened to overflow into physical rage. But he contained it. He continued his mission.

Pain, whether his or another's, always set him off. The most sublime of all experiences, and quite the efficient tool. Only pain could deliver punishment and also retrieve answers. Pain accompanied birth and death in equal measure. And pain created strength, invulnerability.

Essentially, for Tyr, pain—was life.

He couldn't understand anyone's aversion to sweet torment, especially when it was as succulent as the agony being created tonight. He'd truly missed this practice, this form of retribution.

"Now walk." Tyr issued the harsh order and crossed his arms over his bronze chest.

Glassy-eyed, the man stared back at him. "*Heelp meee.*"

"Walk!" Tyr thundered, and the investigator flinched.

Ross took one of the P.I.'s arms and gave a tug, showing him what he was supposed to do. After a few steps, the shifter let go and stood back to watch with that crazy light in his pool-blue eyes. Tyr had always known the dog was insane.

"Walk. Walk." The shifter clapped like a kid at recess.

Scarlett put a hand to her stomach.

And Tyr roared his amusement.

When the man completed a full circumference, Tyr jerked his head, making it clear that Don the P.I. was supposed to take another turn.

"Why?" the man asked, his face fallen into the flatness that preceded unconsciousness.

"Walk," was all Tyr said.

The man looked down at the opening in his abdomen,

the line of his intestines that was still fixed to the tree trunk, now partially wrapped around the wooden base. His insides trailed along the path he had walked. "I'm dying," he pleaded one last time.

Tyr lowered his head and glowered. "That," he ground out, "is the point."

24

Paige closed her bedroom door and leaned against the wooden panel. She was still wearing her dress from the wedding and reception, still in the damnable high heels and, she mused, looking down to her hand, still holding the bouquet. Gently, not clutching or crushing, but with a soft grip, she kept the flowers close.

Part of her viewed the flowers as a representation of Shauni's happiness, so for that reason alone she would treat the arrangement kindly. Another, more surprising piece of her psyche, now viewed the bouquet as another type of symbol.

Wives' tale or not, Paige had caught a wedding bouquet, and she'd be a fool to pretend the silly bunch of flowers hadn't awakened a long-lost sense of hope. The pastel-colored fantasy that most young girls occasionally lost themselves in.

Yes, that even she had dreamed about once upon a time. Paige had imagined hearts and flowers for herself in her early teens, but even then she'd been afraid underneath. She'd already begun to connect her father's abandonment to every other person in the world who might actually start to mean something to her, to become important to her.

As Chris had.

He gave every indication that he wanted to be in her life and that he wasn't leaving any time soon. He'd made no professional commitments yet, no promises outside of the coven's war and Paige's trial.

With a rare seriousness in his gaze, he'd pulled her yet again into another slow dance at the reception. Then he'd told her he'd passed on the job in Arizona, assuring her he wasn't making any huge changes in locale. Not any time soon.

And Paige had flooded with relief. He wasn't leaving.

She lifted the flowers and grinned into the petals as she smelled their rosy scent. Chris had used each dance with her as a segue into another of his arguments, explaining in no uncertain terms that he didn't regret the kisses they'd shared, and that he was openly interested in Paige the woman.

Not the destined avenger.

The man had done a complete turnaround, and since he'd changed his mind, for whatever mystical reason, he was openly pursuing her. Chris was forthright in most things, and his interest in her was no exception.

And the rusty heart inside her chest was clunking in response, scraping its way back to life. She'd considered the organ long dead and far past revitalization.

But a swift kick and soft touch from Chris had started the engines running.

She put a hand over the space in her chest. Not simply running…she was practically purring.

So now—she pondered as she walked slowly to her dresser to set the bouquet on top—what was she going to do about her altered mental status? Her drastically changed feelings where Chris was concerned?

She'd laid the flowers next to her picture of Meg and Troy, and she gazed at her aunt and uncle a moment, before shifting to study the smaller photo tucked into the bottom corner of the frame. The one of herself, her mother, and her father, all three smiling as if holding the secret to life itself.

As she had a million times before, Paige wondered what her mother would advise. If they could have a heart-to-heart, as mothers and daughters did, what would this pretty young woman say to her conflicted daughter? What would the gentle female tell the hardened soldier?

A soft rub across her ankles, and Paige looked down to the wizened eyes of her tough little tabby cat. The only other being Paige had allowed herself to care for aside from her aunt, uncle, and the coven.

She adored Tiger Lily, and would see the cat have nothing but a soft bed, full belly, and loving hands to contend with.

And there, she realized with a smile, was her answer.

Her mother would tell her what mothers told their children, what any good parent desired for the ones they'd brought into the world. Paige stared at the photo, looked hard into the eyes so like her own.

And she would swear she could almost hear the words.

Be happy.

With a kick in her stomach that was pure hope, Paige turned to her bed, tossed off her shoes, and began unzipping her dress. The time was late, but not that late.

Not too late for Paige…or her rusty heart.

Once divested of clothing, she hurried into the bathroom and turned on the tub faucet. Rarely did she luxuriate in bubble baths like her friends did, but tonight was a special occasion. And she wasn't referring to the wedding.

Shauni and Michael were curled up at the Mansion on Forsythe downtown, reveling in their newly married status and the love that made them whole. Shauni, Paige recalled, had been wary of her trial but slightly more willing to follow her heart, and the glowing joy she'd radiated today was all the encouragement Paige needed to take a leap of faith for herself.

She wanted to be happy. She needed to trust.

So what was she waiting for?

Yes, she was somewhat afraid, but she'd never been this shaky and excited over any man before. This was Chris she was about to seduce, and the fact that her stomach dropped like a soldier fast-roping from a helicopter told her exactly what he meant to her.

The only man who could make Paige Reilley nervous.

The stream of bubble bath she poured in was probably more than she needed, and the candles that had never been lit were likely an unnecessary touch. But she was preparing herself for what could be a true turning point in her life, and all the little things suddenly seemed to matter.

All the gooey-girlie stuff she'd endlessly teased her friends about were not so trivial anymore.

So it was with a serious face that she scoured her two whole bottles of lotion that she owned. She didn't have perfume or powders, so Lucia's birthday gift of Purple Passion "skin silk" would have to do. But after the bath.

The hot water felt wonderful, and the bubbles a rare and unexpected treat, but Paige was concerned about shriveling her fingers and toes, so she cut the soak to under five minutes. She spent most of the time re-shaving the spots she'd addressed in the shower this morning, before the wedding.

Afterwards, while still moist, she smoothed on the lotion. Her skin did transform to fragrant silk, and she reveled in the change. She was unleashing the femininity she'd always kept inside, but tonight the softness didn't make her feel weak.

Tonight, it was her greatest power.

She had a moment of indecision when it came to what to wear. Unfortunately, she didn't have any lingerie, and wasn't about to go knocking on doors to borrow from her sisters.

Whatever came of tonight was for her and Chris alone. She

wanted it to be private, and special.

With a glance to her closet, she remembered her red silk robe. Perfect, she told herself with a wicked grin. Not only was the robe the color of lust, with a hemline that hit her mid-thigh, but the back was embroidered with a wealth of bright threads.

The picture was of a bold and often dangerous creature. A dragon.

She pulled it from her closet and dropped the towel she still wore. Now all she had to do was take a deep breath, find the courage to knock on his door, and see if he took her inside.

See if he decided to slay her.

On her newly pampered bare feet, Paige made quick work of traversing the corridor from her room to the guest room where Chris was sleeping. The light shining from beneath the door told her he wasn't sleeping at all.

So without giving herself time to reconsider, Paige knocked on his door, not timidly but assuredly, pretending she didn't have what felt like a flock of birds swooping around in her belly.

The door jerked open to reveal a half-dressed Chris.

And whoa, that tattoo was as fierce and sexy as she'd imagined.

His gaze tracked up and down Paige's scantily clad body, but finally he clapped those bottomless green eyes on hers. "You're here."

Fingering the silky belt tied at her waist, she focused on controlling her breathing. "I'm here." She clenched the material, tamping down on nerves that clattered and made her fingers shake. "Um…do you want me to *stay* here?"

The uncertainty in his features switched to dark and greedy passion. "Absolutely." But despite his I'm-about-to-devour-you expression, he didn't crush her to his chest, pinning her body to his, and neither did he shove her against the wall to ravage her mouth.

Instead, he took her hand, encompassing her fingers like warm water, and slowly guided her inside.

Paige wouldn't have minded the other, though. She'd had experiences with hard and fast. She wasn't, however, accustomed to the careful way that Chris was handling her.

Those unruly nerves of hers began to quake.

Paige had felt so in control, so hear-me-roar sexy when she'd left her room, but as Chris continued to study her, she began to feel more like prey. And he the lion about to feast.

His hand slid up to her arm, open palm curving to lightly stroke the underside of her wrist. Then he continued the climb, up and over sensitive skin, sending shivers to every part of Paige's body.

Her eye lit on the tattoo again, a pattern she couldn't identify, possibly tribal, but sporting sharp ends with razor-point barbs on the tips. The ink gave off an absolutely lethal vibe.

Was this the sweet, charming Chris who flirted with Mrs. Attinger? Or the Ranger who could shut down emotions and dive headfirst into the most perilous mission?

Or had she come face to face with the man beneath all those facades? The man of great power, who held his strength in check…but only because he chose to.

"I wouldn't have told you this before, in any other situation," he said, having made his way to her shoulder with his roaming touch. Then both of his hands converged in the center of her robe, where the material split, held in place only by the single belt.

Paige wore nothing underneath, and the feather-soft touch of his fingertips on the hollow between her breasts made her pull in a breath, hold it, and exhale with a slight lift of her chin. Invitation for him to touch all he liked.

"What," she whispered, "were you going to say?"

"Hmm? Oh." His half-grin was feral. "That your legs are amazing, so long and toned." He raked his spread fingers up the side of her thigh, strength and tenderness combining in a way that had her leaning into him for support. "So, thank you."

Now she was the one losing track of her thoughts. "For... for what?"

He leaned down to brush his mouth over hers. His breath heated her lips when he said, "For wearing this robe."

Paige felt herself go limp when his arm snaked around her waist to hold her up for the ravishment she'd expected at the door. The few minutes of staring at each other had been a potent aphrodisiac. And now they simply consumed each other.

Chris gripped both hands in her hair. "I love your hair," he growled.

"Even short?"

"It's practical, just teasing a man to try and grab onto it." He pulled lightly, making his point. Then he lowered his head toward hers. "Incredibly sexy, this angel's hair."

Again he overwhelmed her, stroking and exciting her with his tongue. And she let him.

The angel comparison didn't bother her, since those creatures were often quite fierce in stories. Unlike the more gentle princesses, who always needed a knight to ride in and save them.

Chris didn't mind her sharper, meaner side. In fact, he seemed to love it.

And she loved him for accepting her, bad attitude and all.

Once he finished taking her mouth with his—with

exquisite thoroughness—Chris eased to the side, leaving her in want of his taste. She licked her lips to experience the dark, hot, and spicy bit of himself he'd left behind.

But when he went lower to brand her neck with his tongue—in that sensitive hollow just below her jawline—a knot of heat began to twist and tighten inside of her. Growing heavy with need, she hiked up one of her legs, capturing Chris as surely as he had her trapped with his arms.

She hazarded a peek at his shoulder, the one with the tattoo, and was almost driven over the edge. His muscles were so carved, so cut, and they flexed and danced with the black ink markings.

This man was pure power, but she'd also been introduced to his sweeter side. Knowing he could offer so much of each only made him that much more desirable.

Taking advantage of her new position, Chris pressed his erection against her heat, lifting her upward so she was forced to hold onto him. The pressure he applied was so deep, so delicious, that her head rushed as lust ran rampant.

"I can't stand," she moaned, overcome by the dual pleasures on her throat and between her thighs.

And finally she got a real taste of his strength and speed. With one lightning-fast move Chris had her beneath him on the bed.

His hands were on her wrists, shackling them in place above her head. The tops of his thighs were against the bottom of hers, nudging her legs up and apart, just wide enough for him to tease and tempt with the occasional thrust against her core.

"Now you're just playing with me." But Paige's breath hitched as she spoke, because she was enjoying every stroke, caress, or hard drive he delivered.

Chris was a drug in her system, chasing out every other

sensation and numbing her with ecstasy. Reaching up, Paige grabbed a hank of his dark blonde hair and, employing a bit of her own muscle, she yanked his mouth back to hers, swirling her hips in a tease.

It must have worked, because his body went rigid. He groaned into her mouth. And all of a sudden, things got serious.

Gone was the thread of playfulness, replaced by a raging surge of pure, raw need. His fingers roved over her, hot and quick, driving her upward and into blinding ecstasy. But she took his fierce touch, she yearned for it.

Chris was still wearing his dress pants from the wedding, and Paige was barely covered by the robe. Somewhere along the way, her breasts had become exposed, so had her legs and hips, leaving only the still-tied bow of the belt around her waist.

She reached to finish untying it, but Chris stopped her with a tight grip. "No," he rasped. "Leave it. My pretty and ferocious Paige, all tied up for me in a red bow."

A sassy comeback would have leapt to her tongue, but while Chris's one hand had lifted hers above her head again, his other moved down to unbutton his pants.

Paige locked her gaze on his, and she knew this was the most erotic moment of her life. Staring into those jungle-green eyes, as he positioned himself and prepared to take her. The velvet heat of him pressing into her was too much, and before he'd fully breached her, Paige felt herself spiraling into that aching, increasing pressure that preceded release.

And when Chris began to move inside of her, when he rasped her name in her ear and kissed her mouth, the world went white-hot around them both. And all she knew was him.

25

Chris stared at the ceiling and dragged in ragged breaths, in awe of the woman lying beside him. He'd known Paige was special, and had always had a soft spot just for her, but... *man*. Even he hadn't expected this perfect storm of strong and sexy.

One long leg was lying across his ankle, and as he recovered, he took a long appreciative walk up the limb with his eyes. Leanly muscled, but softly feminine, he could spend a day on her legs alone.

Instinct made him reach for her hand, but listening to her own quick respirations, he chose to forego the sentimentality for now. But the affection would come later. He'd make sure of it.

That didn't stop him from trailing a finger up the creamy thigh, though.

With a sound of contentment, she stretched and released a long sigh. "Give me five minutes," she teased, "then it's my turn to take the reins."

Chris chuckled. "Make it four."

The mattress gave beside him as Paige sat up, righted her robe again. Then he felt her go still. "What's that?" she asked.

Chris lifted his head to glance around. "What?" He didn't know what she meant, but her demeanor was calm, and no alarm registered on her gorgeous face. So he assumed there was no emergency.

She eased off the bed to stand, and then pointed to a chest of drawers across the room. "That," she said with more emphasis.

He followed the line of her finger to the small container sitting atop the bureau. The plastic pot still had the greenhouse label on the side, and he clenched his jaw. Oh well. So much for avoiding sentiment.

He'd put off dealing with the plant, because of the very fear he was feeling now. How would she react? Would she find him too forward? Too romantic? Or would she—as he'd originally imagined—find the gesture a token of friendship and trust?

He was about to find out, because now she'd seen it. No sense trying to dodge.

Sitting up beneath the blue sheet, Chris propped his elbows on his knees. "That's for you." He marveled at the myriad expressions she rolled through in under three seconds. Surprise, joy, intrigue, and finally, perplexity.

"You got me a plant?"

"Yeah." Rolling out of bed, without a speck of modesty for his naked form, Chris crossed the bedroom to retrieve the pot with a small green tip emerging from the soil. "Anna told me how much you enjoy plants, so I picked this up about a week ago. There just never seemed to be a good time to give it to you."

Paige had come up behind him, so he turned and held out the small bulb, recently forced and beginning to show itself. "I was thinking about you and happened to pass a greenhouse. This will have pale blue flowers when it blooms. It's a hybrid made by the man who runs the place where I bought it."

When Paige remained quiet, he flipped the information

card hanging down the side. "The color in the picture is what drew me. Then he told me he'd named it the Fighting Iris." His grin popped out at the reminder. "That was the clincher, and I knew you had to have it."

He'd given his spiel, but Paige zeroed in on only one specific. Her eyes found his. "You were thinking about me?"

Gone was the lopsided smile as Chris grew somber. "It seems I'm always thinking about you." Why wouldn't she just take the damn thing?

He continued to extend his gift, but the longer she stood there staring, the more uneasy he became. Here he was, a well-trained soldier and possessed of supernatural abilities. He'd spent his youth running from an unknown enemy only to face down even more ruthless foes during his many deployments.

But the hand that had easily held an M-4, had gotten up close and personal with the business edge of his Benchmade blade, was now feeling weak and numb. Even worse, his palm was sweating.

Every fear or uncertainty he'd ever known swiftly coalesced into this one pivotal moment. This one crucial gesture.

As he stood before Paige, the woman he'd fallen for, and offered his heart in the guise of a plant.

He almost jolted when she reached out to grab the small pot, and then cradled it to her chest. Her lips turned up and her eyes sparkled. All of his doubts were driven away.

"No one's ever given me a flower before." She gazed lovingly at the half-buried bulb and its tiny green tip. "I mean. Not like this."

Then her grin grew lascivious. "And definitely not while they were standing in the buff."

With his confidence firmly back in place, Chris spread his arms. "I strive to be unique."

Shaking her head, Paige went to the far side of the bed and set the plant on the night table. "Here it will get some of the morning sun."

"I guess I should have given it to you a while ago. It's been neglected."

"Not neglected." Her turquoise eyes found his. "Just forgotten for a while. But it's still alive. It's tough. It will grow."

Chris had the sense she was alluding to more than the young plant, but he didn't ask her, didn't press.

Turning her head to give him her profile, she whispered. "I don't blame you for not giving it to me sooner. I know I can be…"

"Difficult? Stubborn? Suspicious?" He held out a finger. "Hold on, I've got a thesaurus around here somewhere."

"Smartass." Her tone was playful, but with another look to the small bit of greenery, she sighed. "I'm still not sure what to do with you. You keep surprising me."

Chris made his way over to Paige, stood close behind her, and eyed the fierce dragon on the back of her robe. Then he stroked her soft hair. "Take your time, Paige." He ran a finger down her nape, enjoyed the shiver his touch caused. "And when you figure it out," a kiss on the back of her neck, "I'll be here."

She turned around and embraced him, holding him in place as she rested her head on his chest.

With his hand still on her collar, Chris grasped the robe and pulled. As the red silk slipped down, he let his hand follow its path. Admiring the lean, subtle curves of her body, he memorized her landscape and reveled in the feel of steel beneath satin.

She gasped and rolled her head to his shoulder, losing herself in his gentle exploration.

Turning her slightly in his arms, he studied the length of

her back, the lines of her shoulders. Everything about her was shapely, sculpted. Pure artwork.

His finger trailed down her spine, and he thrilled when she released a moan. Now both of his hands were back around front, working on her belt.

But Paige beat him to it, slipping free of the slick material. Mischievous eyes lifted to his as the red silk pooled at her feet. Two hands flat against his abs, she pushed him back until his legs hit the mattress.

Another little shove and down he went.

Paige climbed on top of him. A picture of beauty as moonlight cascaded across her skin. She was an enchantress, an angel of the night. And Chris would swear his heart stopped for a moment.

"This is the part where I take over." She lifted her hips, and slowly lowered herself, taking him deep inside. Her warmth and softness overrode any other thoughts in his head, and all he could do was relinquish control.

As Paige, his angel-warrior, began to ride, the powerful Ranger, the fated guardian, simply gripped his woman, and held on.

~~~

On the mainland, another man woke in the middle of the night. He was sweaty, and breathless, but he wasn't having any fun.

Far from it.

Ian swiped frantic hands at his skin, bared to the waist, since he slept in briefs. In the nightmare, he'd been burning, his body engulfed by flames. Yet despite the fiery agony, he'd been searching the angry crowd around him. Looking for her.

As the angry mob chanted for his death, he'd scanned their twisted, savage faces. He'd been searching for his sister. For Ronja.

Desperate questions had reeled through his mind as he'd suffered. Where was she? Had she escaped? Had those marauding zealots found her too?

Clutching a hand to his side, Ian remembered the piercing pain of the wound beneath his ribs, where the sword wielded by a huge hairy man had been shoved into him. The damaging blow had been the one to bring him down, hampering the use of his own weapon. And his magic.

And as soon as his blade had lowered, his blast of power faltering as well, the horde had taken him over. They'd dragged him to a crudely carved wooden stake, stuck in the ground with rocks at the base for support.

Another huge stone had struck the side of his head when he saw their intent and began to struggle. Once he'd been subdued, the men swiftly tied his hands behind him, around the wooden pole.

They'd doused him in sheep's fat. They'd thrown a torch.

"No!" Ian sat up and shouted to his empty bedroom, in the dead of night, and still in Savannah.

He was no longer living in that bitter day, on the rocky, barren mountain.

"No," he said again, needing to hear himself speak, to feel his own voice instead of the stranger's that had roared from his throat only moments ago. When his poor, punctured body had burned like flint.

The images wouldn't stop pounding at him, and he felt an undeniable urge to declare his resistance, his denial of this mental impersonation. "I am Ian Keller. I don't know Vanir. I am not him."

He crushed a hand to his face and let loose a deep, raking

sigh. "Not anymore." He could no longer hide from the possibility that he'd lived another life before this one. The emotions that had invaded his mind, and his heart, had been too real, too familiar.

With a flip of the sheet to uncover himself, he sprang from the bed and shouted. "But if I was ever this man, I promise you one thing!"

Who the hell was he talking to? Why did he sense a presence? Eyes, unholy eyes, watching him. "I will fight as hard as he did, until the end! To protect my life." He rammed a fist against his chest. "Mine!"

Dizziness swamped him then, accompanied by a cool flowing sensation, like a winter storm inside his home. He shook his head, determined to drive out what had to be a trick of the mind.

But the light-headedness, the frigid cold, they persisted. "Get out of my house," he ordered, his jaw clenched in equal parts fear and fury.

Someone was here with him. No, some *thing*. Had that bitch sent some mystical being to harass him? A spirit or demon? Or was it her, using magic? Did Ronja think these tactics would actually work and bring him around to her side?

If so, she didn't know him very well.

And judging by what he'd sensed of Vanir, the honorable impression he'd felt in the nightmare, she didn't know her brother all that well either.

How could this other man have felt such sweet and tender feelings for the monster that Ian now firmly believed Ronja to be? The images of the young girl, and later the young woman, they were of a good person, a caring healer, and a responsible witch. One who would never misuse her power.

Ronja was no longer of that gentle nature, and Ian finally

had to admit he didn't know a thing about her. But that was going to change.

Why hadn't he heard back from Don yet?

He took a step with the intent of moving to his bedside table and his phone charging atop the tawny wood. But the coolness that had brushed over him before abruptly changed into an arctic swell. The frozen assault took his breath way.

He couldn't move, as what felt like icy ropes began encircling his body. Everywhere. All over. His legs were being encased so he couldn't walk. His arms so he couldn't reach. And his torso—cold, so cold—the things were squeezing the life from his lungs.

Then finally, a creeping, searching tentacle curled around his neck and began a slow taunting climb up and around his head. He couldn't cry out for help now if he wanted to.

When the crushing embrace of the long frigid cord covered his eyes, his vision blurred. He wasn't able to see this creature, but the damn thing had substance.

Soon, the very real need for air caused Ian's chest to burn, as if filled with acid. Ronja must not care if he came over to her side anymore. She must be finished with him.

Because he was sure he was about to die.

The pain in his chest spread to his head. How could there be so much pressure inside when he couldn't draw any air? *God.* His brain was going to burst!

What little he could see grew gray and hazy, not because his eyes were covered, but from the lack of oxygen. This was it. He was going out.

And then. As any good sadist would do, the creature released Ian's mouth and allowed him a short, panicked gasp of air. Then it sealed his mouth again.

No. No. Is it going to suffocate me over and over? How could he defend himself against something he couldn't even see? A shape that took no recognizable form and was likely not even from this world?

The short answer. He couldn't.

He was completely at the mercy of this monster, and beneath the cold he felt something else entering his flesh. A seeking energy, testing, tasting.

I won't be Ronja's plaything! He shouted in his mind. *That sick bitch doesn't deserve me. Or her dead brother!*

Anger was the last thing Ian would have expected a dying person to experience, but beside the pain blasting though his upper body, there was also rage.

All at once he was released, legs, arms, everything. In his weakened state, and without the support of the tentacles, he fell to the floor in a pile of useless limbs. He lay there unmoving, drawing in deep, gulping breaths of sweet, sweet air.

Eventually he wiggled his fingers and used his arms to push up into a kneeling position, hands flat against the floor. His head still felt foggy, but his vision was clear again.

Screw you. "And your little witch too." He heard the words leave his mouth and realized he was still not quite himself. Being choked to death by a cold, invisible bunch of ropes would do that to a guy.

Diving deep into himself, he channeled what strength he had and flexed his leg muscles. When they stopped tingling, he stood. He reached for his phone, still determined to speak with Don, no matter the hour.

The sleek smart phone buzzed in his hand, emitting mechanical beeps. The number was local, though not in his contact list. Unknown. "Yes," he answered, his stare fixed on the wall.

The person requested to speak to him, and he listened as the man introduced himself as a member of the Savannah

P.D. Ian nodded in silence as he continued his introductory statements. But then the detective—Lonergan was his name—asked a question that made Ian's flesh run cold.

The chill on his skin was less severe but somehow more awful than before. "Yes," he said hoarsely into the phone. "I know Don Jacobson."

26

The first thing her friends commented on the following morning was Paige's choice of breakfast food. As Willyn, Kylie, and Anna entered the kitchen, Claudia made a beeline to where Paige stood with a hand on her hip, waiting for the steam emission to decrease.

Claudia gaped at the square silver device. "You're making waffles?" Her eyes bugged.

"Yeah." Paige said. "What of it?"

"Only that every day since you came to this island you've made your disgusting, brown, salmonella-ridden smoothies for breakfast." Claudia held out her hands. "Every single day."

Paige feared the redhead might explode from shock at any minute, but then Claudia turned around and started laughing. "Paige is making waffles."

"And bacon," Paige uttered under her breath. But she wasn't sure she really wanted to press the point.

Willyn and Anna both remained quiet yet observant while Kylie leaned on the crescent-shaped island on her elbows. "I know why her taste in breakfast has suddenly changed."

Paige expected a crude remark about how she and Chris had expended so much energy last night. No matter how one tried, keeping a secret in a house full of witches was near impossible.

But instead, Kylie tilted her head to the side and said,

"You're smitten."

Paige sputtered like an indignant horse. "Smitten. What a ridiculous word." She lifted her hand. "Can we please just keep some perspective here? This is me we're talking about."

Kylie bounced once. Twice. "Which is why watching this happen to you is the most fun of all."

Paige didn't ask what was supposedly happening, she wouldn't give the coed any more reason to pursue this subject. She returned to the novel act of cooking instead.

Whether the thing was ready or not, Paige decided the waffle was coming out. However, she was pleased to note the golden-crispiness and glorious scent wafting from beneath the raised lid.

Perfect. She'd cooked the perfect waffle.

And her delirium could not be attributed to the pastry alone. Far be it for her to admit it to Kylie, but she was immersed in a brand new feeling this morning.

And if she didn't know any better, she might say the fluttery, giddy feeling could be described as...*smitten*.

And who the hell would have thought it? She forked the waffle onto her waiting plate. *Not me. That's for sure.* It appeared her days of making fun of her friends for having hearts in their eyes were over.

Paige was in no position to say anything. Not with her own heart pulsing like a cartoon character who'd just spied the love of their life.

As much as she'd never imagined wanting a man the way she did Chris, she had to admit, everything seemed to be falling into place. And she felt sure the killer, or killers, that she and Chris were after were members of the Amara. So if she was really destined to end them, then that had to bode well for the success of her trial, as well as for the coven and their prophecy.

It was a win-win. Win.

Slicing the end off of the stick of butter, she dropped the pat onto her steaming and delicious smelling meal. Since she was feeling wild this morning, she might even add a few berries to top it off.

Paige was still floating in her dreams of victory and love when clipped, quick footsteps jerked her back to harsh, cold reality. Eschewing the waffle as it melted the yellow square, she, along with the others, hurried into the grand hall.

When she saw Trevor's and Cole's faces, she had a bad feeling the harsh reality was about to become much worse.

She stayed where she was, just outside of the kitchen doorway. With expectation, she waited, knowing they would deliver the news whether she questioned them or not.

Cole looked to Trevor and nodded, prodding his partner to tell whatever misery they'd come here to share. "The Amara had a busy night last night," Trevor said. "While we were enjoying the reception, they were making hits all over town."

Paige's gut clenched.

"More missing people," Trevor continued as Hayden eased closer to him in a show of support. "More dried out corpses." He paused, looked to Anna. "And a separate murder."

Perceptive in more ways than the magical, Anna breathed deeply before saying, "And there was something different about this other death. What was it?"

"It was a man, but the way he was killed was brutal and torturous." Now Cole took over the explanation. "He was eviscerated slowly, methodically. And his eyes were taken."

"Taken?" Willyn asked on a gasp.

Cole nodded grimly. "Maybe because he'd seen too much. Also, another detective said he checked up on the method, and it's an old practice of some Native Americans."

"Tyr," Anna said.

"And if that's the case, his eyes may have been taken so, according to legend, he wouldn't be able to see in the afterlife. Considering his job as a P.I., it's easy to make the connection." Cole spoke evenly and with a flat tone. "However…" he hedged, "we believe he was chosen for a specific reason."

"What reason?" Paige asked, angst growing and crowding inside of her, spreading like the dirty roots of overgrown weeds.

"He had connections to Ian Keller." Cole fixed Anna with his gaze. "I spoke with Mr. Keller, and he confirmed that the man was working on a file for him. He told us it was Ronja, but then he got dodgy."

"And we didn't push," Trevor said. "Whatever the P.I. was doing, it drew the Amara's attention. And truly pissed them off."

"Mr. Keller could be in danger," Anna said, surprising Paige with the level of concern in her voice.

"He's well aware," Trevor confirmed. "He said he was taking steps to protect himself."

"Whatever that means," Paige snapped. Then she said, "I'll just go get his ass and haul him out here to the island where he'll be safe. What's one more person going to matter?"

She was being a bitch, and she knew it. Just as she knew the source of her fury was a toxic trio of shame, regret…and wounded pride. "That's it." She pounded her hands together, fist into palm. "No one else dies."

A spiked and brittle sensation crept from inside of her, a hardness pulled from her darkest recesses. From here on out, she would do whatever she had to do to protect herself from all the weak, foolish emotions that had steered her off course.

She should have never taken her mind off of her duty. She was supposed to defend the citizens of this city. She was supposed to be the strongest of the coven, the warrior.

Yeah, right.

Curling her fingers inward, she clamped down until her nails drew blood.

She was no protector, no forward-leaning soldier worthy of anyone's respect. She was a disgrace and had failed to follow the most basic rule. People first, mission always.

And because of her slack-assed attitude, her...*diversions*... more people had been harmed or killed during her trial, on her watch, than in the previous seven challenges combined.

She whipped around, unable to face the gathering any longer. "No more."

Ignoring Anna when she called after her, Paige marched through the house toward the back. Normally she would have sought solace from her plants in the greenhouse, but in her current mood, she feared her own destructive abilities.

Outside. To the gardens. She would go where stone might withstand her temper. And the growing, living greenery was stronger, more firmly rooted.

Wind whipped against her face as soon as she barged out the doors. And as she fought for command of her runaway emotions, she marveled at how quickly her day had gone from sugar to shit.

Which is why she never should have let her guard down.

She'd had the audacity, the hubris to believe everything was falling into place? She mimed a punch, striking only air and feeling not at all satisfied. *I'm an idiot.*

Everything was falling apart.

And all because she'd let herself believe the fantasy, the bedtime story where all little girls got a happy ending if they spoke softly and wore pink. "That's not me! I'll never be her!"

"Who?"

Paige spun, panting with her unspent anger to find that Chris had followed her. She growled.

Of course he'd come after her. What else did he do but chase her down again and again, telling her how wrong she was and how she could have it all?

"The woman you want me to be. The girl you remember…" Paige shook her finger at his handsome face, already mourning the loss of what they'd had last night, and what they could have had in the future.

If only she were different.

"What? You don't like this?" She curled her arms and posed, displaying her taut muscles. "This is me. This is what I know. Fighting. For peace of mind, against rejection, the unanswered questions." She was working herself up but didn't care. "Against Al Qaeda, the Amara, and all the badasses you throw at me."

She dropped her hands. "That's what I do. What I know. Just take this dog off its chain and point me to the target."

She flashed over to him, got in his face. "Then let me go."

"Paige—"

"No." She slapped away the hand he tried to lift to her face. "That's what I'm made for." Somewhere along the way self-pity had leaked its way into her tirade, but she would have none of that. "I know how to do my job."

Chris's eyes squinted as if he were trying to maintain his own self-control. He worked his jaw.

Still, Paige raged on. "Until you got in my way. Just like I knew you would." She laughed mockingly at herself and stepped away, her hands held aloft. "I got clouds in my eyes. Hell, I was worried about you leaving me, when I should have been worried you would stay. No matter what I thought or said, you just convinced me to do what you wanted."

"I didn't set your path, Paige. I was only following my own."

"But it was all a waste." She put a hand to her forehead, trying to tame the headache resulting from her tirade. "The

Daevo is with the Amara. I would have fought it eventually, with or without you and this worthless…quest."

"So now, suddenly, you feel this has all been for nothing?"

She heard the underlying question. He wasn't simply asking about their hunt for the Daevo or the mission to avenge their parents.

Paige looked at him. He was asking about them.

"Yeah," she said, wishing her heart was as hard as the inflection of her tone. Maybe then it wouldn't be breaking. "The only thing we've gotten from my trial is more death. Everything you and I did, it was all for nothing."

Again, she gave him her back. Her very cold shoulder. "But don't say I didn't warn you."

"You were wrong then and you're wrong now," Chris said. "This is all supposed to happen. I know it."

"All?" Paige cast a withering stare over her shoulder. "The missing people, the murders. That was supposed to happen?" She sneered. "You really are Fate's bitch, aren't you?"

"Careful." His voice had grown eerily soft. Hard.

"Here I am dressing up like a harlot, hoping to impress you, and meanwhile, the innocent people I'm supposed to be protecting are dying left and right. I'm supposed to guard their safety. Me!" She slapped a hand to her chest. "Not you."

"I care about these people as much as you do."

She choked out a laugh. "That's simply not possible." Hands on her head, she paced away from him and groaned. "Ohhh. I don't need this distraction."

"Maybe I was the one who was wrong." Now his voice was lifeless and cold. "Maybe I was wrong about you." Chris's words, said so simply, were like a dagger driven deep into her center.

"You're right. And yeah, you told me." He exhaled his remorse. "Maybe I should have listened, because you aren't the person you used to be. Open, soft, giving. No, you're tough, Paige, real tough. And even if you had to be while growing up, you've let your defensiveness color your whole personality."

"You don't know anything." She was still acting the part of the tough girl, the defensive one, and things would get a lot worse if he stayed. Because the more Paige hurt, the more belligerent she became.

As if he'd reached the end of his patience, Chris hardened his tone. "At least your father pushed you away and deserted you for selfless reasons. At least he did it because he was protecting you."

Oh, now he was going for the jugular, but she just threw a careless wave at him. "We've been through this."

He ignored the dismissive gesture. "But you're pushing me away for selfish reasons." Now Chris moved fast, like only they could, and was at her ear with a harsh, furious whisper. "Because you're scared, and too damn proud to admit it. That's two sins as far as I'm concerned."

Paige's breath shook as it moved in and out, she trembled all over, his contempt for her a poison in her veins.

"Get out of here," she told him, still unmoving. "Before this gets ugly."

Chris hissed near her head, "Roger that."

In the distance a bird cried, the sun still shone, and palm fronds still danced in the wind, but Paige stood frozen, willing him to go, to stop talking before he destroyed her.

She forced herself to keep staring out at the garden, to the gazebo where soft kisses beneath flowers might happen for a lucky few, like her sisters. But not her, never her.

And hadn't she always known that?

Chris's barely audible footsteps sounded for a moment and then swiftly receded. A few seconds later, the doors to the house opened and closed almost as silently.

He was leaving, just as she'd requested. No. As she'd demanded.

The wind picked up and caressed her face again, this time as if to console. The suspicious burn in her nose, the wetness in her eyes brought forth a fresh wave of antagonism. So she directed it all at Chris.

He'd come into her life and messed everything up, no matter how she'd tried to prevent it. He'd gotten past her defenses, into her soul, and now she was the one who would pay the price.

But damn it all, no one had ever gotten to her this way. No one.

She hadn't opened herself up and let herself care for—no, she hadn't let herself love a man, because of exactly what she was feeling now. That slow ache, that blackness that expands inside a person until it swallows them completely.

Her anger was no longer helping. It couldn't disguise the sorrow that was gradually overwhelming her. All the things she thought she'd done right now fell away. Worthless and wasted.

She'd never shirked her duty. She'd never been in love.

And she hadn't let herself cry in years.

Paige sniffed and shook her head, trying to deny the truth. But the slow roll down her cheek was proof enough. Her long run had ended.

27

Ian rested his hand on the white linen tablecloth, doing his best to appear calm and stoic. He'd specified the Tea Room for this meeting in the hopes its elegant atmosphere would ground him in reality, the present, and, he told himself as he took in the décor, a world without supernatural phenomena.

The restaurant had once been a pharmacy, and some clever person had ensured the antique medicine drawers on the wall had been retained. Raised seating areas were situated near the windows on each wall, while ornate pillars, shelves of books, and a papered ceiling created nineteenth century ambience.

He wanted his guest to feel relaxed, amenable, and willing to speak freely. Yet he also yearned for some peace of mind. Perhaps the stylish surroundings would help with both.

Ian had had enough of late night intrigue, dirty deals, and…murder.

He wished for a drink suddenly, and not the plain tea this place was known for. Rarely did he imbibe, but the strange things he'd been exposed to recently filled him with disquiet. He was ready to accept the unbelievable. He was ready to know the truth.

If he had his way, he'd leave the eatery with a few more answers. That is, if the woman he was waiting for was willing to be completely honest with him, because at this point, Ian trusted no one.

As if carried in by a wind of deliverance, he noticed a figure that might be her. Oh, yes, he thought with a wry smile, he'd recognize that regal walk anywhere. No matter what she thought she was or what she knew about him, Ian would be damned if this woman made him feel inferior in any way.

Personally, he didn't give a damn if she was a witch.

He rose, as a gentleman should, but didn't go so far as to pull out her chair. They weren't quite that friendly. "Thank you for meeting me, Ms. St. Germaine."

Her blue gaze was cool and assessing as she inclined her head, the nod almost imperceptible. "Please, call me Anna."

"Ian," he said sternly, meeting her halfway but in no way fawning over her insignificant token of amiability. So she'd allow him to address her familiarly; that hardly eradicated the rancor he still carried from their last meeting, their only face to face before today.

She'd essentially forced her way into his office, and had demanded his attention, going so far as to inquire about a client. And on that day, he'd defended that client, protecting her right to privacy.

Now he knew Ronja hadn't deserved his allegiance, but Ian always stood by the letter of the law. Another reason he'd ended his representation of her, so he'd never be required to defend her again.

Putting the one woman out of his mind, he focused on the lady before him now. When he'd been unwilling to give Ms. St. Germaine what she'd wanted, she'd grown somewhat hostile, flashing a strange blue light in her hand as if he would automatically understand. As if he would realize she was showing him magic and would fall at her feet in reverence.

Ian didn't care if she was a witch or a congresswoman. No one intimidated him or tried to pull rank, especially in his own office. These supernatural...*beings* might not believe that human regulations applied to them, but Ian was here to say differently.

He was now paying closer attention to the stories of strange deaths in the city, as well as the skyrocketing reports of missing persons. Ever since his P.I.—his acquaintance, if not his friend—had been murdered, desecrated, in a way that filled Ian with guilt, he'd begun to assess everything with a much more critical eye.

He would give Anna St. Germaine a little time, likely until their drinks arrived, to convince him that he and she were on the same side. As it stood, he couldn't differentiate good from bad. He only knew that both Anna and Ronja were talented in ways he didn't understand.

He was human. So that made the two women foreign entities, maybe even enemies. But he was done hiding, finished playing fairly. Holding his suspicions close had only resulted in his being attacked, accosted in his home by that cold, malicious presence.

And, he was afraid his reticence had also gotten Don killed.

He'd no longer follow the precedential and civil path. He might as well come out swinging, and just see what a few well-placed punches gained him.

After they'd both placed orders for the tea sandwich plate and beverages—he black coffee and she cappuccino—Anna finally sighed and settled her curious gaze on him. "I have to say, I was surprised to hear from you. Especially after you ousted me from your office."

"Were you?" His skepticism came through more so than he'd intended, thus Anna's hiking brows.

"Yes." Her tenor was a little more frosty in response. "I was."

He detected motion beneath the table and surmised she

was crossing those lovely legs…er…Her legs.

Irrelevant detail. Ian told himself to focus. "You can't blame me for being cautious, not after what you told me that day." He directed a pointed look to her hand. "And what you showed me."

"Cautious? Is that what we're calling it?" Her expression didn't give anything away. "I came to you that day in good faith and only in an attempt to prevent a very devious and dangerous person from gaining property I suspected would give her…" She trailed off as uncertainty flashed in her brilliant blue eyes.

"Power?" Ian ventured. "Or magic? Is that what you were going to say? That land is tied into all of this, isn't it?"

Her gaze shifted. "All of what?"

"It's too late to retract your earlier statements, Anna. You… Ronja…" He waited a beat. "I know something unnatural is going on in this city."

Mimicking her posture, back straight, head held high, Ian met her stare squarely. "And I believe you can give me answers."

"Then you believe wrongly. You did your part to assist Ronja, and now you'll have to live with—" She sucked in a breath, tapped her fingers on the armrests of her chair. Finally, she let the air flow out through pursed lips, as if she were releasing the annoyance he'd aroused. "I'm sorry, Mr. Keller. What I said was uncalled for."

He waited for her to expound, using the ultimate tool of interrogation. Silence.

But oddly enough, he sensed it was genuine guilt that made her say, "I know Mr. Jacobson was your friend, and whatever happened between you and Ronja, you did nothing to cause his death."

Regret careened into Ian despite her assurances. "Yes." He

put his fist to his knee beneath the table. "Yes, I did."

The coffee and cappuccino arrived then, allowing them both time to regroup and decide how to move forward. As antagonists or allies.

"Why do you think that?" she asked soon after, stirring the foam into her drink.

"Mr. Jacobson was looking into Ronja at my behest, and following some of her known acquaintances."

"Oh." The single drawn-out word confirmed what an egregious mistake he'd made.

"I can't just sweep this under the rug, Anna. I have to find out why they killed him and make sure they're held accountable. I owe him that much."

Sympathy rolled from her when she met his gaze. "Would you take me at my word if I promised you I would see to it for you?"

The woman across from him had transformed as he'd watched. She'd entered like an empress at a gala in her honor, changed to a defensive sentry, and finally had morphed into a kind, comforting friend.

Anna St. Germaine was a chameleon. Or an actress.

No, somehow he didn't think that was right. Why then had she revealed so many sides of herself to Ian?

Maybe she felt a little guilty too. The two of them could have prevented Ronja's acquisition of the property, yet neither of them had. Whether it had been through her inability or his ignorance, it no longer mattered.

But it was up to them to redress the situation.

"I'm afraid I can't just turn this over to you." Ian chose to take a leap. He just hoped Anna St. Germaine was worthy of his faith. "Not anymore."

Her head tilted, like a bird picking up on an intriguing sound. "Why not?" She stared at him, into him. Her eyes delved deeply, as if she were listening to a song playing in his very soul.

"Ronja didn't seek me out because of my litigation skills alone." He took a drag on his coffee, wishing it were laced with Jack. Or Jim. He wasn't particular at the moment.

Anna would either help him, brush him off with whatever advice a witch could spare, or she'd consider him mentally deranged. Just as he'd accused her of being when she'd first presented her argument that day.

Ian inhaled slowly, and rolled his shoulders. "I started having what I'll call visions a couple of weeks ago. They involved a place I've never been and people I've never met."

She listened patiently, so he went on. "They were more like memories, and in each of them was a girl, or an idea of her." He refused to look away from Anna when he said, "My sister. Ronja."

Her mouth opened but no sound came out.

In commiseration with her shock, Ian nodded and took another drink.

Finally, she released a pent-up breath. "I have to tell you, Ian. *That,* I did not see coming."

He studied her, sure there was more to her statement than what he could take at face value.

"But I think you're right." She smiled, half sympathy, half acceptance. "You're not going to be able to just turn this over to me. You're probably going to be involved in this until the end."

She reached across the table for his hand. "And I'm sorry for that."

He would have replied, but as soon as she touched him, she gasped and tightened her grip. Her eyes fixed on a place beyond him, and her pupils wavered from pinpoints to deep, dark pools.

Then just as abruptly, she pulled her hand from his and covered her eyes.

"Are you all right?" Ian waved at the server, intent on ordering her a water.

"I'm fine. But…" She shook her head. "I don't have time to explain everything, but please, please, be careful until we can speak again. In fact, we should meet. Soon." She tried to smile, to alleviate the seriousness that was now stifling their conversation. "Um, tomorrow. I believe you have my number."

Anna stood, but looked down at him earnestly. "I apologize, but I'm going to let you cover the bill today."

"It's no problem," Ian said. "But what's going on—"

"I promise you," she said, breaking in, "I *promise*." She made a small fist, curling it against her stomach. "I will help you."

Ian wasn't stunned speechless very often, but as she whirled and hurried away, all he could do was watch. He'd just spilled some very dark secrets to her, but for the first time since he'd had a vision of the past, he wasn't filled only with misgiving.

Beside the heavy dread that had followed him for weeks, was a tiny glimmer of promise.

Though he was still uneasy, and not at all prepared to simply let her handle it, Ian had uncovered one truth this day. Anna St. Germaine might be a witch, and a determined one at that, but something told him that from this day forward, he'd be wise to listen to her.

No matter what crazy things she might say.

~~~

Paige was in the kitchen staring into the refrigerator when she heard Anna calling the names of all the witches. She looked out the kitchen door in time to see her friend hurry straight through the mansion, and down the rear hallway.

She'd eased out into the grand hall and was staring after the coven's leader with a perplexed stare, when the other women came racing down the stairs. All but Kylie and Willyn, who were on the couch, also looking down the corridor where Anna had disappeared.

"Was that Anna?" Hayden's forehead was compressed into wrinkles.

"She was saying something about the koi pond," Willyn said, springing off the couch to go after their leader. Rarely did Anna display overt emotions, so when she all but ran through the house yelling for her sisters, they came running too.

Naturally, Paige was the first one outside, spotting Anna where she stood next to the rock wall encircling the pond Willyn had mentioned. She sped over to her friend. Anna had her hands out as if to catch the sun in her palms.

"What is it?" Paige asked, her hand going to Anna's shoulder.

By now the others had assembled around them, with Viv bringing up the rear and still wearing her black-framed reading glasses. They listened as Anna summarized her meeting with the lawyer Ian Keller.

Then she concluded with the stunner. "He believes he was Ronja's brother in his past life." Anna nodded. "And I have no doubt that he's correct."

"Why?" Claudia asked, slipping on the shoes she must have grabbed as she darted from her room.

"Please, all of you, circle around the pond. I need your energy to see." Anna looked at the calm water, its surface essentially a huge reflecting pool.

And Paige understood what she meant by "see." "You had

a vision," she guessed, receiving a harried nod from Anna in response.

Quickly, the women spread themselves in equal distances around the rock wall. Finally lowering her hands, Anna appeared somewhat composed, but her eyes still cast shadows of fear. "I had the vision when I touched Ian's hand." She tossed her sable hair over her shoulders. "Like a blast of dynamite. Images catapulted into my head."

Anna glanced around to include each of the coven members in her explanation. "Ian is connected to Ronja, and I was able to link to her through him." She extended her hands, grasping those of the women on either side of her, Paige and Willyn. "And I saw that the Amara have another attack planned."

Paige's mind felt like it began to boil, the collision of particles responding to her fury, her determination. She refused to let them harm anyone else, during her trial or after. "Where?" she demanded. "When?"

"That's why you're all here," Anna said. "I want to take another look, but I need the coven's strength behind me."

"Like when you looked for me," Kylie said, having heard the story of the bonfire the witches and men had used when she'd been kidnapped by the Amara.

"Yes. I want to use a reflective surface, like my looking ball." Anna inclined her head toward the pond, a slight smile tugging at one side of her mouth. "This is the only one we'll all fit around and that's ready for immediate use."

"Then let's do it," Lucia said, taking Willyn's free hand and then Hayden's on her other side.

Paige silently echoed the sentiment. *Yes.* She relaxed her body and prepared to funnel her magic to Anna. *Let's do it.* She linked to Viv who then reached for Shauni.

As soon as Kylie and Hayden completed the circle, Paige

instantly felt the rush of power. They all understood the urgency of the situation, so their normally powerful coven magic was even more extreme.

Usually they performed rituals and cast their circles in the great room, the oldest portion of the mansion and the source of their strength. But the presence of wind and bright sun felt right to Paige, as if nature would help reveal the coven's enemies to Anna.

Time passed quickly before Anna gripped Paige's hand more tightly. Paige only hoped that was a positive sign. Still, she concentrated on letting her gift flow into the woman who would be the next to stand trial. The last of them.

And the one who would face the beast.

On a gasp, Anna's eyes popped open. "It's today, this afternoon." She stared up at the sky. "It will be raining."

Kylie and a few others eyed the cheery blue and cloudless horizon. "Not anytime soon, then," the younger woman said.

"You know how fast Savannah weather can change." Viv looked across the pond to Anna. "Do you have any idea where?"

"Not specifically, but I got enough for us to work with." Anna released Paige's hand. "Ronja and her bastard followers have no shame."

Paige was taken aback. Anna hardly ever used profanity.

"They mean to attack a funeral," Anna said, contempt dripping from her tone. "Plenty of victims in one place."

"And the rain will make sure the attendees of the funeral are isolated. Few others will visit a graveyard during a storm, not when they can just wait for a better time." Paige envisioned the morbid scene. People who were already in mourning, in pain, would not only be placing their loved one in the ground under a gray day, but would then have their lives destroyed.

A funeral. What a horrible time to be set upon by monsters.

"We have to stop it," Paige said. "What do you have to go on?"

"A description of one area in the cemetery. A few names." Anna's lips were pinched, making her appear as anxious as Paige felt. "We'll figure it out in time, Paige. We'll get you there."

"I know. We'll make it happen." Paige acquiesced with a tiny nod, but wasted no more time on discussion. They had until the clouds rolled in to discover where the Amara would attack. And they had to be on the mainland, in Savannah, ready to defend.

Before the first drop of rain hit the ground.

28

As the vehicle roared through the historic district, Paige sat in the front passenger seat with Hayden behind the wheel of Joe's huge SUV. Viv, Kylie, Claudia, Willyn, and Anna filled the backseats while the others followed in another vehicle.

All except Cole and Trevor, who were up ahead with Dare, Ethan, and Quinn. Their cruiser flew through the streets, sirens screaming and lights flashing.

All of the coven men were either on their way to the Laurel Grove Cemetery or already part of the convoy. With nine women and seven men, the coven army was coming out in force, no longer willing to give the Amara the smallest advantage.

Then again, Paige silently worried, with Searenn involved the evil group had a mobile infantry of their own. An almost endless supply of demons.

She wondered if Fate had bound all of the men to the witches not only for love but also as reinforcements. Because on a day like today, every able body was in demand.

Thankfully, behind every good witch in the coven, there stood a great man.

She scowled at the rivulets of rain streaking down her window, trying valiantly to forget her own solitary status. The shit was going down. Today. Right now.

Yet Paige would still be standing alone.

Pretending not to feel the crack spreading across her heart, she told herself Chris's absence didn't matter. His desertion didn't mean anything. But all the nonsense she repeated internally couldn't block her memory of the night they'd spent together.

Neither could she forget the words he'd said, the promise he'd made to be there for her.

Because look now. He was nowhere in sight.

She didn't care if she was being unfair. Sure, they'd had a fight. And, yeah, she'd pushed him away, but she'd expected Chris to be made of sterner stuff.

Even more than that, he should have realized how turbulent her emotions were, particularly after the report of more kidnappings, more deaths. But had he understood? Had he just waited for her temper to pass?

No. At the first sign of trouble, the big, tough Ranger had cut and run.

Well, fine. Paige popped her knuckles, one hand and then the other. She didn't need him. She didn't need any man. She had her circle, her sisters.

And even the crack—now a chasm—creeping through her chest, would heal eventually. Over time, she would stop aching for the soldier with whom she'd foolishly fallen in love.

Up ahead, she saw wrought-iron gates standing wide, and was almost grateful for the distraction of their arrival at Laurel Grove. A curving black metal sign overhead announced the cemetery's name, though much of the lettering was obstructed by dangling Spanish moss.

Trees enshrouded the entry and beyond, and when the cars drove beneath them the impact of the rain drops lessened, absorbed by the thick canopy of leaves. In front of them, Trevor and Cole killed the lights and sirens. They slowed, but Hayden stayed tight on the bumper while they weaved along the interior roads.

The lanes inside were split, like veins consisting of gravel and dirt, branching with no set pattern. On any other day, Paige would have been intrigued by the massive cemetery with its crowded plots, the crypts and monuments all shrouded romantically by giant live oaks and the ever-present moss.

But now she and her friends had lives to save. She only prayed they weren't too late.

As they drove, she noticed that most of the tombstones and monuments boasted dates from the seventeenth and eighteenth centuries. Only the occasional marker was new and shiny, with more legible engraving.

The last available plots had been sold over a century before, but some far-reaching people had made preparations for their children, grandchildren, and beyond, purchasing massive familial burial grounds. Interments in the present day were extremely rare and, aside from the attendees of today's funeral, no one would be prowling the graveyard in the rain.

The perfect setup for an Amara attack.

Another wide turn took them through a forest enclosure before leading into another massive area. Here, there were more crypts, larger and with more elaborate designs, clearly where wealthier families had bought a luxury afterlife.

"There," Hayden said, indicating the spot ahead where several cars were parked along each side of the road.

Without bothering to pull over, Cole and Trevor stopped the cruiser in the road and jumped out. Paige and all the others did likewise. Once outside, they all gathered their weapons, Paige with her trusty dagger on her hip and the mean sword sheathed across her back.

A smaller path, barely wide enough for a hearse, divided two sections, each filled with the trappings of burial. Massive statues, memorials, crypts, and gravestones. Most larger plots were enclosed by thick metal fences with intricate designs that screamed Victorian Era.

Midway down the trail, a group of people were cloistered in front of a white marble structure with a design reminiscent of a Greek Parthenon with six vaults of the same milky marble situated on the raised floor. One with a brand new wreath of flowers to commemorate the family's most recent loss.

As one, the gathering turned as Cole and Trevor started toward them. Despite their troubled stares and curious whispers to each other, the group seemed calm, only grieving. If the somber demeanor of the crowd was any indication, Ronja and her cohorts had yet to arrive.

Paige sighed with relief. She and the others had beaten the Amara, if not the rain.

Even now black umbrellas shielded the funeral-goers from pattering droplets.

Surveying the terrain, Paige realized her first assessment might have been wrong. The Amara members could be right around any number of corners, since there were far too many places to hide. Thick oak trunks, crypts, huge statues and effigies.

Ronja's thugs could be anywhere.

"We should spread out, form a perimeter while a few of us get these people to safety." Paige made the suggestion to her friends. They were hanging back, trying to keep from overwhelming the family of mourners. "If the Amara aren't here already, they will be soon."

Falling quickly into two teams, they all went in opposite directions down the gravel trail while Cole and Trevor tried to talk the mourners into leaving. Paige and the others began to peel off one at a time to guard both the main entry as well as the individual plots, because while the fences were everywhere, they could be easily vaulted over.

Paige cursed under her breath. There was almost no line of sight to the areas beyond the immediate plots because of the crypts and tombs along both sides. This was probably the least defensible type of location. There were entry points everywhere, yet the enemy wouldn't be seen until they were on top of Paige, her friends, or the innocent people.

Cole and Trevor were conversing quietly with a tall white-haired man in a charcoal suit when a familiar war cry rang out in the rain. The eerie sound echoed through the cemetery, bouncing off stone monuments, making it difficult to pinpoint its origin.

Falling immediately into a fighting stance, Paige jerked her head back and forth, searching for the bastard it belonged to. A devil she knew too well.

Tyr. She'd recognize his call to battle anywhere. She'd heard it before, on an awful night far out in the marsh. That terrible time when the coven had its first true casualty.

The previous manager of Nick's pub, Jen, had been scooped up off of the streets by the Amara and later gutted in the woods on a sacrificial altar. The brutal man responsible had been killed soon after, in an unexpected twist when Sylvie had chosen light magic over dark, and had stabbed her own ally, R.J., to save an innocent woman.

Paige wouldn't mind seeing the Amara lose a few more members today, but first, they'd have to show their faces.

She continued to scour the area, peering through the now skittish crowd of people. She listened past the soft plink of rain, looked beyond the presumably quiet and peaceful scene.

Because she knew better. Her witch's instinct was pulsing, beating out a warning in her brain.

Then she saw him. Tyr, emerging from behind a vault, rising with the mists. His dead black eyes clapped onto Paige, but he made no aggressive move.

One by one, the Amara members showed themselves, popping out from behind gravestones, standing on top of crypts, or walking boldly down the narrow lane.

Paige spun slowly in a three-sixty, seeking every devious face. The whole group was here, even Ronja, standing in front of an obsidian tomb, getting her deep indigo dress wet.

And judging by the curl of her upper lip, the Nordic witch wasn't pleased to find her planned assault on the humans interrupted by the coven. With a toss of her corn-silk hair, she turned to Searenn, speaking heatedly to the Droehk.

Paige expected Searenn to lift her hands, to summon a demon, but instead the Droehk lifted an arm like a general leading troops into battle. In a foreign tongue, understood only by ancient demons, the hooded woman threw her hand forward with a fierce and commanding bellow.

To her horror, Paige realized the Amara had made preparations. They'd come ready for this eventuality.

A battle with the Savannah Coven.

Demons materialized all over the graveyard, forming their own border outside the coven and the funeral gathering. The witches had surrounded the innocent people to protect them, but the huge beasts holding crude yet lethal weapons were forming this boundary for an entirely different reason.

So that none could escape.

These were the warrior caste the witches had first fought during Hayden's trial. They held their arms above their heads in a threatening manner, each wielding a weapon—maces, axes, scythes.

And they weren't alone. Paige recognized the skinless shapes creeping up behind the larger demons. The beasts Chris had dubbed "leeches" now advanced on their eerily thin legs. They eyed the humans hungrily.

Packed together as they were, the poor people were like a herd awaiting slaughter.

The demons had likely made themselves visible to the humans as a scare tactic.

And it was working. The mourners began to shift and murmur, a few emitting cries of distress, others staring in astonishment. Then, the shock began to wear off. And panic set in.

One woman broke ranks, screaming as she ran down the path. She was brought up short when Dare grabbed her and tried to calm her down.

Unsure of who or what was attacking them, other people started to spread out, eyeballing the fences, looking for a way out.

A demon jumped down from a nearby crypt, and true bedlam broke out.

Pushing and shoving, as any panicked mob would do, the people bolted, running for safety with no clear plan or destination in mind. They were driven by sheer and mindless horror.

A few retreated to hide behind the marble columns or vaults but no true refuge could be found. Though the stones, crypts, and trees were everywhere, none provided any coverage from the monsters that were slowly closing in.

Across from the small Parthenon, a trio of women were cowering together between a huge crepe myrtle and the backside of a cement crypt. Others dashed back and forth, but wherever they went they were met by fences, crypts walls, or beasts too horrible to face.

Trevor and the other men tried to corral the people into one mass, better to control the situation and provide protection. But fear had its hold on the poor people who'd come to this rainy graveyard to say goodbye to a loved one.

Their minds had been overtaken by the madness of terror. So they either ran blindly or hunkered down. Either way, there were too many to contain.

A swift motion caught Paige's eye, and she looked up to see one of the leeches on top of the crypt across the way. The three women were still huddled against the stones, crying, covering their eyes, and holding onto one another.

Above them, the leech hung its head over the edge of the roof, getting a good look at its prey. Its wiry body seemed to tense, ready to spring.

But Paige moved with the agility she'd been blessed with. Using the raised concrete dais in front of the crypt as a springboard, she leapt up, past the crepe myrtle, and onto the small roof. When she landed, the demon reared up on its hind legs and opened its mouth, baring the three razor-teeth that pierced flesh and sucked the life force from its victims. The thing emitted a high-pitched and gurgling scream.

So Paige held up one hand and rammed a shot of blue light special down its ugly throat. The leech erupted into a plume of white-gray ash, quickly beaten down by the rain.

There was no time to rejoice in her kill with so many demons to contend with in addition to the Amara. She glanced around, trying to formulate a plan. Maybe she could flash a couple of people out, past the border of demons.

No. This was a free-for-all. She'd do just as well to put down each creature she came across. That would be faster, and it would reduce the level of danger. Even if she got people out, she'd still have to turn around and confront the Amara and their army of devils.

She heard a woman scream. "Jeremy! Jeremy! No, not my son!"

Following the horrible shriek, Paige located the woman, saw her trying to scramble over the fence surrounding the

Parthenon-like temple, and then followed her desperate stare to a teenage boy who was being carried away by one of the larger demons.

So they had come to attain new human bodies. This wasn't a massacre, but a mass kidnapping. More skins for the imposter demons to inhabit.

She was about to jump across the path in pursuit, when a car screeched to a halt on the far side of the cemetery. Michael and Nick piled out, both pulling their weapons of choice as they ran.

Both men lit up the creature with borrowed coven magic. Michael nailed the demon with his knives, and Nick darted in from the opposite side to stab and jab with a mean-looking dagger.

Paige's attention was torn away, drawn back to the poor, hysterical mother. The woman was still screaming, but the tenor and the cause had changed. A leech had clamped its mouth onto her leg, and Paige could see the awful beast's throat working as it sucked.

She was across the path and over the iron fence before the monster ever saw her coming. This time, Paige pulled her dagger, and buried it to the hilt in the bastard's ropy back.

"Are you okay?" Paige asked the woman, and despite the pain she had to be feeling, the female nodded quickly. "But Jeremy…" She stood, whipping her head around.

Paige looked along with her and was relieved to see Nick and Michael with the teenage boy. Other than being covered in ash, he seemed fine.

Tossing the woman over a shoulder, she decided on a combination of her previous plans. She leapt across the fence to zip between a collection of tall headstones and crosses and deposited the woman on the ground next to her son.

"We'll take care of them," Michael told Paige.

With a sharp nod, she accepted the assurance and returned to the melee.

A foolish warrior demon ran from behind the Greek-styled structure and tried to bash her head in with its mace. She fired off a stream of blue at its chest and kept the line of magic flowing until the creature puffed into dust.

Glancing around, she saw the other witches and the men engaged in various battles. Anna, Trevor, Cole, and Hayden had finally managed to regroup many of the funeral attendees. They were pressed into a tight mass inside the Parthenon, while the two witches and the detectives defended them from all sides.

Paige was struck with sadness for these people. Their farewell to the person laid to rest there would forever be marred by this nightmare. If they remembered.

But she didn't have time to consider whether Dare could erase the memories from this horrible day. The priority was to get the people out of here, away to safety. No one was going to bother changing their recall first.

She was surveying the confusion and various brawls and deciding which beast to target next when she saw a streak of black come down the path. She had a second to recognize the fast-moving object as Jack before the vile bitch came up behind Claudia and rammed both hands into her back.

Claudia was thrown forward several yards where she fell on her front and skidded over the gravel, scraping the side of her face in the process. She rolled over and was on her feet, ignoring her wounds and ready to face her attacker.

But Jack was no longer interested in the flame-haired woman. She was staring at Paige, lifting the middle finger of both hands.

And Paige knew the show, the assault on her sister, had been all for her benefit.

"You want me, Jack? Why don't you be woman enough to just say so?"

Turning on her full speed, Paige was over the fence again and flying the last few feet toward Jack, her hands reaching to encircle—maybe even break—the nasty little bitch's throat.

Jack was expecting the move, but Paige's momentum still threw her back. Together, they landed on the rocks and dirt and began grappling as they always did. The two were evenly matched in speed and strength, but Paige wasn't wasting her magic on her.

She had to save every drop for the demons.

So it wasn't a great surprise when Jack kneed her in the stomach and took advantage of Paige's brief grunt and clutch to roll aside and stand. Another burial area had been built a couple of feet above ground on a platform. Still watching Paige, she stepped up into the fenced-in section.

The family segment held several large effigies, a tall brown monument with a long inscription on front, and several more aboveground vaults of cement. Paige followed the Amara woman up onto the raised level.

And Jack continued to retreat.

Another stone chest was positioned near the back of the plot, and had a life-sized statue of an angel standing at one end, her hand on top of the sealed lid. Jack stood next to the heavenly figure, smirking, waiting.

Paige closed in, her focus all for the ink-haired viper.

So she never saw Tyr coming.

The huge man appeared from behind the brown statue and grabbed Paige's arms, holding them behind her back. He was naked from the waist up and had his bronze skin oiled with a strong smelling herbal substance, but Paige could still easily defeat him in a hand-to-hand fight.

Only she wasn't just fighting Tyr. Jack had moved in

immediately to begin pummeling Paige in the stomach. Between Jack's blows and Tyr's greater than average strength, Paige was starting to feel some hurt.

She and Jack were equal opponents, but with Tyr's additional strength, Paige was folding. She couldn't force her way out. Every twist or turn she took, every attempt to grapple her way free just seemed to result in a harder viselike grip from Tyr. And a punch to the face from Jack.

A blow to her right eye made Paige slump, and the break in her stamina was all Tyr had been waiting for.

"Hold her arms," he barked to Jack, and the black-haired woman quickly complied. She also kneed Paige hard in one thigh, causing her leg to buckle. She then shoved Paige farther back, pressing her shoulder against the rusted iron of the surrounding fence.

With Paige immobilized, Tyr clasped both hands on her temples. He torqued her face to one side and started pressing her down. She struggled and shook, but to no avail. Then she looked down and understood his intent.

Using all his strength, Tyr continued to force her down. Paige resisted with all her might, but Jack was also applying pressure, ensuring Tyr only had to contend with the muscles in Paige's neck.

And as strong as those muscles were, they were beginning to fail.

The spike on the fence rail was inching closer and closer, and was soon just a huge blur of rusted iron in her field of vision. Tyr was going to impale her eye on the sharp point, possibly even pushing the metal spike all the way through her brain.

Kylie had already come back from the dead. That had been the one act she'd had to do to complete her trial. She'd had to die, so she could rise again.

But Paige didn't think the same miraculous act was part of her destiny.

The tip was coming closer. She felt it brush her lashes.

"Kill her, Tyr. Shove it into the bitch's skull." Jack jeered and laughed at Paige with the lust for blood in her voice. Cruel, merciless, the epitome of evil.

But no matter how angry she got, how much power she summoned, Paige was losing. She couldn't push back.

Here it comes. She squeezed her eyes shut in an instinctual effort to protect herself. A wave of shivering terror rushed through her when the sharp point touched the outside of her lid.

Then suddenly the pressure on her head was gone, and she felt a draft as Tyr simply disappeared. She turned in time to see Jack fly backward as well, but in her distraught and weakened state, Paige couldn't tell what was happening.

Something or someone had smashed into the Amara members, and as she sagged against the fence she saw Tyr's nose gushing blood.

And Jack was out cold. Something Paige had never been able to do herself.

Then she was gripped from behind, hands coming over the fence to pull her back and flip her over the railing. She had a moment of panic, wondering just who or what had a hold on her.

But she landed with a safe, soft thud.

Right into Chris's strong arms.

29

Chris had never been so happy to look into Paige's Caribbean blue eyes as he was at this moment. A breath of relief escaped him as he studied her face, checking every inch for any signs of injury.

"Chris," she said, her raspy voice betraying her shock. "You're here."

Before he could say a word, she gripped his head with both hands and pulled him in for a quick kiss. "You saved me."

Now his breath rushed out, pent up relief spilling over. "Somebody has to watch your blind side." He gripped her tighter in his arms. "But I've got you now."

Paige's breath hitched, and she brushed his cheek with the back of her fingers. "Yes, you do."

Then she patted her palms against his chest. "But quick. Put me down before anyone sees."

With a chuckle, he let her feet drop to the grass, but then his attention shifted to the man who had risen and was now towering over them. Chris's blood pounded through his veins, his hands clenched into fists.

The son of a bitch who'd almost blinded Paige, almost killed her, was standing atop some type of stone casket. Glaring down at them, Tyr swiped a hand across his face, streaks of blood creating a macabre imitation of war paint.

If the son of a bitch wanted a fight, he'd come to the right man.

Chris noticed Jack was rousing as well, but when she gained her feet, still leaning, she chose to station herself farther back, almost hiding behind the stone angel's wings. The tiny yet terribly fierce woman had a hesitant expression on her face.

"Yeah. Not as much fun when it's fair odds is it?" Paige called to her.

But instead of letting pride rule her and make her jump over to face Paige, Jack jerked her head to the side and yelled, "Searenn!" Then she waved a hand forward as if requesting backup.

Instinct rose in Chris, and he wanted to stand in front of Paige. He wanted to take the blows meant for her. Yet he'd promised never to do so.

That had been the guardian speaking.

But the man who was in love with Paige Linen Reilley? He would protect her from anything.

Even at the risk of pissing her off.

However things went from here, Chris wasn't finished with Tyr. Not by a long shot. He would tear a few more pieces from his exposed flesh before the battle was done.

He didn't wait for the evil man with the dark, hawkish looks to come to him. No, Chris reached over the fence and latched onto his legs, curling his fingers into the backs of his knees.

Then he wrenched his ass down to the ground.

No rules. No conscience.

Chris drove his foot into the man's ribs when he tried to gain his feet.

No forgiveness.

When Tyr tried to scramble away on his hands and knees, Chris was there, catching him by the long raven braid and wrenching him upright for another blow.

No mercy.

He grabbed Tyr's oil-slickened shoulders and spun him around, forcing him to stay on his feet. The fist that plowed into his nose this time issued a satisfying crunch and sent the bastard flying.

"Tyr!"

Chris heard the cry, he heard the underlying alarm. Someone was worried about the black-hearted bastard? Well, then they were about to be very, very upset. He flashed to stand over the bare-chested man. "Get up."

Tyr groaned and covered his face, but the eyes that glared at Chris through spread fingers were enraged. The sadist wasn't down for the count. Not yet. Apparently, the man could endure great pain.

Good thing, Chris told himself. Because he had more to deliver.

Tyr tried to roll and crawl to his knees.

Chris moved in to finish the job.

This was what he'd been meant to do. He would guard the gifted child and ensure she had vengeance.

No one was going to touch Paige the way Tyr had, to threaten her life or hold her down in any way. Not without swift and hard retribution from Chris.

As he watched his opponent fall over once again, Chris realized he was letting hate and rage override his judgment. His thirst for revenge was averting him from his duty.

Tyr was down. He was done for the day. So Chris needed to get back to Paige. And not let her out of his sight again.

He turned to find her amid an explosion of ash, which told him she'd just offed another demon. As he scanned the cemetery, he could tell the coven allies were making a push for victory. Even the troops of battle-demons were being methodically cleared out.

Willyn was bent over an older man who had a wound on his head, and at least four witches and three men were guarding the funeral attendees inside the burial chamber. Meanwhile, Viv was using her telekinesis to toss demons into the air for Kylie or Lucia to zap with their magic.

It was now raining ash along with…well, the rain.

Paige was walking toward him with a crooked smile on her beautiful but dirty face. Was that rust on her cheek or red mud?

He knew he should apologize as soon as they got a break in the madness. Tell her he should never have left her, even for a single hour.

In fact, he should tell her a lot of things, but he'd wait until the right moment.

As she strode toward him on those long powerful legs, her light hair darkened from being wet, and a sword strapped across her back, Chris thought she'd never looked more gorgeous. He took a deep breath, held out his hand to her.

"You will pay for this!"

Chris spun to see a furious woman, kneeling on the wet ground, her hands roaming over the bruised and bloody Tyr. The man was trying to sit up, but she put her hand on his chest and pressed him down. Not with her strength, but with an unspoken authority.

Was this the notorious Ronja? He had yet to meet her, but if her blotchy face and narrowed eyes were any indication, she was irate with Chris for the beating he'd given Tyr.

Paige was at his side in an instant. "Careful," she told him quietly.

The red-haired witch Scarlett sauntered up as well, hovering just behind the couple on the ground. She protected herself from the downpour with a pale blue umbrella that perfectly matched her fancy top. The beige pants and boots she wore were not in sync with the somber occasion or the foul weather.

Chris wondered what type of mad witch she really was.

As if on cue, Scarlett rolled her attention over to him. "So you're the little boy we missed that day."

Her words were a blow to the chest, knocking the breath from his lungs as surely as a round hitting Kevlar. He heard Paige gasp beside him as she too made the connection.

Scarlett pursed her lips, angled her head to the side. "And here you are helping the coven. What a small, small world."

Chris dragged air in his nose, his muscles tightening as he held his growing rage in check. Scarlett had been at the commune. She'd been part of the massacre that had destroyed both his and Paige's young lives.

But had her hands dealt the killing blows to their parents? The children?

With a sigh, the red-haired woman twirled her umbrella. "That's what we get for not being more thorough. I told him we should have waited to make sure we'd gotten everyone." She shrugged. "But now we've found you, and you must know it's inevitable. You will die by my hands."

Was that an admission? Who did she mean by "him"?

Chris was repulsed by how carelessly she spoke of what she'd done. He remembered the carnage, the burns, the other kids lying on the ground, having fallen right where they'd likely just been playing or laughing. And if he and Paige had been there, they would have been brutalized right along with them.

He wanted to rush straight for Scarlett and rip her throat out. But he couldn't do that. He had to maintain control and get the answers both he and Paige needed. They had to be sure Scarlett was the one.

Stepping out from behind Ronja—who was now cradling Tyr in her lap—Scarlett took three casual steps toward Chris and Paige. "I didn't want to believe that one of the coven witches was the gifted child. Honestly, what are the odds?" She put a finger to her lips, her expression bemused. "One destiny? Two? Who can keep track anymore?"

The red witch's features hardened then. She indicated Paige. "I didn't want to believe that one of the few damned brats we missed was now one of the coven witches." Her hand tightened on the umbrella's handle. She seemed to be clenching her fingers and then releasing her grip. Again. And again.

She turned her glare to Chris. "I didn't believe, until I saw *you* that day at Factor's Walk." A thousand accusations were in the statement.

He hazarded a glance at Paige, but she stood quietly, her expression flat and dazed as she listened to what Scarlett was revealing.

The bold witch continued, taking one step closer. "I recognized you," she told Chris. "I just knew I'd seen you before. Then I realized…not you. No." She smiled cruelly. "But your father."

A shockwave rolled through Chris. She was talking about his biological father.

He took in the woman's expensive clothing and made-up face. Scarlett didn't look anything like the monster he'd been chasing in his head for years. His entire life.

But he could no longer deny the truth as it literally walked up to him. He felt as if the sky was tilting, as if the ground beneath him was suddenly unstable. "You killed my parents."

Scarlett held his gaze. "You do look so much like your father. But I wonder, will you die the same way? With your arms held out in a feeble attempt to protect your woman?"

The images her words conjured stabbed into Chris. But her mockery of his parents only confirmed his resolve. "My father was a brave and honorable man. I'm not surprised you don't recognize those qualities. Since you have neither."

Dismissing him with a growl and a wave of her hand, Scarlett sneered and turned to Paige. Her stare might as well have thrown daggers.

Chris edged closer to the woman he loved. Paige's face was pale, her hair flat against her head and dripping from the rain. As her blue eyes stared at Scarlett, they were wide, bruised with torment.

She stood there looking more vulnerable than Chris had ever seen her.

Be strong, Paige. I'm here.

"And what about you?" Scarlett asked her. "The coven's warrior." The witch made a sound of scorn, as if coughing up something bad. "Will you look like your mother, Paige?

"Shut up." Paige's words were but a whisper. But Chris heard.

"Will you scream and plead? I see now that you have her eyes." Scarlett leaned in to peer more closely. "How did I miss that before? Denial? Maybe." She pointed a shaking finger at Paige. "But I'm not afraid of you. If Ronja has taught me anything, it's that destinies can be altered. Fates can be changed."

In a move that seemed in contrast to her character, Scarlett threw down the umbrella and let the rain pelt her red curls, her pretty, powdered face. "Will you look like your mother did when I slit her from gash to gullet? As she bled out slowly, crying…Paige…Paige." Scarlett's voice was an awful imitation of the poor woman's final moments.

"Shut up!" Paige screamed, but still, she didn't move.

Chris was also furious, but he had to restrain himself.

As much as he wished to crush the bitch's face in, he had to stand down. His duty was to protect Paige. To ensure she had vengeance and fulfilled her destiny.

And if he just held on. If he stayed his course, he knew she would deliver. He had faith in her, his beautiful angel of death. She would ensure justice for them both.

For their parents. The innocent people at the commune. All the little children so unjustly murdered.

A slick, scraping noise drew Chris's notice, and he saw Jack sneaking up on Paige's far side, edging around a large headstone that listed to the right. He knew a flanking action when he saw it.

Whipping his head, he looked to his left to discover Searenn also coming closer. She was a level above them, inside the fenced-in plot where Tyr and Jack had attacked Paige.

But she wasn't alone. The hooded woman had a small gang of demons with her.

"Yes, she had your pretty blue eyes." Scarlett continued taunting Paige.

Chris steeled himself for the impending battle.

"It's just too bad," the red witch simpered with false concern, "that your poor little mother…didn't have your strength."

~~~

Of all the times in her life when she should have let her anger run free, Paige could only stare in shock as Scarlett confessed her crimes. Her body trembled, and her hands clenched, but all she could do was feel the pain and disgust the Amara witch was causing.

"I can't believe, all this time I was so close to you. Never knowing." Paige's tone was surprisingly mild. Casting a quizzical look to the Amara witch, she asked, "Are you the

Daevo?"

Scarlett put a hand to her chest, with her manicured nails and soft, pampered skin. But she was a lie. Her pretty clothes and mannerisms were nothing but pretense, yet all the frills and makeup in the world couldn't disguise her rotten and putrid soul.

"Me?" Scarlett's laughter was a tinkle of disbelief. "Do I seem the type of person to undergo torture willingly?"

"Maybe not." Deep inside Paige, a flame was suddenly struck. Fury like she'd never known before began to lick and burn, spreading throughout her body as if she were coming back to life.

Her good friend was returning, coming back to give her the push she needed.

Her dear, old friend. Anger. Only this time as her rage flared, Paige felt absolutely no shame. She wasn't worried about losing control and hurting someone. In fact, she was about to let her fury-flag fly.

The burning sensation was in her gut now, spreading farther, burning hotter. The flames moved into the hands that wielded her magic, down to the legs that carried her so swiftly. And to her mind, which was now afire with the knowledge that she faced her mother's murderer.

Scarlett had stolen so much from her. And from Chris. She hazarded a slide of her eyes to where he stood. He was braced, surveying the scene as the Amara crowded around them.

"I've changed my mind," Scarlett said abruptly. "There's no reason for you to live and to complete your challenge. In fact, today is when your coven will fall to defeat." She flicked her hands up and formed a miniature hurricane of red between them, still unmindful of the falling rain and her ruined silk blouse. "Today your coven will feel death."

"I've heard that one before," Paige said. Oh, yeah. She was definitely back.

As rage turned her eyes bright red, Scarlett lashed out with a jagged bolt of her magic. Paige was ready, but the deathblow wasn't aimed at her. The wily and cruel witch sent her streak of death toward Chris.

But he too leapt aside easily.

The bolt continued on and struck one of Searenn's huge demons in the stomach. The creature seemed to both dry out and sizzle with red energy at the same time, before falling to the ground in a pile of russet soil-like material.

The black scythe it had been holding dropped on top of the mound with a soft *thunk*.

Paige chuckled and slid her gaze back around. "I thought you weren't scared of me, Scarlett?" Getting into her rhythm and ready to serve some vengeance, she flashed to her right, drawing the red witch's gaze. Then she moved again, far behind Ronja and Tyr.

When Scarlett pivoted to find her, Paige notched her chin up. "Bring it, you two hundred-year-old saloon whore."

"I may not be the Daevo," Scarlett growled, "but I will take you down!" She hurled the second crimson ball.

Paige dodged it as easily as Chris had the one before. She borrowed a move from Jack and lifted her middle fingers to the red witch.

Scarlett screamed her fury, clenching and shaking her fists. Then she looked over her shoulder and yelled at Searenn. "Kill them all! Kill them all!"

Paige watched as Searenn flung her hands above her head and cried out in her strange language. The demons she'd brought to surround them went into fight mode. And they all stared at Chris.

The other witches and their men were engaged with the

other Amara members, Ross and Carson. Paige assumed Beth and Valentina had already decided to run for it. The Amara were outnumbered by the coven now.

At least, on the other side of the cemetery.

But here, behind the raised burial ground? Paige and Chris were on their own against a small army of evil.

Falling back on her training, Paige zipped over to stand with Chris, back to back. Paige fired a line of blue into another warrior beast with a sword raised high. From behind her she heard Chris grunt before falling against her.

He quickly righted himself, but Paige turned back to find him wrangling with another of the huge armed demons. Oh, shit. Chris had never gotten a magic-infused weapon. He was fighting bare-knuckled and had already sustained red marks on his arms where the demon had grabbed him.

"Get out of here, Chris!" Paige unloaded her magic into the creature, and it dissipated into the air. But several more closed in to fill the gap.

Paige's dagger moved faster than the eye could see, stabbing into any demon body part that came too close, but she was afraid to pull her sword with Chris pressed up next to her. She glanced around wildly and was relieved to see Willyn, Lucia, and Claudia running down the path to the end so they could come around to the backside where she and Chris were facing off against a larger number.

She just had to hold the monsters off until then.

A streak of red flew by and singed her hair, and she heard Scarlett's spiteful laugh. "You die today, *gifted* child." Her voice reeked sarcasm and hate.

When Scarlett raised her hand, Paige shouted a warning to Chris. "Go, Chris!"

"No. I'm not leaving you!"

Scarlett laughed again and reared back her hand. Then

aimed the ball of magic at Paige.

There was a haze of movement, a flash of body, and too late, Paige realized it was Chris. He'd thrown himself between her and Scarlett's last punch of power. The blow glanced off his arm and sent him cartwheeling sideways through the air.

As soon as he landed, stunned, Searenn called out in her contemptible demon-speak and in an instant, a leech fell upon Chris. It bit down on his neck. And began to suck.

"No!" Paige screamed and would have jumped, but Scarlett was already throwing out more of her lethal ruby-toned sorcery.

She threw herself to the side and rolled before springing back to her feet. She searched out Chris, only to see another leech had fallen on him, bleeding him of his life force.

Searenn had sent another of the creatures. To kill Chris faster. *Oh, God, no. Please don't take him from me.*

Scarlett rushed closer, her features contorted with rage. One swing of her sword and Paige could end her. Here. Now. She could fulfill her destiny and be done with it.

But Chris was in trouble, and there was no way anything else was coming before him. Paige had to get him away from the leeches before they drained him dry.

She raised her sword. She ducked another red missile.

Screw Scarlett. Screw fate. Paige locked her eyes onto Chris as he struggled against the monsters. She could kill the red bitch any day.

Saving the man she loved was her top priority.

Her body was filled with a surge of determination. Yes, she loved him. And no one was taking him away from her. *Not Chris.*

She summoned a mystical echo of the emotions running rampant through her heart. Fear. Fury. Power.

As hate filled her up, Paige reminded herself that she had

magic too. And a speed like none of the Amara could match. Even Jack couldn't keep pace with her. Not when Paige was this killing mad.

And right now, every particle of her being was pure rage.

In a split-second, she was behind the beasts that were attacking Chris. Latching onto the back of the leeches' necks—even as Scarlett continued to launch her killing missiles—Paige literally dug her fingers into the ropy flesh and enjoyed their responding screeches of pain.

Then she lit those bastards up in blue. And they disintegrated.

Chris lay like a corpse, pale and somewhat shriveled. "Chris!" She fell to his side. "Get up, soldier!" She yelled into his face, pain and grief spiraling straight into wrath.

Because she refused to lose him.

Lifting him over her shoulder, she flashed down the path and across the main road to another section of graves. She laid him on the grass in front of a Gothic style tomb.

He was breathing. He had a pulse. "Come on, Chris." She held his face in her palms. "I know you want to come back out here and tell me what to do. I know it!" She was on the verge of tears but couldn't spare the time to let them gather in her eyes and spill.

"Get back here and protect me!" She was on the edge of delirium. Her heart was being ripped from her, a long, agonizing pull.

Lifting her head, she searched frantically for Willyn, but the healing witch was already racing toward them. She too fell to the grass and began running her hands over Chris's body.

"Don't you let him die on me, Willyn." Paige knew she was being unfair to her friend, but once her true fury was unleashed, it was a dragon of a thing to get back under control.

But to her surprise, Willyn met her toe-to-toe. Because she knew Paige. She knew what she needed.

She was her sister.

"Get your ass back to the front line and let me do my job," Willyn bit out, her brow furrowed. Then, because she was Willyn, she relented and bit her lip. "Too much?"

"No." Paige laughed, and she was sure Chris would be just fine in her friend's gentle care. "It was perfect." She grasped the back of Willyn's head and pulled her forward to smack a kiss on her forehead. "I love you."

Willyn nodded but was already working on Chris, her magic puffing his skin back to normal as Paige watched.

She was on her feet with a ninja-esque move and slowly pivoted, scanning the field for those who'd shot to the top of her target list. Even through the falling gray lines of rain, she spotted the gray hoodie, the curly red hair, soot black hair and even—yes, even—the sleek blonde head of the woman herself.

Searenn. Scarlett. Jack. Ronja. They would all feel Paige's vengeance this day.

While she'd been with Chris and Willyn, Claudia and Lucia made it around back and were putting down the last of the demons.

Paige continued her trek toward Scarlett and the other Amara members who were standing at the ready, watching as another of their schemes deteriorated. In her anger, though, Scarlett was still firing her magic.

Paige could see the red witch was tiring and running out of power, so she didn't move in her special way. She didn't speed over to confront her.

No, this time, she marched across the road with slow deliberate steps. She wove through the various stones and statues.

And as Paige drew nearer, Scarlett focused her attention on the woman walking toward her. The gifted child who was about to reap her vengeance.

Scarlett let her hands drop and stood unmoving. Saving her last push of magic for Paige?

Fine, because for once in her life, Paige wasn't in a hurry. She stopped while plenty of space was still between her and the red witch. She crossed her arms. And smiled.

Scarlett glowered back at her, flexing her fingers as if the crimson poison inside of her was making her hands itch. Her breathing was heavy and ragged. She was terrified.

Ronja glanced between Paige and Scarlett, her face twisted with an emotion Paige couldn't quite identify. Lifting the wet, dirty hem of her dress, the Amara leader stood over Tyr, who was still sitting on the ground but apparently somewhat recovered. "Get up now," Ronja told him. "Go back to the house."

"What?" Tyr gave her an affronted look. Finally, he stood up. "I'm not leaving you."

Scarlett whirled around. "You're sending him away?"

Ronja ignored her long-time friend. The woman she'd fed demon-enchanted blood to for more than two centuries. She focused on Tyr. "Leave. Now!"

When Tyr crossed his arms over his chest, Ronja issued sharp commands to the other Amara members standing in various spots amongst the clustered headstones and crypts. They and the witches were all watching to see what would happen.

"Jack, Ross!" Ronja ordered. "Take him to the plantation house!" Then she snapped her fingers at Carson who was closer. "Help them."

What was going on? Paige studied Ronja, confused by her

panic over removing Tyr from the confrontation. All of the demons had been destroyed, and now she was sending some of her best fighters away?

But Beth and Valentina had reappeared, they moved in with Searenn to flank Ronja and Scarlett. The five of them formed a line, but even with Ronja's power, they couldn't defeat the entire coven and the men.

Ronja spoke to Searenn. "How many more demon dregs are in reserve?"

Giving no actual answer, the Droehk simply began to chant, calling forth whatever creatures she had at the ready. Several of the acidic monsters popped into view, but after a quick scan of the area, Paige counted only six.

She smiled directly at Scarlett. "They won't save you. None of them will."

As if Paige spoke with the command of destiny itself, Scarlett took a step back. Why didn't she run?

When Ross and Jack fell on Tyr and began to drag him away, he bellowed his displeasure at being forcibly removed. Scarlett flinched.

But Ronja lifted a hand as if to slap her. "What are you waiting for?"

Scarlett looked wounded, but she quickly hid her reaction to Ronja's mistreatment. She called forth the smarmy bravado that was her norm. Again the witch summoned her magic, a roiling ball of crimson in each hand.

A strong wind lifted Paige's hair, and the sudden presence beside her told her she was no longer standing alone. Sliding her gaze to find him, she gave Chris a wink. "What took you so long?"

He rolled his shoulders. "I had to ditch sick bay and a very insistent nurse."

Go, Willyn. Paige smirked at the imagery. The sweet healer had probably even tried to hold him down.

Returning her attention to their enemies, Paige saw Scarlett speaking quietly yet heatedly with Ronja.

Then she turned to glare at Paige. "Come," she challenged. "If you will."

"You think I should run from you?" Paige said, again progressing step by step.

"You've hidden from me your whole life. Why shouldn't you cower again?"

Shaking her head, Paige scoffed. "I never hid from anyone or anything. I never even knew my mother had been murdered." She continued to close the distance between herself and the witch she'd been born to destroy. "But I know now."

Scarlet flung one of her bright red balls, but Paige met the blast with a streak of blue. The two magical shapes slammed into each other and formed a violet star that erupted and scattered with the wind and rain.

"You've lived lifetimes," Paige said. "Longer than I have."

"True." Scarlett purred her response, but the effect was forced. Her fierceness now was all an act.

Paige was only fifteen feet from her enemy. "Some might even call you immortal."

"I *am* immortal." Scarlett sneered. "You. Are. Nothing."

"And even I have to admit," Paige offered as her body began to tingle with anticipation, "you're a much more powerful witch than I am."

"Yes."

"You just have one problem, Scarlett." The very air seemed to guide Paige's arm, her grip had never been truer as she pulled the sword from the sheath across her back.

"Ha!" Scarlett barked. "What would that be?"

Paige leveled the red bitch with a glower of pure hatred.

"You're slow as hell."

In one move, Paige flashed closer and swung her sword in an arc so clean and smooth it whistled through the air.

Scarlett's eyes were still turned up at the corners with a wicked grin when the blade sliced through her neck. And her head toppled to the ground.

There was a moment of stunned silence as coven members and Amara alike all stared.

Then a soft sound rose from the amulet Paige wore, a somber yet hopeful tune, appropriate for the surroundings and the scene. Paige had completed her trial, but she'd had to kill Scarlett to do so.

Her two destinies had been one after all.

Suddenly, Ronja began to scream. "No! No! No! You vicious bitch!" The Nordic witch ran to Scarlett's body as it sank slowly to the ground, gravity winning out over the mass that was no longer controlled by red witch's evil mind.

The scene was almost comical, yet disturbing, as Ronja picked Scarlett's head up—the ruby-hued curls now matted with grass and mud—and tried to put it back onto the dead witch's severed neck.

After long minutes of fumbling with the gory, decapitated body, Ronja finally clutched Scarlett's head to her chest and lurched to her feet, taking a step toward Paige.

But now she was the one being detained, as Searenn and the other women grabbed her arms and shoulders, pulling her back from certain death. Paige felt a quick urge to finish the Nordic witch off, but she knew that wasn't how things were supposed to play out.

She wouldn't steal Anna's trial from her, or the coven's true and final victory.

She stood in the falling rain as the wailing and screaming Ronja was pulled away, past a large black tomb and out of sight. She looked at Scarlett's body, wondering if any of the Amara would return to collect her.

With a sigh, she turned and found Chris watching her. So she went straight to him, fell into his arms, and breathed in the warm life force still running through him. "You're safe," she said, clutching him tightly.

"So are you." He kissed the top of her wet head. "I have so much to say, but let's—"

"Go somewhere else," she finished for him, wanting to get away from the mutilated corpse before she told him she loved him.

As the others milled around with each other and talked about what to do about the funeral attendees, Chris and Paige walked to a white stone bench near the crypt where she'd laid his battered body on the grass.

She sucked in a breath, and felt like crying. *No more of that.*

Still, she and Chris really did make a good team, and today, they had saved each other. They had both been guardians.

Because that's what love was all about.

"So that sound was your amulet?" he asked her, brushing at something on her cheek.

"Yes. My challenge is over." She looked up at him and was sure big, pumping cartoon hearts were in her eyes. "I did just what I was supposed to do."

His hand was in her wet hair now, cupping the side of her head tenderly. "I'm so proud of you. You were amazing. So strong and—"

"I love you." She blurted the words, cutting Chris off mid-sentence. "And I'm sorry for the argument we had. I was being selfish." She steeled herself and admitted, "And I was scared."

"I'm sorry I left." Lifting her chin with his fingers, he promised, "But I never will again." He gave her one of his charming smiles, and Paige's once-rusty heart began a healthy gallop.

She leaned in for a kiss, hugging him close as his hands wrapped around her. And then they pulled apart to stare at their hands. "Ugh," she said. "You're muddy."

"So are you. Guess we kicked it up a bit."

She gave him a flirtatious look. "We'll just have to take a hot shower when we get home."

"Hm-mm." His forest eyes were clapped onto her face. "Home," he said. "With you. I like the sound of that."

"I want you to stay, Chris." She took his hands—mud and all—in hers. "I won't ask for guarantees or promises. I just want to be with you. I don't know what will happen in the future—"

Now it was his turn to interrupt. "But we'll handle it together."

Deciding this was a day for surprises and bravery, Paige took a deep breath. "I think the first thing we should do together…" she swallowed, "is call my father. Matthew. He deserves to know that it's over, and that the one who hunted us is dead."

She sniffed against tears. *Damn it.* "I want him to know we didn't spend our lives apart for nothing."

That burning wouldn't leave her eyes, so she pinched the bridge of her nose. But Chris moved her hand away. "I told you it's okay to cry, princess."

"No. Oh, no."

He raised a brow. "I still can't call you that?"

Paige shook her head, sure her joy would dry the tears for good. "Only if I can call you little Christian."

He tilted his head toward her. "Okay then. Angel."

Paige just laughed, and then she bit her bottom lip. How could she refuse him when he looked at her like he was doing now? She threw her arms around his neck and pressed her cheek tightly to his. "I do love you, Chris."

He squeezed her tighter, with a strong, possessive arm.

And she absolutely loved it.

Dropping her head backward, she let the rain wash over her cheeks. When her gaze met his again, she said, "You know, I thought you were a crazy man that night in City Market. I just wanted to get away."

"Because you had no idea how persistent I would be." His thumb brushed her bottom lip and sent a tingle straight through her. "But I found you."

"You did. You never gave up." Tracing a finger under his firm jaw, Paige looked up into the greenest eyes she'd ever seen. She let her guard down. She let her love flow freely. "And it didn't matter how fast I ran. You caught me after all."

30

Ronja slammed into the plantation house and fell to her knees on the dark hardwood floor. She screamed a sound of grief and rage, just as she'd done countless times on the return trip from the cemetery.

Scarlett was gone. Beheaded like a worthless animal. And right in front of her.

Oh, Ronja slammed her palms against the floor, how far she had fallen.

She'd found Vanir, a miracle after so long, but even he'd rejected her. She'd lost eight times now to those goddess damned witches, and Bastraal had punished her before for much less.

They'd lost so many demons today, so that meant she had to work double time to bring more over from the abyss of the underworld. Searenn could summon them as well, but only so many at a time.

And Bastraal still demanded his army.

Ronja could have dealt with all of that. No. She *would* deal with it all.

But she'd never imagined the Amara's wonderful victory would come without Scarlett by her side. "My dear, sweet Scarlett." Ronja moaned and let her head fall forward, ignoring the sound of the other women as they crept through the door and stood nearby.

The only thing worse than actually being beaten was to allow her submissives to believe she'd been defeated. So, gathering her strength and fortitude, Ronja stood up. She pushed her wretchedly wet and dirty hair back from her face.

She wiped away the tears.

Staring down the hallway, she noticed Carson step out from the dining room. The Amazon scanned the three women and said, "Where is—"

She cut herself off when Valentina sliced her hand down in a motion to stop speaking. Dark understanding entered Carson's eyes.

"Have the preparations been made?" Ronja asked, her voice calm and steady, with no hint of the sorrow still throbbing inside.

"Yes. Tyr is already down below."

"I want to start. Immediately." Ronja stood and dropped her soaked and muddy gown to the floor, standing naked with no embarrassment. "Bring me a robe," she snapped at Beth. The young girl ran off and was back in seconds with one of Ronja's favorites, silver silk.

Covered up once again, she marched to the door that opened to the basement stairs. Down she went, until she entered the dungeon. Then she made her way back to the room with the pit.

The dirt walls remained unchanged, but the contents of the subterranean room had not. Bastraal's altar of blood and bone was no more. Ronja had destroyed the monolith, spreading the pieces over the dirty floor.

There was much work to be done down here, and she wanted as much dark magic scattered throughout the room as possible.

A new altar had been erected, this one of pure granite with the breadth and width to hold the body of a large man.

The leather cuffs and heavy chains, those were attached for caution's sake. For when the first outcast demons tried to take command of the body lying atop the stone.

Tyr stood near the granite slab, arms crossed over his chest. Ronja could see he was still angry she'd sent him from the cemetery, but her next words wiped the emotion away entirely. "Scarlett is dead."

She walked down the dirt steps to the pit to greet her one living lover. No longer would she split her demon-laced blood between two people. No longer would she be loved by her scarlet-haired minx.

A tiny dart of pain struck the center of her chest.

But all of the loss and pain would be worth it in the end, when Bastraal reigned and Ronja ruled a bloody and savage world alongside the great demon.

She went to Tyr, whose demeanor had changed, becoming tender as he opened his arms, his black eyes full of consolation. He had never cared for Scarlett, but Ronja knew he loved her and hated to see her in pain.

After a long embrace, she retreated. She stood a foot apart from Tyr and spoke. "My love, as you endure the coming days, as you suffer and bleed, please know that you have my gratitude, and my eternal devotion."

"As you have ever had mine," he said.

A flicker of true love passed between them, but then, as Ross and Jack moved in to prepare the restraints, Tyr slowly lowered his gaze to the altar. He scanned the earthen hole in which he would be entombed for the next week.

When Ronja spoke again, her face was a mask of stoicism, her voice stiffened by fortitude. "You will be successful. I am sure of this." She sent a hard stare to Tyr. He would survive the ceremony.

As he had once before. "I'm counting on you." She drilled

her stare into him.

But Tyr gave no sign of emotion, simply closed his eyes and exhaled.

Her strong, virile warrior. He would withstand the torture. His spirit would become more powerful for all the pain…the endless pain.

No more will I think of this. Ronja whirled in a flurry of shiny silk and climbed the steps out of the pit. She stood beside Carson, and wished pitifully for Scarlett. Her dear, fallen lover and friend.

But retribution was finally going to come to those witches. They would pay penance through untold agonies, and suffering the like of which none of them had ever conceived.

"You know what to do," she said to Carson, the Amazonian child she'd rescued from the jungle. Her new second female in command, with wild and carnivorous ways.

"Yes, Ronja." Carson crossed her lean, powerful arms and stood with the proud stance of her ancestors. "Tyr will know unspeakable assaults on his body and psyche. I will make sure of it."

"Yes." Ronja wouldn't use the word "good," for as necessary as this ritual was, even she did not relish the idea of Tyr suffering such excruciating torment.

Carson's voice was sharp, infused with the exact intensity Ronja needed in her new second. "The more he endures, the stronger he'll be after rebirth."

Nodding firmly, Ronja stared down into the pit. She studied the angular features of the man chained to the granite. So calmly did Tyr lie in repose, even though he knew what was coming.

"He will be successful," Ronja stated plainly.

"Yes."

"He will become the creature of darkest power."

Carson remained silent.

With fingers curling into the silver silk of her robe, Ronja growled as the face she pictured in her mind changed, as the features softened from Tyr's hawkish handsomeness, to the softer, leaner face of another.

"Anna St. Germaine will see her own end." She bit her bottom lip, drawing blood to taste and savor, in honor of her lost friend. And as a tribute to her male lover, who even now was receiving his first cut of many.

But this was only the beginning. His injuries, his torment, would be legion.

But his agony will ensure our triumph. And that imperious St. Germaine bitch would die, but only after an amount of suffering that would surpass even this ceremony. Ronja would personally abuse Anna in ways that would make the awful Jin Deva seem tame in comparison.

The final witch would have her trial. Anna would have the long-overdue confrontation with Ronja. But this time when the Amara came for her, they would be coming with the saints of Hell on their side. Every horror known to man or devil.

They would be coming…with the Daevo.

If you enjoyed this book, we would love to read your review on your favorite retail or review site.

Thank you!

Suza Kates writes both paranormal romance and suspense. She lives in Savannah, Georgia with her family and three ridiculously spoiled cats.

For more on Suza and her books visit

www.suzakates.com